SOLO

SOLO

Women on Woman Alone
Edited by Linda Hamalian and Leo Hamalian

DELACORTE PRESS/NEW YORK

Published by
Delacorte Press
1 Dag Hammarskjold Plaza
New York, New York 10017

Designed by MaryJane DiMassi

Library of Congress Cataloging in Publication Data
Main entry under title:

Solo: women on woman alone.

1. Women—Fiction. 2. Short stories, American—
Women authors. 3. Short stories, English—Women
authors. I. Hamalian, Linda. II. Hamalian, Leo.
PZ1.S687   [PS648.W6]   813'.01   77-11861
ISBN 0-440-08068-1

ACKNOWLEDGMENTS

"A Stroke of Luck" by Kathy Roe: Used by permission of the author.

"Sweets to the Sweet" by Jane Mayhall: Used by permission of the author. First published in *Aphra*.

"Dreamy" by Sherry Sonnett: Copyright © 1973 Sherry Sonnett. Used by permission of A. Watkins, Inc.

"I Love Someone" by Jean Stafford: Reprinted with the permission of Farrar, Straus & Giroux, Inc. from THE COLLECTED STORIES OF JEAN STAFFORD, Copyright © 1952, 1969 by Jean Stafford.

"Success Is Not a Destination but the Road to It" by Katherine Harding: Reprinted by permission of the author and her agent, Blanche C. Gregory, Inc. Copyright © 1976 by Katherine Harding.

"The Lover" by Joy Williams: Reprinted by permission of *Esquire* magazine, © 1973 by Esquire, Inc.

"Secretive" by Jane Augustine: Used by permission of *Aphra*. First published in *Aphra*.

"World of Heroes" by Anna Kavan: From JULIA AND THE BAZOOKA AND OTHER STORIES by Anna Kavan. Copyright © 1970 by Rhys Davies and R. B. Mariott. Reprinted by permission of Alfred A. Knopf, Inc. and Harold Ober Associates Incorporated.

"And the Soul Shall Dance" by Wakako Yamauchi: Reprinted from *AIIIEEEEE: An Anthology of Asian-American Writers* edited by Frank Chin, Jeffery Chan, Lawson Inada, and Shawn Wong, published by Howard University Press. Copyright © 1974 by Wakako Yamauchi.

"The Good Humor Man" by Rebecca Morris: Reprinted by permission of Curtis Brown, Ltd. Copyright © 1967 by Rebecca Morris. First published in *The New Yorker*.

"Lunch" by Rebecca Rass: Used by permission of the author.

"Reena" by Paule Marshall: Reprinted by permission of the author.

"Let Them Call It Jazz" by Jean Rhys: From TIGERS ARE BETTER-LOOKING by Jean Rhys. Copyright © 1962 by Jean Rhys. By permission of Harper & Row, Publishers.

"Dynastic Encounter" by Marge Piercy: Reprinted by permission of Wallace, Aitken & Sheil, Inc. Copyright © 1970 by Marge Piercy.

"A Cold-Water Flat" by Elizabeth Pollet: Used by permission of the author.

"An Old Woman and Her Cat" by Doris Lessing: Reprinted by permission of John Cushman Associates, Inc. Copyright © 1972 by Doris Lessing.

"Tuesday Night" by Ann Beattie: Reprinted by permission of The New Yorker. Copyright © 1977 The New Yorker Magazine, Inc.

"Pure Will" by Harriet Zinnes: Used by permission of the author.

"In Place of a Preface": from the poem "Requiem" in ANNA AKHMATOVA: A Poetic Pilgrimage by Amanda Haight. Copyright © Oxford University Press 1976. Reprinted by permission of the publisher.

CONTENTS

IN PLACE OF A PREFACE

". . . a woman with blue lips standing behind me,
who had of course never heard my name, suddenly
woke out of the benumbed condition in which we
all found ourselves at that time and whispered in
my ear (in those days we all spoke in a whisper):

Can you put this into words?
And I said:
I can."

Anna Akhmatova
Requiem

INTRODUCTION

Whether living by themselves or surrounded by friends, lovers, husbands, children, or parents, women are just now beginning to perceive their existence the way men have always seemed to perceive theirs—as separate from anyone else's. To be separate means to be alone. Although aloneness is a state of being all men and women must experience at some time in their lives, women have regarded it as damnation exemplified, whereas men have taken it as a natural, inevitable aspect of their emotional development.

Until very recently women have not been encouraged to plan lives of their own by their parents, teachers, employers, or the institutions that subtly govern growing up. Instead, they have been taught to see themselves, as Adrienne Rich points out in *Of Woman Born*, as part of a relationship—as a mother, a daughter, or a wife, but rarely as an independent individual. Often women are the ones who promote this view of themselves. The stories in this anthology, all of them written by women, reflect the particular dilemma that most women face even today: how to conquer that self-destructive longing for dependency without denying the deep satisfactions of emotional sharing and security.

These stories often deal with mundane events and musings in the ordinary life of ordinary women. The authors are not concerned with what has come to be known as "existential loneliness," that human condition so searingly dramatized in *Oedipus Rex, Hamlet, King Lear,* and the work of Camus, Sartre, Duras—that feeling of overwhelming, nonspecific anxiety generated in the person who becomes aware that he or she is alone in an alien, indifferent universe, that shocking conviction that the individual belongs to nothing but his or her own self. Everyone on one occasion or another has felt a flash of such existential anxiety, but unless it is reinforced by a prolonged state of isolation, it may vanish as inexplicably as it descends upon us. The writers of these stories look beneath—or beyond—the philosophical. Their intention is not to derive ontological lessons from the lives of their protagonists, but to examine closely, often compassionately, the shards and fragments of the everyday lives that women live every day. Often the stories seem to be moral tales without a moral, and many of them have epilogues but not endings.

We have tried to derive some order from the typical dilemmas that the women of these stories find themselves in. To this end, we have divided the stories into three categories or thematic trends: struggle, tragedy, and independence. The theme of struggle centers on women who, neither independent nor dependent, understand the rewards inherent in autonomy. Forced to confront the challenge of aloneness, they meet it stoically, if not with pleasure. Their stoicism is a form of resignation rather than a surrender—a fine but necessary distinction. The theme of tragedy explores the lives of women who are too fragile to fight the temptation to be passive and malleable. They are the "men junkies." Under the theme of independence, there are stories about women who are coping with, even enjoying, the state of singleness. In this group of stories, the women are not only effectively managing solitary existences they may not have sought, but they are actively creating self-contained existences that leave them relatively free of what those forces that govern growing up, previously referred to, had defined to them as a "natural need"—dependence on men. We see them in the process of "kicking the habit."

In the following pages, we would like to take a closer look at these stories and the women whose lives they depict.

STRUGGLE

Margaret Lamb's "Management" is the story of an old woman's fierce determination to maintain her independence. Despite her poverty and physical feebleness, Bitsy does not want to surrender her freedom to a nursing home. Instead, she figures out a way to outfox the man who robs her of her meager welfare check, accepts the patronizing contempt of those who administer welfare, outwits her nasty landlady, and rents a room less comfortable and more expensive than the one she had occupied for years. For the sake of her independence, she tolerates heavy abuse. Though we sense that she will eventually be defeated by her circumstances, we admire the spirit that will command her to fight with her last shred of strength against the bitter end that lies in store for her.

In Willa Cather's "Nanette: An Aside," a middle-aged opera singer named Tradutorri has all the material wealth and freedom of movement that Bitsy never had. Ironically, Tradutorri's good fortune has made her less capable of coping with loneliness than the impoverished Bitsy. When Nanette, Tradutorri's servant and confidante, chooses romantic love and domesticity over her more exotic, adventurous life with Tradutorri, the famous artist is overcome with grief. Despite her talent, ambition, and devotion to her art, she has not yet learned how to live alone or how to achieve a healthy, equal relationship with another person. She will retain her independence, but she knows at the end that the struggle for independence does not always yield happiness. Does the struggle avail naught? That question is left hanging.

Joyce Carol Oates, in "6:27 P.M.," depicts the same picture in the setting of a contemporary wasteland. Glenda is a divorced hairdresser who is engaged in a quiet but inexorable struggle to become an individual rather than an invalid. Her son, who constantly alludes to his absent father, seems to be more of a burden than a source of joy and comfort. Glenda works hard to maintain the severance from the married life that she despised, but she can expect no reward for her efforts other than the grim recognition that she has achieved financial self-support. By the end of her workday, she feels worn out, used up, and trapped between the boredom of her job and the isolation of her private life. But she persists when her pessimism is at its greatest, and there is the suggestion that she may survive the difficult years ahead without irreparable damage to her psyche, or to her son's.

In Penelope Gilliatt's "As We Have Learnt from Freud, There Are No Jokes," marriage is clearly not an onerous experience for Emm. Indeed, she experiences the fulfillment of a good, simple, loving relationship with a man who absurdly, accidentally is removed from her life. Saddened by her husband's death, she somehow preserves a sense of humor about widowhood. Her friends do not understand Emm's particular (and to them peculiar) strategy for staving off the paralysis of sorrow, and hence her sense of isolation is intensified by the miscommunication between her friends and herself. In a sophisticated milieu, her malady seems to be a form of bad manners. Life has played a poor joke on her, and this woman of exquisite sensibility is left to contend with a well-meaning but inept Bulgarian.

The protagonist in Elaine Gottlieb's "Go with Love, He Says," also a widow, is made desperate by the discovery of something that she always knew: that although she may be willing to put away the weeds of mourning and to reach out for renewing relationships, she is doomed to disappointment. In her widowhood she is no less vulnerable to the risks of new encounters than the younger, more innocent females she teaches at the university. She has achieved a degree of independence and yet wonders: Will she be betrayed by her hope that one of these relationships will prove to be enduring? Should she measure out her remaining life in whatever solace she can derive from one-night stands? Like the widow in the Gilliatt story who tries to overcome loneliness, the protagonist in Elaine Gottlieb's story is becoming aware that isolation breeds itself—and that in spite of this knowledge, she must hold fast to its small blessings.

In "A Negative Balance," April Wells depicts the eccentric behavior that often accompanies the isolation of widowhood. Unlike the women in the stories by Gottlieb and Gilliatt, Wells's protagonist does not attempt to issue out of her isolation. The cocoon of her hermitlike existence is threatened by a visit from a young cousin of her dead husband. She realizes when his visit ends that she is becoming a lonely person on the road to paranoia. Will this insight save her, encapsulated as she seems to be by the loneliness that she clings to like a protective cloak? The question remains unanswered, but there is the hint that the young man, a symbol of life, may have touched a source of vitality hidden within her.

An attractive, young woman who has missed the affection and security of parents is the central figure in Sallie Bingham's account of a quest, "Mending." She seeks affection and approval from a succession of men who respond only to her sex appeal. Finally, after trying vainly to seduce her psychiatrist, she comprehends the folly of smothering herself in fantasy as a way of conquering her loneliness. For her, mending means an end to romantic dreams, acceptance of a reality wherein handsome knights do *not* rescue the beautiful maiden.

Martha, the protagonist of Edna O'Brien's "The Love Object," is strong, decisive, and disciplined in her professional career, but in the presence of her lover, a man married to another woman, her judgment is suspended and her intelligence melts like tallow: "He simply said my name. He said 'Martha,' and once again I could feel it happening. My legs trembled under the big white cloth and my head became fuzzy, though I was not drunk." So possessed is she by her passion that she saves the ashes of her lover's cigars—perhaps a suggestion of what is left to her in the relationship. What strikes us as sad about Martha, despite the ecstasy that almost transforms her flesh, is the discontinuity, the disconnection between the faculties of mind that bring her success in her career and the vulnerability of her emotions that turns her erotic life into a shambles. Martha embodies a condition that T. S. Eliot called "the dissociation of sensibility"— a fancy term for a common modern malady. In prose

both poignant and precise, sensitive and forceful, Edna
O'Brien captures the anguish and sense of isolation that
accompanies such dissociation. Yet Martha's spirit, we
note, is far from spent, and like many of her contem-
poraries in the real world, she has learned the unhappy
knack of surviving on the horns of such a predicament.
The title, ambiguously, seems to allude to Martha's lover
no less than to Martha herself, implying that in such
impossible couplings both participants are victims of their
affections.

TRAGEDY

In the stories of the first section, the women protagonists
manage to maintain the structures of a normal life even
though they are engaged in warding off loneliness, disappointment, or isolation. That they struggle against total
silence testifies to their continuing connection with the
world. They are not completely lost or submerged. In
the second section, the women are not so fortunate. The
authors of these stories reveal with a chilling accuracy the
devastation that loneliness creates among people who
have nothing within themselves to marshal against the
advancing vacuum. In some instances, the physical or
social environment seems to be the cause of the tragedy;
in others, some quirk of personality or flaw of character
appears to be responsible. In all these stories, the fault
lies not in the protagonists, but in their stars—that they
were born women. Their gender is like an ancient curse
that time cannot wash away.

Death, the ultimate form of isolation, offers a release
of sorts for the protagonists of both the Susan Hill and
Kathy Roe stories. With the demise of her friend, Miss
Bartlett in "How Soon Can I Leave?" realizes that she
took pride in her false strength and that the future looms
as bleak as the winter weather that grips the English
coastal town where she lives. The old woman in "A
Stroke of Luck" summons the courage to articulate her
misery and loneliness only as she is about to be rendered
inarticulate. Miss Bartlett grieves, perhaps for the first

time, for her own misery, and the old woman finally
expresses the bitterness and resentment she has nursed for
years.

Many of the people in this group of stories seem damaged in one way or another. Miss Bartlett and the old
woman lock up their emotions until it is too late to escape
self-suffocation. Other protagonists in the stories in this
section cannot confront human emotion on any level
either. Elsie in Jane Mayhall's "Sweets to the Sweet" is an
obsessive chocolate eater. Consuming candy, she is reminded of a time when she was young and desirable to
many people. Her aunt who raised her never loved her;
her husband loved her only at the beginning of their
marriage; her daughter whom she raised without love
despises her. Elsie can only connect with a memory of
what her life was before she was married. Bitter and
beaten in her abandoned state, she stuffs herself with
sugar—a modern symptom of that condition.

The protagonist in Sherry Sonnett's "Dreamy" fantasizes
a life uncontaminated by human emotion. The true luxury
of life, in her eyes, is the life free of emotional attach-
ments to other beings—a life in which order and reduc-
tion replace passion and uncertainty. The stress of
interpersonal relationships repels her. This ascetic,
machinelike, programmed existence is secure, as secure
as life would be in a straitjacket. Is this a response to a
world dominated by masculine will? Perhaps. Although
this story may be superficially reminiscent of "A Negative
Balance," the protagonist here does not stop to consider
that her perceptions may be off-kilter.

Jenny Peck, in Jean Stafford's "I Love Someone," cannot connect with other human beings either. The recent
suicide and funeral of a friend shocks her into an awareness that she has "unfailingly taken all the detours around
passion and dedication," and she is more dead than her
friend buried in the suburban cemetery. Passions are as
dangerous for Jenny as they are for the woman in
"Dreamy." She fears the risks and perils of emotional
commitments.

In Katherine Harding's "Success Is Not a Destination
but the Road to It," the lonely, alienated protagonist

wants exclusively superficial relationships with her friends
—or, more accurately speaking, her contacts. She ruins
the potential for intimate friendship with a person who
genuinely responds to her by pretending that she does
not care for him. Determined that she will not suffer as
her mother (whose husband left her) did, she leaves her
men and devotes her passion to an inanimate object—a
car. The car creates the illusion of power, but in reality
it isolates her in steel.

The woman by herself in Joy Williams's "The Lover"
has no illusions about her incapacity to love or care about
anyone. There is a catatonic solitude about her that Williams emphasizes with flat language and paucity of dialogue. Each night the woman listens to the "Answer Man"
on the radio to forget her misery, but the disembodied
voice has little power to pardon her from the sentence of
solitary life. For her, love is a quantum, a supply that she
has exhausted. She has run out of gas.

Another woman who sounds as lost, as psychotic, perhaps, as the woman in "The Lover" is the protagonist
in Jane Augustine's "Secretive." She rivets her attention
on buying lining material for a bright new coat because
spending money will keep her from feeling what would be
an uncontrollable anger. Her marriage is a disaster; her
husband beats her. Her only friend is an imaginary one
who keeps her, she thinks, from going mad. The internal
monologue in this story is quite effective for illustrating
the degree of isolation and loss of contact this woman is
experiencing.

Anna Kavan's protagonist in "World of Heroes" is a
young, rich woman whose mother wanted her to be a boy
and whose father is dead. A character reminiscent of
Katherine Harding's protagonist, this woman puts her
libido into automobiles. She becomes a companion of racing
car drivers and is accepted into a glamorous jet-set type of
group. After an accident, she is jolted into the knowledge
that her relationship with these people is superficial and
that she will always be an outsider.

A different perspective on the tragedy of isolation is
present in Wakako Yamauchi's "And the Soul Shall
Dance." Through the eyes of a child who is surrounded

by the warmth of a loving family, we perceive the pain of a Japanese woman transplanted to an arid, alien land, living a lonely, barren life. Mr. Oka, her husband, is solicitous about his daughter's loneliness but indifferent to his wife's. For him she occupies a different position on the scale of concern. To make her life bearable she drinks. One evening she surprises her spying young neighbor by dancing with the grace and abandon of the happy person she may have been before she was locked into the loneliness of the new world, where familiar friends and customs are not there to alleviate masculine tryanny.

INDEPENDENCE

The last group of stories is closer in theme to the first group, with one difference. The protagonists in this group are more successful in resisting the force within themselves to yield—and the force within their friends and society that tries to persuade them to yield—to dependence. The people in these stories do not completely conquer loneliness; probably no one ever does. Rather, they are consciously preserving or rebuilding their autonomy. Often the protagonists in these stories achieve a distance from the situations they are involved in and have a healthy perspective on them. There is more room for self-analysis in these stories, and less time spent in anguish.

Recently separated from her husband, a newly appointed college professor, Anne, in Rebecca Morris's "The Good Humor Man," wanders over the familiar places, disconsolately seeking ghosts of her former love. Finally she takes a room in Greenwich Village and allows herself almost imperceptibly to be picked up by the pulse of the city's vitality. For the entire summer she resists the pull of destructive sex and survives into a new selfhood. Unlike the women in the Sonnett, Stafford, and Harding stories, she does not have to deaden her emotions to be by herself.

The protagonist in Rebecca Rass's "Lunch" is a divorced woman who has the option of starting a new relationship with her former husband. She rejects the proposal as she gradually understands that her real life began with her divorce. "War waged inside her between what she was and what she wished to be, between the dependent crawling snail looking for a master, and herself as the master of herself." She will not play the role of victim again, and cheerfully she leaves him after a good fuck on the beach.

It is quite possible to renounce personal emotional involvement and remain a functioning, socially committed individual. Reena, in Paule Marshall's story by that name, does so. A confident, professional, politically active woman, Reena is tired of the pull and drain of human emotion. She too is divorced, and like Anne in "The Good Humor Man" and the protagonist in "Lunch," she plans to stay free of confining, demanding relationships. By herself she can lay plans that are not subject to the whims of interfering men.

Selina Davis, in Jean Rhys's "Let Them Call It Jazz," is a young Caribbean woman who comes to London with a passing skill at sewing and little else. Broke and desperate, she falls in with a pimp who provides her with a place to live in a crumbling old house. She is imprisoned for disturbing the peace, but when she is released she finds work in a dress shop and discovers the formula for survival: forget what is past and plan for the future. Her spirit and her will to live help her run the gantlet of lower-class existence in a foreign city. She traps a reservoir of resourcefulness within herself which sets the direction of her life.

Maud, an aspiring poet in Marge Piercy's "Dynastic Encounter," is introduced to the corrosive, hierarchical structure of the literary and academic world. Duncan, a teacher at the college where she used to teach, arranges a meeting with his friend, a well-known poet named Saltzman, because he (Duncan) wants to have an affair with her. Saltzman has agreed to meet her because he wants Duncan to get him an appointment at the college. Her integrity tested, Maud rises above the game of petty politics. She decides that she no longer requires the stamp of approval from "influential" people whose behavior contradicts their purported values, nor will she allow herself to be used to advance her position. The price of integrity leaves her unfazed.

Having reached "the age of consent," the heroine of Elizabeth Pollet's "A Cold-Water Flat" runs away from home to become a writer. As she moves among the shadows who populate the world of New York's literati, she feels like Christopher Robin of "Solitude," her favorite poem. After she loses a boring job and sheds a tedious lover, she decides to seek alternatives to the reality offered by a male-dominated world. Rather than allow her experience to embitter her into inertia, she determines as a feminist to be as responsible as possible for her life. This remarkable story was written before the feminist movement of our time had surfaced.

Doris Lessing's "The Old Woman and Her Cat" follows the career of an aging woman, Hetty, who has lived alone since the death of her husband in World War II. Her children have grown up and lost touch with her, and her loneliness has made her a little "strange." She refuses to settle into decrepitude as she ages. She begins to peddle junk in the streets and learns to enjoy her new life to the brim. She adopts a kitten that turns into a tough, independent cat much like herself in temperament. The days pass swiftly and sweetly until civilization closes in on Hetty. She flees from city officials who want to put her in a home for the aged. She eventually dies in hiding, on the second floor of an abandoned building during a bitter cold spell, but she has triumphed over the forces that would have controlled a weaker-willed person in the name of social concern.

Other women in these stories seek or crave aloneness. In Ann Beattie's "Tuesday Night," the protagonist is surrounded by her ex-husband, lover, brother, and son. All of them are puzzled by her wish to be alone on Tuesday nights. Similarly, the heroine of Harriet Zinnes's "Pure Will" decides that if she can't have time alone then she will at least have her own space, shut off to intruders, where no one can make demands upon her. Friends and family misinterpret her motives. These two women know that they must—symbolically, at least—remind those around them that they are keeping their separate iden-

tities intact. At the risk of offending their dearest human
companions, they insist that their individuality and
separateness be respected.

As we look back on the discussion of these stories,
loneliness may appear as more than an arresting or interesting theme for stories by women. A woman writing
about the loneliness of women is not merely developing
a theme or examining a subject. She is assuming an angle
of vision, a way of relating to what for men is the real
world. The very position of a woman in the world grants
her this special angle of vision, this manner of relating.
Her traditional absence from the sphere of influence in
politics, business, law, international affairs especially
equips her to respond with radical clarity to questions and
issues related to these fields. Her displacement and dislocation in life lend power and penetration to her understanding of the tragic potential of loneliness in everyday
life. Men, too, share these experiences, but perhaps suffer
them less intensely because they are far more in command
of their own lives, because they can and could make
choices that only recently became available to women.
The short stories in this collection are mirrors of a movement toward a new understanding and appreciation of the
woman's place in the emerging world.

LINDA HAMALIAN

MANAGEMENT

by Margaret Lamb

On the first of the month everyone is out on the stoop early, looking for the postman. All along the block people stand or sit, talking or just waiting. Most of them are on welfare; some never look for any mail except the half-monthly check.

That's all the mail that comes for Bitsy Larkin. She remembers being on the city roll since it began, when no one had work and they gave out clothing and food tickets, not money. Bitsy was at the end of her working days then.

No one knows how old she is. Bitsy was never told the year she was born, only that it was in freedom.

Despite the sun and her sweaters, she shivers. She is so old and thin that she is always cold, and holds her arms tight across her wishbone chest. Her nose and chin, once sharp, are fallen, but she holds her neck stiff.

"Man comin'?"

"You lookin' with your blue eye, Miz Larkin!"

Bitsy laughs too. One eye is so blind it's blue. The other is getting cloudy but isn't all grown over yet.

She is right. At last the postman has come to put in her hand the envelope with the little window. She doesn't look at the amount as other people do. Putting the unopened envelope in the big pocket of her dress, she starts right off to the bank.

The bank is on the avenue, three blocks up. Bitsy takes her time. The wide avenue is sunnier than the street. Her good eye sees straight ahead of her, not too far, but always further than her slow, shuffling feet. She can't see at all to the sides but isn't taken aback when a stranger suddenly speaks in her ear.

"Can I help you?"

She always nods and lets herself be helped. The man thinks she wants to get to the hospital on the other side of the avenue. She explains that she is going to the bank on this side. The man is in a hurry. He wants to move her along, almost picks her up and moves her, but Bitsy is stubborn. She holds him back to make him walk at her pace. She is used to walking slowly, one foot at a time.

She wins out. After a block the man tips his hat and leaves her. Many people—men and women, colored and white—want to help her when she goes out; but they usually get nervous. She tolerates their aid and their excuses.

As she walks, her hand in the pocket feels the stiff check move back and forth over the hip bone.

There is already a line at the bank. Bitsy goes to a high table, takes a pen and signs her name on the back of the check. She draws the letters very carefully, always keeping in her mind the picture of her name in full. She waits in line, then has to find her identification card in the other pocket. They give her the money.

"How much, Miss?" she asks.

"Fifty-one dollars and fifty-five cents," says the girl behind the glass.

Bitsy is relieved. It is always the same amount.

Going home, she goes over her budget. Twenty-six dollars for the room at Mrs. Frazer's, one-half month's rent. The rest is for the food she will buy to cook in the landlady's kitchen, and whatever else she might need until the next check. Sometimes she puts her few things in Mrs. Frazer's laundry bag and pays a little for that.

Bitsy always goes straight home from the bank, to put aside the rent money. This way there is never the danger of being put out—or of having to ask the welfare for more money. Many people she knows cannot live on their check; they eat the rent, and then the landlord wants his room. But Bitsy eats less as she gets older. She is always very careful in her spending, and so she gets along.

No one is sitting outside on the stoop at her house. Everyone has gotten a check and gone to spend it. Bitsy is the only one who returns right from the bank.

She feels her way along the dark hall and starts up the stairs. Suddenly she falls backward, she is pulled back roughly and her hands go up—lifted right up out of her pockets, with the money falling from her fists! She falls in pain, shattering like glass, to the damp crumbling cement. She tries to rise, tries to warn—

"Ah-ah-ah—"

Her voice is broken too. In the near dark hands move over her, scrambling for the money. As she rises on all fours a foot comes down at her. Her side is smashed. The pain is so great she curls up around it. It's like the time her hip broke, and she prays to be saved. The man runs along the hall away toward the light.

Bitsy lies still, then cries for a while. She calls for help, but no one hears. They are all gone, spending their checks.

After a long time she can stand up. She feels her way slowly up the stairs, crying softly.

She can hardly see to unlock the door of Mrs. Frazer's apartment. When she goes into the empty kitchen with the big bare table, she remembers: Mrs. Frazer has gone to visit her sister in New Jersey.

Bitsy opens her mouth wide to stop the sound of her crying. She is hungry, but she can't eat: as is her custom, she ate every speck last night, so she would have room for the new groceries on her refrigerator shelf. Mrs. Frazer's food she doesn't dare to touch.

Her little room is dark; the shade is down. Bitsy goes to the bed. Lying there, she feels for the hole in the mattress, the nest in the soft horsehair, where she always stores her money.

She is still lying there, moaning and weeping softly, when Mrs. Frazer returns next day. . . .

The day after check day there are always people waiting in the welfare center, hoping to see their investigators. Bitsy sits holding a scrap of paper with a number written on it.

"Eighty-two."

They repeat the number. The girl next to Bitsy nudges her. "That's you." Flustered, Bitsy tries to speak but can't.

She stands up and goes up the aisle to the man who called out her number, a colored man with gray hair.

He takes her to his office, a tiny room with a desk and two chairs. Pasted on the frosted glass partitions are cartoons from newspapers.

Bitsy tries to explain what happened. She can't explain very well, and is glad to have the notes the doctor and the police gave her. She is afraid the welfare interviewer will scold her for losing her money, but he doesn't.

"This is awful. Your investigator will be right down. Those people stop at nothing!"

He is angry, but not at her, it seems. Included among the respectable, Bitsy is encouraged. Her new investigator, a young white girl with glasses and long straight hair, is also upset. Bitsy starts to explain all over again for her.

"They want to keep me at the 'mergency ward. I told them I has to see my investigator."

"Will Mrs. Frazer wait for the rent?"

After a pause, Bitsy offers, "Hard to say."

"We'll call her. Don't worry, Mrs. Larkin."

On the phone the investigator sounds young and sad. Mrs. Frazer's voice comes loud and clear:

"No, I wouldn't put out an old woman—if you all give your word on the rent. I needs it this week. I'm a widow woman, that's my income—"

"I'm sure we can—"

"Miz Larkin is a very peculiar person. I don't know if I should keep on with her, person of her age. Too much responsibility for me!"

The investigator sighs as she hangs up. Bitsy writes her name three times for the stolen money.

"Was it a young man?"

"They kick me and hit me. . . ." Bitsy feels her side. "Doctor say to come back tomorrow, he want to look it over again."

The investigator walks Bitsy back to a chair in the big waiting room.

"We can give you some cash today, to last until the new check comes. You just wait here."

The white girl goes away. A great weight leaves Bitsy:

she understands that welfare will give her another check, and the landlady will wait for it. Now she feels confident again. After a long time the investigator returns with two dollars and ninety-five cents.

"Food money for three days. I'm sorry. . . ." The investigator is embarrassed because welfare gives so little. She goes to the door with Bitsy, jiggling Bitsy's elbow.

"Are you sure you can get home by yourself?"

"I'm growin' foolish, child, but I ain't a baby yet."

As soon as the new welfare check comes, Mrs. Frazer takes her rent and stops calling Bitsy peculiar. To Bitsy the robbery is like a bad dream. In the daytime she forgets about it; in the night, when her side hurts, or when she feels with her hand the money-hole in the mattress, she remembers. The only trouble is that getting her check five days late and in a different amount confuses Bitsy in her management. Welfare explains that the cash issued has to be subtracted from the check replacement.

"You folks know what you doing," Bitsy says.

But something is wrong. Bitsy buys rice and collard greens, and some days a bit of meat, starting out with bacon and ending up with chicken feet. The adventure and the lingering aches and pains have given Bitsy an appetite. Her old investigator told her once she could spend twenty-five dollars and fifty-five cents out of each check for "food and other." But two days before the next check she runs out of both money and food.

Rather than tell Mrs. Frazer, who might call the investigator, Bitsy pretends she is sick and doesn't want to eat.

"I'll call the welfare doctor," the landlady threatens.

"No . . . I be on my feets tomorrow."

On the sixteenth Bitsy takes her check right to the bank. She buys a bag of chicken parts to cook and goes straight home. Again in the hall she is attacked and robbed. This time the thief doesn't hurt her. This time she wants to die.

"Nobody's fault but my own," says Mrs. Frazer; but she is angry at Bitsy. She puts herself and Bitsy on the bus to go over to the welfare center.

"You all look after her," Mrs. Frazer tells the investigator. "I has my own troubles, scuffling hard, looking for the rent. I can't carry her over here every time."

Four chairs are squeezed into the cubbyhole office. Mrs. Frazer and the investigator and the welfare supervisor—a plump white woman with gray hair—all look at Bitsy in a way that makes her feel ashamed. Bitsy tries to explain; but this is impossible, and she cries instead.

"Now, now, no tears," says the supervisor. "Let's try to think what's best."

"Do you have any relatives, Mrs. Larkin?" the investigator asks. The white girl frowns, embarrassed and worried.

The supervisor leans her red face toward Bitsy. "Did you ever have any children? Were you ever married, Mrs. Larkin? Our records are very confused. First you say you have children, then you say no kin at all."

Bitsy shakes her head. From time to time the welfare people ask her these questions, and Bitsy never answers the same way twice. It isn't so much that she is forgetful: more that she has come such a long way to such a different life from the one they want to bring back; and in order to get on with her present life she always has to concentrate on what she is doing *right now*. So she can never answer.

"You don't have anyone?"

"I don't see no need for questions," says Mrs. Frazer. "Bitsy don't know her own Christian name. Why don't you all take and put her in a nursing home where she belong? If a person can't help themself, that's where you all sends them. She get the best care there."

The supervisor looks at the investigator, who looks down at her hands.

Bitsy does not dare to speak. Hearing the words "nursing home" is like being struck down a third time. Once before, in the hospital, she was threatened with a nursing home. Now she holds her breath.

The supervisor smiles reassuringly at Bitsy but speaks to the landlady. "Mrs. Larkin seems to have a management problem. We'll work it out."

"I don't want her in my house—"

"We want Mrs. Larkin where she will be happiest."

The supervisor stands up. They all stand and file out of

the little room. This time the supervisor helps Bitsy to a chair in the waiting room.

Mrs. Frazer doesn't want to wait with the clients, but she agrees to sit with Bitsy until the emergency check replacement is issued. Mrs. Frazer also agrees to cash the check for Bitsy and give her the food money day by day. Bitsy is eager to be agreeable.

So a second check is replaced. The supervisor warned it would be difficult to do this, but it is permitted after all for Bitsy.

Bitsy lives in terror of being sent to a nursing home. Her fear of meeting a thief again on the dark stairs is nothing compared to her expectation of being taken off in the night, by taxi. An old man in the building was taken away like that because his son signed the papers. Bitsy thought she would be safe because she always managed well. Besides, she has no child to sign the papers.

A nursing home is like the hospital, she knows. The time she broke her hip, they took away her clothes and things so she couldn't see them. She had to lie in a big room with many beds where people were always crying.

"The welfare ain't forgot about that nursing home," Mrs. Frazer tells her. "They put you on the waiting list. Soon's they find you a bed, my troubles be over."

Mrs. Frazer tells all the neighbors how the welfare handed over Bitsy's check to her, to be doled out day by day. She says she doesn't like it, she doesn't like to have to do with welfare money.

"What you mean, you been takin' half of Bitsy's ever' check," says Mrs. Thompson, who gets welfare money for her grandchildren.

"See if I take in another person on relief. Nothing but trouble!"

The neighbors turn against Mrs. Frazer for her airs and her social security. Bitsy never did anyone any harm, and suddenly everyone wants to help her.

"You don't watch this house nohow," Mrs. Thompson says to the super. "Junkies sleeping under the stairs—now they are robbing the old people."

"Tell the judge," says the super, shrugging.

He has three other buildings to take care of. No one knows who the landlord is, and the case is in court.

They are all sitting out on the stoop. Different women try to tell Bitsy to stand up to Mrs. Frazer and the Welfare Department. Bitsy feels very confused. A man who is helping the super load a washing machine on a wheelbarrow stops to listen.

The other women go up to start supper, but Bitsy stays out on the stoop. The sun is still warm, and she doesn't want to go back up to Mrs. Frazer. By and by the man with the wheelbarrow comes by again.

"Good evenin'."

"Good evenin'."

"Miz Larkin?"

"Ye-es." Bitsy has been thinking about the nursing home again and is almost ready to cry.

"I'm Mr. James Taylor. Sorry to hear about your troubles."

Bitsy's chin trembles.

"This house ain't no good for you, Miz Larkin, with the junkies waitin' on your check. I was thinkin' I might be some help to you."

Bitsy sits with her legs shaking and looks up at him. Mr. Taylor is a middle-aged man, nice appearing, with gray hair. He wears work clothes.

"They going to put me in a nursing home."

"Friend of mine got a nice room empty. No junkies there. Maybe you could go see it."

Bitsy lets herself be persuaded to go see the room, which is several blocks away. She is afraid of returning after dark, but Mr. Taylor says he will walk her back. He walks beside Bitsy, but doesn't worry her elbow or urge her to go faster. He is interested in her troubles and just asks her questions.

"I s'pose Miz Frazer charge fifteen dollars a week for that little bitty room."

Bitsy shakes her head and smiles. She is pleased but flustered at Mr. Taylor's interest.

"More? Less?"

"She take twenty-six dollars out of my ever' check."

"O Lord! And make you climb all them stairs. This room you going to see is on the first floor."

Mr. Taylor stops in front of an old brownstone house.
The street lights are already on, and Bitsy is suddenly
afraid to go into a strange house. Mr. Taylor helps her up
the steep outside steps.

The inside hall is lighted with one bulb. Mr. Taylor
leads Bitsy past the staircase to the back of the house.
There is no noise here, unlike Bitsy's building in the
evening. Mr. Taylor takes out a key and opens the door
of a room, then switches on the light.

Bitsy follows him in. There is a cot covered with a
blanket, a wooden chair, and a little table stuck up against
the wall. The walls are high and bare except for clothing
hooks. To Bitsy, turning her head gradually to see these
things, the room looks very strange.

At Mrs. Frazer's she has a big bed with a headboard,
a chest with a mirror, and an overstuffed chair with pillows. In her old room the furniture is so crowded that
Mrs. Frazer, a fat woman, can hardly walk around in it.
This new room seems empty. At Mrs. Frazer's she has a
window looking down on the street.

"There ain't no window."

"You see how clean it is here. No dirty people here."

The room does look clean. Bitsy feels sad and weary.
She knows that if she doesn't take this room she will
certainly go to the nursing home.

Mr. Taylor reads her thoughts: "Here you don't have
to worry about no Mrs. Frazer and no nursing home."

Mr. Taylor snaps off the light and leads her out. He
goes to a door under the stairs and calls down. A man
comes up the stairs and stands in the doorway.

"Miz Larkin here was lookin' at your room. She can
move in on the first."

The man smokes his pipe and looks at Bitsy without
saying a word. Mr. Taylor nods. The man nods and goes
back down to the basement.

Mr. Taylor shows Bitsy the hall bathroom and tells
her the kitchen is upstairs. "You just explain to the welfare
that you be living with a family. That way they don't
have to bother with no papers."

On the way back Bitsy thinks about the bathroom and
kitchen in Mrs. Frazer's apartment; but Mr. Taylor jokes
with her until she forgets her fears and questions. He

seems very happy that she won't have to go to the nursing home.

"You just listen and learn how to get along with the welfare. They won't carry you off to no nursing home!"

Gradually Bitsy accustoms herself to the idea of moving. She likes her old room although she is afraid of Mrs. Frazer. But she has lived in so many furnished rooms, in rooming houses and in other people's apartments, that the idea of moving again is not strange. Her main fear is that the Welfare Department will find a nursing home place for her before she can move.

Mr. Taylor stops by to see her once, while she is sitting on the stoop watching the children dance to radio music. He arranges to move her on the first, when the check should be coming.

"We won't tell Miz Frazer 'til you get the money safe in hand. You just get on down here early in the mornin', Miz Larkin. We won't let that thief get near your check."

On check day Bitsy goes downstairs early, long before the postman can be expected. No one is waiting outside yet except Mr. Taylor, who wears a hat and stands on the sidewalk, his arms folded.

"Good mornin'! Movin' day!"

"Hope so," says Bitsy.

He steers her down the block and across the street to the projects. There they sit on a bench facing the empty playground. Mr. Taylor explains he has brought her over there to get a good view of the postman when he first appears around the corner.

"You can pick up your check without everybody seein'. All you know, that junkie is sittin' on the block right now, waitin' for you to appear."

Mr. Taylor takes the newspaper out from under his arm and looks in it. Bitsy sits looking at the cobblestones underfoot.

After a long while, Mr. Taylor suddenly jumps up. He pulls Bitsy up and makes her run with him across the street. The postman is just turning in from the avenue.

Bitsy has tears in her eyes, out of breath from hurrying. The postman frowns but hands over the envelope.

"I wants to get to the bank early," she explains.

But Mr. Taylor does not take her to the bank. Instead of passing her building again, with all the people waiting in front, he makes her go around the way the postman came. Bitsy has to give over the check to a man in a little office on the avenue there. The man gives her the money in dirty bills, then keeps back a quarter. When Bitsy protests, Mr. Taylor tells her the man is paid for cashing the check.

"That don't matter," he says. "You don't do the way you done the last two checks—went to the bank and got your money stole. Here, let me put it away for you."

Alone with him, Bitsy might have protested. But the man who kept her quarter watches her from behind his little cage, and Bitsy feels shy. Still she shivers as Mr. Taylor takes all her money from her hand and folds the bills in his shirt pocket.

Outside, he gives her instructions; but Bitsy feels all cold and sick inside her and can hardly listen. Her hand trembles as she takes little pieces of paper and a white card with writing on it. The day looks different, pale and chilly.

"You tell that investigator you took your whole check and moved this mornin' to the new room. That's the truth anyways! Here's the address: 'Andrews family,' so they knows you the *sole* lodger. Now, you going to say you *already* moved and paid out twenty dollars for the truck. That way they be sure to give you the money. I needs the money before so's I can get a hold of that truck. The movin' company name is right here, on the card, with the telephone. Then you ask for new dishes, pots and pans, since you ain't going to use Miz Frazer's no more. The Andrews family uses all they own. You understand?"

"Pots and pans . . ." Bitsy hasn't asked for a check for special needs since underwear two years ago.

"The new rent is fifteen dollars a week. So now you paid a week rent, week security, and the movin' expenses." He taps his pocket with Bitsy's money inside. "That's fifty dollars. Here's the receipts all wrote out to show them."

"I needs my food money," Bitsy begins timidly.

"They going to give it to you, honey. You got legitimate expenses! Now you go on over to the welfare while I start

to work on the movin', I got to get home if the welfare
wants to call."

Mr. Taylor makes her go over the cards and receipts
and repeat the requests she is to make. Bitsy is shy and
uneasy at having turned over her money, yet excited and
pleased as if they share a joke. Mr. Taylor waves, leaving
her a block from the welfare center.

"Remember, you going to move away from the people
takin' your money. You don't need no nursing home, you
be safe!"

"I don't need no nursing home. I be safe there," Bitsy
says.

The investigator looks at the little papers laid out on
the desk. "The new rent is higher. . . ."

"I be safer!"

"Well . . . this Mr. Taylor seems to want his moving
money today. . . ."

"He the only one to help me," Bitsy says firmly.

The white girl goes away and comes back with the gray-
haired supervisor.

"So now we have all these new requests," says the
supervisor. "You know, Mrs. Larkin, the department has
gone to a lot of trouble on your account."

Bitsy says nothing.

"Mrs. Larkin is managing very well," says the young
investigator. "She's managed to move out of a building
where people rob her. We're supposed to help people help
themselves, not railroad them—"

"Twenty dollars for moving! You don't have furniture,
do you, Mrs. Larkin?"

Bitsy is ready with Mr. Taylor's arguments, but the
supervisor waves her hand and sifts through the bits of
paper.

"At least the primary tenant knows how to make a
receipt properly."

"I'll be glad to go with Mrs. Larkin to look at this
new room," says the investigator.

"You won't go anywhere. You have two emergencies
today besides this."

The supervisor folds her hands over her stomach and
sits looking at Bitsy for a moment. Bitsy sits up straight

and looks right back at her. She has repeated what Mr.
Taylor told her to say, and the women at welfare have
listened; this gives her confidence.

"All right," says the supervisor, nodding at Bitsy but
speaking to the investigator. "Make out the emergency
checks. And transfer the case *today* to the new building
worker. Since Mrs. Larkin seems to have solved her
management problem"—the supervisor's eyes look deep
into Bitsy's—"we can put her back to six-month visits.
Cancel the nursing home memo—I'm doing you a favor!"

The girl writes very fast in her black notebook. She
looks up at Bitsy and smiles, her glasses falling down on
her nose.

"Now, Mrs. Larkin," says the supervisor, "we're giving
you another chance. If you let your money get taken from
you one more time, it's the nursing home. If you ever
don't have enough to eat over a check period—if you
have to ask Miss Robbins for too many extra things—
then we'll think it's better for you to be where you'll be
taken care of. Do you understand?"

The investigator and supervisor go away. Bitsy sits in
the waiting room, thinking, for a long while, until the
investigator returns with three checks and a list, which
Bitsy can't read, of what each dish or pot will cost.

It is late afternoon when she returns to Mrs. Frazer's.
Many people are outside on the stoop, and Bitsy knows
she won't have to worry about going up those stairs again.
This time she has checks in her pocket instead of cash.

Mrs. Frazer is in the kitchen, waiting for her rent.

"Ain't no rent," says Bitsy.

"They rob you again?!"

"Fixin' to move out," says Bitsy. She retreats to her
room.

She tries to concentrate on gathering together her
belongings, but Mrs. Frazer stands in the doorway and
tries to find out where she is moving.

Bitsy puts her clothes in a cardboard box she has kept
for a long time, and all her other personal effects in
another box. There are two lamps, a winter coat too big
for her, quilts, an old radio, a pile of withered shoes, a
framed church membership certificate, a plant.

"What's that?" Mrs. Frazer points to the plant.

"They calls it creeping Charlie."

Remembering the windowless room, she decides to leave the plant with Mrs. Frazer.

Bitsy finishes her packing, feeling very tired and stiff. She sits on the bed between the two cardboard boxes, an arm around each one. Mrs. Frazer does not move from the doorway of her room; she has checked each item as it went into the boxes.

Bitsy remembers the chill that passed through her when she handed over her check money to Mr. Taylor. Again she shivers. He promised to come before supper. Bitsy is hungry and has eaten nothing.

"You owe rent since noon," says Mrs. Frazer.

She snaps off the light in Bitsy's room and goes off, leaving Bitsy in the near dark.

Bitsy sits listening to the sounds of people passing outside and the sounds of Mrs. Frazer making supper in the kitchen. Soon it will be dark. Bitsy closes her eyes. Again she sees the rent and food money passing into Mr. Taylor's hands.

She is ready to cry. They will take her, packed and ready, straight to the nursing home.

At last there is a man's voice in the kitchen. Mr. Taylor has arrived. Bitsy clings to him, but he shakes her off.

"I was waitin' downstairs," he says, looking away from her.

He goes straight to the bedroom to get the boxes. He scarcely glances at Mrs. Frazer, who keeps looking at him as he works.

"I guess they ain't never too old," the landlady says.

Mr. Taylor takes one box at a time to the apartment door. He takes the big horsehair mattress too, which Bitsy forgot belongs to her until Mrs. Frazer insists they carry it out. Mr. Taylor rolls up the mattress.

"Glad it ain't going to go on in *my* house," says Mrs. Frazer.

Mr. Taylor opens the door and shoves the big boxes outside in the hall.

"Maybe I'll call up the welfare—"

Mr. Taylor's forehead bulges out, and he says, "After the way you treated this lady—"

"But it ain't none of my business. I'm quit of her."

They are safely outside in the hall. Mr. Taylor makes three trips with the boxes and mattress in the time it takes Bitsy, carrying a pillow, just to walk down once. When she reaches the stoop, Mr. Taylor is standing on the sidewalk, waiting.

Bitsy looks around for the truck. Out in the street stands a large wooden fruit cart on which are piled the two boxes and the mattress.

"I couldn't get a hold of no truck for today. Don't need it anyway for these little things." He walks out into the gutter, turning away from her. "Can't always get just what you wants." He sounds angry. He takes Bitsy's coat, which has fallen into the street, and flings it over one of the boxes.

Mr. Taylor takes up the two handles of the cart and trundles it along like a big wheelbarrow. Bitsy walks down the steps and across the sidewalk to the street.

Mr. Taylor has to walk very slowly behind the cart, so he goes just fast enough for Bitsy.

"I sure hope things be better now," she says.

Mr. Taylor says nothing. After a while Bitsy tells him that welfare has given her the checks.

He stoops to set the cart down.

"You let me hold them for you," he says.

Bitsy stands in the street and looks at him. She giggles.

"They safe now," she says. "They hid good. I ain't undressin' in the street."

He picks up the wheelbarrow again, and they turn up the avenue. It is lighter there, with more sky. The street lights turn on. A few cars whiz by. Bitsy tries to forget about the cars and concentrate on Mr. Taylor, who is puffing behind the creaking cart. She has to be clear what she wants to say.

"That old coat come from the garbage," says Mr. Taylor. "You ask the welfare, they give you a new one."

"The welfare don't want to give too much."

"They give you the checks today."

Bitsy remembers the red face of the supervisor. She tries to recall the words.

"The welfare only let me stay by myself if I ain't going to bother them too much. That what they say." She puts her hand on Mr. Taylor's moving elbow. "They tole me if my money get took again . . . I got to go to that nursing home."

Mr. Taylor looks straight ahead. The strain of the weight he pushes has brought tears to his eyes. Bitsy keeps on talking. Just as repeating his words to the welfare people gave her confidence before, so repeating theirs to him helps now.

"They tole me, 'Miz Larkin, anytime you unhappy, you come right on over.' They got that bed ready for me. I tole them I ain't decided on takin' it yet. Maybe yes, maybe no. Depend how I feel."

Mr. Taylor turns to look at her.

"I just needs my few bitty things," she says. "Don't need much. Once I goes into that nursing home the check stops for good. Nothin' for nobody."

She walks along beside Mr. Taylor. They turn into the darkening street where she will live. Mr. Taylor keeps nodding to himself. Bitsy is glad she has spoken her piece, yet fearful. Will he leave her as not worth his trouble? She steals little looks at Mr. Taylor. He is peeking right back at her the same way.

At last he says, "I could find you a bargain on the pots and pans."

"You can help *some*. . . . A person don't need so many pots and pans," she says.

He nods. "You going to do fine, Bitsy," says Mr. Taylor.

NANETTE: AN ASIDE

by Willa Cather

Of course you do not know Nanette. You go to hear Tradutorri, go every night she is in the cast perhaps, and rave for days afterward over her voice, her beauty, her power, and when all is said the thing you most admire is a something which has no name, the indescribable quality which is Tradutorri herself. But of Nanette, the preserver of Madame's beauty, the mistress of Madame's finances, the executrix of Madame's affairs, the power behind the scenes, of course you know nothing.

It was after twelve o'clock when Nanette entered Madame's sleeping apartments at the Savoy and threw up the blinds, for Tradutorri always slept late after a performance. Last night it was *Cavalleria Rusticana*, and Santuzza is a trying role when it is enacted not merely with the emotions but with the soul, and it is this peculiar soul-note that has made Tradutorri great and unique among the artists of her generation.

"Madame has slept well, I hope?" inquired Nanette respectfully, as she presented herself at the foot of the bed.

"As well as usual, I believe," said Tradutorri rather wearily. "You have brought my breakfast? Well, you may put it here and put the ribbons in my gown while I eat. I will get up afterward."

Nanette took a chair by the bed and busied herself with a mass of white tulle.

"We leave America next week, Madame?"

"Yes, Friday; on the *Paris*," said Madame, absently glancing up from her strawberries. "Why, Nanette, you are crying! One would think you had sung 'Voi lo sapete' yourself last night. What is the matter, my child?"

"O, it is nothing worthy of Madame's notice. One is always sorry to say good-bye, that is all."

"To one's own country, perhaps, but this is different. You have no friends here; pray, why should you be sorry to go?"

"Madame is mistaken when she says I have no friends here."

"Friends! Why, I thought you saw no one. Who, for example?"

"Well, there is a gentleman—"

"Bah! Must there always be a 'gentleman,' even with you? But who is this fellow? Go on!"

"Surely Madame has noticed?"

"Not I; I have noticed nothing. I have been very absentminded, rather ill, and abominably busy. Who is it?"

"Surely Madame must have noticed Signor Luongo, the head waiter?"

"The tall one, you mean, with the fine head like poor Sandro Salvini's? Yes, certainly I have noticed him; he is a very impressive piece of furniture. Well, what of him?"

"Nothing, Madame, but that he is very desirous that I should marry him."

"Indeed! And you?"

"I could wish for no greater happiness on earth, Madame."

Tradutorri laid a strawberry stem carefully upon her plate.

"Um-m-m, let me see; we have been here just two months and this affair has all come about. You have profited by your stage training, Nanette."

"O, Madame! Have you forgotten last season? We stopped here for six weeks then."

"The same 'gentleman' for two successive seasons? You are very disappointing, Nanette. You have not profited by your opportunities after all."

"Madame is pleased to jest, but I assure her that it is a very serious affair to me."

"O, yes, they all are. *Affaires très sérieuses.* That is scarcely an original remark, Nanette. I think I remember having made it once myself."

The look of bitter unbelief that Nanette feared came over Madame's face. Presently, as Nanette said nothing, Tradutorri spoke again.

"So you expect me to believe that this is really a serious matter?"

"No, Madame," said Nanette quietly. "He believes it and I believe. It is not necessary that anyone else should." Madame glanced curiously at the girl's face, and when she spoke again it was in a different tone.

"Very well: I do not see any objection. I need a man. It is not a bad thing to have your own porter in London, and after our London engagement is over we will go directly to Paris. He can take charge of my house there; my present steward is not entirely satisfactory, you know. You can spend the summer together there and doubtless by next season you can endure to be separated from him for a few months. So stop crying and send this statuesque signor to me tomorrow, and I will arrange matters. I want you to be happy, my girl—at least to try."

"Madame is good—too good, as always. I know your great heart. Out of your very compassion you would burden yourself with this man because I fancy him, as you once burdened yourself with me. But that is impossible, Madame. He would never leave New York. He will have his wife to himself or not at all. Very many professional people stay here, not all like Madame, and he has his prejudices. He would never allow me to travel, not even with Madame. He is very firm in these matters."

"O, ho! So he has prejudices against our profession, this garçon? Certainly you have contrived to do the usual thing in a very usual manner. You have fallen in with a man who objects to your work."

Tradutorri pushed the tray away from her and lay down laughing a little as she threw her arms over her head.

"You see, Madame, that is where all the trouble comes. For of course I could not leave you."

Tradutorri looked up sharply, almost pleadingly, into Nanette's face.

"Leave me? Good Heavens, no! Of course you cannot leave me. Why, who could ever learn all the needs of my life as you know them? What I may eat and what I

may not, when I may see people and when they will tire
me, what costumes I can wear and at what temperature I can
have my baths. You know I am as helpless as a child in these
matters. Leave me? The possibility has never occurred
to me. Why, girl, I have grown fond of you! You have
come entirely into my life. You have been my confidante
and friend, the only creature I have trusted these last ten
years. Leave me? I think it would break my heart. Come,
brush out my hair, I will get up. The thing is impossible!"

"So I told him, Madame," said Nanette tragically. "I
said to him: 'Had it pleased Heaven to give me a voice
I should have given myself wholly to my art, without one
reservation, without one regret, as Madame has done. As it
is, I am devoted to Madame and her art as long as she
has need of me.' Yes, that is what I said."

Tradutorri looked gravely at Nanette's face in the glass.
"I am not at all sure that either I or my art are worth it,
Nanette."

2

Tradutorri had just returned from her last performance
in New York. It had been one of those eventful nights
when the audience catches fire and drives a singer to her
best, drives her beyond herself until she is greater than she
knows or means to be. Now that it was over she was
utterly exhausted and the life-force in her was low.

I have said she is the only woman of our generation
who sings with the soul rather than the senses, the only
one indeed since Malibran, who died of that prodigal expense of spirit. Other singers there are who feel and vent
their suffering. Their methods are simple and transparent:
they pour out their self-inflicted anguish and when it is
over they are merely tired as children are after excitement.
But Tradutorri holds back her suffering within herself;
she suffers as the flesh-and-blood women of her century
suffer. She is intense without being emotional. She takes
this great anguish of hers and lays it in a tomb and rolls
a stone before the door and walls it up. You wonder that
one woman's heart can hold a grief so great. It is this
stifled pain that wrings your heart when you hear her,

that gives you the impression of horrible reality. It is this, too, of which she is slowly dying now.

See, in all great impersonation there are two stages. One in which the object is the generation of emotional power; to produce from one's own brain a whirlwind that will sweep the commonplaces of the world away from the naked souls of men and women and leave them defenseless and strange to each other. The other is the conservation of all this emotional energy; to bind the whirlwind down within one's straining heart, to feel the tears of many burning in one's eyes and yet not to weep, to hold all these chaotic faces still and silent within one's self until out of this tempest of pain and passion there speaks the still, small voice unto the soul of man. This is the theory of "repression." This is classical art, art exalted, art deified. And of all the mighty artists of her time Tradutorri is the only woman who has given us art like this. And now she is dying of it, they say.

Nanette was undoing Madame's shoes. She had put the mail silently on the writing desk. She had not given it to her before the performance as there was one of those blue letters from Madame's husband, written in an unsteady hand with the postmark of Monte Carlo, which always made Madame weep and were always answered by large drafts. There was also another from Madame's little crippled daughter hidden away in a convent in Italy.

"I will see to my letters presently, Nanette. With me news is generally bad news. I wish to speak with you tonight. We leave New York in two days, and the glances of this signor statuesque of yours is more than I can endure. I feel a veritable *mère Capulet*."

"Has he dared to look impertinently at Madame? I will see that this is stopped."

"You think that you could be really happy with this man, Nanette?"

Nanette was sitting upon the floor with the flowers from Madame's corsage in her lap. She rested her sharp little chin on her hand.

"Is anyone really happy, Madame? But this I know, that I could endure to be very unhappy always to be with him." Her saucy little French face grew grave and her lips trembled.

Madame Tradutorri took her hand tenderly.

"Then if you feel like that I have nothing to say. How strange that this should come to you, Nanette; it never has to me. Listen: Your mother and I were friends once when we both sang in the chorus in a miserable little theatre in Naples. She sang quite as well as I then, and she was a handsome girl and her future looked brighter than mine. But somehow in the strange lottery of art I rose and she went under with the wheel. She had youth, beauty, vigor, but was one of the countless thousands who fail. When I found her years afterward, dying in a charity hospital in Paris, I took you from her. You were scarcely ten years old then. If you had sung I should have given you the best instruction; as it was I was only able to save you from that most horrible of fates, the chorus. You have been with me so long. Through all my troubles you were the one person who did not change toward me. You have become indispensable to me, but I am no longer so to you. I have inquired as to the reputation of this signor of yours from the proprietors of the house and I find it excellent. Ah, Nanette, did you really think I could stand between you and happiness? You have been a good girl, Nanette. You have stayed with me when we did not stop at hotels like this one, and when your wages were not paid you for weeks together."

"Madame, it is you who have been good! Always giving and giving to a poor girl like me with no voice at all. You know that I would not leave you for anything in the world but this."

"Are you sure you can be happy so? Think what it means! No more music, no more great personages, no more plunges from winter to summer in a single night, no more Russia, no more Paris, no more Italy. Just a little house somewhere in a strange country with a man who may have faults of his own, and perhaps little children growing up about you to be cared for always. You have been used to changes and money and excitement, and those habits of life are hard to change, my girl."

"Madame, you know how it is. One sees much and stops at the best hotels, and goes to the best milliners—and yet one is not happy, but a stranger always. That is, I mean—"

"Yes, I know too well what you mean. Don't spoil it

now you have said it. And yet one is not happy! You
will not be lonely, you think, all alone in this big strange
city, so far from our world?"

"Alone! Why, Madame, Arturo is here!"

Tradutorri looked wistfully at her shining face.

"How strange that this should come to you, Nanette.
Be very happy in it, dear. Let nothing come between
you and it; no desire, no ambition. It is not given to everyone. There are women who wear crowns who would give
them for an hour of it."

"O, Madame, if I could but see you happy before I
leave you!"

"Hush, we will not speak of that. When the flowers
thrown me in my youth shall live again, or when the dead
crater of my own mountain shall be red once more—
then, perhaps. Now go and tell your lover that the dragon
has renounced her prey."

"Madame, I rebel against this loveless life of yours!
You should be happy. Surely with so much else you
should at least have that."

Tradutorri pulled up from her dressing case the score
of the last great opera written in Europe which had been
sent her to originate the title role.

"You see this, Nanette? When I began life, between me
and this lay everything dear in life—every love, every
human hope. I have had to bury what lay between. It is
the same thing florists do when they cut away all the buds
that one flower may blossom with the strength of all. God
is a very merciless artist, and when he works out his pur-
poses in the flesh his chisel does not falter. But no more
of this, my child. Go find your lover. I shall undress alone
tonight. I must get used to it. Good night, my dear. You
are the last of them all, the last of all who have brought
warmth into my life. You must let me kiss you tonight.
No, not that way—on the lips. Such a happy face tonight,
Nanette! May it be so always!"

After Nanette was gone Madame put her head down on
her dressing case and wept, those lonely tears of utter
wretchedness that a homesick girl sheds at school. And
yet upon her brow shone the coronet that the nations had
given her when they called her queen.

6:27 P.M.

by Joyce Carol Oates

7:30 A.M. Squinting in the bathroom mirror. Her eyebrows are growing out coarsely—shouldn't have shaved them—a mistake. She steams her face and plucks her eyebrows. That looks better. A thin, arching curve. She pats pink moisturizer on her face, rubs it into her skin in small deft circles, mechanically, hurrying. Hears Bobby fretting at the table. "Hey Bobby, you finish that cereal yet? Eat that cereal, it's good for you," she calls over her shoulder. She can hear the tinkle of his spoon against the bowl: but is he eating it or not? Her face, seen so close, is enormous like a balloon. After the pink moisturizer comes the liquid makeup—expensive stuff, eight dollars for the medium-sized bottle—which she rubs into her skin quickly, with upward strokes, up toward the outsides of her cheeks—and then her lips outlined with a lipliner, and then her lipstick, then rouge—very lightly on her cheekbones—and then the eye makeup, which will take ten minutes—"Hey Bobby, you're eating that stuff, aren't you? You better eat it all down," she cries. The kid had bad dreams last night and who can blame him, with a father like his? Glenda strokes mascara on her eyelashes, swift upward strokes, frowning into the mirror. Already she is chewing gum—no cigarette this morning—and her jaws are moving constantly, agreeably, as she appraises her face and her high-puffed pink-blond hair, hair like cotton candy. She looks all right.

8:00 A.M. Lets Bobby off at the nursery school. His collar is wrinkled—a mass of wrinkles that look baked solid, how'd she manage that?—"You be good now, y'hear?" she says, and Bobby swings his short legs across the car seat, manages to get the car door open without any help from her. He looks back at her and says, "Is Daddy coming back tonight?" and Glenda feels her face go sour. "I sure as hell hope not," she says with a shudder. Bobby doesn't let on whether this is the answer he wanted or not.

8:15 A.M. Fifteen minutes late. She struggles into the pink uniform—tight around the hips—and snaps on the radio. Coral is fussing around at the counter up front and yells back to Glenda, "Who's this supposed to be at eleven? Looks like 'W' something—" "That's Mrs. Wieden," Glenda yells up front, plugging in the hot plate—she's dying for some coffee—and glancing at herself in the mirror. The mirror runs the entire length of the shop, so Glenda has to parade around in front of it all day long. Always strutting in front of mirrors, her mother used to scold—Glenda pauses, thinking of her mother. Gray-faced and sour, the old woman, but not a bad old gal—except she wouldn't do anything for Glenda's wedding, and she paid out a lot for Glenda's kid sister—but she had it rough on that farm, a few acres in Texas, down in the southeast corner. Glenda is staring at herself in the mirror and her gaze becomes vague, watery.

8:30 A.M. Roxanne is doing her first customer, but Glenda's first customer—a regular named Babs—hasn't showed up yet, so Glenda answers the telephone when it rings. "Hello, Coral Hardee's," she says, but there is no one at the other end—must have been a wrong number. She hangs up. Coral, who is going over some bills, looks over at her. "Nobody there?" she says suspiciously. "Must of hung up when I answered," Glenda says. Glenda inspects her fingernails—it's been almost a week since she did them—thick gold lacquer, very attractive, worth the extra dollar. The telephone rings again and she answers it and this time it's her eight o'clock customer, Babs, with an excuse Glenda doesn't believe for one minute. But she says, "Sure, okay, Babs, I'll put you down for eleven-thirty. Sure." She hangs up. Coral says, "That one is always late." Glenda grunts in agreement. She tears the

wrapper off a stick of peppermint gum and pops the gum
in her mouth, wishing she could smoke a cigarette instead,
after the rotten night she had . . . four or five hours of
sleep, maybe less, ruined by the kid's nightmares . . . then
the kid has to go and ask, "Is Daddy coming back tonight?" Jesus Christ.

10:15 A.M. A woman with a northern accent, her hair
practically down to her hips, looking at Coral with big
blue innocent eyes and asking if it costs more for long
hair. "Afraid so, honey," Coral says. The bitch blinks as
if she'd never heard of such a thing and Glenda holds
her breath, hoping she'll walk out, but she decides to have
her hair done anyway. Just Glenda's luck to be free for
the next twenty minutes. So she spends ten minutes washing that haystack (inky black hair, probably dyed with
a do-it-yourself kit) and ten minutes setting it up, using
the biggest rollers in the place, and the woman is watching her in the mirror all the time, sharp-eyed as a lynx,
trying to make small talk. Glenda notices a big diamond
on her finger. "Are you from Miami?" she asks Glenda.
"No, Port Arthur in Texas," says Glenda with a businesslike smile. "I'm from Chicago," the woman says, in that
harsh whiny accent Glenda can't stand, "and I want to
tell you that my husband and I just love it down here . . .
everybody is so friendly down here. . . ." The woman
chatters and Glenda nods, barely listening. When she had
long hair herself, long wavy blond hair, she sure as hell
didn't go to a beauty parlor to have it done; she'd have
been sitting under the drier all day. She washed it herself
and let it dry loose, running around barefoot, and at five
o'clock on the dot she'd stop whatever she was doing and
get fixed up for Guy, brushing her hair until it gleamed,
putting on fresh makeup, checking herself from every
angle. Guy liked her in slacks best. Her white slacks.
She'd stand sideways and pose, assessing herself in the
mirror critically—a nice trim waist, broad hips, a big
bosom—she was all right. They had lived in Pensacola
then. "You married, honey?" the woman with the black
hair says, as Glenda packs her away for a nice two-hour

session under the drier. "Was," Glenda says with a fast, tight smile, to shut her up.

11:35 A.M. Babs finally shows up, wearing a red play-suit, a girl blobbing all over—you'd think she would be ashamed to walk on the street like that, half a mile from any beach. She calls out hello to Coral and Roxanne, has to be friendly to everybody. Glenda is a little put out this morning and deliberately keeps still for the first few minutes, as she brushes out Babs' hair—the set is still stiff from last week, sticky with hairspray—and Babs winces. Glenda begins the washing, notices that the spray is hot, but Babs doesn't complain—probably embarrassed for coming late. Glenda says, grudgingly, "How're you this week?" She gets Babs all toweled up and leads her over to the counter, to her chair. A big orange plastic container of hair rollers and pins is on the counter; it says "Glenda" in nail polish on its side. In the next chair Roxanne—with a new red wig, looking good—is toiling with a little old lady who drifted in from the street; in the other chair Coral herself is doing an old customer, Sally Tuohy, an ex-dancer at one of the clubs, the two of them chatting loudly and smoking so that Glenda's eyes water. She would give anything for a cigarette herself. But she won't give in, she absolutely will not give in. . . . "You heard from *him* lately?" Babs asks. Glenda, winding a strand of blond hair around a pink roller, wonders who Babs is talking about—then she remembers that she was telling Babs about a new friend of hers, Ronnie Strong, the racetrack man . . . or was it her other, fading friend W. J. Hecht, the mystery man? She doesn't think it was Guy; she doesn't talk about Guy if she can help it. So she says with a little grin, "Can't complain."

12:25 P.M. A guy in baggy shorts and sunglasses leads an elderly woman in—says to Coral, "Can you make her beautiful? Make her beautiful, okay? I'll be back in two hours." Thank God Roxanne is free, so Roxanne gets stuck with this dilly; the poor old woman is so feeble she can hardly walk. Glenda and Roxanne and Coral all glance at each other in the mirror—at the same instant—

all thinking the same thing, what hell it is to be old, dod-
dering like that, especially in Miami. Glenda goes across
the street to get some sandwiches and coffee for them.
When she strides in the restaurant people glance at her.
Men glance at her. For some reason this makes her nervous
today—maybe because she has been thinking of Guy so
often. She dreads running into him. Maybe seeing him in
a place like this. He'd be sitting at the counter and waiting, waiting. . . . Guy with his cowboy hat and his denim
work-clothes, walking sort of bow-legged, showing off to
her or anybody who would watch. Guy with his bleached-
out hair and face, looking weathered at the age of thirty-
one—reddened skin, a boil on the side of his neck, his
looks ruined from too much sun and too much alcohol.
Jesus, she thinks in amazement, she was married to that
man for six years. . . . She feels a kind of kick in the
belly—the memory of a kick from when she was carrying
the baby—and the men's eyes up and down the counter
make her shiver, they are the same eyes, Guy's eyes,
always the same. "Hey, Pink Princess," one of the men
whispers, referring to the "Pink Princess" stitching on
Glenda's collar, but Glenda ignores him. Her uniform is
too tight. Should lose a few pounds, or buy another uniform. "Hey, Pink Princess, are you snooty?" the man
says, but Glenda pays no attention to him. She waits
nervously for the sandwiches and the coffee. She has
always liked men to look at her, but today she feels
different . . . today everything seems different. . . .

1:15 P.M. Shelley, the part-time girl, who is a hat-check
girl also at one of the clubs, hurries in to pay back the
ten dollars she owes Glenda; she is all perfume and clattering heels. Glenda likes Shelley even though the kid is
pretty stupid. She's twenty-three and Glenda is a few
years older, she's a few decades wiser, but Shelley won't
listen to her advice. It's always hurry, hurry, hurry with
her. Shelley got out of her marriage without any kids, no
threats, no crazy telephone calls, no spying . . . now she's
heading into trouble with a married man, but do you
think she'll listen to Glenda? Glenda feels irritated with
Shelley's excitement. The girl is always in a hurry, a sweaty

erotic daze, her perfect lips curled up into a mindless, pleased smile. . . . Her eyes catch onto Glenda's in the mirror and she whispers, "Murray says he saw Guy the other night. Is he back in town? Is he bothering you again?" Glenda's heart begins to pound. "No," she says, "No. I got an injunction against him." "Yeah, well, Murray says he's back in town, says to tell you," Shelley says, on her way out. Her white skirt is so short it looks like a slip, nothing more, straining tight against her thighs. Glenda stands staring after her, holding the ten-dollar bill in her fingers.

2:05 P.M. The telephone rings. Glenda is in the middle of brushing out a customer and Coral is out and so Roxanne finally dashes up to the desk at about the tenth ring. Glenda's nerves are on edge. She pauses in her brushing of this woman's hair, her rather square chin contemplative, stern, hoping the telephone isn't . . . isn't for her. . . . But Roxanne yells, "Hey Glenda, for you!" So Glenda hurries up front, just knowing that it is Mrs. Foss at the nursery, that sorry old bat, with some bad news, or maybe W. J. with some far-out story about why he hadn't called her for two weeks, as if she gave a damn. . . . But when she picks up the receiver the line is dead. Not even a dial tone. "Hello? Hello?" she says sharply. "Hello?" She slams the receiver down, since Coral isn't in. Roxanne, lighting a cigarette, asks her what it was—Glenda shakes her head, nothing, no one—Roxanne says whoever it was was a man, and asked for Glenda in person. "Well, that could be anyone, couldn't it," she says sharply, and goes back to her customer. She hates Roxanne always snooping into her business.

2:15 P.M. One of her regular customers, Mrs. Foster, is being teased and brushed and sprayed. The poor old gal is withered on the bottom and puffed out on the top, her hair a bright burnished red, glowing from the tint—you'd swear she was a kid until she turned around and you saw her face. She always gives Glenda a dollar tip. Coral is back, chatting over the telephone with someone. So the telephone can't ring. Glenda stops herself from thinking of that call—the dead line—stops herself from thinking of Guy, because it never does any good to think about him. That's over. Gone. He has enough sense to leave her alone, since that night in the parking lot when he tried to beat up a boy friend of hers and the police carted him off—he never was stupid—he's got enough sense to leave her alone.

3:05 P.M. Cute little Bonnie from the insurance place down the block comes in for a shampoo and set; Glenda likes her, approves of her petite figure, no more than a size 5—Glenda is a size 12 now, going on 13, she's going to have to lose a few pounds. She approves of Bonnie's long pink fingernails and her golden tan. She's cute, all right, but most of it is make-up . . . some of it gets on Glenda's fingers when she washes Bonnie's hair. Bonnie is getting married next month. "Ma wants to have three hundred people, isn't that wild?" Bonnie laughs. "How many'd you have to yours?" "Oh, not more than a hundred," says Glenda, adding a few people, and reluctant to think again about that hot Texas afternoon, getting drunk and squabbling all during the reception with one another and with Guy—not wanting to think about the hotel in Houston that stank of insecticide, and the bed with its musty covers and mattress. No, she doesn't want to think about that Saturday, or about how it all ran down to a day last July, also a Saturday, with Guy screaming at her that he was going to kill her. Washing Bonnie's hair, briskly, she rubs a row of very small pimples just at Bonnie's hairline, and the pimples begin to bleed, just thin trickles of blood mixed in with the water . . . and while Bonnie is chattering about her wedding gown Glenda is trying to blot the blood with a towel. She leads Bonnie over to the chair, sees that the bleeding seems to have stopped, it looks O.K., tosses away the stained towel, then sprays Bonnie's hair with the bluish hair-set mixture. She puts two rows of pink rollers on Bonnie's head, a back row of green rollers, and pins down the back hair carefully. Sprays it all. The spray stinks—almost chokes Bonnie. Godawful stuff. Glenda reaches down, grunting, to fish out a pair of ear-protectors. They are made of flesh-pink plastic.

She fastens them over Bonnie's reddened ears, puts a hairnet over the whole business and draws it tight. Fixed up like this, Bonnie looks small and trivial; her face looks pasty. "There you are," Glenda says, leading Bonnie over to the hair drier where Angel Laverne is all set to come out.

3:30 P.M. Angel Laverne strolls with Glenda up to the front desk to make next week's appointment. Angel always asks for Glenda. She is a dancer at the Cutless Club and much admired by everyone for her long trim legs and her expensive clothes. "It looks great," Angel says, admiring her high-stacked orange hair, with the row of stiff curls across the front. It is an open secret that Angel had silicone injected into her breasts and that the operation was a marvelous success; Angel sucks in her breath, glances at herself in the mirror approvingly. Once in a while she tells Glenda, seriously, that Glenda should try out at the club—"You'd make a great dancer," she tells Glenda—and Glenda laughs in embarrassment, not mentioning the fact that she tried out for something like that back in Houston, but with no luck, and she was younger and better-looking then. Angel thanks her again and says good-bye. Glenda goes to the book to see who's next but someone starts shouting—an old biddy under the hair drier—"Glenda, Glenda, what time is it?" She has a hoarse, froggy voice; her double chins tremble. Glenda tells her the time, though she knows the old girl won't be able to hear—why the hell do they always try to talk under the hair drier? So Glenda strides over and holds out her arm so that the woman can see her wristwatch. "Oh. Three-thirty," she says stupidly, as if she thought it might be some other time. Glenda feels sorry for her, the old dame is a widow and probably hasn't anywhere to get to; this town is filled with widows. It occurs to Glenda that Coral Hardee's Pink Princess Salon is like the backstage of a theater—the audience is men, made up only of men, who know what they want to see and who are impatient with anything else. She goes back to check the book. God, is she tired, and it's only three-thirty. . . .

Three more customers coming up, one right after the other, and the first one wants a permanent. . . .

4:10 P.M. And the call does come from the nursery: a very unconvincing story about Lynda going home early, having to babysit for a neighbor who's had a baby, or some such lying crap, so could Glenda come pick up Bobby early? "No, I cannot," Glenda says in a soft furious voice. "I'm going to report you to the Better Business Bureau if this keeps on!" On the other end Mrs. Foss stammers, no doubt she's been drinking and the kids have been running wild, no doubt, Glenda is fed up with Mrs. Foss's problems and says firmly: "Look, you know I have a job here and I can't leave early. It's your responsibility to take care of those children until the mothers get there—Mrs. Foss—" Mrs. Foss hangs up. Glenda wonders if she should call back, maybe the old bat is passed out, or whether this means she has won. Scaring her with the Better Business Bureau probably did the trick.

4:45 P.M. "Did you read here about Jackie Kennedy and Onassis, what's-his-name, they spent twenty million dollars in one year?" Glenda's customer, a woman with thinning brown hair, is tapping a movie magazine angrily on the counter.

Roxanne, standing next to Glenda, says, "He can't be such a geek, or else how could he make all that money? Or is the twenty million just the interest, you know, the interest on the stuff they own?"

"Jesus, twenty million," Glenda says, whistling through her teeth, "that's—that's like more than what all of us make in a year, or in our lives—"

She is backcombing her customer's hair energetically.

"What I feel sorry for is the kids, those two little kids —"

"Yeah, those two little kids."

"Caroline, you know, she has a shrine devoted to her father. It's in their New York apartment. What do you think Onassis thinks about that?"

"If he wants to have any opinion on it, let him get himself assassinated. He's only a guest in this country."

"I wouldn't want his nose—"

"Isn't he ugly?"

"Caroline has a whole staff of servants to occupy her mind, and all the allowance money she wants to occupy the rest of her mind," Roxanne says. "Think of all the clothes and stuff she could buy—"

"How Onassis got started," Glenda's customer explains, "he bought some ships from the United States for ten million dollars. Just bought them. The United States gave up some navy ships, I mean fighting ships—"

"Really?"

"They gave them to him, and he went back to Greece—which is incidentally just about the poorest country in Europe—he went to Greece with them—now, ten million dollars' worth of boats, in a country like that—that's why the United States can't get the money back. That's what was behind all that to-do about Onassis not being allowed in the country."

"Which country?"

"*This* country. He was barred, until he married Jackie Kennedy. That was in the newspapers."

"Well, he can't be such a geek if he made all that money. But I wouldn't want to be married to him!"

"If you can prove you're a blood relative of his, he'll pay you $25,000 a year interest-free for life. That's what they say. But he never gives any money to charity, not one dime."

"I wouldn't want to be related to him," Glenda says with a laugh. "You ever see his sister? Her nose? I wouldn't want that family nose, Christ!"

"Yeah, there's a picture of his sister or somebody in one of these magazines, a few months ago, she's all pockmarked and's got eyes sunk ten miles back in her face, all bags and stuff—I wouldn't want to look like that just to be that guy's sister!"

"Me neither!"

5:00 P.M. Coral has to go to the lawyer's—some fuss about a customer who got her eye poked by one of the part-time girls, the girl stuck her little finger in the woman's eye, just an accident, but Coral has bad luck. Glenda takes over. She tries on a red wiglet, remembers when she was a redhead, smirks at herself, exchanges wiglets with Roxanne—they always fool around when Coral is out of the shop—and wonders if maybe she should invest in a red wig. Only forty dollars with her discount. Maybe. Maybe for a change. But seeing herself in the mirror, that striking face—like a billboard, that face—she feels uneasy, because the red hair will make people look at her, men, men will look at her, men will look at her in that certain way, and does she want this to happen? To happen again?

5:10 P.M. Telephone rings. Coral isn't back yet, so Glenda goes to answer it. Begins to perspire even before she picks up the receiver. She approaches the desk, legs working hard, fast, the muscles of her thighs straining against the tight skirt, *she can feel, remember, the football-sized baby inside her,* she picks up the pink plastic receiver breezily. . . .

"Hello!"

No answer.

"I said hello. This is Coral Hardee's. Hello . . . ?"

Be calm. Calm.

"Hello . . . ?"

She begins to pick at one of her fingernails. The gold polish is chipping. She says suddenly, "Listen, Guy, if this is you you'd better cut it out. I'm going to call the police—" She can see him suddenly: the grimy cowboy hat crooked on his head, his grin that had nothing to do with his eyes, his wise-guy grin, his little-boy wise-guy grin, the way he'd sit with a toothpick in his mouth and stare at her. At first she liked it, but then after they'd been married for a while she could feel him staring at her even while she was in another room, staring through the walls at her. Sometimes he'd joke with her, slapping her rear, *Hey, is all that mine?* he'd say. He liked her best in slacks. Out on the street he got mad if other men looked at her, but he liked her to wear slacks, especially that pair of white knitted slacks. . . . "I'm going to call the police!"

she says, hanging up. She is about to cry. Roxanne is watching her, hesitating . . . not knowing if she should say anything or stay out of this. . . .

5:15 P.M. The door opens. A man enters.
Glenda stares at him, frowning. He is short, stocky, wearing neat beige trousers and a shirt and, in spite of the 85-degree temperature, a dark green wool sweater, armless, and a large wristwatch. Glenda feels a dull automatic tug in his direction, wondering how his face will change when he sees her. Their faces always change, always; she shivers with excitement, though the man is homely himself—a swarthy face, too small, a very small receding chin, sunglasses with cheap plastic frames, hair that looks a little kinky.
"Hiya, Jere, that you?" says Coral, who has just come in.
He takes off the sunglasses with a grin, and Glenda, shocked, sees that this isn't a man after all, but that woman—"Jere"—who comes into the Salon every two weeks to have her hair cut.
"Hiya, Coral. How's business?"
"Can't complain."
"I can't complain either."
Jere smiles and waves at Glenda and Roxanne, but shyly: she knows they won't smile back.
Ugh.
Glenda glances at the book to see who's stuck with this character—too bad, Roxanne!—Roxanne is down for 5:15. Last customer of the day. Glenda ignores Jere and starts tidying up her things. Feels sorry for poor Roxanne, but thank God it isn't her. Coral, bustling by with an armful of wigs, winks at Glenda and Glenda winks back.

5:30 P.M. Sits with Coral in the back room, smoking. Her first and only cigarette of the day. "Tomorrow I'm giving it up permanently," she tells Coral, "but today I feel kind of nervous. Real jumpy." Coral chain-smokes and drinks coffee all day long. "How come you're jumpy?" she says. "I don't know," Glenda says slowly, "on account of Guy. . . ." "Oh, hell! Is he back in town again?"

says Coral. "That I don't know," says Glenda. She hesitates, wanting to tell Coral about the telephone calls. She can't stop shivering. Coral says with a harsh expulsion of breath, "Listen, kid, frankly I never liked his looks. I mean he's nice-looking and all that, he's a handsome guy, but, you know, he *knows* he's handsome, and . . ." She glances out to see if the last customer is gone. Yes, Jere is gone and Roxanne is gathering up the towels. "And handsome men, when they go to bed with you, you know, they're going to bed with themselves. I read that."

Glenda stares at her. "They *what?*"

"They're doing it to *themselves.* The woman is just a mirror or something. I read it in a psychiatrist's column in the newspaper."

"I don't get it."

"Well, that's what he said. A good-looking man is apt to be a son of a bitch and the woman doesn't count, I mean he wants a good-looking woman himself, I don't mean that, but whichever one it is doesn't count because, you know, he's doing it to him*self* and the woman is the mirror he looks into. I read it. It was real convincing."

Glenda shakes her head, confused. "Yeah, well, Guy's handsome and all that . . . but . . . Coral, could you maybe come over to my place with me after work? After I pick up Bobby?"

"What? Why?"

"Oh, we could have supper together and then go to a movie, all three of us, you know, like we did that one time. . . . I was just thinking . . ."

"I don't know, Glenda, I got a lot of work to do tonight."

"Bobby ain't no trouble, is he?"

"Bobby is a real sweet kid. Does he still wet the bed?"

"Not so much now."

"How's that what's-her-name, Foss? She any better?"

"Oh, she's all right," Glenda says nervously. "We could send out for some Chinese food or maybe a pizza. . . ."

Coral lights another cigarette and gets to her feet. "The problem is I got to look through the bills and stuff tonight . . . start making out some refill orders, you know. . . ."

"Bobby ain't no trouble, he sits real still in the movies."

"Oh Bobby is sweet, he's a sweetheart," Coral says vaguely. "Oh, hey, Roxanne, don't forget that peroxide thing—"

"I put it away," Roxanne calls back.

"Half-full, did you?"

"Yeah, it's half-full."

"Did you put it down for reorder?"

"Okay, I'll do it now," Roxanne says wearily.

"She always lets things go, it never fails," Coral mutters to Glenda.

Glenda has finished her cigarette and is staring at it, at the dry lipstick stains on it.

"So you can't make it tonight, then?" Glenda says.

"Some other time, maybe . . . okay?" Coral says.

Glenda puts out her cigarette. For some reason the cigarette made her feel cold.

5:50 P.M. Double parks by Mrs. Foss's, and what the hell—there comes Bobby running up the street! "What are you doing out by yourself?" Glenda shouts. Bobby climbs in the car; his mouth is stained with something greenish. He looks a little sick. "What happened, did she kick you kids out on the street?" Glenda cries. Bobby says, vaguely, "She said you was s'posed to come at five-thirty and you didn't." Glenda has half a mind to leave her car out on the street here and run up to Mrs. Foss's door and pound on it until the old bitch answers. . . . "Oh, goddam her, goddam everybody," Glenda whispers, so angry she could almost cry, and now somebody is honking his horn behind her. . . . "You gonna cry now?" Bobby asks scornfully, fearfully.

6:05 P.M. The A & P, very crowded, Glenda has picked a cart with wobbling wheels, just her luck. Bobby is muling and whining and pulling at her. She moves as fast as she can up and down the aisles, her stomach jumpy, she buys a barbecued chicken wrapped in greasy cellophane and some potato chips that Bobby starts to eat right away—probably didn't get any decent lunch—probably got slapped around all day. But Glenda has no

time to think about Bobby and Mrs. Foss, she has to get
this stupid limping cart over in line, she is perspiring with
strain or with worry, something seems to be wrong with
her nerves today. If she got married again . . .
But she isn't going to get married again. No.
But if . . .
The cashier has pink-blond hair, like Glenda's, ringing
up the items one-two-three, very efficient and skillful.
Glenda notes approvingly the girl's pierced ears and tiny
gold earrings, her large rather sullen red mouth, her
red-polished nails. Men would like her looks. She probably
does well with men.

6:15 P.M. Parks crooked at the curb, runs into the drugstore for some sleeping pills—a new brand called *Sleepeez*,
might as well try something new—and some laxatives, the
usual. She feels a little sick, like rocks in her intestines,
her stomach is bad again and has been for the last week;
on her way out she remembers that she needs some toothpaste, she'll have to get it tomorrow—hell—and her first
customer is due at eight, that fussy skinny bitch with the
"sensitive scalp." . . .

6:25 P.M. Parks behind her apartment building. Bobby
groggy, sniffing; what if he's coming down with another
cold? She checks his forehead and it seems very warm.
She notices that the garbage men haven't come yet to
pick up the enormous piles of junk out behind the apartment building, there was talk of a slow-down this
week. . . . Hell, she is so tired of slow-downs and strikes
and demonstrations. . . . "Bobby, come *on*, carry one of
these packages," she says in exasperation, because he is
just sitting there, staring. "What are you staring at?" she
says. He shakes his head. Nothing. She looks and sees
only the back of the building, the dreary entrance and the
stacked boxes and damp, scattered newspapers. There is
nothing there. No one there. She lives on the first floor,
her apartment is nearby, there is nothing to worry about.
"Bobby, come on, please," she says, and this time he
rouses himself and starts moving.

AS WE HAVE LEARNT FROM FREUD, THERE ARE NO JOKES

by Penelope Gilliatt

I married my Manhattan landlord. If I were a local, I suppose I would put that more delicately. But I come from Tobermory, a Scottish island village where it would not be such a craven blunder.

The beginnings with him were not auspicious, though.

I waited for him for an hour, outside his half-built apartment building. You could see him coming a block away. He wore a bright mustard suit. One of the Mafia? An evil-looking briefcase contributed. On the other hand, and leaving the suit aside, there was something pleasant about his stoop.

"Are you married?" he said at once, head turned toward the din from his workmen as he stepped past me over the rubble and put a key into the lock of the, I should have thought, not yet apt to be plundered building.

"I've been waiting an hour," I said. "The foreman promised you'd be here. I've got to find somewhere to live."

He scraped his shoes free of the mess outside, an act which interested, considering the dirt he was to step into. A piece of grit flew backward from his heel into my eyeball. I had an impulse to say "Sorry," owing to my nationality, but managed to quench it.

"I'd like one of these apartments," I said.

He went in. "Married?" he said.

"No," I said, holding my eye. I suppose a New Yorker would have said "Yes," for prudence, but there wasn't much lust in the air.

"I can't have unmarried women," he said. "They're always getting raped on the way to the laundry."

As I left, with all speed, I noticed a sign outside the apartment building that said "Beware of the Dog." Rage

weakened here, and I thought quite fondly of the work-
man within who must be in the habit of bringing some
overloyal pet to the site.

The next day, after the thirty-third night spent on the
exitless side of a bed that was shoved up against a wall
and that also housed a physiotherapist called Daphne, an
air hostess called Olga, and Olga's dopey Teddy bear, I
got out of the bottom of the bed unheard and thought, *No.*

I rang the building site. The foreman said the owner
was there.

"Can I speak to him?"

"He don't speak on the telephone."

So.
Do something else. Buy a birthday present for my
grandmother on the way to work.

"I want a nightdress to send airmail," I said to a saleswoman in a fair-to-lousy cut-price shop. "For an old
lady."

"This."

"No, something to the floor, I think."

"This."

"Haven't you got anything that goes to the floor?"

"This is waltz-length."

"She's eighty-one. I think she'd rather have something
full-length."

"Everything is waltz-length or bikini. You want she
should trip over and break her neck?"

So.
Push on to work. My employer, Simpson Aird, a
friendly capitalist who calls me Miss Nib when he feels
rumbustious, dictated letters in bed. His wife, Tessa, ate
fried bread and tomatoes. Their six-month-old son was
kicking on the bottom of the eiderdown. I picked him up
while Mr. Aird thought. The baby treated me hospitably,
being the age he is and therefore still inclined to interpret
the rest of the world as an annex of himself. To be or-
ganic to somebody else's idea is an experience not to be
sneezed at, in these divided times or any other. The Aird
baby has a strong cast of thought and he imposes him-

self, philosophically speaking; as he stared at me, lying
on my lap, he seemed like a hand of mine. Self and
others. The usual tautology.

"How's the apartment hunt?" Mr. Aird said.

"Plugging on," I said.

"No luck?"

"Not yet."

Tessa said, "You'll suddenly find one."

"Or gradually," I said.

"You don't *gradually* find an apartment. You *suddenly*
find an apartment," said Tessa.

"I might be inching up on it, mightn't I?"

"No," said Tessa, who sees things her own way as
resolutely as any baby. "One day you'll simply have it,
and then you won't remember what it was like to be
without it."

"No?"

"You need some new clothes," said Tessa.

"Shall I get on with the letters?" I said.

Simpson peered at our two faces, scenting a row. Or a
wound. "My dear Miss Nib," he said, hurling himself out
of bed and into the bathroom, "take a letter. I think you
look first-rate." He imitated my Scots accent. "Furst-rate.
Scrumptious." He sang "D' ye ken John Peel?" into
the bathroom mirror.

So.

Revived, go back in the lunch hour to the apartment
building, even if the landlord has twice more refused
to come to the telephone. Swine.

He was standing in the foreman's office, looking
troubled. Mustard jacket off; black pullover underneath.
That stoop. A brooding and somewhat majestic effect. If
swine, then big wild boar, hunting quietly in the woods
for something, mooching about and turning things up.

The foreman was putting down the telephone. "They
won't pay," he said to the landlord. "I told you."

"I've come about an apartment," I said. "I don't see
why I have to be married. If it comes to getting raped on
the way to the laundry, married women with a lot of
washing must get raped more."

"Get them back on the phone," the landlord said to the foreman.

"You'll have to talk to them yourself," the foreman told him. "They're your insurers."

"No."

"You know what you've got, not talking on the telephone?" the foreman said. "You've got a hangup."

The landlord went on standing there, turned away from me.

"I want one of these apartments," I said to the foreman, who was drinking a Coke.

"Can't you see I'm busy?" he said.

"I've something on my mind," the landlord said softly to a concrete wall.

"What's happened?" I said.

"A *dog's* been stolen," the foreman said impatiently.

"Oh dear," I said. "Was it his?," looking at the large black back.

"It was to guard the plumbing," said the foreman, crushing the Coke tin with his hand and throwing it into a corner.

"What?" I said.

The landlord said, fast, "It was supposed to be guarding the plumbing, and if you think that's crazy then ask him about it. He told me to."

"It's you that's crazy," said the foreman. "What sort of a boss are you, doing what *I* say?"

"Trained to look after *plumbing*?" I said.

"These dogs are highly skilled," said the foreman.

"This one wasn't," the landlord said.

"Well," the foreman said, "what do you expect for eighty bucks a week? You got it cheap."

"It seems a heavy thing to steal, a bath," I said. "Let alone baths."

"I know it was only eighty bucks a week," the landlord said over me. "But eight *hundred* for the loss of the dog."

"You should've taken out insurance. You should've thought of that," said the foreman.

"Also, it was a nice dog," the landlord said, now sorrowing and private.

The foreman yelled something to the ceiling in another

language and stomped toward the door saying, "The whole world is crazy, I tell you. Make your own telephone calls. What kind of a landlord are you, not speaking on the telephone?"

"You should've got the four-inch ducts finished on schedule," the landlord said. He took a couple of steps toward the man. "Then the plumbing would have been connected and we'd never have had to *have* your guard dog."

"Listen," said the foreman, swinging the door handle to and fro. The landlord had come to a halt. "I'm going to take time out to tell you something."

"Well, I pay for the time," the landlord defended himself, though not as intimidatingly as I could have hoped.

"One: Plumbing has to be bought in *ahead of schedule*, in case you lose a month's rent, O.K.? Two: The four-inch ducts were finished *last month*. It's the Mayor's *inspector* we're waiting on now. And why? Because you were too goddam mean to drop the five-hundred-buck payment to City Hall for *special services*."

"Five-hundred-buck *bribe*."

"*Payment*. For *special services*, for getting it *done*. See what happens when you waste your time in line?"

The foreman left. The landlord stood there. Now, to contradict myself, he didn't look like one of the Mafia at all. On the contrary.

"Shall we have some lunch?" he said.

"Yes, please. Could I have an apartment as well?"

He laughed. His eyebrows looked permanently as if they had just shot up. They had big half circles of pure white skin below. His hair was dark brown, and his face so asymmetrical that a reflection of it in a piece of broken mirror on the wall was unrecognizable. An exuberant man, nervous, poetic, with a way of pulling his long fingers one by one when something was making him laugh to himself. He was fun. I have never had such fun with anybody.

At our first lunch I asked for canneloni to fill myself up.

"Good. Girls are always thinning themselves," he said.

"What's your name, by the way?" I said.

"Murray Lancaster," he said. Pause. "Huh?" he said. "What are you looking like that for?"

"Well," I said, "I thought you were in the Mafia, but it's not much of a Mafia name."

"Why do you think I was in the Mafia?"

"Because you're a landlord, I suppose," I said, holding back the next thing I had been going to say and then deciding he might not mind. "Perhaps also because of your mustard suit."

He looked angry. It took me some time—weeks—to discover that he was poor and wore clothes handed on by a negligently competent brother-in-law in the soft-drink business.

He asked my name.

"Emm," I said. "Emm McKechnie. My parents christened me Empyrean, but there had to be a way out."

"Do you believe that, in general?" he said.

"Yes, with luck," I said. He looked up fast, extremely pleased in a philanthropic way but still hanging back for himself. One could tell. Something more needed to be said, obviously. Wondering whether this was it, I told him I had a mustard suit, too. Ah, no. He concentrated on the menu. Hell, I thought. Patronage. The British abroad at their old work. But when I bent down on some pretext and could see into his face it seemed possible that he was laughing at himself as well as flustered.

Still with his head down, he ordered his own lunch. "A very rare steak," he said. And then, to me, "Vegetable?"

"Could I have a green salad?"

"And a very green salad," he said to the waiter before he could stop himself.

The foreman victimized him. Waiters made him feel a fool, this clever man. Spectres of poverty beset him, and he hankered after anything that would last. Perhaps that was why he had embarked, without capital, on trying to put up a building, though God knows this would have no long life in Manhattan. The little money he had saved was kept in seven different banks and also in his apartment, in the freezer locker of the fridge, inside a string-beans packet. He made piles of quarters in his sock drawer when he emptied his pockets at night. After a few months, despite our best efforts, he went bankrupt and his knavish contractors were awarded all he had. We kept the loot that was in the freezer. We got married in a while. By then we were living in a dirt-cheap place on the Bowery. He hung on to his car. No bailiff would have touched it. He was deeply fond of it. It was a very old dark green Hispano-Suiza, held together with beautiful leather straps like the ones my grandparents had on their steamer trunks.

He was a moving man, bashful but debonair. He was the only man I have ever known who once actually fell out of a hammock with laughing.

He slept on his back, at the edge of the bed by the telephone, near the door. I think he was frightened something would happen to us.

The following year he turned over in his sleep and crashed his leg onto my hipbone. It was like a piece of falling timber. Next morning I limped.

"What's happened?" he said from bed.

"You hit me with five ton of leg in your sleep. I didn't know a leg could be so heavy. It was like being socked with a Wellington boot full of mud."

"Should you go to a doctor?"

"Oh, no."

"What's a Wellington boot?"

"Gumboot. Rubber boot."

"I'm so sorry."

"I was rather pleased. It's the first time you've ever slept anywhere near the middle of the bed."

He groaned and looked away. "And the first time I do it I hurt you. I do things wrong too often. One of me is too many."

He thought of himself as a bungler. He thought he was infinitely dispensable and replaceable. From things he said in his sleep, I know he thought I was going to fall in love with somebody else. But we were allies. We were some sort of kin.

My husband died, my love, died in his car, on the night we put the clocks back, on the night of the extra hour that everyone else was glad of, though for my part I found

no use to put it to. It was a Saturday night and I had a
fortnight of holiday ahead of me while the Airds were
unexpectedly away, not to speak of the obligatory Sunday
to get through, the one that would have fallen to me in
any case. I did what one does, moving myself about, reading the news, maintaining the circulation of the blood,
for the accepted reasons. The heart and lungs carried on
willy-nilly, keeping me awake. The need for sleep wasn't
as merciful as it might have been. I would have to get my
clothes cleaned, if I was to go on. I would have to telephone the grocer, if I was to go on. A pound of tea, I
said; no, half a pound, thank you, and any bread that's
got a European type of crust, and have you some Dundee
marmalade? I don't like it here very much, not at the
moment, I said, no doubt sounding like a dangerous re-
cluse and a chauvinist to boot. Which would have been
doubly misleading, for I had never felt more in search of
company, nor indeed more indebted to Manhattan, the
city without him being a great deal more like the city
we had lived in together than anywhere else without him
would have been. After a few days, nine or ten, I wondered if it would aid things to pay a visit to Scotland, but
I hadn't the purpose for it, let alone the money. So I
went and lived in public libraries and all-night cafés for
a time. Someone moved me out, sooner or later, and
it was probably just as well, for my attempts to find anyone to talk to had not prospered. "Do you think I could
have a cup of tea, please?" I had said to a promising-
looking man behind a counter, but it seems I should have
said "Cup of tea" and left it at that, for he put his hands
on his hips and shouted, "What's stopping you?"

When my holiday had the goodness to be over, I stood
on the usual rush-hour bus and read a schoolboy's comic
strips over his shoulder. There was sun outside. Life had
several appearances of being on the mend. Halfway up-
town, after a setback caused by a reminiscent cheekbone
at the other end of the bus, I got a seat between a Chinaman and a Puerto Rican woman. I seemed to be taking
up more than my share of the space, and the grief was
bad again. I tried thinking of others, more as a device than
a good, and clenched my thigh muscles for a start, to
give half an inch more room to the neighbors.

"Excuse me," I said to the Chinaman. "My husband is dead."

The Chinaman grunted and dug his heel-shaped chin into his collar. It started to rain.

"Every morning this time the bus is full of nuts," the driver said with violence, not even visibly addressing me, though his right eye was glaring at me in his driving mirror. I spread my muscles again and took all the room I wanted. I should get my hair done, I thought. Widows slip if they let their hair go. Queen Victoria went downhill. It's a mistake to be wearing his watch.

"Hello," I said to the Puerto Rican child who was sitting on the lap of the woman beside me.

"Doan speak English," the mother said in the voice of a record, turning the child on her lap so that its back now faced me.

"Hi," said the Ukrainian doorman at the Airds' building, using the sum of the English that I had ever heard him speak, apart from "God bless," "Cab, sir?," and "You bet your ass." This morning he followed "Hi" with "How's life treats you?," so I thought he must have learned more English while I was away.

I said, "My husband's dead."

He laughed and said, "You bet your ass."

In the Airds' duplex apartment I hung my raincoat over Tessa's second mink with a malign hope that it would drip, which involved me in turning in my tracks after a minute or two to take the gesture back. The Chinese manservant caught me at it. I'm afraid nothing of the sort is hidden from him. There is no meanness he does not recognize. He winked in the direction of the Airds' bedroom and said, "Having late breakfast."

"Yes," I said coldly.

He winked again and said, "Nice holiday? Nice time with hubby?"

"My husband isn't well," I said, having no mind to hand him the truth at that moment.

The Airds were good to me. Cheerful. They made me move in to live with them as something they called their *au pair* girl, mostly to exercise two new Great Dane puppies. The manservant, Wu, took me in hand in his own

way and gave me makeup lessons. He sold cosmetics on
commission. He had a fine and steady hand with an eye-
line brush, like a miniaturist.

"You should go take Spanish at night school," he said
one evening in the Airds' downstairs lavatory when we
were clearing up after they had gone out to dine. He put
one of their cocktail nuts into my mouth off a silver tray
that he had balanced for the moment on the washbasin,
and set himself to work on my mascara. "Meet Mr. Right,"
he said, twirling one of his makeup brushes in a half-empty
glass of Simpson's after-office bourbon. Then the Airds
came back for something they had forgotten. Wu panicked
and locked the door.

One of the Airds tried to come in.

"Who's there?" said Simpson's voice.

Wu clapped his hand over my mouth and daftly said
nothing himself.

"Who is it?" Simpson said again, firmly.

"It's only us," I said like a fool, through Wu's palm.
Inapt. Wu and I were not us—not in any way.

The Great Danes slept in my room, unfortunately. I
walked them for three or four hours a day, but nothing
tired them or won their love. They seemed quite unde-
voted, except to each other. From an air hostess with a
Teddy bear to two Great Dane pups. I lived in a room
off the kitchen, so thin-walled that it was impossible not
to hear what was happening in the dining room unless
Wu had a gadget going. The garbage disposal, say, would
drown things, but then it would stop and there I was, a
living wiretap.

"We could send you our *au pair*," Tessa was saying one
night. "She has a genius for sorting things out. You could
pay her whatever you wanted."

"Can she really do filing?" said a woman's voice.

"She's Simpson's secretary," Tessa said. "She's got high
speeds. She can even cope with the baby. She looks after
the dogs at the moment to keep herself busy. She can do
anything."

"It doesn't sound as if she's got much spare time."

"She doesn't know what to do with it. Her husband . . ."

Wu ran a beater for a short while. I had thoughts about the awesome hearings of eavesdroppers, of spies, of babies before memory. Then the beater was turned off, unmercifully.

"To tell you the truth, it'd be a relief to me if she did something adult. The dogs are too much of her life," Tessa said.

"She's a handsome girl," Simpson said. "She'll marry again. She's funny."

Tessa laughed gently. "Simpson worries about her. I think he's a bit in love with her." There was the sound of a kiss. Merriment.

". . . two defunct types of people now," the woman was saying. "Have you ever thought of that? It struck me the other day. The man of letters and the maiden aunt. Your *au pair* may be a born maiden aunt. From the sound of it, she's more like a relative to you than a servant."

"I don't think she wants to be a maiden aunt," Simpson said. "I don't get that feeling."

No, I thought. Though one can pretend, if required.

Some other day, Tessa came gaily into my room and pulled the dog off the bed. "And what are you doing here, pray?" she said to them. "Emm doesn't want to see you today. It's Emm's day off." She kissed them.

"How can they tell it's my day off?" I said. "I'm here and they're here."

Tessa looked at me as if I had said something odd. "You should go out more," she said. "Take my charge plate and go shopping. How would you like to buy me a black cashmere sweater? No, that wouldn't be much of a holiday. Why don't you go and buy yourself a sweater, on me?"

"Or not?"

"That's something you say, isn't it? O.K., not, but for Christ's sake go out and enjoy yourself, my dear. You're sitting there like death warmed over."

It might be preferable, I thought, not to shop?

"She should get married again," I heard Tessa say to her mother-in-law on the telephone. "I'm going to send her to my doctor. She's got this thing about saying 'not' all the time."

So.

I went to her doctor. Tired to death, for some reason, and answering his questions in a doze.

"Perhaps you should get married again," he said.

"Why?"

"Sleeping all right?" he said, head down, plowing on.

"Who with?" I said, without thinking. Poor man.

"I meant, would you like some sleeping pills?"

"I'm fine. I don't need putting out. Do you think I should go and live in a commune in San Francisco? Somebody once asked me to. I wouldn't mind that."

"If you like the idea. Though people can get over-individuated in communes."

"Does that mean lonely?" I started to laugh.

He leaned forward. "Aha. Interesting. Now we have to ask ourselves why you're laughing, don't we? What you're avoiding." He shook his kindly head. "As we have learnt from Freud, there are no jokes."

So.

I coped with the amazingly uninteresting savories for one of the Airds' cocktail parties. I met a Bulgarian as I was handing round the cheese dip. He made some measure of pass at me. Given the circumstances of a cheese dip, it was cheering. However off the point.

Much later, I came back in to help Wu clear up the debris and to take the puppies out for a walk. Simpson looked at me. At this tall, broad-shouldered girl. I tried to shrink. One of the puppies suddenly flung itself through the air and banged its wet nose against my right eye in its flight to a tray of vol-au-vent. Wu looked at me and gestured to his own right eye and giggled. He meant that my mascara had been licked off. "Brrr," I said, shaking my head and pretending to myself that I had dog's jowls. Any disguise to slink into, any animal mask.

"Perhaps you should go to an analyst," Tessa said. She put her arm around me. I laughed, and she said, "Laughing is a way of protecting yourself from the truth."

What? I thought, a laugh being pretty well the only dealing with the truth that offered itself at the moment, and so nothing to run down.

The Bulgarian took me out. I think he thought I was younger than I am. I think he thought I didn't recall anything about the war.

"I had to leave Bulgaria," he said. "You know where Bulgaria is?"

"Yes."

"You English girls are so educated."

"Scottish. But thank you."

"I had to leave," he said heavily, "because my conscience dictated that I inform on the Nazis."

"So you came here what year?"

"You have heard of the Nazis?"

"Yes."

"They were brutes. My conscience shouted that I had to inform. Bulgaria is a proud country."

"Bulgaria wasn't so proud in the war," I said. I thought about this, and then said, "I'm sorry," for he was a good-natured man. "I'm sorry. I've never even been there."

But he took no notice of either thing I had said, anyway, and laughed heartily at nothing evident about Sixth Avenue, and grabbed at my knee. "I do what I have to do, as they say in Western films," he declaimed, ogling my car. "Bulgarians are masterly. In Bulgaria the woman is the man's slave."

"Are you hungry?" I said.

"Where shall we eat?"

"Where would you like?"

"When I take you out, you have to be my slave. You have to decide," he said, looking waggish, and also beginning to whine.

"What do you mean, your slave?"

"The man is superior."

"Oh," I said, glad of surrealism, though wondering who was to cope.

Silence unseated him. "What is it you do for the Airds, our friends?" he said desperately. "Apart from making succulent eats such as sardines?"

"I'm their nanny," I said. "To their Great Danes. Also their secretary, sometimes."

"So the Airds are Danish," he said. "Danish in ancestry. A proud race." He beat his chest and sang a song that turned out to be the old monarchist Bulgarian anthem.

"Slave," he said when it was over, "where shall we eat?"

"I like being mastered," I said, not sure how much money he had.

He looked suddenly suspicious that I was making fun of him, which I wasn't, and grabbed me to look down the front of my dress. "Aha. I spy a bra," he said. "I was thinking you were a member of Women's Liberation."

"I told you, I'm a sort of nanny."

"Women are inferior."

"Yes," I said. But now he looked inescapably furious, and also seemed stalemated about what to say to the cabdriver. So I tried for a calming course, feeling thankful to this man for his dogged clasp on difficulties that wouldn't cause me any recall of my dead love in a million years, and I pursued the wisp of a path suggested by the word "nanny." "Women have babies," I said firmly to my redeeming friend, "so it's men who have to decide about spending money, such as money on restaurant bills."

"Bulgarian women have babies in hedges," he said, looking vaguely about him at the north end of Sixth Avenue.

I got him out at an ice-cream parlor after a while. I paid for the taxi because he had no change. We ate waffles. Perhaps he had no money whatever.

"You see," he said, maple syrup on his chin, "we are celebrating."

Celebrating, my fellow in farce, although neither of us belongs, to waffles or to one another. Of course, belonging may be gone by the board, historically speaking, she advises herself, wiping her face with this American paper dinner napkin and not wishing to be personal, to use a bygone phrase.

"What shall we celebrate?" I said.

"I give you a toast," he said, waving a doubled-over piece of waffle on his fork in salute. "To your beauty," he said, though my looks at the time were nothing to

write home about, "coupled with the birthday of the King
of Bulgaria."

"The ex-King?" I said, which was hurtful, so I toasted
the man in coffee. "His Majesty," I said. "Will he be having a party?"

"We have sent him a loyal birthday telegram in exile,"
he said. "My name is at the head of the list. Boris Blagov,
chairman."

"Chairman?" Now I knew his name.

The heartening nature of repetitions. Obviously fortified
by my inane echoing, Boris clutched my knee. "I am the
leader of the forty-five members of the Bulgarian Monarchist Front," he said.

"Forty-*five*?" I said. It seemed best.

"After our celebration I shall take you to a solemn
service," he said, gripping my left ankle between his shoes.
At the same time he looked at his watch. We left in
haste. He took me to a church where the other forty-four
members of the Bulgarian Monarchist Front were mus-
tered outside the front doors. All entrances were locked.

"I myself shall get the keys," Boris said to me stylishly.
"Because I am the leader. The keys are in New Jersey."

We took a cab to New Jersey and back. I paid. We
went through the service at two in the morning. Some of
it was very fine. The priests were out of voice through
tiredness. At three, Boris took me home. He tiptoed from
the elevator to the apartment door with erotic wheezes.

"I cannot lovemake to you," he said at the door, "in
the house of our ancient Danish friends where you are
the nanny."

"Never mind," I said.

But he came in all the same, not apparently wounded.
He wanted a drink. The Airds had long since gone to bed.
I felt no right to sit in their drawing room but no call to
take Boris to my bedroom. So we went to the dining room.
He dived gaily at my legs, like a football player. I thanked
him in my head for so thoroughly putting paid to the past,
at least for the moment. One of the Great Danes was
simultaneously clambering into my lap, trying to get all
four legs fitted into the available footage, under the delu-

sion that she was some other size. It is a delusion that many of us have, including Boris and possibly myself.

"How I am jealous of the young puppy in your lap," Boris said.

Liar, I thought, and so feeling a trifle low but at the same time in his debt. By half past five he had drifted off to sleep underneath three paws of the other dog, which had taken to him. He had been muttering vows of romantic love, rather sullen. He slipped into Bulgarian and became not absurd. Other people, alive and kicking. Other people to blot out a face.

I went to sleep near him, on the floor.

Tessa came in at half past eight and looked overjoyed. She drew me into the kitchen and stretched out her arms, leaning backward a bit, and said, "How I love people who say 'Yes' to life." Then she asked why I was laughing again, and I said that that wasn't what had happened, and she looked angry, and I had a shower. I don't like showers, but the bathroom was the only place in the apartment where I could lock a door on myself. I wondered why the best-off nation in the world should have chosen showers instead of baths. Dreams of childhood garden sprinklers, perhaps. I sat on the step of the shower and went to sleep and then wept. The voice of the dead rang in my ear. "Say 'No.'" The only time I cry now is in my sleep.

Days later, when I had decided to find myself a less cushy job, someone telephoned me and said, "You are ruining my life."

"Who is it?" I asked, unforgivably.

"So soon you forget a passion," said Boris.

Apologize. Explain. Say "How are you?"

Boris moaned. Silence.

"Thank you for the other night," I said.

"I am a wreck," he said. "You are making me a wreck."

"Why? Oh dear." Again, silence. I said, "Boris, I didn't mean why; I meant how? How am I making you a wreck?"

"You force me to sleep with a Great Dane puppy. I am a proud man." I started to laugh, but I don't believe he heard. "A Great Dane puppy. I am a Bulgarian," he said.

"I'm sorry. You'd dozed off," I said.

"My life is ruined. I have laid my life at your legs and yet you say nothing. What can I do to get off the phone?"

"Should I ring off?"

"I'll kill myself if you ring off."

I looked at my watch. "Could you get yourself some lunch?" I said. "Treat yourself to a *nice* lunch, and go to bed? Could you?"

"I'd choke," he said, putting the receiver down. He rang back again at once and mistakenly carried on with the Airds' answering service, not realizing that the woman there had picked up by the time I got to the phone.

"You English girls are so cruel," he was saying.

The answering service said, "One moment, please."

"I'm here," I said. "It's me. I was getting your number from Tessa."

"You are ruining my life, I tell you."

"Could I take you out to lunch?"

"You ruin my life all by one little word."

"Which little word?"

"The most terrible word in your cruel language," he said, putting the phone down.

He rang back several times to say that the word was "no." Twice he had his mouth full. Once he said it to the answering service.

Tessa grew testy about the line's being used all the time, and said that the Bulgarians were the worst lovers in the Balkans, as though that were a world-known fact, like the trying nature to others of our gentle Scottish weather. I was laughing, which was the debt I owed him. But what if he wasn't faking? What if he wasn't funny?

GO WITH LOVE, HE SAYS

by Elaine Gottlieb

You admire my scarf. We are in one of those crowded basement restaurants. A fireplace of chunky gray stones. Shadowed walls studded with deer heads, bisons, guns, Indian headdresses. At the bar, men turn about, glasses to lips, and gleam at women. Table candles illumine other glances.

You have moved close to me, and lifting my purple silk sari scarf, caress it. You admire my purple dress and I am embarrassed, though trying to remain amused. I remark that you observe more than most men. You explain that it is perhaps because you have been in the theater. Smiling. Teeth a white lie to your smoking.

I smile back, hesitantly. I want you to know that I can no longer accept your bow-taking smile or those manicured hands on which I see a silver ring with an opal at its center. You place your hand next to mine to indicate that my ring, a gift from my husband, is almost a duplicate of your own. Our hands, you say, are nearly the same shape.

What is your astrological sign? you tease.

But even as I tell you I want to protest: my students believe that sort of thing.

Yet all you can say, looking at me in a way I have not been looked at since my husband sat up in the hospital bed and watched me come down the hall toward him for the last time, is: You have grace.

You are one of the friends of my fellow teacher, Laurie, who taught in this city the year before. Our pushed-together tables join her friends with our department members. Laurie decided to attend this convention because she missed her group, and I came along out of boredom, having lived in New York most of my life. The college where Laurie and

I teach is in a town so small and remote it is almost a village. In the midst of farm land, hunters' land, it has one main street, one theater, one restaurant and our small state college. The natives are all Republicans.

Laurie is overjoyed to be eating shrimps in beer.

Laurie appreciates also the gossip with which her other friends entertain her. They laugh together in that academic way. You do not listen to them. You keep scrutinizing me. You love novels, you say, though it is drama you teach. You prefer the erotic writers: Henry Miller, Jeffers, Lawrence, Colette, Singer. We discuss *Portnoy*, but you don't seem to listen when I tell why I think it is funny.

You have been glancing at my thigh and now your hand falls on my knee. I do nothing about it. Somehow it doesn't seem too soon. I have had several drinks.

Snow falls lightly on my hair and face as we leave the restaurant and emerge into an evening of Christmas lights, green and scarlet, diffusing on the snow. We are all on our way to another party, some English department that someone knows. Laurie and I in a car belonging to another friend of hers. You disappear around the side of the restaurant and I am almost sure I will never see you again. But there you are when we arrive, striding through the chandeliered lobby of the oldest, best hotel in town, and you smile your flash of welcome.

The party is in a glass-enclosed suite that looks down at a snow-blown city. With our backs to a golden darkness of bellowing cars and window lights and street lamps, we sit talking to each other. Separated from the rest who sit or stand, holding glasses, we are lost in each other's strange and fabulous past.

About your life as an actor, you name the cities, the big hotels, the famous persons you have known, how you always loved well-made clothes, fine restaurants, how you cooked gourmet dishes.

You say: I always travelled first class.

You bought paintings too, you tell me, when you could afford them. You love color, but more than that, creatures in flight, dancers, birds, horses, airplanes, Chagall. In the army you were a pilot.

As we walk outside to a nightclub you tell me I have the legs of a dancer.

In my hand your palm feels rough; it is peeling at the center.

Tension and altitude, you explain.

In parting, you sweep up my hand and kiss it, smiling me into a sense of youth. I see your eyes taking me in. I try to imagine myself as you are imagining me. Entering the lobby, I see none of it. In the elevator, aware of my bare arms against the soft lining of my fur cape, I rise through a sphere of amazement. We are to have lunch together the following day.

2

In the lobby of the hotel, I run to meet you, arms extended. I realize how tall you are. How oddly your head tilts; it sets you in another dimension. I speak urgently, trying to pull you down to the region where I don't want to orbit alone.

The lobby appears incongruous, the wrong setting; tall, straight chair-backs against pillars, a few solemn guests. On the mezzanine there is rock music, the rush of festive dialogue, and Oriental people packed into American clothes. I glimpse the mango face of a Chinese bride in white satin as she raises her veil to receive an eclipsing kiss. Children crawl and scramble up and down stairs. Suddenly the lobby door opens and a Chinese beggar in an old dark tunic shuffles in. Two splendidly sober Chinese girls, poised at the foot of the stairs, dash upward.

We escape into a street over-luminous and slushy.

People stare as if, I think, they can't understand how we came together. Nor can I. After my husband's death it had not seemed possible that I could know a man again. It seems to me, as I look up at you, in daylight, that neither do you know why we have found each other. Surely I must appear older. And what new thing can we expect?

Nor do you seem to know where you are going. This is your city but you keep making false turns, unable to locate the skyscraper with the penthouse restaurant. Then, through a sidestreet, you glimpse the building. We leap over puddles.

The restaurant has walls of windows, the day is sunny, the sky a flaming blue, snow on the mountains touched with violet and a pale rose nimbus. Visitors to the restaurant jump about, crouch, walk around, trying to trap exactly the right shot.

I wish I had my camera, I say.

The mountains disappear on film, you tell me.

(The moments?) my mind echoes.

You take me by the shoulders and turn my head in another direction toward the highest snow-capped peak.

See? There it is. Something to remember.

I can't really distinguish it, but I want to share this impulse of yours to show me what you think beautiful. A living thing, a mountain, destroyed by a photograph. That moment, trying to see, feeling you next to me. When you are in a plane, you say, you love to see the mountain at dawn. It is one reason why you still fly, though now you are only in the Civil Air Patrol.

Your hand burns my shoulder.

I invite you to my room for a drink.

We talk and drink for a while in my room, telling about our loves. So many people, I say. And children. None of them with me. You speak of your daughter, an actress. You tell me about friends in other cities, and of the old man for whom you buy groceries. You say nice things about the young people who study with you. . . . I like to help people, you tell me. . . . Your actor's smile has become imbued with graciousness.

Suddenly you are on your knees, clasping my legs, your head in my lap. I am startled, but I place my hand on your black soft hair. You draw my face down to your own.

It will be good, you say, almost as if you are sobbing. Yes, I know this time it will be good. . . . (I am trembling.)

In bed. The remembered ritual of clothes. Close to yours, my body bursts awake, even before your hands begin their quest. I want to swim into your legs.

We rock together, sweating. I have forgotten that the room has grown cold and that snow is drifting down again outside the window.

As if a cry lodged in my throat is about to release that one name which will free it from silence, my body rises taut, and attempts to enclose you. But then there is a knock on the door. You fall away. I reach toward you; you've become alert. Why does it matter? I want to ask. I open my eyes. There is horror on your face.

It's only Laurie; she's gone, the door's locked, I whisper.

But you're shivering, say you're cold, and rise to find your shirt and a cigarette.

After a few puffs you are in bed again. Putting out the cigarette, you hold me and mutter: Damnit, damnit . . . and kiss my hair.

But it's the first time, I say.

You're not smiling now.

3

Arriving home I am ill, lie within a fever of memories and possibilities, grappling with loneliness. I recall that he said: Maybe I'll visit you. I might want to be your man.

All day, all night I send unwritten messages to him. My body twists in protest. I desire. Not only do I desire; there is something else. A sense of his warmth, the feeling he has for people, so sympathetic. He held me in his arms a long time, as if he wished to console me. I want to say: Come out, come over, meet me. My fever goes up. I tell myself: It is too late. Men only like younger women. I have given him no illusion of dawn. . . . But I cannot dismiss that fine sense of his considerateness. I turn and groan. Why do I delude myself?

If only someone could tell me what to expect. There is no one to ask except Chrystal, who believes in the impossible. Though I am barely well, I invite Chrystal and her husband Eric and Laurie to dinner. They arrive, visibly exhaling as if something other than their physical selves has entered. They hand me their Ouija Board. I place it on the buffet and offer sherry.

We play a folk song on the record player. Chrystal sways around the room, glass in hand. Laurie sits upright, modestly sipping.

Chrystal is tall and handsome in a British way, with long red hair; she wears a pink velvet gown. A silver pendant of some arcane design dangles between her breasts. Her husband wears an old sweatshirt, down over one shoulder. He has been working all day at his dissertation, and apologizes, sleepily. Laurie, as usual, is tailored, unobtrusive, with the straight back of a blue-ribbon horsewoman.

Seated at the table, Eric watches his wife, smiling at her, touching her hair: Doesn't she look great in that color? I really like that dress, don't you?

He places his hand on her shoulder and she moves away as if avoiding a draft. He studies the movement of her lips, which are small, plump and exquisitely articulated. His eyes succumb to adoration. He touches one finger to her cheek.

I don't think you're listening, she drawls.

Oh I am, I am. You know I always listen to you. I'm fascinated by your occult experiences. Tell about some of them, honey. Isn't she wonderful? he adds.

But the more his glance engulfs her the more she struggles to be free of it, until the resonance in her voice sets her apart from us all.

When I was a child, Chrystal says, I saw extraordinary jewels of every shape and color in the dark . . . some area of my mind hears music from another plane . . . music I never heard before . . . creatures appear to me, forms transmuting sex, changing color, regarding me with expressions I understand but can't explain; they want me for something. I don't know what, excite me in an indescribable way. Strange hands caress me, whispering: It is time to leave; take me with them on nocturnal flights. I dream of a man in a red car. Yesterday I saw that car. I didn't get the license number. My fortune teller informs me I am destined for great things. I will be rich, I must travel. Soon . . . they say. Agents are beginning to call me. Modeling jobs in the city. A part in an Italian movie . . . I had to wear pink tonight . . . something told me. . . .

. . . But Eric, she adds, doesn't really care about my career. He'd prefer me to stay home with the baby and keep things quiet so he can get through his dissertation. Isn't that true, Eric?

I? Don't I always let you do as you please? What good would it be to keep you back? You're not the average girl. Photographers don't find someone like you, with your looks, on every street corner. Why should I hold you back? Don't I read the Tarot cards for you? I know what they've been saying. . . .

You're not really clairvoyant and you know it, she decides.

His eyes lose their luster; his face grows pale and older.

Chrystal flings up her arms; the sleeves of her dress roll down to her shoulders.

Oh spirits of the earth and air . . . she begins, but interrupts herself: They don't like to be mocked. . . .

We rest our fingers on the planchette, in the center of the board. In the silence I feel my fever weakening me; pain compresses my head. The hands moving the planchette seem to separate from me, I move through them, they drive me into myself. I submit to an avalanche of yearning.

Someone is there, Chrystal says. I don't know who, standing behind your chair.

I grow hunched.

Chrystal reads the letters swiftly. The planchette slides about. I can't keep up with her.

Give us your name, she says.

Ed—war-d . . . (His name.)

I feel a violent heat.

. . . I love . . . Ada . . . it spells.

They look at me. Laurie's proper eyes widen. I attempt to appear skeptical, though I want to believe.

Chrystal furrows her brow as if she sees through me.

To keep her from being certain I ask: Is he dead?

But Chrystal returns to the planchette. The board repeats phrases he has spoken. No one could have known them. Is she reading my mind? Or . . . what if he is dead? Can one reach a live person? I ask, my thighs weak.

Hurriedly she informs me about dreams, telepathy.

She spells out: You are a good woman. You will live again. I am coming. . . .

Our hands begin to make fuller, more rapid circles; the planchette seems to fly out of control. I grow warmer. My clothes cling; sweat rolls down between my breasts.

I am coming . . . you are a good woman . . . you will live again. . . .

Unable to speak, we look at each other. All of us are breathing hard, we all say we are exhausted. My chest hurts.

What does it mean? I ask. Can he possibly be dead? . . . I feel terrified.

I don't think so, she tells me. He could be sick, feverish or simply sleeping.

He did mention that he might be coming down with something, I say. Maybe I caught it from him. Yes, he could be sick. But is it really him, reaching me? What does it all mean?

It means what it says. He will call you, will write. . . .

Eric searches in his pocket and comes up with a tissue in which he rolls some "grass," and then hands it to his wife. She takes a long, languid draw and then another, and offers it to Laurie, who declines, and then to me. I shake my head. She gives it to Eric.

With her usual precision, in her clear, cool voice, Laurie asks: But do you know Ed that well? She taps a cigarette against the table.

I believe my fever has returned, I say. I feel I must go to bed. I'm sorry.

They leave quietly. As I mount the stairs, strange promises circle in my head, not unlike the jewels Chrystal said she'd seen in the dark when she was a child. Or perhaps more like sea coral or pearls or whatever eyes and bones become when they have lain too long in the channels of the spirit.

I float undulantly through the pillow, sink into damp sheets smelling of hope.

A tidal wave of fever plunges through the room, rocking the bookshelves and tearing the past from its moorings. My husband's photograph shatters into globules that waver against the wall. The clock he gave me tells the hours upside down. My closet turns inside out; all my dresses slide into a heap of wasted anticipation. Only the purple remains.

The purple silk scarf floats overhead like the dove at the end of the flood. I try to twist it around my head, catch it around my throat, revive its perfume; my fingers reach for its threads as if to restore the caress in which it had been crushed.

He was so affectionate, I think.

. . . Until he went out the door, as if walking offstage.

When the fever leaves me I rise and go downstairs for tea. Sitting at my dining room window I look through a plastic colored sunburst at greywhite skies and coalsmoke roofs.

I tell myself he must be dead. Only then could I receive such messages. I look in the mirror. What right do I have to expect what belongs to youth? I lift up my head and pull back the skin of my face. I hear a cosmic laugh. Through the catalyst of Chrystal I have acquired a ridiculous conviction that my own personal life can continue.

Still, I think, only Chrystal can tell me what it means.

I telephone. But Chrystal isn't in. Her husband answers. He regrets that I have been sick again, but he had no time to call and inquire about my health. Chrystal has left him, having had, she said, an irresistible revelation. I hear the baby cry behind him or in his arms.

Yes, he says. That's the way it is. The Tarot cards told her to go to New York and so did the Ouija board, the I Ching and the lady in the Gypsy Tea Room. She was to meet God knows who and make a million dollars modeling.

But a friend of mine, he adds, bitterly, saw her walking the streets, picking up men. She sniffs cocaine. That's where her visions come from.

I hang up, submissive to fate.

. . . I am related to nothing, to no one, I conclude, I live in fever and fantasy.

Impatience casts me back to the telephone.

Does Ed have the right to mystify me? Don't I have the right to know?

I dial Information for his number.

But as I do so I can hear the window rocking with a wind that leaps from the cellar and throws itself shrieking up the stairs. I hear another wind moan around the corner of the house. Forces seem to be watching, warning. Love will shame you, they say. You must not expose this absurd love when you are not sure of how he feels.

At the same time others tell me: Go ahead. There is too much distance between knowing and supposing.

But as I dial his number I am appalled. What can I say? What question was left unanswered? Did I lend him a book? Did he ask me to send him something? I could say I thought I remembered that he wanted a certain . . . But suddenly I see how ridiculous I am. A chance encounter. Conventions. That's what they're for, I'd been told. Like artists' colonies, shipboards, resorts. Love on the run. The brandy after the meal. The footnote to a lecture. A telephone call. A meeting. Hello and good-bye.

A widow at a convention.

You know what widows are like, I once heard a man say.

But I didn't know.

Nor divorcees.

You had to be a man to know, perhaps.

One of those things.

I can hear them laughing, those spirits, who are accustomed to dangling before us the appearances of love.

Incredibly, his voice on the phone. Warm, as if he were beside me. Interested.

Impossible to describe that voice, a voice that has lived in me since I met him. It strikes just the right note. Comforting. Flattering. Radiant. So delighted that I have called. Wanted to call me. But was so busy. His divorced wife demanding money. Things. But that's unimportant. You're so close to me. Oh, it's so good to hear you, he says. I can see you. I feel your body next to mine. If I could only be with you.

I murmur something, expecting a suggestion from him.

What are you wearing? he asks, rapidly. It's later now where you are, isn't it? Are you ready for bed, in bed?

I'm dressed.

And underneath?

I laugh. I have the feeling that he is making clever dialogue. Laughing at sex. Like Noel Coward. Sophisticated irony. In the same supposed mood I describe my underwear minutely, examining it to be sure of the stitching, the shape of the cups and where the lace is situated.

If I were only there, he says.

I am amazed that he sounds so serious.

Just hearing you gets me hot. I want to see you. If I were only there. Damnit. I'd fuck you hard.

You did mention making a trip here.

I want to come. God, I want to see you. You made such an impact on me. And on the phone it's almost as if I have you with me again. You're real. A real female. How lovely you are! And I want to give you what you want, Ada. You know that's what I want, don't you? There's nothing more beautiful than sex, darling, and don't you forget it.

When can we get together?

Darling, I would in a minute. Oh, if I only had the money. But my wife . . . You don't know how much I have to give her, how she carries on. She's castrated me. I have no money. But darling, if my stocks go up . . . Oh if I could. Maybe the stocks. I wouldn't lie to you. . . .

Why haven't you written?

I just can't write. Believe me. I try and can't. I've started letters so many times. If only I had some money.

Write to me. Please.

I'll write. I'll start a letter tonight. I've thought of you so much. A nice long letter. Oh how I wish I were with you. I'd crawl up your belly. Tonight I know I could fuck you. You're so female. Why didn't I insist you stay a day longer?

Will I ever see you?

There'll be a letter for you at the end of the week, a nice long letter. I'll try to work something out. Maybe I can borrow something. I know a few people. . . . If my stocks would go up . . . We'll meet somewhere. I promise. I'm not putting you on. *Go with love,* he says, *go with love.*

4

It is the last day of the term, the week before finals, and in my literature class we are discussing Charles Williams'

Descent into Hell. I speak of "Lily Sammile." Lilith, I
explain. Samael. The devil. Satan. I write the names on the
board. Don't they recognize them? They look at me with
rural complacancy.
   What is it Lily does? I ask.
   They await the answer to the riddle.
   Look in your books, I say.
   Finally, after a flurry of pages, one of the girls: Lily
promises.
   Yes. I agree. She is full of promises. Arrives with packages wrapped like gifts, arms full of easy answers.
   There are no easy answers, another girl is quick to
intercede.
   No love without pain. I tell them, no pleasure without
suffering. If there is to be rebirth someone must die on a
cross. We carry our crosses within us and must remember
that the climb to Gethsemane is an analogical one. That
the nails dug into His flesh have been dug into ours. Only
with nails in our flesh and blood emptying the wounds can
we hope to rise from the torturous cross that is the earth
itself.
   As if it were historical fact, they take notes.
   We return to the book. Lily Sammile, we find, lives in
the earth. In a shadowy hole, almost a cave, with the resur-
rected dead who cling to her, waiting for gifts she has
promised. But she never opens the packages. She herself
is tied up in the wrappings, glittering, tawdry, singed and
above all frightened, because one must realize that such
packages were not meant to be opened. Who could bear
the disenchantment of what is not to be found within
them? Huddled together, the dead know what they have
suspected and feared in their lifetimes, yet they still look
toward Lily with hope. Surely the packages are not there
for nothing! They are so fastidiously wrapped! Won't they
open to some umbilical pleasure that will sustain them for
all eternity? Lily, as they watch her, imploring the dream
tales to spin again, grows even older, old beyond the possibilities of age, until she has reached the time of Adam,
her first lover, still strong, still willing and unpunished by
God, Adam who has clasped and dismissed her, knowing
how old she will become, how old and ugly her beauty can

be, how touching her leaves nothing but the memory of touch.

How does the book define pleasure? I ask them.

An intent Catholic girl with dark, tilted eyes, pale skin, long black hair, who looks like an Indian goddess but comes from Irish-Spanish parents, quotes:

Happy, rich, insatiate yet satisfied . . . how delicious everything would be. I could tell you tales that would shut everything but yourself out.

Look at Wentworth, I say. They scurry through their books again.

Isn't his life satisfying yet insatiate? What does his pleasure consist of?

Again the Catholic girl raises her hand while the others try not to show their faces.

He has everything he wants, she says, everything within the realm of sensation. A phantom mistress created by his imagination. Who conforms to every spoken or unspoken wish. He pulls down the shades and is alone with her. In other words, with himself. He needn't go out, needn't risk himself.

In other words, I add, risking interruption, negation, contradiction, the failure to please and be pleased. Since he only dreams, everything remains as he wishes.

Is he saying, a quiet boy in the front row inquires, that if Wentworth really had this woman whom he only knew as a phantom answer to his lust, he would still have nothing because he could see her as nothing more than what he desired?

. . . And therefore not really loved? the Catholic girl asks.

She came to him too easily, I tell them again. She came because he wanted her to come in the phantom way she appeared. And with the shades drawn that's all there was for him, this phantom mistress, these imagined caresses.

Every day I have passed over the snow-packed streets to open my box at the post office . . . a box because I wanted to insure myself against loss. Yet I gather mostly ads and unpaid bills. Still the post office lures me. I feel sure, my intuition tells me, that I will find the letter there this time or the next. I open the post office doors, seeking inwardly that note, that one true note of foreknowledge. I am full of promises and dread. I run over during my lunch hour. Sometimes twice a day. What did the cards say last time Eric read them for me? Even on Sundays I am drawn to my box. I open it, wanting and not wanting to see.

Later that day, as I am planning an exam, a student enters my office and asks permission to speak with me. She has one of those locality-stamped faces, bland as an oyster. Her smile reflects cool colors. It is the smile of a docile girl.

I'm getting married, she says. I'll have to miss the final.

She drops her eyelids as though to scatter petals between us.

I'm making a C now. She smiles sweetly.

Petals float before me in mud puddles.

If you miss the final (I resist her vulnerability. I astound her with lack of pity) you'll get an Incomplete.

Oh. . . . She tiptoes away. And yet I can see that she will keep looking for someone to reassure her that it is just a story and will turn out all right.

Fool! I want to run after her, shake her.

Fool! I write on my calendar, circling the date, exactly a month since meeting him.

My windows are broad. The leaves of the trees are gone. Snow covers and distresses everything, confusing the distinction between earth and sky.

A NEGATIVE BALANCE

by April Wells

Almost before the sound of the engine dies away down the street, she begins to clean away the traces of his visit. Small clumps of mud on the carpet, a spilled ash, a used coffee cup are pieces of her world that have been nudged out of order; she wants things back in place. She rattles dishes in the sink with perhaps a bit more zest than usual, loving the silence and choosing to break it. But somewhere between the wiping of dishes and the straightening of chairs, part of her mind brings him back, as though he were refusing to be vacuumed up with the cookie crumbs, refusing to let her find an orderly place in her mind for what has happened.

His body was a visual disruption in her carefully proportioned living room; beside him chairs, lamps, end tables looked like doll furniture. She stiffened her spine, forced a smile, and offered him the only chair in the room in which he would fit, her favorite chair of pale corduroy by the window.

She remembers searching for something to say. Finally, "What brings you to the West Coast?"

Grimy fingers reached for a cookie, carried it upward, stuffed it whole into the beard approximately where a mouth should be.

"Bummin'."

She takes a breath, tries again. "Where have you been staying along the way?"

The answer comes through cookies, not between them. "Crashin' with friends."

Three questions in a row, that's too many, that would be rude. She sips coffee, seated—no, posed, really—on the end of the couch.

"Nice pad you got here."

"Thank you. John did a lot of work on it just before he went into the hospital. It helped to keep him occupied when he couldn't go into the office anymore."

There is a short silence, then:

"Um, I forget—what'd he do for a living?"

"He was an accountant."

"Oh. Yeah."

She sees clearly that he is uncomfortable with the subject of John's death, but she has dealt with her widowhood; she seeks to make it easier for him.

"We knew, you know, before it happened. I had time to adjust, although you never really do until afterward. It's been a year, now. I'm okay."

He does not reply. He has finished the cookies, is looking out the window. Late afternoon shadows lie across the lawn; down the block, children have gone in from play; fathers are coming home from work in station wagons. Until recently it had been her worst time of day, knowing others were drawing together, coalescing into families at this hour. She is brushed faintly by loneliness.

"Would you care to stay for dinner?" she asks, then immediately regrets it; she has learned to cope with being alone—it is his presence that is disrupting. Say no, please.

He had said yes, he hadn't got much bread, that would be fine.

She moves now to the pale chair which seems to still bear traces of his weight. She scans its velvety surface for smudges of dirt. How in the world did he get so dirty? Working on his car? Heavy machinery? He was here an entire evening and she knows nothing, really, about his life, how he spends his days. Still, yesterday, she made her judgment. Such judgments are necessary to her sense of order for she keeps her emotions like her house, the way one keeps a ledger, meticulously neat. She had learned from John, who ran his own life like a balance sheet, with its carefully attended system of debits and credits. She retained these habits, even now; she thinks they are, perhaps, all she has left of him.

Despite the chair's apparent freedom from stains, she fetches detergent and a damp brush and goes to work on the fabric.

The kitchen and its automatic motions had been a relief
from the strain of attempted conversation. She feels like a
fugitive, hiding behind the dinner preparations, dreading
the meal itself. Then, reaching for garlic salt or pepper or
Worcestershire sauce, there is the smooth green shape of
a bottle in her hand instead, offering if not a way out at
least a way to ease the tightness in her stomach. They will
enjoy wine with dinner, and perhaps it will not be so difficult to tolerate this awkward young man.

She picks at her food. He eats hungrily, with gulping
noises. She tries not to look at him, sips her wine instead.
He drinks his wine like he drank his coffee, in large swallows. She refills their glasses, aware of the effects of the
wine; the tightness in her stomach is nearly gone, her disapproval is not so urgent, her dislike of him is muffled.

"How old are you?" she asks.

"Turned twenty yesterday."

"Happy birthday, then."

He smiles a little beneath the beard, wipes his mouth
with the back of his hand, pushes his chair back from the
table.

"Yeah," he says, "figured it was about time to see the
country before I got to find me a job."

Thank heaven, a topic. "What sort of work are you looking for?"

"I dunno. Something different." He leans back, relaxed
from the wine. A sudden grin splits the beard. "You know
what I'd really like to do?"

"No, what?"

"I maybe shouldn't say this, you'll probably get the
wrong impression, but, you know, if I didn't have to worry
about the consequences, I'd sort of like to try being a con
artist."

"A what?"

"Yeah. Try to see if I could get people's money away
from them without getting caught." He is tipped back in
his chair, arms crossed behind his head, smiling. "Oh, I'd
probably never really do it, but, you know, every once in
a while I like to think just maybe I could get away with it.
Be fun, I think."

She feels he can't be serious; still, she is inclined to bait him a little, argue the point, talk him out of it. "Stealing, you mean. Taking people's money, something they've worked for."

"Look," he says leaning forward again, "is that so different from your average ad man or marketing executive? My old man, now, he pulls down a healthy salary doing just that, only what he does is supposedly legitimate. The hype is still there, just packaged differently."

She is relaxed now, almost enjoying herself. "But there is a difference. The person who's selling a product gets your money, true. But when you've paid it, you've got the dishwasher or the car or whatever. The con artist is different. There's no exchange. He leaves you with nothing, sometimes less than nothing, a negative balance."

They leave the table and move to the living room, where again he fills the pale chair. "Haven't you ever been conned?" he asks. "Haven't you ever had the feeling, after some transaction, that you've been taken?"

She remembers briefly the unctuous man in the too-discreet suit in the funeral parlor, trying to talk her into buying a more expensive casket. But she had been firm despite her grief. "No," she replies. "You don't have to buy something just because it's advertised."

The whiff of memory has made her uncomfortable, and she searches for a new topic, manages to ask him something about his friends. They seem to be street people, very hip, and he obviously admires them. The wine is wearing off; she begins to dislike the talk; it is too close to the subject of his strangeness in her house. Her edginess begins to surface again. She wishes he would go.

The memory of that discomfort propels her, now, into the bedroom, where with violent movements she strips from her bed the sheets she had changed only the day before. Tense moments had come and gone, last evening, as she sat making small talk, bound and gagged by good manners, unable to ask him to go. Later, lying awake in the shadows of her room, she wondered if her living-room couch was perhaps the most comfortable bed he'd had in a long time. She cannot hear him breathing, for the walls are thick and the door is closed—and locked. But he is there, and that is enough. She tries to push away her sense

of confinement, but a corner of her mind is busy with an
alertness that will not let her sleep.

How is she to know, really, if he is who he says he is?
She had asked for no proof, trusting instead to her recognition of John's mother in his face. Yet she had never met
his family, and at dinner he had talked of his pipe dream
of conning people; perhaps it was no whim at all. A
young man, pretending to be a travel-dusty young relative,
calls on the widow, hoping she will be naive enough to
extend her hospitality. . . .

In the fuzzy darkness she can hear small noises as the
house responds to the cool of night. There is a faint breeze
through the barely open window, making shadows of leaves
move on the wall. She is listening for other sounds. The
night is a blurry reality where imagination supplies the
missing details. She begins to fancy the creak of the couch,
a footfall in the hallway, perhaps the handle is turning. . . .
Oh, stop it.

She sits up in bed, runs fingers through her hair to shake
out the fantasy. She knows the rest: the sense of another
breathing in the room, a movement, the flash of a knife.
Refusing the plot, she settles back, turns over on her side.
And a moment later is listening again, imagining the soft
sliding sound of drawers being opened, the clink of silver as
it is removed, the small sharp click of the front door
latch. . . .

And this time the click is clear in the night, distinct and
real, leaving a deeper silence behind. She is still and tight
in her panic, there beneath the bedclothes. I will not move,
not move, not move. A very long time later, she had drifted
off into sleep.

But today the bedroom is a place of sunlight and smooth
sheets. She and the sun have worked a magic on it, a
minor exorcism. It waits for a peaceful night, this time,
filled only with the sounds of her privacy. There is one
room left.

She opens the shower door, looking at the still damp
tiles. She finds it difficult to bring an image of him to
mind here, though she recalls her surprise at waking to the
sound of running water. She tries to picture him here,
standing under the spray of water—and can't. Were the

clothes, then, really that important, so important that she can't think who he would be without them?

She had hurried to put on coffee, passing on her way to the kitchen a suitcase opened on the floor of the living room. She stood watching the water boil, glad she had not jumped up in the night when he went to his car for the suitcase. Pouring the coffee into cups, she looks up; he has finished his shower and stands in the kitchen doorway. He is wearing clean slacks and a fresh, light-colored shirt. His hair is combed; the beard has been trimmed.

"Please don't bother with breakfast," he is saying. "I'll stop later on down the highway."

Perhaps it is her relief that he is going, perhaps it is his appearance, so different in the sunny morning, but she insists he stay for cereal and toast at least.

Over a second cup of coffee: "I haven't said much about the family, I know." He looks apologetic. "The truth is, I'm sort of missing them, and last night I was feeling a little homesick. I guess it takes a while to get used to being out on your own."

He pulls out his wallet, then, and shows her snapshots: two rather ordinary-looking teenage boys, a smiling ten-year-old girl with his coloring. "My brothers look like Mom," he says, "but in some ways my sister and I take after Dad; she's afraid she's going to get as big as me." He smiles, and she can see the affection in the smile.

"Here's Mom and Dad. Hard as the dickens to get them to pose for this one." John's aunt and uncle, then; standing in front of a blossoming apple tree, their arms around each other's waists, squinting into the sun.

She looks at the snapshots a moment, then returns them. "You seem very proud of your family."

"Yeah." Momentarily awkward again, he sits looking out the window at the bright day. After a moment he turns to her and smiles, squares his shoulders, gets up from the table.

"Thanks for everything," he says at the door. At the end of the walk he turns and, almost shyly, raises his hand in a V-shaped salute.

She lifts her arm to wave and is surprised to find that, inadvertently, she has returned his peace sign. Embarrassed, she steps inside, closes the door carefully and locks it. She leans against the hard surface of the doorjamb, listening to her breathing, aware of her receding tension, feeling in its place the slow unfolding of a question.

His words of the night before occur to her again: Haven't you ever been conned? She had seen him as a grubby, street-wise young man, flaunting against her ordered world a sophistication entirely repugnant to her. And then, in the morning, she had discovered that he had taken a shower and changed—not just his clothes, but himself. Confused totally, she does not know, now, which one of these he truly is.

She hurries to the window, looks out across the street at the dusty old car where he sits attentively warming up the engine; a motion of his shoulder and the car begins to move off down the street. Through the window she watches him go: half man, half bum, somebody's older brother, somebody's son; for all his loneliness, unafraid to change.

So, after all, she had been conned. And now, above the marble countertop two hands, palms pressed together, wipe at each other, two faces catch each other's eye and stare. The mimic in the mirror has faint lines at the corners of her mouth, a slight frown drawing the brows together: an anxious face. She does not like this woman who is caught like this, unguarded in her fussiness. The phrase "over thirty" slides into her head, a silent caption and an indictment. She turns from the mirror, leaving it blank.

MENDING

by Sallie Bingham

On Fifth Avenue in the middle fall, the apartment buildings stand like pyramids in the sunlight. They are expensive and well-maintained, but for me their grandeur stems not from the big windows with the silk curtains where occasionally you can see a maid dusting with vague gestures but from the doctors' names in the ground-floor windows. Some buildings have bronze plaques for the doctors' names beside the entrance door. Whether those doctors are more magical than the ones who are proclaimed in the windows is one of the puzzles I amuse myself with as I ply my trade up and down the avenue.

My trade is not the trade which might be expected from the height of my red-heeled sandals or the swing of my patent-leather bag. I am, after all, a good girl, a fairly young girl, although I have a few lines and a tendency to wake up at five in the morning. Taxi drivers still comment on my down-home accent, and although for a while I tried to dispel that impression by buying my clothes at Bloomingdale's, I have given up the effort.

My trade is doctors, and it is essential. I have a doctor for my eyes and another for my skin; I have a special man for my allergies—which are not crippling—and I also have a specialist for the inside of my head. For a while it seemed that my head was as far as he would go, with an occasional foray down my throat. Finally a choking sensation forced me to cancel my appointments. I suppose I should not expect anyone to take that at face value. He was a very handsome man; he is still, and it is still painful for me to imagine the man whose lap I longed to sit on presiding behind his profession, gazing with those curious green, unshadowed eyes at the women (why are they all women?)

—the young ones, the old ones who hang their coats on his rack and sling their bags beside their feet as they sit down, with sighs, or in silence, on his couch.

My childhood was made to order to produce a high-heeled trader in doctors on Fifth Avenue, although my childhood would never have provided the money. My mother was blond and a beauty, and she had a penchant for changing men. My favorite was a truck driver from Georgia who used to let me ride with him on all-night trips down the coast. Mother didn't approve of that, but it took me off her hands. He would sing and I would doze in the big high cab, which seemed to me as hot and solid as a lump of molten lead—as hard to get out of, too, as I discovered when I tried to open the door. Oh, that truck cab was ecstasy. That was as close as I could come. My mother lost interest in him when I was six and replaced him with a white-collar worker. She thought Edwin was a step up, but for me, he never had any kind of appeal; he was the first of her men to carry a briefcase, and I learned an aversion then I have never been able to overcome to men who tie their shoes with very big bows and carry cow-smelling leather briefcases.

There were many others after Edwin, but they washed over me and I do not remember disliking them at all. They did not make much of an impression, as my mother would say; that was left to my first doctor, a personable Cincinnati gynecologist. My mother, who had settled in that town with a railroad man, made the appointment for me. She wanted me to know the facts, and she did not feel up to explaining them. Of course by then I knew everything, as well as the fact that if you turn a boy down, he will suffer from an excruciating disease. I did not really need to know that to be persuaded, since the interiors of those 1950 Chevrolets smelled just like the cab of Ronny's truck.

The gynecologist armed me with a strange rubber disk that flew across the room the first time I tried to insert it. The second time I was successful, but I was never able to find the thing again. It sailed like a moon through the un-charted darkness of my insides. I knew it was not right to have a foreign body sailing those seas, but it took me a month to summon the courage to call the gynecologist. I was so afraid he would be disappointed in me. He rescued the thing the next day as I lay down on his long table; he was disappointed, and the thing had turned bright green.

After that my mother married an Air Force man who was going to be stationed in Honolulu. I still think of her little black boots when I think of brave women leaving for parts unknown. She tripped up the steps to the airplane, an indomitable little mountain climber, with tears in her eyes. The Air Force man was in tears, too, and smiling as though their future lay shining on the tarmac. There was no room for me in that arrangement, and so I was farmed out to my mother's only prosperous relative, a hard-working doctor who lives in Greenwich and had the luck to marry my aunt.

I was nineteen, too old to be educated, too young to be employed. It made sense for me to do what I could to help Aunt Janey run her large house. There were people to do everything that needed to be done, but no one to organize them. Often the window washer arrived on the same day as the man who put up the screens, or the children needed to be picked up at friends just as Aunt Janey was going to bed with her second cousin. (He was no relative of mine: another briefcase man.) So it was vital to have someone she could rely on to make telephone calls and draw up schedules.

Since I was not being paid in money but in good food and a fine room with roses on the wallpaper, Aunt Janey felt responsible for finishing me. She had been a brilliant woman once, and she still had her books from those days. She wrote my assignment every morning while I started the telephoning. I had to do it before I could do the bills. I can't say the reading meant a great deal to me, but the swing of the sentences—*Jane Eyre*, for example—seemed to carry me out of my ordinary way. I had thought that life was quite plain and obvious, with people coupling and breaking apart like the little snot-colored dots I had seen under the microscope in fifth-grade biology. The only lesson I had learned so far was to stay out of the way of those dots. After I read about blind Rochester's cry, I began to want some of that for my own.

I had not been demanding until then. No one could

have complained that I made a fuss over a quick one in the
back hall—that was the furnace repairman—or took it
more seriously than the roar of the crowd at a construction
site. I was never a prude, and my body did not do me that
kind of helpful disservice. At home, in the upper South, in
the Midwest, in Florida, they talked about boobies or the
swing on my back porch. Greenwich is more refined, even
New York City is more refined, and the repairmen used to
praise my eyes. When it came to seeing one of the men
twice, I would shy away, not only because I was waiting
for the voice across the miles but because I did not want to
spend any time with a man who might begin by praising
my eyes and then go on to feeling things himself—I did not
mind that—but then would expect me to feel things, as
well.

In feeling, I was somewhat deficient. It had not mattered
before. I could remember the smell of Ronny's cab and
glory in it, but I was not able to enjoy the particular flavor
of a man's body. A naked man, to me, was like a root or
a tuber. I can't say I was afraid. But I never could see the
gleam, the light before the dawn, the pot at the end of
the rainbow when a naked man stood in front of me. It
seemed to me that women were seemlier, more discreet,
without that obtrusive member I was always called on to
admire. I could not touch it without conscious effort, and
that showed in my face. For a long time, it did not matter
to me, but it mattered to those men. They wanted me to admire, they wanted me to feel something. Even the man who
came to prune Aunt Janey's forsythia insisted that I had to
feel. "What's wrong with you?" he complained, when we
were lying under the bare branches of the big bush. I
knew he was feeling that it was somehow his fault.

I have never wanted to hurt anyone. I have wanted to
help, if possible. And so I decided I would stop going out
with men.

The trouble was that I wanted a pair of arms. I needed
a pair of arms with a pain that even now I can't bring myself to describe. That, of all things, I had carried out of my
childhood. When my mother was between men and feeling
the ache, she would call me into her bed and squeeze me
until suddenly she would fall asleep. I was more the holder

than the holdee. It did not matter. The warmth of her
thin arms, the wrists hardly wider than milk-bottle necks,
the bones as fine as glass splinters, would last me through
the next day and the next. Chronic cold was one of my
chief complaints. But after she had held me, I didn't even
need to button my school coat. I would walk down whatever gray street we were living on in whatever more or
less depressed small-city neighborhood in whatever indistinguishable section in the middle of this country with no
scarf over my head, no gloves on my hands, and the wind
that comes from the Great Plains or the Mississippi or the
Rockies or some other invisible boundary lifting the ends
of my mouse-colored hair like a lover. Of course the trick
was that my mother didn't expect anything of me, except
not to wet the bed. She didn't expect me to feel anything
in particular or to praise the way she looked in her nylon
slip. She gave me the warmth of her long, skinny arms, and
I gave her the warmth of mine, and before I was ten years
old, I was addicted.

When the new man moved in, I had to spend the night
in my own bed with my fist in my mouth, not because the
sounds they made frightened me—they were no more
frightening than the chittering of the squirrels in the little-
city parks—but because there was no more warmth for
me. Mother got into the habit of buying me bunny pajamas
and woolly sweaters before she installed a new cousin.

After the forsythia man and my decision to do without
men, I started to get cold in that old way. Aunt Janey
noticed the gooseflesh on my arms one morning when I
brought up her breakfast tray. She made me sit down on
the satin blanket cover. "We haven't had a talk in I don't
know how long." She was the prettiest woman I'd even
seen—the best, the brightest, with her jewelry box turned
upside down on the pillow and her list of the day's duties,
prepared by me, balled up and thrown on the floor. I could
think of her only in silly ways—still that's the best I can
do—because when I think of her eyes and the way her
lips curled when her second cousin rang the doorbell, I
know I will always be lonely for her. So I describe her to
myself as a fickle woman who cheated on what my mother
(who never had her luck) called, reverently, a perfectly

good husband, and fed her children peanut butter out of the jar when I made the mistake of leaving a meal to her, and was happy. So happy. Outrageously happy. She had my mother's long, skinny arms—the only family resemblance—and although she very seldom held me in them, I knew she had the same heat. The difference a diamond wristwatch and a growth of fine blond hair made was not even worth thinking about.

(And he, the second cousin, did she make him groan with happiness, too? She used to come downstairs afterward in her Chinese kimono with her pearls hanging down her back, but I never saw much of him.)

We had our talk that morning. It was fall and Jacob the gardener was burning leaves. I insisted on opening the window, although Aunt Janey hated fresh air, and so I was able to flavor her words with the leaf smoke. She told me that I was unhappy, and there was no way I could deny that. So for once she took the pad and the telephone book and asked for the telephone, which had a crook on the receiver so that it could perch on your shoulder. And she began to make me appointments.

She had noticed my teeth, she said between dialings. Was there an implication about my breath? She had noticed that I squinted a good deal over the print in the telephone directory, and so she was sending me to have my eyes checked. She was also not certain that I should be as thin as I seemed to be growing, and so she was making an appointment with her own internist on upper Fifth Avenue. Unfortunately in his office I felt my old enemy, tears rising like an insurrection of moles, like a walking army of termites. When I cried on the leatherette chair, the doctor, who was as friendly as the repairman my mother had left after six months of too much loving, suggested that I ought to go and see the other kind.

That was all right, too, as far as I was concerned. I was ready to take anyone's advice. It did not seem possible to go through the rest of my life trying to get warmth from the eyes of construction workers; it did not seem possible to go on spreading my legs for men who took it personally that that part—"down there," as my mother called it—had no more feeling than the vegetable it so closely resembles: a radish, fancy cut.

The next waiting room was soft and beige, like the
tissuey inside of an expensive shoe box, and I could have
lain there forever, till the robins covered me with magazine
leaves. Of course I had to get up and go and lay myself
down when the time came—why this eternal lying?—on
an even softer, browner couch in a smaller, safer room. I
asked the doctor right away to let me stay forever. He held
my hand for a moment, introducing himself, and my cold
began to fade. Can it fade from the hand up and will the
heart in the end be heated, like a tin pot on a gas burner
turned high? I had always assumed that my body warmed
up independently and that my heart, at the end, would
always be safe and cold. He did not want anything from
me—you can't count money in a desperate situation like
this—except my compliance, so that he could try to help.
And I believed him.

My mother would have said there is no such thing as a
disinterested man; she would have gone on to add that since
he had green eyes, he must have other things in view. He
did have green eyes, pale, finely lashed, and a pale, tired
face. He seemed to have spent himself warming people up.
By the second session, I hated the idea of any particle of
him going to other people, and I ground my teeth when I
passed the next patient—always a woman—in his little hall.
I wanted him all to myself and it seemed to me that this
was my last chance. My day was flooded with sights I had
never seen in my life, views of my lean body folded up on
his lap or the back of my neck as I knelt to kiss his feet. I
had been cross and mean all my life and now, like a three-
year-old with a lollypop, I was all syrup and sunshine.
Shame had no part in it. As I went my rounds to the other
doctors, letting them fill my teeth or put contact lenses in
my eyes, as patiently as I have seen horses stand to be
bridled and saddled, I imagined myself in my doctor's arms.
Of course he did not respond. How could he respond? He
wanted to help and, as he explained, holding me in his
arms for a while or even for fifty minutes could not do me
anything but harm. It is true that afterward I would never
have let him go.

I thought I could push him. After all, other men had always wanted me. So I started to bring him little presents,
bunches of chrysanthemums from Aunt Janey's garden,

jars of my own grape jelly, poems on yellow paper that
would have embarrassed a twelve-year-old. He made me
take them all away, always neutral, always kind, always
ready to listen, but never won or even tempted. My wishes
were making me wild and I wanted to gather myself up and
wrap myself in a piece of flowered paper and hand myself
to him—not for sex or compliments, but only to be held
by him.

Aunt Janey caught me crying after three months of this
and offered a trip to Paris as a distraction. I told her I
couldn't go because I couldn't bear to break a single appointment with my doctor; she was taken aback. We had a
long talk in the late-night kitchen where Uncle John had
been making pancakes. She told me that analysis works but
not in that way. "I can understand you wanting to go to
bed with him, that's what everybody wants, but I can't
understand you letting it get so out of hand."

"I don't want to go to bed with him," I said. "I couldn't
feel him any more than I could feel the furnace repairman.
I want him to hold me on his lap and put his arms around
me."

"Yes, that's childish," she said, tapping her cigarette out.

"If I can't persuade him to do it, I'll die. I'll lie down
and die." It was as clear to me as an item on the grocery
list.

"You will not die," she said firmly. "You will go to Paris
with me and we will shop for clothes and visit the museums
and we will find you a nice free man."

"With green eyes and rays around his eyes and long
hands with flat-tipped fingers?"

"That I can't promise," she said. "But he'll be free."

"I won't go if it means missing an appointment."

She started to figure how we could leave late on a Friday
and come back on a Sunday, but then she saw it was no
use and decided to go for a longer time with the second
cousin.

So I was left alone for two weeks, except for Uncle John
and the children. He was gone most of the time, coming
back at night for his ginger ale and his smoked salmon and
a spot of conversation before the late news. He wouldn't
let me fix real coffee in the morning; I think, being old

and tired, he was afraid of the obligation. (The quid pro quid, my mother called it; nothing was free in her world, especially first thing in the morning.) The two girls spent most of the day in school and when the bus brought them home, I would have our tea picnic ready and we would take it out to the field behind the house. Late autumn by now and not many flowers left to pick, so we found milkweed pods and split them into the air. The little girls sat on my lap, either one at a time or both together, and when I kissed them, their hair smelled of eraser dust. I was in pain because the hours between my appointments were the longest hours of my life, and yet I never saw anything as beautiful as that field with the willows at the far end and the two little girls in their navy skirts and white blouses running after the milkweed parachutes.

By then I had discovered that my doctor had a wife and three children, and they all loved one another and managed well. More than that he would not tell me, and I was forced to believe him. After all, the owners of pale green eyes and flat-ended fingers tend to find the wives and get the children they can enjoy, the way a girl I met in one of my many schools knew exactly—but exactly—what to say to win a smile, and what flavor of milkshake would bring out the angel in her.

As my mother used to say, "Those that know what they want, get it." But she had feeling all over her body, not just lodged here and there in little pockets.

Meanwhile my doctor was trying to take the bits and pieces I gave him and string them together to make me a father. I had never known or even asked which one of the cousins was my father, and so I gave him all the pieces I remembered from the whole bunch of them. Ronny and his truck. He had thick thighs that rubbed together when he walked and made him roll like a seafaring man. He liked to hold me between the thighs and comb my hair. Edwin with his briefcase that reminded me of my doctor's (although Edwin's was more expensive) and which, he once told me, held a surprise. The surprise, it turned out, was my cough medicine. Louis the railroad man who said he would take me with him on the train except that white girls brought bad luck; it was just like in the mines. The

Air Force regular who yelped with joy and hugged me the
day my mother said she would go to Honolulu.

My doctor wanted to know which one was my father,
and he proposed that I write my mother and ask. I wrote
her because I did everything he even hinted at and I would
have as soon slit my own throat. Word came back a week
later; she thought I had known all along. My father had
been a Kansas boy stationed at Fort Knox one summer
when she was working at a diner called the Blue Boar. I
remembered then that she had always kept a picture of a
big-faced smiling boy on the mantelpiece, when there was
one, or on the table by her bed. She said he had been killed
in Korea.

My doctor did not try to do much with that scrap. Probably my father never even saw my mother's big stomach;
if he had, he might have told her what to do about it, as a
farm boy familiar with cows. So we had to start all over
again with the scraps and pieces, trying to undo the way
my memory simplified everything, trying to get behind
the little pictures I wanted so desperately to keep: the
shape of men's hands and the ways they had let me down.

We were still at work when Aunt Janey came back from
Paris and she made me get on the scales that first evening.
I told her the work we were doing was wearing me down;
it was like ditch digging, or snaking out drains. She knew
I was better, and she told me not to give up now with the
end in sight. I wasn't sure what she meant, but I knew
I had to keep on. There was some hope for me somewhere
in all that. At my doctor's, the sweat would run down my
face and I would have to pace the floor because there were
months and even years of my life when all I could remember was the pattern a tree of heaven made when the sun
shone through it on a linoleum floor. My doctor thought
some of the scraps might have forced me into bed, but I
only remember being tickled or chased with the hairbrush
or locked in the car while they went into a road house.
Nothing high or strange but only flat and cold. Something
killed off my feeling, but it wasn't being raped by Ronny
or Edwin or any of the others. Mother had sense enough
to find men who wanted only her.

I told my doctor I believed I had been an ugly, squalling

baby who kept my mother up at night, screeching for more milk. That was the only thing Mother ever said about me, and she said it more to criticize herself. She hadn't had sense enough, she explained, to realize I was hungry and to give me more bottles. Instead she slapped me once or twice. That wasn't enough to kill off much feeling, although it is true that if I were asked to draw a picture of myself, I would draw a great mouth.

By then I was almost in despair about getting what I wanted from my doctor, even a kiss or a lap sit or holding his hand. I kept having faith in him, the kind he didn't want, the kind that keeps you from eating and wakes you up at night. That faith woke the saints with visions of martyrdom and woke me with visions of lying in his arms. I kept believing that nature and its urges would triumph over the brittle standards of his profession; I kept believing that his calm attention was the marker for a hidden passion. I also believed that if he would take me, I would begin, magically, to feel. Or lacking that, light up like a torch: joy, like Aunt Janey with her pearls hanging straight down her back.

But he would not.

So for me it was a question of quitting—which of course I would not do, because at least during the sessions I saw him—or of going on with the work, keeping to the schedule, getting up in Greenwich in time to dress and catch the train. It was a question of opening my mind to the terrible thoughts that flashed through it like barracuda through muddy water. It was a question of making connections between one thing and another that did not come from the expression in his eyes—the looks I called waiting, eager, pleased—but from some deep, muddy layer of my own, where the old dreams had died and lay partially decayed.

The result was that I lost what ability I had. The children went back to eating peanut butter out of the jar although I had gotten Aunt Janey to lay in a supply of bread. The little skirts and tops we had bought at Bloomingdale's began to stink with sweat, and I stopped washing my hair. It did not seem possible to stand under the shower and come out feeling alive and new. It did not seem worthwhile even to try.

I didn't care anymore about getting better—that was a sailing planet—but I did care about the little fix of warmth which I got from sitting next to my doctor. I cared about his words, which were for me and not for all the other women, and after a while I began to care about the things he said that hurt me and seemed at first unacceptable. There were, in the end, no answers. Yet he seemed to see me, clearly, remotely, as I had never seen myself, and he watered me with acceptance as regularly as he watered the sprouted avocado on his windowsill. Is it after all a kind of love? By January, I was back inside my own bleached mind; I knew it the day I went out and bought myself a bunch of flowers.

Aunt Janey washed my hair for me and insisted on new clothes and a trip to Antigua; when I said I would go, she hugged me and kissed me and gave me a garnet ring. Uncle John told me I was looking like a million dollars, and the little girls, who had been scared off by my smell, began to bring their paper dolls again so that I could cut out the clothes. I was still, and always would be, one of the walking wounded; I was an internalized scab, and when I looked at myself in the mirror, I understood why people call naked need the ugliest thing in the world. I broke two appointments with my doctor and went to Antigua with Aunt Janey, and one night, I danced with an advertising man. I was no queen, but I was somebody, two legs, two arms, a body, and a head with a mouthful of choice words. I wouldn't sleep with him because I knew that I wouldn't feel a thing, but the next day we played some fine tennis.

When I came back to New York, the pyramids on Fifth Avenue were no longer shining. The gutters were running with filth and melted snow, and the doctors' names in the windows and on the plaques were only names, like lawyers' and dentists'. My doctor was on the telephone when I walked in, and I looked at his free ear and knew he would never be mine. Never. Never. And that I would live.

THE LOVE OBJECT

by Edna O'Brien

He simply said my name. He said "Martha," and once
again I could feel it happening. My legs trembled under
the big white cloth and my head became fuzzy, though I
was not drunk. It's how I fall in love. He sat opposite.
The love object. Elderly. Blue eyes. Khaki hair. The hair
was graying on the outside and he had spread the outer
gray ribs across the width of his head as if to disguise the
khaki, the way some men disguise a patch of baldness. He
had what I call a very religious smile. An inner smile that
came on and off, governed as it were by his private joy in
what he heard or saw: a remark I made, the waiter remov-
ing the cold dinner plates that served as ornament and
bringing warmed ones of a different design, the nylon
curtain blowing inward and brushing my bare, summer-
ripened arm. It was the end of a warm London summer.

"I'm not mad about them either," he said. We were engaged in a bit of backbiting. Discussing a famous couple
we both knew. He kept his hands joined all the time as if
they were being put to prayer. There were no barriers between us. We were strangers. I am a television announcer;
we had met to do a job and out of courtesy he asked me
to dinner. He told me about his wife—who was thirty like
me—and how he knew he would marry her the very
first moment he set eyes on her. (She was his third wife.) I
made no inquiries as to what she looked like. I still don't
know. The only memory I have of her is of her arms
sheathed in big, mauve, crocheted sleeves and the image
runs away with me and I see his pink, praying hands
vanishing into those sleeves and the two of them waltzing in
some large, grim room, smiling rapturously at their good
fortune in being together. But that came much later.

We had a pleasant supper and figs for afters. The first figs I'd ever tasted. He tested them gently with his fingers, then put three on my side plate. I kept staring down at their purple-black skins, because with the shaking I could not trust myself to peel them. He took my mind off my nervousness by telling me a little story about a girl who was being interviewed on the radio and admitted to owning thirty-seven pairs of shoes and buying a new dress every Saturday, which she later endeavored to sell to friends or family. Somehow I knew that it was a story he had specially selected for me and also that he would not risk telling it to many people. He was in his way a serious man, and famous, though that is hardly of interest when one is telling about a love affair. Or is it? Anyhow, without peeling it I bit into one of the figs.

How do you describe a taste? They were a new food and he was a new man and that night in my bed he was both stranger and lover, which I used to think was the ideal bed partner.

In the morning he was quite formal but unashamed; he even asked for a clothes brush because there was a smudge of powder on his jacket where we had embraced in the taxi coming home. At the time I had no idea whether or not we would sleep together, but on the whole I felt that we would not. I have never owned a clothes brush. I own books and records and various bottles of scent and beautiful clothes, but I never buy cleaning stuffs or aids for prolonging property. I expect it is improvident, but I just throw things away. Anyhow, he dabbed the powder smear with his handkerchief and it came off quite easily. The other thing he needed was a piece of sticking plaster because a new shoe had cut his heel. I looked but there was none left in the tin. My children had cleared it out during the long summer holidays. In fact, for a moment, I saw my two sons throughout those summer days, slouched on chairs, reading comics, riding bicycles, wrestling, incurring cuts which they promptly covered with Elastoplast, and afterward, when the plasters fell, flaunting the brown-rimmed marks as proof of their valor. I missed them badly and longed to hold them in my arms—another reason why I welcomed his company. "There's no plaster

left," I said, not without shame. I thought how he would
think me neglectful. I wondered if I ought to explain why
my sons were at boarding school when they were still so
young. They were eight and ten. But I didn't. I had ceased
to want to tell people the tale of how my marriage had
ended and my husband, unable to care for two young
boys, insisted on boarding school in order to give them, as
he put it, a stabilizing influence. I believed it was done in
order to deprive me of the pleasure of their company. I
couldn't.

We had breakfast out of doors. The start of another
warm day. The dull haze that preceded heat hung from
the sky and in the garden next door the sprinklers were
already on. My neighbors are fanatic gardeners. He ate
three pieces of toast and some bacon. I ate also, just to put
him at ease, though normally I skip breakfast. "I'll stock
up with plaster, clothes brush, and cleaning fluids," I said.
My way of saying, "You'll come again?" He saw through
it straight away. Hurrying down the mouthful of toast he
put one of his prayer hands over mine and told me solemnly
and nicely that he would not have a mean and squalid
little affair with me, but that we would meet in a month or
so and he hoped we would become friends. I hadn't
thought of us as friends but it was an interesting possibility. I remembered the earlier part of our evening's conversation and his referring to his earlier wives and his older
grown-up children and I thought how honest and un-
nostalgic he was. I was really sick of sorrows and people
multiplying them even to themselves. Another thing he did
that endeared him was to fold back the green silk bedspread, a thing I never do myself.

When he left I felt quite buoyant and in a way relieved.
It had been nice and there were no nasty after-effects. My
face was pink from kissing and my hair tossed from our
exertions. I looked a little wanton. Feeling tired from such
a broken night's sleep I drew the curtains and got back into
bed. I had a nightmare. The usual one where I am being
put to death by a man. People tell me that a nightmare is
healthy and from that experience I believe it. I wakened
calmer than I had been for months and passed the remainder of the day happily.

Two mornings later he rang and asked was there a chance of our meeting that night. I said yes because I was not doing anything and it seemed appropriate to have supper and seal our secret decently. But we started recharging.

"We did have a very good time," he said. I could feel myself making little petrified moves denoting love, shyness; opening my eyes wide to look at him, exuding trust. This time he peeled the figs for both of us. We positioned our legs so that they touched and withdrew them shortly afterward, confident that our desires were flowing. He brought me home. I noticed when we were in bed that he had put cologne on his shoulder and that he must have set out to dinner with the hope if not the intention of sleeping with me. I liked the taste of his skin better than the foul chemical and I had to tell him so. He just laughed. Never had I been so at ease with a man. For the record I had slept with four other men but there always seemed to be a distance between us, conversationwise. I mused for a moment on their various smells as I inhaled his, which reminded me of some herb. It was not parsley, not thyme, not mint, but some nonexistent herb compounded of these three smells. On this second occasion our lovemaking was more relaxed.

"What will you do if you make an avaricious woman out of me?" I asked.

"I will pass you on to someone very dear and suitable," he said. We coiled together, and with my head on his shoulder I thought of pigeons under the railway bridge near by, who passed their nights nestled together, heads folded into mauve breasts. In his sleep we kissed and murmured. I did not sleep. I never do when I am over-happy, over-unhappy, or in bed with a strange man.

Neither of us said, "Well here we are, having a mean and squalid little affair." We just started to meet. Regularly. We stopped going to restaurants because of his being famous. He would come to my house for dinner. I'll never forget the flurry of those preparations—putting flowers in vases, changing the sheets, thumping knots out of pillows, trying to cook, putting on makeup and keeping a hair brush near by in case he arrived early. The agony of it!

It was with difficulty I answered the doorbell, when it finally rang.

"You don't know what an oasis this is," he would say. And then in the hallway he would put his hands on my shoulders and squeeze them through my thin dress and say, "Let me look at you," and I would hang my head both because I was overwhelmed and because I wanted to be. We would kiss, often for a full five minutes. He kissed the inside of my nostrils. Then we would move to the sitting room and sit on the chaise longue, still speechless. He would touch the bone of my knee and say what beautiful knees I had. He saw and admired parts of one that no other man had ever bothered with. Soon after supper we went to bed.

Once he came unexpectedly in the late afternoon when I was dressed to go out. I was going to the theater with another man.

"How I wish I were taking you," he said.

"We'll go to the theater one night?" He bowed his head. We would. It was the first time his eyes looked sad. We did not make love because I was made up and had my false eyelashes on and it seemed impractical. He said, "Has any man ever told you that to see a woman you desire when you cannot do a thing about it leaves you with an ache?"

The ache conveyed itself to me and stayed all through the theater. I felt angry for not having gone to bed with him and later I regretted it even more, because from that evening onward our meetings were fewer. His wife, who had been in France with their children, returned. I knew this when he arrived one evening in a motor car and in the course of conversation mentioned that his small daughter had that day peed over an important document. I can tell you now that he was a lawyer.

From then on it was seldom possible to meet at night. He made afternoon dates and at very short notice. Any night he did stay he arrived with a travel bag containing toothbrush, clothes brush, and the few things a man might need for an overnight, loveless stay in a provincial hotel. I expected she packed it. I thought how ridiculous. I felt no pity for her. In fact the mention of her name—it was Helen—made me angry. He said it very harmlessly. He

said they'd been burgled in the middle of the night and
he'd gone down in his pyjamas while his wife telephoned
the police from the extension upstairs.

"They only burgle the rich," I said hurriedly, to change
the conversation. It was reassuring to find that he wore
pyjamas with her, when he didn't with me. My jealousy
of her was extreme, and of course grossly unfair. Still, I
would be giving the wrong impression if I said her existence
blighted our relationship at that point. Because it didn't.
He took great care to speak like a single man, and he
allowed time after our lovemaking to stay for an hour or
so and depart at his leisure. In fact it is one of those
after-love sessions that I consider the cream of our affair.
We were sitting on the bed, naked, eating smoked-salmon
sandwiches. I had lighted the gas fire because it was well
into autumn and the afternoons got chilly. The fire made
a steady purring noise. It was the only light in the room.
It was the first time he noticed the shape of my face because he said that up to then my coloring had drawn all of
his admiration. His face and the mahogany chest and the
pictures also looked better. Not rosy, because the gas fire
did not have that kind of glow, but resplendent with a
whitish light. The goatskin rug underneath the window
had a special, luxurious softness. I remarked on it. He
happened to say that he had a slight trace of masochism,
and that often, unable to sleep at night in a bed, he would
go to some other room and lie on the floor with a coat over
him and fall fast asleep. A thing he'd done as a boy. The
image of the little boy sleeping on the floor moved me to
enormous compassion and without a word from him I led
him across to the goatskin and laid him down. It was the
only time our roles were reversed. He was not my father.
I became his mother. Soft and totally fearless. Even my
nipples, about which I am squeamish, did not shrink from
his rabid demands. I wanted to do everything and anything for him. As often happens with lovers my ardor and
inventiveness stimulated his. We stopped at nothing. Afterward, remarking on our achievement—a thing he always
did—he reckoned it was the most intimate of all our
intimate moments. I was inclined to agree. As we stood
up to get dressed he wiped his armpits with the white

blouse I had been wearing and asked which of my lovely dresses I would wear to dinner that night. He chose my black one for me. He said it gave him great pleasure to know that although I was to dine with others my mind would ruminate on what he and I had done. A wife, work, the world might separate us but in our thoughts we were betrothed.

"I'll think of you," I said.

"And I, of you."

We were not even sad at parting.

It was after that I had what I can only describe as a dream within a dream. I was coming out of sleep, forcing myself awake, wiping my saliva on the pillow slip, when something pulled me, an enormous weight dragged me down into the bed and I thought: I have become infirm. I have lost the use of my limbs and this accounts for my listlessness for several months when I've wanted to do nothing except drink tea and stare out of the window. I am a cripple. All over. Even my mouth won't move. Only my brain is ticking away. My brain tells me that a woman downstairs doing the ironing is the only one who could locate me but she might not come upstairs for days, she might think I'm in bed with a man, committing a sin. From time to time I sleep with a man but normally I sleep alone. She'll leave the ironed clothes on the kitchen table, and the iron itself upright on the floor so that it won't set fire to anything. Blouses will be on hangers, their frilled collars white and fluid like foam. She's the sort of woman who even irons the toes and heels of nylon stockings. She'll slip away, until Thursday, her next day in. I feel something at my back, or, strictly speaking, tugging at my bedcovers, which I have mounted right up the length of my back to cover my head. For shelter. And I know now that it's not infirmity that's dragging me down but a man. How did he get in there? He's on the inside, near the wall. I know what he's going to do to me and the woman downstairs won't ever come to rescue me, she'd be too ashamed or she might not think I want to be rescued. I don't know which of the men it is, whether it's the big tall bruiser that's at the door every time I open it innocently, expecting it's the laundry boy and find it's Him with an old black carving

knife, its edge glittering because he's just sharpened it on
a step. Before I can scream my tongue isn't mine any
more. Or it might be the Other One. Tall too, he gets me
by my bracelet as I slip between the banisters of the stairs.
I've forgotten that I am not a little girl any more and that
I don't slip easily between banisters. If the bracelet had
snapped in two I would have made my escape, leaving him
with one half of a gold bracelet in his hand, but my
goddam provident mother had a safety chain put on it
because it was nine carat. Anyhow he's in the bed. It will
go on for ever, the thing he wants. I daren't turn round
to look at him. Then something gentle about the way the
sheet is pulled down suggests that he might be the New
One. The man I met a few weeks ago. Not my type at
all, tiny broken veins on this cheeks, and red, actually red
hair. We were on a goatskin. But it was raised off the
ground, high as a bed. I had been doing most of the loving;
breasts, hands, mouth, all yearned to minister to him. I
felt so sure, never have I felt so sure of the rightness of
what I was doing. Then he started kissing me down there
and I came to his lapping tongue and his head was under
my buttocks and it was like I was bearing him only there
was pleasure instead of pain. He trusted me. We were two
people, I mean he wasn't someone on me, smothering me,
doing something I couldn't see. I could see. I could have
shat on his red hair if I wanted. He trusted me. He
stretched the come to the very last. And all the things that
I loved up to then, like glass or lies, mirrors and feathers,
and pearl buttons, and silk, and willow trees, became
secondary compared with what he'd done. He was lying
so that I could see it: so delicate, so thin, with a bunch of
worried blue veins along its side. Talking to it was like
talking to a little child. The light in the room was a white
glow. He'd made me very soft and wet so I put it in. It
was quick and hard and forceful and he said, "I'm not
considering you now, I think we've considered you," and
I said that was perfectly true and that I liked him roughing
away. I said it. I was no longer a hypocrite, no longer a
liar. Before that he had often remonstrated with me, he had
said, "There are words we are not going to use to each
other, words such as 'Sorry' and 'Are You Angry?' " I had

used these words a lot. So I think from the gentle shuffle of the bedcovers—like a request really—that it might be him and if it is I want to sink down and down into the warm, dark, sleepy pit of the bed and stay in it forever, coming with him. But I am afraid to look in case it is not Him but One of the Others.

When I finally got awake I was in a panic and I had a dreadful urge to telephone him, but though he never actually forbade it, I knew he would have been most displeased.

When something has been perfect, as our last encounter in the gaslight had been, there is a tendency to try hard to repeat it. Unfortunately the next occasion was clouded. He came in the afternoon and brought a suitcase containing all the paraphernalia for a dress dinner which he was attending that night. When he arrived he asked if he could hang up his tails, as otherwise they would be very creased. He hooked the hanger on the outer rim of the wardrobe and I remember being impressed by the row of war medals along the top pocket. Our time in bed was pleasant but hasty. He worried about getting dressed. I just sat and watched him. I wanted to ask about his medals and how he had merited them, and if he remembered the war, and if he'd missed his then wife, and if he'd killed people, and if he still dreamt about it. But I asked nothing. I sat there as if I were paralyzed.

"No braces," he said as he held the wide black trousers around his middle. His other trousers must have been supported by a belt.

"I'll go to Woolworths for some," I said. But that was impractical because he was already in danger of being late. I got a safety pin and fastened the trousers from the back. It was a difficult operation because the pin was not really sturdy enough.

"You'll bring it back?" I said. I am superstitious about giving people pins. He took some time to reply because he was muttering "damn" under his breath. Not to me. But to the stiff, inhuman, starched collar which would not yield to the little gold studs he had wanted to pierce through. I tried. He tried. Each time when one of us failed the other became impatient. He said if we went on

the collar would be grubby from our hands. And that
seemed a worse alternative. I thought he must be dining
with very critical people, but of course I did not give my
thoughts on the matter. In the end we each managed to
get a stud through and he had a small sip of whisky as a
celebration. The bow tie was another ordeal. He couldn't
do it. I didn't dare try.

"Haven't you done it before?" I said. I expect his wives
—in succession—had done it for him. I felt such a fool.
Then a lump of hatred. I thought how ugly and pink his
legs were, how repellent the shape of his body, which did
not have anything in the way of a waist, how deceitful his
eyes that congratulated himself in the mirror when he succeeded in making a clumsy bow. As he put on the coat the
sound of the metals tinkling enabled me to remark on their
music. There was so little I could say. Lastly he donned a
white silk scarf that came below his middle. He looked like
someone I did not know. He left hurriedly. I ran with him
down the road to help get a taxi, and trying to keep up with
him and chatter was not easy. All I can remember is the
ghostly sight of the very white scarf swinging back and
forth as we rushed. His shoes, which were patent, creaked
unsuitably.

"Is it all-male?" I asked.

"No. Mixed," he replied.

So that was why we hurried. To meet his wife at some
appointed place. The hatred began to grow.

He did bring back the safety pin, but my superstition
remained because four straight pins with black rounded
tops that had come off his new shirt were on my window
ledge. He refused to take them. He was not superstitious.

Bad moments, like good ones, tend to be grouped together, and when I think of the dress occasion I also think
of the other time when we were not in utter harmony. It
was on a street; we were searching for a restaurant. We
had to leave my house because a friend had come to stay
and we would have been obliged to tolerate her company.
Going along the street—it was October and very windy—I
felt that he was angry with me for having drawn us out
into the cold where we could not embrace. My heels were
very high and I was ashamed of the hollow sound they

made. In a way I felt we were enemies. He looked in the windows of restaurants to see if any acquaintances of his were there. Two restaurants he decided against, for reasons best known to himself. One looked to be very attractive. It had orange bulbs inset in the walls, and the light came through small squares of iron grating. We crossed the road to look at places on the opposite side. I saw a group of rowdies coming toward us and for something to say—what with my aggressive heels, the wind, traffic going by, the ugly, unromantic street, we had run out of agreeable conversation—I asked if he ever felt apprehensive about encountering noisy groups like that, late at night. He said that in fact a few nights before he had been walking home very late and had seen such a group coming toward him, and before he even registered fear he found that he had splayed his bunch of keys between his fingers and had his hand, armed with the sharp points of the keys, ready to pull out of his pocket should they have threatened him. I suppose he did it again while we were walking along. Curiously enough I did not feel he was my protector. I only felt that he and I were two people, that there was in the world trouble, violence, sickness, catastrophe, that he faced it in one way, and that I faced it—or to be exact that I shrank from it—in another. We would always be outside one another. In the course of that melancholy thought the group went by and my conjecture about violence was all for nothing. We found a nice restaurant and drank a lot of wine.

Later our lovemaking, as usual, was perfect. He stayed all night. I used to feel specially privileged on the nights he stayed, and the only little thing that lessened my joy was spasms of anxiety in case he should have told his wife he was at such and such a hotel and her telephoning there and not finding him. More than once I raced into an imaginary narrative where she came and discovered us and I acted silent and ladylike and he told her very crisply to wait outside until he was ready. I felt no pity for her. Sometimes I wondered if we would ever meet, or if in fact we had already met on an escalator at some point. Though that was unlikely because we lived at opposite ends of London.

Then to my great surprise the opportunity came. I was invited to a Thanksgiving party given by an American magazine. He saw the card on my mantelshelf and said, "You're going to that too?" and I smiled and said maybe. Was he? "Yes," he said. He tried to make me reach a decision there and then but I was too canny. Of course I would go. I was curious to see his wife. I would meet him in public. It shocked me to think that we had never met in the company of any other person. It was like being shut off . . . a little animal locked away. I thought very distinctly of a ferret that a forester used to keep in a wooden box with a sliding top when I was a child, and once of another ferret being brought to mate with it. The thought made me shiver. I mean I got it confused; I thought of white ferrets with their little pink nostrils in the same breath as I thought of him sliding a door back and slipping into my box from time to time. His skin had a lot of pink in it.

"I haven't decided," I said, but when the day came I went. I took a lot of trouble with my appearance, had my hair set, and wore a virginal attire. Black and white. The party was held in a large room with paneled walls of brown wood; blown-up magazine covers were along the panels. The bar was at one end, under a balcony. The effect was of shrunken barmen in white lost underneath the cliff of the balcony, which seemed in danger of collapsing on them. A more unlikely room for a party I have never seen. There were women going around with trays, but I had to go to the bar because there was champagne on the trays and I have a preference for whisky. A man I knew conducted me there and en route another man placed a kiss on my back. I hoped that he witnessed this, but it was such a large room with hundreds of people around that I had no idea where he was stationed. I noticed a dress I quite admired, a mauve dress with very wide, crocheted sleeves. Looking up the length of the sleeves I saw its owner's eyes directed on me. Perhaps she was admiring my outfit. People with the same tastes often do. I have no idea what her face looked like, but later when I asked a girlfriend which was his wife she pointed to this woman with the crocheted sleeves. The second time I saw her in profile. I still don't know what she looked like, nor do those

eyes into which I looked speak to my memory with anything special, except, perhaps, slight covetousness.

Finally I searched him out. I had a mutual friend walk
across with me and apparently introduce us. He was un-
welcoming. He looked strange, the flush on his cheekbones
vivid and unnatural. He spoke to the mutual friend and
virtually ignored me. Possibly to make amends he asked,
at length, if I was enjoying myself.

"It's a chilly room," I said. I was referring of course to
his manner. Had I wanted to describe the room I would
have used "grim," or some such adjective.

"I don't know about you being chilly but I'm certainly
not," he said with aggression. Then a very drunk woman
in a sack dress came and took his hand and began to slob-
ber all over him. I excused myself and went off. He said
most pointedly that he hoped he would see me again some
time.

I caught his eye just as I left the party and I felt both
sorry for him and angry with him. He looked stunned, as
if important news had just been delivered to him. He
saw me leave with a group of people and I stared at him
without the whimper of a smile. Yes, I was sorry for him.
I was also piqued. The very next day when we met and
I brought it up he did not even remember that a mutual
friend had introduced us.

"Clement Hastings!" he said, repeating the man's name.
Which goes to show how nervous he must have been.

It is impossible to insist that bad news delivered in a
certain manner and at a certain time will have a less awful
effect. But I feel that I got my walking papers from him
at the wrong moment. For one thing it was morning. The
clock went off and I sat up wondering when he had set it.
Being on the outside of the bed he was already attending
to the push button.

"I'm sorry, darling," he said.

"Did you set it?" I said, indignant. There was an ele-
ment of betrayal here, as if he'd wanted to sneak away
without saying good-bye.

"I must have," he said. He put his arm around me and
we lay back again. It was dark outside and there was a
feeling—though this may be memory feeling—of frost.

"Congratulations, you're getting your prize today," he

whispered. I was being given an award for my announcing. I am a television announcer.

"Thank you," I said. I was ashamed of it. It reminded me of being back at school and always coming first in everything and being guilty about this, but not disciplined enough to deliberately hold back.

"It's beautiful that you stayed all night," I said. I was stroking him all over. My hands were never still in bed. Awake or asleep I constantly caressed him. Not to excite him, simply to reassure and comfort him and perhaps to consolidate my ownership. There is something about holding on to things that I find therapeutic. For hours I hold smooth stones in the palm of my hand or I grip the sides of an armchair and feel the better for it. He kissed me. He said he had never known anyone so sweet or so attentive. Encouraged, I began to do something very intimate. I heard his sighs of pleasure, the "oy, oy" of delight when he was both indulging it and telling himself that he mustn't. At first I was unaware of his speaking voice.

"Hey," he said, jocularly, just like that. "This can't go on, you know." I thought he was referring to our activity at that moment because of course it was late and he would have to get up shortly. Then I raised my head from its sunken position between his legs and I looked at him through my hair which had fallen over my face. I saw that he was serious.

"It just occurred to me that possibly you love me," he said. I nodded and pushed my hair back so that he would read it, my testimony, clear and clean upon my face. He put me lying down so that our heads were side by side and he began:

"I adore you, but I'm not in love with you, with my commitments I don't think I could be in love with anyone, it all started gay and light-hearted. . . ." Those last few words offended me. It was not how I saw it or how I remembered it: the numerous telegrams he sent me saying, "I long to see you," or, "May the sun shine on you," the first few moments each time when we met and were overcome with passion, shyness, and the shock of being so disturbed by each other's presence. We had even searched in our dictionaries for words to convey the specialness of our regard for each other. He came up with "cense," which meant to adore or cover with the perfume of love. It was a most appropriate word and we used it over and over again. Now he was negating all this. He was talking about weaving me into his life, his family life . . . becoming a friend. He said it, though, without conviction. I could not think of a single thing to say. I knew that if I spoke I would be pathetic, so I remained silent. When he'd finished I stared straight ahead at the split between the curtains, and looking at the beam of raw light coming through I said, "I think there's frost outside," and he said that possibly there was, because winter was upon us. We got up and as usual he took the bulb out of the bedside lamp and plugged in his razor. I went off to get breakfast. That was the only morning I forgot about squeezing orange juice for him and I often wonder if he took it as an insult. He left just before nine.

The sitting room held the traces of his visit. Or, to be precise, the remains of his cigars. In one of the blue, saucer-shaped ashtrays there were thick turds of dark gray cigar ash. There were also stubs, but it was the ash I kept looking at, thinking that its thickness resembled the thickness of his unlovely legs. And once again I experienced hatred for him. I was about to tip the contents of the ashtray into the fire grate when something stopped me, and what did I do but get an empty lozenge box and with the aid of a sheet of paper lift the clumps of ash in there and carry the tin upstairs. With the movement the turds lost their shapes, and whereas they had reminded me of his legs they were now an even mass of dark gray ash, probably like the ashes of the dead. I put the tin in a drawer underneath some clothes.

Later in the day I was given my award—a very big silver medallion with my name on it. At the party afterward I got drunk. My friends tell me that I did not actually disgrace myself but I have a humiliating recollection of beginning a story and not being able to go ahead with it, not because the contents eluded me but because the words became too difficult to pronounce. A man brought me home and after I'd made him a cup of tea I said good night over-properly; then when he was gone I staggered to my bed. When I drink heavily I sleep badly. Wakening, it was still dark outside and straight away I remembered the previous morning, and the suggestion of frost outside, and his cold warning words. I had to agree. Although our meetings were perfect I had a sense of doom impending, of a chasm opening up between us, of someone telling his wife, of souring love, of destruction. And still we hadn't gone as far as we should have gone. There were peaks of joy and of its opposite that we should have climbed to, but the time was not left to us. He had of course said, "You still have a great physical hold over me," and that in its way I found degrading. To have gone on making love when he had discarded me would have been degrading. It had come to an end. The thing I kept thinking of was a violet in a wood and how a time comes for it to drop off and die. The frost may have had something to do with my thinking, or rather with my musings. I got up and put on a dressing gown. My head hurt from the hangover but I knew that I must write to him while I had some resolution. I know my own failings and I knew that before the day was out I would want to re-see him, sit with him, coax him back with sweetness and my overwhelming helplessness.

I wrote the note and left out the bit about the violet. It is not a thing you can put down on paper without seeming fanciful. I said if he didn't think it prudent to see me, then not to see me. I said it had been a nice interlude and that we must entertain good memories of it. It was a remarkably controlled letter. He wrote back promptly. My decision came as a shock, he said. Still he admitted that I was right. In the middle of the letter he said he must penetrate my composure and to do so he must admit that above and beyond everything he loved me and would always do so. That of course was the word I had been snooping around for, for months. It set me off. I wrote a long letter back to him. I lost my head. I oversaid everything. I testified to loving him, to sitting on the edge of madness in the intervening days, to my hoping for a miracle.

It is just as well that I did not write out the miracle in detail because possibly it is, or was, rather inhuman. It concerned his family:

He was returning from the funeral of his wife and children, wearing black tails. He also wore the white silk scarf I had seen him with, and there was a black, mourning tulip in his buttonhole. When he came forward toward me I snatched the black tulip and replaced it with a white narcissus, and he in turn put the scarf around my neck and drew me toward him by holding its fringed ends. I kept moving my neck back and forth within the embrace of the scarf. Then we danced divinely on a wooden floor that was white and slippery. At times I thought we would fall but he said, "You don't have to worry, I'm with you." The dance floor was also a road and we were going somewhere beautiful.

For weeks I waited for a reply to my letter but there was none. More than once I had my hand on the telephone, but something cautionary—a new sensation for me—in the back of my mind bade me to wait. To give him time. To let regret take charge of his heart. To let him come of his own accord. And then I panicked. I thought that perhaps the letter had gone astray or had fallen into other hands. I'd posted it of course to the office in Lincoln's Inn where he worked. I wrote another. This time it was a formal note, and with it I enclosed a postcard with the words YES and NO. I asked if he had received my previous letter to kindly let me know by simply crossing out the word which did not apply on my card and sending it back to me. It came back with the NO crossed out. Nothing else. So he had received my letter. I think I looked at the card for hours. I could not stop shaking and to calm myself I took several drinks. There was something so brutal about the card, but then you could say that I had asked for it by approaching the situation in that way. I took out the box with his ash in it and wept over it, and both wanted to toss it out the window and preserve it for evermore.

In general I behaved very strangely. I rang someone who knew him and asked for no reason at all what she thought his hobbies might be. She said he played the harmonium, which I found unbearable news altogether. Then I entered a black patch and on the third day I lost control.

Well, from not sleeping and taking pep pills and whisky I got very odd. I was shaking all over and breathing very quickly the way one might after witnessing an accident. I stood at my bedroom window, which is on the second floor, and looked at the concrete underneath. The only flowers left in bloom were the hydrangeas, and they had faded to a soft russet, which was much more fetching than the harsh pink they were all summer. In the garden next door there were frost hats over the fuchsias. Looking first at the hydrangeas, then at the fuchsias, I tried to estimate the consequences of my jumping. I wondered if the drop were great enough. Being physically very awkward I could only conceive of gravely injuring myself, which would be worse because I would then be confined to my bed and imprisoned with the very thoughts that were driving me to desperation. I opened the window and leaned out, but quickly drew back. I had a better idea. There was a plumber downstairs installing central heating—an enterprise I had embarked upon when my lover began to come regularly and we liked walking around naked eating sandwiches and playing records. I decided to gas myself and to seek the help of the plumber in order to do it efficiently. I am aware—someone must have told me—that there comes a point in the middle of the operation when the doer regrets it and tries to withdraw, but cannot. That seemed like an extra note of tragedy that I had no wish to experience. So I decided to go downstairs to this man and explain to him that I *wanted* to die, and that I was not telling him simply for him to prevent me, or console me, that I was not looking for pity—there comes a time when pity is of no help—and that I simply wanted his assistance. He could show me what to do, settle me down, and—this is absurd—be around to take care of the telephone and the doorbell for the next few hours. Also to dispose of me with dignity. Above all I wanted that. I even decided what I would wear: a long dress, which in fact was the same color as the hydrangeas in their russet phase and which I've never worn except for a photograph or on television. Before going downstairs I wrote a note which simply said: "I am committing suicide through lack of intelligence, and through not knowing, not learning to know, how to live."

You will think I am callous not to have taken the existence of my children into account. But, in fact, I did. Long

before the affair began I had reached the conclusion that
they had been parted from me irrevocably by being sent
to boarding school. If you like, I felt I had let them down
years before. I thought—it was an unhysterical admission—
that my being alive or my being dead made little difference
to the course of their lives. I ought to say that I had not
seen them for a month, and it is a shocking fact that although absence does not make love less it cools down our
physical need for the ones we love. They were due home
for their mid-term holiday that very day, but since it was
their father's turn to have them, I knew that I would only
see them for a few hours one afternoon. And in my de-
spondent state that seemed worse than not seeing them at
all.

Well of course when I went downstairs the plumber took
one look at me and said, "You could do with a cup of
tea." He actually had tea made. So I took it and stood
there warming my child-sized hands around the barrel of
the brown mug. Suddenly, swiftly, I remembered my lover
measuring our hands when we were lying in bed and saying
that mine were no bigger than his daughter's. And then I
had another and less edifying memory about hands. It was
the time we met when he was visibly distressed because
he'd caught those same daughter's hands in a motor-car
door. The fingers had not been broken but were badly
bruised, and he felt awful about it and hoped his daughter
would forgive him. Upon being told the story I bolted off
into an anecdote about almost losing *my* fingers in the door
of a new Jaguar I had bought. It was pointless, although a
listener might infer from it that I was a boastful and heartless girl. I would have been sorry for any child whose
fingers were caught in a motor-car door, but at that
moment I was trying to recall him to the hidden world of
him and me. Perhaps it was one of the things that made me
like him less. Perhaps it was then he resolved to end the
affair. I was about to say this to the plumber, to warn him
about so-called love often hardening the heart, but like
the violets it is something that can miss awfully, and
when it does two people are mortally embarrassed. He'd
put sugar in my tea and I found it sickly.

"I want you to help me," I said.

"Anything," he said. I ought to know that. We were friends. He would do the pipes tastefully. The pipes would be little works of art and the radiators painted to match the walls.

"You may think I will paint these white, but in fact they will be light ivory," he said. The whitewash on the kitchen walls had yellowed a bit.

"I want to do myself in," I said hurriedly.

"Good God," he said, and then burst out laughing. He'd always known I was dramatic. Then he looked at me and obviously my face was a revelation. For one thing I could not control my breathing. He put his arm around me and led me into the sitting room and we had a drink. I knew he liked drink and thought, It's an ill wind that doesn't blow some good. The maddening thing was that I kept thinking a live person's thoughts. He said I had so much to live for. "A young girl like you—people wanting your autograph, a lovely new car," he said.

"It's all . . ." I groped for the word. I had meant to say "meaningless," but "cruel" was the word that came out.

"And your boys," he said. "What about your boys?" He had seen photographs of them, and once I'd read him a letter from one of them. The word "cruel" seemed to be blazing in my head. It screamed at me from every corner of the room. To avoid his glance, I looked down at the sleeve of my angora jersey and methodically began picking off pieces of fluff and rolling them into a little ball.

There was a moment's pause.

"This is an unlucky road. You're the third," he said.

"The third what?" I said, industriously piling the black fluff into my palm.

"A woman further up, her husband was a bandleader, used to be out late. One night she went to the dance hall and saw him with another girl; she came home and did it straight away."

"Gas?" I asked, genuinely curious.

"No, sedation," he said, and was off on another story about a girl who'd gassed herself and was found by him because he was in the house treating dry rot at the time. "Naked, except for a jersey," he said, and speculated on why she should be attired like that. His manner changed considerably as he recalled how he went into the house, smelled gas, and searched it out.

I looked at him. His face was grave. He had scaled eyelids. I had never looked at him so closely before. "Poor Michael," I said. A feeble apology. I was thinking that if he had abetted my suicide he would then have been committed to the memory of it.

"A lovely young girl," he said, wistful.

"Poor girl," I said, mustering up pity.

There seemed to be nothing else to say. He had shamed me out of it. I stood up and made an effort at normality—I took some glasses off a side table and moved in the direction of the kitchen. If dirty glasses are any proof of drinking, then quite a lot of it had been done by me over the past few days.

"Well," he said and rose and sighed. He admitted to feeling pleased with himself.

As it happened, there would have been a secondary crisis that day. Although my children were due to return to their father, he rang to say that the older boy had a temperature, and since—though he did not say this—he could not take care of a sick child, he would be obliged to bring them to my house. They arrived in the afternoon. I was waiting inside the door, with my face heavily made up, to disguise my distress. The sick boy had a blanket draped over his tweed coat and one of his father's scarves around his face. When I embraced him he began to cry. The younger boy went around the house to make sure that everything was as he had last seen it. Normally I had presents for them on their return home, but I had neglected it on this occasion, and consequently they were a little downcast.

"Tomorrow," I said.

"Why are there tears in your eyes?" the sick boy asked as I undressed him.

"Because you are sick," I said, telling a half-truth.

"Oh, Mamsies," he said, calling me by a name he had used for years. He put his arms around me and we both began to cry. He was my less favorite child, and I felt he was crying for that as well as for the numerous unguessed

afflictions that the circumstances of a broken home would
impose upon him. It was strange and unsatisfying to hold
him in my arms when over the months I had got used to
my lover's size—the width of his shoulders, the exact
height of his body, which obliged me to stand on tiptoe
so that our limbs could correspond perfectly. Holding my
son, I was conscious only of how small he was and how
tenaciously he clung.

The younger boy and I sat in the bedroom and played
a game which entailed reading out questions such as
"A River?," "A Famous Footballer?," and then spinning
a disc until it steadied down at one letter and using that
letter as the first initial of the river or the famous footballer or whatever the question called for. I was quite slow
at it, and so was the sick boy. His brother won easily
although I had asked him to let the invalid win. Children
are callous.

We all jumped when the heating came on, because the
boiler, from the basement just underneath, gave an al-
mighty churning noise, and made the kind of sudden
erupting move I had wanted to make that morning when
I stood at the bedroom window and tried to pitch myself
out. As a special surprise and to cheer me up the plumber
had called in two of his mates and between them they got
the job finished. To make us warm and happy as he put it,
when he came to the bedroom to tell me. It was an awkward moment. I'd avoided him since our morning's drama.
At tea time I'd even left his tea on a tray out on the landing. Would he tell other people how I had asked him to
be my murderer? Would he have recognized it as that? I
gave him and his friends a drink, and they stood uncom-
fortably in the children's bedroom and looked at the little
boy's flushed face and said he would soon be better. What
else could they say!

For the remainder of the evening the boys and I played
the quiz game over and over again, and just before they
went to sleep I read them an adventure story. In the
morning they both had temperatures. I was busy nursing
them for the next couple of weeks. I made beef tea a lot
and broke bread into it and coaxed them to swallow those
sops of savory bread. They were constantly asking to be

entertained. The only thing I could think of in the way of facts were particles of nature lore I had gleaned from one of my colleagues in the television canteen. Even with embellishing, it took not more than two minutes to tell my children: of a storm of butterflies in Venezuela, of animals called sloths who are so lazy they hang from trees and become covered with moss, and of how the sparrows in England sing differently from the sparrows in Paris.

"More," they would say. "More, more." Then we would have to play that silly game again or embark upon another adventure story.

At these times I did not allow my mind to wander, but in the evenings when their father came I used to withdraw to the sitting room and have a drink. Well, that was disastrous. The leisure enabled me to brood; also I have very weak bulbs in the lamps and the dimness gives the room a quality that induces reminiscence. I would be transported back. I enacted various kinds of reunion with my lover, but my favorite one was an unexpected meeting in one of those tiled, inhuman, pedestrian subways and running toward each other and finding ourselves at a stairway which said (one in London actually does say), "To central island only," and laughing as we leaped up those stairs propelled by miraculous wings. In less indulgent phases, I regretted that we hadn't seen more sunsets, or cigarette advertisements, or something, because in memory our numerous meetings became one long uninterrupted state of lovemaking without the ordinariness of things in between to fasten those peaks. The days, the nights with him, seemed to have been sandwiched into a long, beautiful, but single night instead of being stretched to the seventeen occasions it actually was. Ah, vanished peaks. Once I was so sure that he had come into the room that I tore off a segment of an orange I had just peeled and handed it to him.

But from the other room I heard the low, assured voice of the children's father delivering information with the self-importance of a man delivering dogmas, and I shuddered at the degree of poison that lay between us when we'd once professed to love. Plagued love. Then some of the feeling I had for my husband transferred itself to my lover, and I reasoned with myself that the letter in which he had professed to love me was sham, that he had merely written it when he thought he was free of me, but finding himself saddled once again, he withdrew, and let me have the postcard. I was a stranger to myself. Hate was welling up. I wished multitudes of humiliation on him. I even plotted a dinner party that I would attend having made sure that he was invited and of snubbing him throughout. My thoughts teetered between hate and the hope of something final between us so that I would be certain of his feelings toward me. Even as I sat in a bus, an advertisement which caught my eye was immediately related to him. It said, DON'T PANIC, WE ADAPT, WE REMODEL. It was an advertisement for pearl-stringing. I would mend and with vengeance.

I cannot say when it first began to happen, because that would be too drastic and anyhow I do not know. But the children were back at school, and we'd got over Christmas, and he and I had not exchanged cards. But I began to think less harshly of him. They were silly thoughts really. I hoped he was having little pleasures like eating in restaurants, and clean socks, and red wine the temperature he liked it, and even—yes, even ecstasies in bed with his wife. These thoughts made me smile to myself, inwardly, the new kind of smile I had discovered. I shuddered at the risk he'd run by seeing me at all. Of course the earlier injured thoughts battled with these new ones. It was like carrying a taper along a corridor where the draughts are fierce and the chances of it staying alight pretty meager. I thought of him and my children in the same instant, their little foibles became his: my children telling me elaborate lies about their sporting feats, his slight puffing when we climbed steps and his trying to conceal it. The age difference between us must have saddened him. It was then I think that I really fell in love with him. His courtship of me, his telegrams, his eventual departure, even our lovemaking, were nothing compared with this new sensation. It rose like sap within me, it often made me cry, the fact that he could not benefit from it! The temptation to ring him had passed away.

His phone call came quite out of the blue. It was one
of those times when I debated about answering it or not
because mostly I let it ring. He asked if we could meet, if,
and he said this so gently, my nerves were steady enough?
I said my nerves were never better. That was a liberty I
had to take. We met in a café for tea. Toast again. Just like
the beginning. He asked how I was. Remarked on my
good complexion. Neither of us mentioned the incident of
the postcard. Nor did he say what impulse had moved him
to telephone. It may not have been impulse at all. He
talked about his work and how busy he'd been, and then
relayed a little story about taking an elderly aunt for a
drive and driving so slowly that she asked him to please
hurry up because she would have walked there quicker.

"You've recovered," he said then, suddenly. I looked at
his face. I could see it was on his mind.

"I'm over it," I said, and dipped my finger into the
sugar bowl and let him lick the white crystals off the tip of
my finger. Poor man. I could not have told him anything
else, he would not have understood. In a way it was like
being with someone else. He was not the one who had
folded back the bedspread and sucked me dry and left
his cigar ash for preserving. He was the representative
of that one.

"We'll meet from time to time," he said.

"Of course." I must have looked dubious.

"Perhaps you don't want to?"

"Whenever you feel you would like to." I neither welcomed nor dreaded the thought. It would not make any
difference to how I felt. That was the first time it occurred
to me that all my life I had feared imprisonment, the nun's
cell, the hospital bed, the places where one faced the self
without distraction, without the crutches of other people—
but sitting there feeding him white sugar I thought, I
now have entered a cell, and this man cannot know what
it is for me to love him the way I do, and I cannot weigh
him down with it, because he is in another cell confronted
with other difficulties.

The cell reminded me of a convent and for something
to say I mentioned my sister the nun.

"I went to see my sister."

"How is she?" he asked. He had often inquired about her. He used to take an interest in her and ask what she looked like. I even got the impression that he had considered the thought of sleeping with her.

"She's fine," I said. "We were walking down a corridor and she asked me to look around and make sure that there weren't any other sisters looking and then she hoisted her skirts up and slid down the banisters."

"Dear girl," he said. He liked that story. The smallest things gave him such pleasure.

I enjoyed our tea. It was one of the least fruitless afternoons I'd had in months, and coming out he gripped my arm and said how perfect it would be if we could get away for a few days. Perhaps he meant it.

In fact we kept our promise. We do meet from time to time. You could say things are back to normal again. By normal I mean a state whereby I notice the moon, trees, fresh spit upon the pavement; I look at strangers and see in their expressions something of my own predicament; I am part of everyday life, I suppose. There is a lamp in my bedroom that gives out a dry crackle each time an electric train goes by and at night I count those crackles because it is the time he comes back. I mean the real he, not the man who confronts me from time to time across a café table, but the man that dwells somewhere within me. He rises before my eyes—his praying hands, his tongue that liked to suck, his sly eyes, his smile, the veins on his cheeks, the calm voice speaking sense to me. I suppose you wonder why I torment myself like this with details of his presence but I need it, I cannot let go of him now, because if I did, all our happiness and my subsequent pain—I cannot vouch for his—will all have been nothing, and a nothing is a dreadful thing to hold on to.

HOW SOON CAN I LEAVE?

by Susan Hill

The two ladies who lived together were called Miss Bartlett and Miss Roscommon.

Miss Roscommon, the older and stouter of the two, concealed her fear of life behind frank reference to babies and lavatories and the sexing of day-old chicks. It was well known that she had travelled widely as a girl; she told of her walking tours in Greece, and how she had driven an ambulance during the Spanish Civil War.

Miss Bartlett, who was only forty, cultivated shyness and self-effacement, out of which arose her way of leaving muttered sentences to trail off into the air, unfinished. Oh, do not take any notice of anything *I* may say, she meant, it is of no consequence, I am sorry to have spoken. . . . But the sentences drew attention to her, nevertheless.

"What was that?" people said, "I beg your pardon, I didn't quite catch . . . Do speak up. . . ." And so, she was forced to repeat herself and they, having brought it upon themselves, were forced to listen. She also protested helplessness in the face of everyday tools. It was Miss Roscommon who peeled all the potatoes and defrosted the refrigerator and opened the tins.

Their house, one of two white bungalows overlooking the bay, was called Tuscany.

When Miss Bartlett had finally come to live with Miss Roscommon, seven years before, each one believed that the step was taken for the good of the other. Miss Bartlett had been living in one of the little stone cottages, opposite the harbour, working through the winter on the stock that she sold, from her front room and on a trestle outside, in summer. From November until March, there were

no visitors to Mountsea. Winds and rain scoured the surface of the cliffs and only the lifeboat put out to sea. Miss
Roscommon had taken to inviting Miss Bartlett up to the
bungalow for meals.

"You should have a shop," she had begun by saying,
loading Miss Bartlett's plate with scones and homemade
ginger jam, "properly equipped and converted. It cannot
be satisfactory having to display goods in your living room.
Why have you not thought of taking a shop?"

Miss Bartlett made marquetry pictures of the church,
the lighthouse and the harbour, table lamps out of lobster
pots and rocks worked over with shells. She also imported
Italian straw baskets and did a little pewter work.

The idea of a shop had come to her, and been at once
dismissed, in the first weeks after her coming to Mountsea.
She was too timid to take any so definite a step, for, by
establishing herself in a shop, with her name written up
on a board outside, was she not establishing herself in the
minds of others as a shop*keeper*? As a girl, she had been
impressed by her mother's constant references to her as
dreamy and artistic, so that she could not possibly now
see herself in the role of shopkeeper. Also, by having her
name written up on that board, she felt that she would
somehow be committing herself to Mountsea, and by
doing that, finally abandoning all her hopes of a future
in some other place. As a girl, she had looked out at the
world and seen a signpost, with arms pointing in numerous
different directions, roads leading here, or here, or there.
She had been quite unable to choose which road to take,
for, having once set out upon any of them, she would
thereby be denying herself all the others. And what might
I lose, she had thought, what opportunities shall I miss if
I make the wrong choice?

So that, in the end, she had never chosen, only drifted
through her life from this to that, waking every morning
to the expectation of some momentous good fortune
dropped in her lap.

"That cottage is damp," said Miss Roscommon, allow-
ing her persuasions to take on a more personal note as
they got to know one another better. "I do not think you
look after yourself properly. And a place of business
should not have to double as a home."

At first, Miss Bartlett shrank from hints and persuasions, knowing herself to be easily swayed, fearful of being swept along on the tide of Miss Roscommon's decision. I am only forty years old, she said, there is plenty of opportunity left for me. I do not have to abandon hope by retreating into middle age and life with another woman. Though certainly she enjoyed the meals the other cooked; the taste of home-baked pasties and stews and herb-flavoured vegetables.

"I'm afraid that I cannot cook," she said. "I live on milk and cheese and oven-baked potatoes. I would not know where to begin in the kitchen." It did not occur to her that this was any cause for shame, and Miss Roscommon tut-tutted and floured the pastry-board, relieved to have, once again, a sense of purpose brought into her life.

"There were nine of us in the family," she said, "and I was the only girl. At the age of seven, I knew how to bake a perfect loaf of bread. I am quite content to be one of the Marthas of this world."

But I will not go and *live* there, Miss Bartlett told herself toward the end of that summer. I am determined to remain independent, my plans are fluid, I have my work, and besides, it would never do, we might not get on well together and then it would be embarrassing for me to have to leave. And people might talk.

Though she knew that they would not, and that it was of her own judgment that she was most afraid, for Mountsea was full of ladies of indeterminate age sharing houses together.

The winter came, and the cottage was indeed damp. The stone walls struck cold all day and all night, in spite of expensive electric heaters, and Miss Bartlett spent longer and longer afternoons at Tuscany, even taking some of her work up there from time to time.

At the beginning of December, the first of the bad storms sent waves crashing up over the quayside into the front room.

Of course, Miss Roscommon is lonely, she said now, she has need of me, I should have realized. That type of woman, who appears to be so competent and strong, feels the onset of old age and infirmity more than most, but she cannot say so, cannot give way and confess to human weakness. She bakes me cakes and worries about the dampness in my house because she needs my company and concern for herself.

And so, on Christmas Eve, when the second storm filled Miss Bartlett's living room with water up to the level of the window seat, she allowed herself to be evacuated by the capable Miss Roscommon up to the white bungalow.

"It will not be for good," she said anxiously. "When the weather improves, I shall have to go back, there is the business to be thought of." "We shall make plans for a proper shop," said Miss Roscommon firmly. "I have a little money. . . ."

She filled up a pottery bowl with leek soup, having acquired her faith in its restorative powers when she had set up a canteen at the scene of a mining disaster in the nineteen-twenties.

Miss Bartlett accepted the soup and a chair close to the fire and an electric blanket for her bed, thereby setting the seal on the future pattern of their relationship. By the beginning of February, plans for the shop were made; by mid-March, the work was in hand. There was no longer any talk of her moving; she would sell her goods from the new shop during the summer days, but she would live at Tuscany. The garage was fitted with light, heat and two extra windows, and made into a studio.

"This is quite the best arrangement," said Miss Roscommon. "Here, you will be properly fed and looked after, I shall see to that."

Over the seven years that followed, Miss Bartlett came to rely upon her for many more things than the comforts of a well-kept home. It was Miss Roscommon who made all the business arrangements for the new shop, who saw the bank manager, the estate agent and the builder, Miss Roscommon who advised with the orders and the accounts. During the summer seasons, the shop did well, and after three years, at her friend's suggestion, Miss Bartlett started to make pink raffia angels and potpourri jars for the Christmas postal market.

She relaxed, ceased to feel uneasy, and if, from time to time, she did experience a sudden shot of alarm, at seeing herself so well and truly settled, she said not, "Where else would I go?" but, "I am needed here. However would she manage without me? It would be cruel to go." All the decisions were left to Miss Roscommon. "You are so much better at these things. . . ." Miss Bartlett said, and drifted away to her studio, a small woman with pastel-coloured flesh.

Perhaps it was her forty-seventh birthday that jolted her into a renewed awareness of the situation. She looked into the mirror on that morning and saw middle age settled irrevocably over her features. She was reminded of her dependence upon Miss Roscommon.

I said I would not stay here, she thought, would never have my name written up above a permanent shop, for my plans were to remain fluid. And now it is seven years, and how many opportunities have I missed? How many roads are closed to me?

Or perhaps it was the visit of Miss Roscommon's niece Angela, and her husband of only seven days, one weekend in early September.

"I shall do a great deal of baking," Miss Roscommon said, "for they will certainly stay to tea. We shall have cheese scones and preserves and a layer cake."

"I did not realize that you had a niece."

Miss Roscommon rose from the table heavily, for she had put on weight over the seven years. There had also been some suspicion about a cataract in her left eye, another reason why Miss Bartlett told herself she could not leave her.

"She is my youngest brother's child. I haven't seen her since she was a baby."

Miss Bartlett nodded and wandered away from the breakfast table, not liking to ask why there had been no wedding invitation. Even after seven years, Miss Roscommon kept some of her secrets, there were subjects upon which she simply did not speak, though Miss Bartlett had long ago bared her own soul.

The niece Angela, and her new husband, brought a slab of wedding cake, which was put, to grace the centre of the table, on a porcelain stand.

"And this," said Miss Roscommon triumphantly, *"this*

is my friend, Miss Mary Bartlett." For Miss Bartlett had
hung behind in the studio for ten minutes after their
arrival, out of courtesy and because it was always something of a strain for her to meet new people.

"Mary is very shy, very retiring," her own mother had
always said. "She is artistic, you see, she lives in her own
world." Her tone had always been proud and Miss Bartlett
had therefore come to see her own failure as a mark of
distinction. Her shyness had been cultivated, readily
admitted to.

The niece and her husband sat together on the sofa, a
little flushed and self-conscious in new clothes. Seeing
them there, Miss Bartlett realized for the first time that
no young people had ever been inside the bungalow since
her arrival. But it was more than their youthfulness which
struck her, there was an air of suppressed excitement
about them, a glitter, they emanated pride in the satisfactions of the flesh.

Miss Roscommon presided over a laden tea table, her
face still flushed from the oven.

"And Miss Bartlett is very clever," she told them. "She
makes beautiful things. You must go down to the shop
and see them, buy something for your new home."

"You make things?" said Angela, through a mouthful
of shortbread. "What sort of things?"

Miss Bartlett made a little gesture of dismissal with
her hand. "Oh, not very much really, nothing at all exciting. Just a few little . . . I'm sure you wouldn't . . ." She
let her voice trail off, but it was Miss Roscommon and not
the niece Angela who took her up on it.

"Now that is just nonsense," she said firmly. "There
is no virtue in this false modesty, I have told you before.
Of course Angela will like your things, why should she
not? Plenty of visitors do, and there is nothing to be
ashamed of in having a talent."

"I wore a hand-embroidered dress," said the niece
Angela, "for my wedding."

Miss Bartlett watched her, and watched the new husband, whose eyes followed Angela's slim hand as it moved
over to the cake plate and back, and up into her mouth.
Their eyes met and shone with secrets across the table.

Miss Bartlett's stomach moved a little with fear and excitement. She felt herself to be within touching distance of some very important piece of knowledge.

"Do you help with this shop, then—?" asked the husband, though without interest.

"Oh, no! Well, here and there with the accounts and so forth, because Mary doesn't understand any of that, she is such a dreamer! No, no, that is not my job, that is not what keeps me so busy. My job is to look after Mary, of course. I took that upon myself quite some time ago, when I saw that I was needed. She is such a silly girl, she lives in a world of her own, and if I were not here to worry about her meals and her comforts, she would starve, I assure you, simply starve."

"Oh, I don't think I really . . ."

"Of course you would," said Miss Roscommon. "Now let me have your cup to be filled."

The young couple exchanged another glance, of comprehension and amusement. How dare you, thought Miss Bartlett, almost in tears with anger and frustration, at being so looked upon and judged and misunderstood. What do you know of it, how can you sit there so smugly? It is because you are young and know nothing. It is all very well for you.

"All the same," said the niece Angela, sitting back in her chair, "it's nice to be looked after, I must say."

She smiled like a cat.

"Yes, that has always been my role in life, that is *my* talent," said Miss Roscommon, "to do all the looking after." She leaned over and patted Miss Bartlett on the hand. "She is my responsibility now, you see," she told them confidently. "My little pussy cat."

Miss Bartlett pushed the hand away and got to her feet, her face flushed with shame and annoyance. "What a foolish thing to say! Of course I am not—how very silly you make me look. I am a grown woman, I am quite capable of looking after myself."

Miss Roscommon, not in the least discomfited, only began to pour the tea dregs into a slop basin, smiling.

When they were about to leave, Miss Bartlett said, "I will walk down the hill with you, and we shall drop in

for a minute at the shop. Yes, I insist . . . but not for you
to buy anything. You must choose a wedding present
from my stock; it is the very least I can do." For she
wanted to keep them with her longer, to be seen walking
in their company down the hill away from the bungalow,
wanted to be on their side.

"You will need a warm coat, it is autumn now, the
evenings are drawing in. Take your mohair."

"Oh, leave me, leave me, do not *fuss*." And Miss Bartlett
walked to the end of the gravelled drive while the niece
and her new husband made their good-byes.

"I am afraid it is all she has to worry over nowadays,"
she said hastily, the moment they had joined her. "It
gives her pleasure, I suppose, to do all that clucking round
and I have not the heart to do anything but play along,
keep up appearances. If it were not for me, she would
be so lonely. Of course, I have had to give up a good deal
of my own life on that account."

The niece Angela took her husband's arm. "It must be
very nice and comfortable for you there," she said, "all
the same."

Miss Bartlett turned her face away and looked out to
sea. Another winter, she thought, and I am now forty-
seven years old. You do not understand.

She detained them in the shop for as long as possible,
fetching out special items from the stock room and taking
time over the wrapping paper. Let me be with you, she
wanted to say, let me be on your side, for do you not see
that I still have many opportunities left, I am not an old
woman, I know about the world and the ways of modern
life? Take me with you.

But when they had gone she stood in the darkening shop
and saw that they had already placed and dismissed her,
that she did not belong with them and there was no hope
left. She sat on the stool beside the till and wept for the
injustice of the world and the weakness of her own nature.
I have become what I always dreaded becoming, she said,
everything has slipped through my fingers.

And for all of it, after a short time, she began to blame
Miss Roscommon. She has stifled me, she thought, she
preys upon me, I am treated as her child, her toy, her

pussy cat, she has humiliated me and fed off my dependence and the fact that I have always been so sensitive. She is a wicked woman. And then she said, *but I do not have to stay with her*. Fortified by the truth of this new realization, Miss Bartlett blew her nose, and walked back up the hill to Tuscany.

"You cannot leave," said Miss Roscommon, "what nonsense, of course you cannot. You have nowhere else to go, and besides in ten days' time we set off for our holiday in Florence."

"You will set off. I am afraid my plans have now changed." Miss Bartlett could not bear the thought of being seen with her friend in all the museums and art galleries of Florence, discussing the paintings in loud, knowledgeable voices and eating wholemeal sandwiches out of neat little greaseproof bags, speaking very slowly to the Italians. This year Miss Roscommon must go alone. She did not allow herself to think of how, or whether, she would enjoy herself. We are always hearing of how intrepid she was as a girl, she thought. Then let her be intrepid again.

Aloud, she said, "I am going back to live at the cottage." For she had kept it on, and rented it to summer visitors.

Miss Roscommon turned herself, and her darning, a little more toward the light. "You are being very foolish," she said mildly. "But I understand why; it is your age, of course."

Appalled, Miss Bartlett went through to her room and began to throw things furiously, haphazardly, into a suitcase. I am my own mistress, she said, a grown-up woman with years ahead of me, it is time for me to be firm. I have pandered to her long enough.

The following day, watched by Miss Roscommon, she moved back down the hill to the cottage. She would, she decided, stay there for a while, give herself time to get accustomed, and to gather all of her things around her again, and then she would look out and make plans, take steps toward her new life.

That evening, hearing the wind around her own four

walls, she said, I have escaped. Though she woke in the
night and was aware of being entirely alone in the cottage,
of not being able to hear the loud breathing of Miss
Roscommon in the room next door.

She expected the Italian holiday to be cancelled on some
pretext, and was astonished when Miss Roscommon left,
on the appointed day and alone. Miss Bartlett took the
opportunity of going up to Tuscany and fetching some
more of her things down, work from the studio to keep
her busy in the evening, and during the days, too, for now
it was October and few people came into the shop.

Here I am, she said, twisting the raffia angels and winding ribbon around the potpourris, etching her gift cards,
here I am, living my own life and making my own decisions. She wanted to invite someone down to stay, someone young, so that she could be seen and approved of,
but there was no one. A search through all the drawers
and cupboards at the bungalow did not yield her the
address of the niece Angela. She would have sent a little
note, with a Christmas gift, to tell of her removal, prove
her independence.

Miss Roscommon returned from Italy, looked rather
tired and not very suntanned. She came in with a miniature
plaster copy of a Donatello statue and some fine art
post cards. Miss Bartlett made tea, and the conversation
was very stilted.

"You are not warm enough here," said Miss Roscommon. "I will send down some extra blankets."

"Oh no, thank you. Please don't do that."

But the following day the blankets, and a Dutch apple
pie, arrived with the butcher's boy.

Miss Bartlett bought huge slabs of cheese and eggs,
which she could boil quite well, and many potatoes, and
ate them off her knee while she read detective stories
through the long evenings. She thought that she might
buy a television set for company, though she was busy,
too, with the postal orders for Christmas. When all this
is over, she told herself, that is when I shall start looking
about me and making my plans. She thought of all the
things she might have done as a girl, the studio in London and the woodblock engravings for the poetry press,

the ballet company for whom she might have been asked to do some ethereal costume designs. She read in a newspaper of a woman who had started her own firm, specializing in computer management, at the age of fifty and was now rather wealthy, wholly respected in a man's world. Miss Bartlett looked at herself in the mirror. I am only forty-seven, she said.

In her white bungalow, lonely and lacking a sense of purpose, Miss Roscommon waited.

On November the seventh, the first of the storms came, and Miss Bartlett sat in her back room and heard the wind and the crashing of the sea, terrified. The next morning, she saw that part of the pierhead had broken away. Miss Roscommon sent down a note, with a meat pasty, via the butcher's boy.

"I am worried about you," she wrote. "You cannot be looking after yourself, and I know that it is damp in that cottage. Your room here is ready for you at any time."

Miss Bartlett tore the note up and threw the pasty away, but she thought of the warm bed, the fires and soft sofas at Tuscany.

Two days later, when the gales began again, Miss Roscommon came herself and hammered at the door of the cottage, but Miss Bartlett hid upstairs, behind a cheval mirror, until she went away. This time there was no note, only a Thermos flask of lentil soup on the doorstep.

She is suffocating me, thought Miss Bartlett, I cannot bear all these unwanted attentions, I only wish to be left alone. It is a poor thing if a woman of her age and resources can find nothing else to occupy her, nothing else to live for. But in spite of herself, she drank the soup, and the taste of it, the smell of the steam rising up into her face reminded her of all the meals at Tuscany, the winter evenings spent happily sitting beside the fire.

When the storms came again, another section of the pier broke away, the lifeboat put out to sea and sank with all hands, and the front room of Miss Bartlett's cottage was flooded, rain broke in through a rent in the roof. She lay all night, too terrified by the roaring of the wind and seas to get out of bed and do anything about it, only whimpering a little with cold and fright, remembering how close the cottage came to the water, how vulnerable she was.

As a child, she had been afraid of all storms, gales and thunder and cloudbursts drumming on the roof, and her mother had understood, wrapped her in a blanket and taken her into her own bed.

"It is because you have such a vivid imagination," she had said. "You feel things that the other, ordinary little children cannot ever feel." And so, nothing had been done to conquer this praiseworthy fear of storms.

Now I am alone, thought Miss Bartlett, there is no one, my mother is dead, and who is there to shelter and understand me? A flare rocket, sent up from the sinking lifeboat, lit up the room faintly for a second, and then she knew who there was, and that everything would be all right. On the stormy nights, Miss Roscommon always got up and made sandwiches and milky hot drinks, brought them to her as she lay awake in bed, and they would sit reading nice magazines in the gentle circle of the bedside lamp.

I have been very foolish, Miss Bartlett thought, and heard herself saying it aloud, humbly, to Miss Roscommon. A very foolish, selfish woman; I do not deserve to have you as a friend.

She did not take very much with her up the hill on the following morning, only a little handcase and some raffia work. The rest could follow later, and it would be better to arrive like that, it would be a real indication of her helplessness.

The landscape was washed very clean and bare and pale, but the sea churned and moved within itself, angry and battleship grey. In the summer, Miss Bartlett thought, refreshed again by the short walk, it will be time to think again, for I am not committing myself to any permanent arrangements and things will have to be rather different now, I will not allow myself to be treated as a pet plaything, that must be understood. For she had forgotten, in the cold, clear morning, the terrors of the previous night.

She wondered what to do, ring the bell or knock or simply open the back door into the kitchen, where Miss Roscommon would be working, and stand there, case in hand, waiting to be forgiven. Her heart beat a little faster. Tuscany was very settled and reassuring in its low, four-square whiteness on top of the hill. Miss Bartlett knocked timidly at the blue kitchen door.

It was some time before she gave up knocking and ringing, and simply went in. Tuscany was very quiet.

She found her in the living room, lying crumpled awkwardly on the floor, one of her legs twisted underneath her. Her face was a curious, flat colour, like the inside of a raw potato. Miss Bartlett drew back the curtains. The clock had stopped just before midnight, almost twelve hours ago.

For a moment she stood there, still holding her little case, in the comfortable, chintzy room, and then she dropped down on to her knees and took the head of Miss Roscommon into her lap and, rocking and rocking, cradling it like a child, Miss Bartlett wept.

A STROKE OF LUCK

by Kathy Roe

Although the grandmother had never actually experienced any violence or illness, a feeling of doom darkened her life, and at 73 when she finally had her collapse it was like a ray of light forming out of the close calls that lurked in her past. Now they would come, she thought, as they shifted her from the stretcher to the starched hospital sheets; now they would listen, as the stern white nurse drove the needle into the muscle beneath her flesh (the pain felt good, at least real); now they would repent, even if it were at her deathbed. While a swarm of hands took her pulse and temperature and blood, she heard the words "emergency," "intensive care," "stroke." One good eye closed and the grandmother smiled for the first time all winter.

The nurse patted her head. "That a girl, Pinky, get some rest."

The grandmother blanched. Her hand returned to the forgotten right eye, which was red and swollen and had shut completely for the first time that afternoon. The Dodge had coughed away without her, she running after her sisters and brother, shouting and waving as the upturned dust from the road flew into her throat and the slit beneath the puffy lid of her eye until the pines and foxtail—in fact, everything to her right—disappeared from her vision. The grandmother picked at the hardened pus on her lash. She had stumbled back to her cottage and combination storeroom-bedroom where she had tied together the café curtains and stretched out in the semidarkness. It would be another week before Esther, the oldest sister and only driver in the family, made the trip out to the highway for groceries again. It was fifteen miles to the nearest store and the grandmother was without provisions for the week. What if one of her children dropped in for the weekend? What would she feed them? And if she told them she needed a ride to the highway, they'd go instead to a restaurant in Rehoboth, leaving her to sit with the grandchildren who sneered at her paint-by-number and checker sets and played their own secretive games behind her back. Her sore body convulsed as the booms of the Air Force fighter planes broke the sound barrier across the bay. She berated herself for not knowing how to drive. They'd given her such indecent notice that she'd barely been able to change her clothes, run to the buffet drawer for her Social Security check and shopping list, and dash across the water-soaked pine shats in her house slippers in time to catch the fumes from their exhaust pipe. Her younger sister and brother, Ruth and Earl, had not looked back, but Esther had seen her in the rearview mirror. And it was just another in a long series of insults that Esther—yes, she was sure it was Esther—had instigated.

It was Esther who'd forced her to join the Stitch and Chatter Club after she'd been rejected by the Colonial Dames. Her papers and family tree had been in good order, but when the sack was passed around the circle, Esther told her, 16 white balls and one black one were dropped in the folds, "And it only takes one, honey." Esther had also insisted that Cora Massey was the one. Cora, said Esther, objected to the grandmother's husband's great-great-grandfather, a Tory and New Englander. The grandmother, however, had her own suspicions. Her husband had worked for the State Highway Department dwarfing trees under telephone wires, and had directed the Methodist Church choir until something inside him had soured and he'd lapsed into drink and trumpet playing. And it was Esther who'd warned her not to marry her husband, Esther who was still punishing her—though her husband had been buried thirty years—for her sin. Esther was a charter member of the Grange, the 78th Club (*her* husband had been a senator in the 78th Congress), the

Organization of Founders and Patriots, and the Colonial Dames; and any blemish, however distant, she said, might jeopardize her position. "Honey, I own half the state of Delaware, and if I had my way I'd run that husband of yours out of here tomorrow." When Esther's husband died, he left his entire estate to Esther, and the grandmother and her husband had to get out of the farm's old servant quarters and take a room in town. Her husband took up with the church organist, the grandmother got a job in a secretarial pool, and her teenage girls moved in with Esther. By the time the grandmother was able to afford more living space, her children had married.

Now the half-acre that surrounded her cottage was her own. Esther had said she hated to charge her but she was short of funds, and after all, at *that* price she was still doing her a favor. The grandmother offered to pay it off in installments, but Esther wanted cash. The grandmother had withdrawn all her savings from the bank— thirty years' worth—and borrowed the difference on her life insurance. But there was no way to get out of debt. Her Social Security check came to $132 a month; it would take more years than she had left to finish off the bank loan. Ruth and Earl, who sniveled and fussed in the face of Esther's wealth, were given their land. She had been robbed, but her final years would be spent with the children and grandchildren; as soon as she had it properly equipped, they would flock to her secluded cottage. And if she skipped an installment or two, she could buy a fifteen-horsepower motor for the rowboat. The children refused to row, and though her brother Earl had a fifty-horsepower Chris Craft, neither the grandmother nor any of her children had ever been for a ride. Earl went out at dawn every day to check the crab traps before the patrol boats came cruising around for illegal traps; and in good weather he took Esther and Ruth for a spin around the point.

This morning, she remembered, she had awakened to the sounds of Earl's dying engine and Ruth's cackling. Still stiff with fear from the night's plane and gun explosions, she brooded over Earl's illegal traps, the grandchildren's carelessness, and the sharpness of the propeller blades on Earl's outboard motor. She was still dressing when the phone went off—two shorts and a long. She panicked, couldn't find a sleeve hole, and when she finally came out of the closet, the ringing had stopped. She tiptoed to the buffet cluttered with framed generations of bare bottoms, buck teeth, and thin brides, and picked up the receiver.

". . . when she's not complaining about some ailment, it's the riffraff on Slaughter Beach. She hears obscene conversations, gunfire, rings up Earl in the middle of the night—"

"All right, all right," another voice interrupted. "Did you hear something?"

"She's not beyond eavesdropping."

"Who's there? Hello, hello?"

"But what really gives me the willies is that she hovers."

She silently laid the receiver back in its black cradle. She opened the porch door, retched, discovered when she was mopping up the mess that the bucket of slops she'd left on the steps the night before was gone.

She tossed on her cot, struggling to link events. Had her oldest daughter been trying to reach her? Had they taken the bucket to frighten her? Were they all in league? Esther, she knew, had purposely kept an acre of pines between the grandmother's cottage and the others so that when the hooligans and mulattoes did attack, she'd be the first to go, a decoy for the others. The grandmother picked viciously at her sty. When they returned from their trip to the store, she'd give them a piece of her mind. She imagined Esther, Ruth, and Earl in the aisles of the Blue Hen, plotting their weekly feast without her. Esther was the only one with a television and every Friday night, after a communal meal, they drank crème de menthe and watched the Lawrence Welk Show. The grandmother had felt ill the last two times and hadn't ventured out; they hadn't bothered to inquire why but when she'd tried to excuse herself, to explain about her illness, Esther had suggested that she buy her own TV.

The grandmother gingerly lowered her bunioned feet to the cold floor and smoothed the wrinkles out of her dress. There were three narrow trails in the room: one to the window, one to the closet, and another to the door. Between the trails stood stacks of *Good Housekeeping* and *National Geographic* dating back to the thirties; boxes of outdated dress patterns; scraps of unused fabric, sepial photos; her children's outgrown clothes; unopened Girl Scout candy; art supplies for unbegun canvases; a disassembled pump-peddle sewing machine; her personal papers, including her last will and testament; the wicker furniture from the porch.

The grandmother wound through the debris, past the guest rooms, to the back door, which she unbolted and cracked. She listened for their whereabouts. A gust of wind dampened her nerve. She decided to approach from behind, even though it meant a long circular hike. She floundered along the gutted back road, clung to the frame of a red billboard that said G U N S in giant black letters, imagined the water line rising above the roofs of their piers, flooding their three clapboard houses, identical except for Esther's, which had been built on a larger scale. She forced her chilled body on to the last fork and Esther's door. Inside, across from the top half of the Dutch door, a yellow, off-centered picture of Ruth and Earl in a baby stroller snickered at her. When the shot had been taken, she had posed by the carriage in her new Red Riding Hood cape, but years ago Esther had cut the picture so that only her hand, placed on the stroller bar by the professional photographer, remained visible.

The grandmother yoo-hooed through the dark halls. When she reached the entranceway to the kitchen, hunched, her good eye squinting against the sudden light, they hushed. Ruth clapped shut the Scrabble board, turned, and grinned. There were several teeth missing in her smile. Her head shook slightly, uncontrollably, and the grandmother closed her eye to keep her own head from shaking, then reopened it and shifted her glance to her brother. Earl, deaf, gaped at the ruined game. Esther broke the silence.

"Where've you been? We must have waited 45 minutes this afternoon." She towered above them, seemed to have grown rather than shriveled over the years. She wore silver, wire-rimmed glasses and orthopedic shoes and although the grandmother once thought she'd detected

a growth on her neck—usually concealed by high collars—
Esther had no other visible defects.

"I knocked and knocked but no one—"

"That's all right, honey. Coffee?" Esther thrust a full
cup between her palms.

The long list of grievances blurred. The grandmother
placed the cup in front of Ruth. "Just half a cup."

"Earl, get another chair."

Earl frowned. The grandmother dragged a rocker in
from the parlor. Esther placed a half-filled cup in front
of the grandmother. The grandmother gazed at the black
liquid; the steam made her eye itch. "I just stopped in to
borrow some salts." She cleared her throat. "For my
eye, I mean."

"Fritters, honey?"

The grandmother followed her sister's corseted buttocks to the deep-fat fryer. "Oh, no." Her body rocked
against the motion of the chair.

Ruth leaned across the table. "Something the matter
with Esther's fritters?"

The rocker tipped. The grandmother grabbed the table
edge on the downswing. "Well, maybe a tiny taste." Her
hands fluttered to the jiggling cup. "My stomach hasn't
been right." She took a sip before she realized the cup
was full. The coffee cut knives through her stomach.
Ruth's cup, she saw, was half empty.

She rose tipsily from the circle and staggered to the
front porch. Behind her, the door banged shut by itself.
She half wheeled to see with her good eye. The kitchen
window was cracked; she peered inside. Earl was con-
structing a word on the board. Esther was drawing up a
new score card. The fritters bubbled in the fryer below the
sill. The grandmother saw her own bare refrigerator, the
unused beds she'd ordered from the Sears Roebuck cata-
logue in the guest rooms, the dusty chest of new Mattel
toys she planned to spring on the grandchildren when
they came around again. Maybe a TV would be the best
bait to draw them down. A feeling of revulsion spread
from her stomach to her arms and legs. She felt her
blood congealing; a slimy clam had entered her blood-
stream.

She reached the end of Esther's frontage of pines and

crossed a strip of land that was a brown tangle of prickers
and vines and forgotten, shriveled berries. Ahead, the
grasses bent and rushed with the wind. She pushed them
apart. They opened and closed behind her. *Bahroom*. A
fighter plane broke the sound barrier. Startled, she
crouched in the marsh grass. Barbed wire pierced the grey
soft mass in her skull. Berry juice seeped down her throat.
A horn-toed lizard slithered away in fright. The grandmother held her breasts—one real, both numb—and
braced herself against the dead weight of her body. The
two stumps that had been her legs lurched forward. As
she approached the scud of the bay line, her head cleared.
The salt spray soothed her blinded eye. The mud was
littered with the horseshoe crabs her grandchildren liked
to take home, swinging them by their tails, for souvenirs.
A crab crunched open on either side of her shoe; she
shuddered. Once they had sent her a package from New
York: inside, underneath a shroud, was a hideous empty
shell painted into a white grinning mask.

The beach line curved gently, then jutted out, forming
a narrow peninsula that separated her from the others. To
the left of the peninsula was her cottage, the bay, the
ocean and beyond; to the right calmer waters. *Bahroom*.
Another jet. She ducked behind her rowboat, staked on
the reeds for the winter. There was a smaller crash. She
peeked over the barnacled bottom. The wind had knocked
the missing slop pail off the bench on her pier and sent it
rolling across the platform. She rushed down the walkway.
The pier swayed. She caught the bucket at the edge. Her
arms flapped and circled. The blood drained from her
head. Sea and sky merged into a grey swirling monotone,
and the grandmother sank into oblivion.

A bay patrol boat making its last afternoon round
found the old woman. They'd expected to see her huddled
on her bench, gazing at the winter sky; instead she was
sprawled wrapperless across the platform. They laid the
soft, limp mass on seat cushions in the bottom of the boat
and sped to the air base hospital. It was the grandmother's
first ride in a motor boat.

When the grandmother woke from the chloral hydrate
injection, she saw a large pink hand squeezing a grey rub-

ber bulb. A piece of cloth tightened around her arm. "Ow."

"Shh." The nurse put her finger to her lips.

The grandmother scanned the right side of the room with her left eye. "Where are they?"

"Who?" The nurse let the air out.

"My family." The grandmother propped herself on her elbow. "Are they waiting outside?"

"Hold still, dearie." The nurse's fingers cooled her wrist.

"Please send them in."

"Try and nap. That bad eye needs a rest."

A large-boned woman in a tweed suit and alligator shoes stopped inside the doorway and looked around. "What a large, lovely room!"

"Sarah!" The grandmother extended her hand.

"Hello, Mother. The nurse at the front desk told me this used to be the solarium." She smiled at the nurse. "It was a stroke of luck to get in here."

The nurse brushed against her. "Make it brief." Sarah nodded and the nurse left.

"It's been dreadful, Sarah. Where're the others?"

"You're looking chipper, mother." Sarah's heels clicked across the linoleum.

"Listen here"—the grandmother struggled to a sitting position—"it's a blessing I'm even alive."

"There, there. Let's not exaggerate."

"I've had a stroke, Sarah."

"It was a pinched artery, Mother."

The grandmother hoisted herself to her knees. "The doctor *said* it was a stroke."

Sarah beat the pillow. "It was a *false* stroke."

"No, it was real." The grandmother pushed her legs over the edge of the bed. "Why won't you ever believe me?"

"Lie back," Sarah's hand pressed against her shoulder.

The grandmother collapsed to her side. "All you children do is belittle me."

"You're impossible, Mother. Now turn over and calm down."

"You never take anything that happens to me seriously."

"Come on, turn over. That's better." Sarah sat on the

edge of a metal folding chair. "Mary Sipple asked about
you. Why don't you invite the Stitch and Chatter Club
down to the cottage? You've always got a stocked refrigerator, and that beautiful view . . . I know they'd love
it."

The grandmother rubbed her eye with a clenched fist.
"It's for you. The cottage is for you—"

"Kevin prefers lakes, Mother. You know that."

The eye throbbed. The grandmother dug into the socket.
"You don't realize what Esther does to me when I'm
alone. She schemes with Ruth and Earl behind my back—"

"Stop it, Mother."

"Steals my things, sneaks off to the store without me."

"You're going to be all right, Mother."

"I'm not all right. I'M NOT!" Juices filled the afflicted,
dammed-up eye. The grandmother pried open the lid but
it wouldn't drain. Her sinuses clogged, now her windpipe;
she clutched her throat. Her good eye bulged.

"What are you *doing*?" Sarah jumped to her feet.
"Nurse!" She loosened the pudgy fingers. "In here, Nurse.
She's working herself into a state. My God, Mother, what's
the matter with you?"

The nurse plunged another needle into the flailing arm.
The grandmother slumped to her pillow.

That night the infected eye opened. Yellow liquid
streamed from the sore and hardened on the grandmother's still, dead cheek. An autopsy was performed and
it was determined that Helen Viola Redmond had died
of geriatric complications. She was buried in the family
plot.

SWEETS TO THE SWEET

by Jane Mayhall

One evening when Elsie Linker was seventeen years old, she walked out on the front porch to wait for her father. He was a streetcar conductor and usually got off his afternoon run at this hour. Elsie went over and sat on the porch step, looking past the gate and up the street. She was not especially anxious to see her father, but she liked to come outside at twilight, just after a fresh bath, and to sit waiting. With her long brown hair neatly combed and her skin smelling faintly of orange water, she felt deeply happy.

It was 1913, and the little house on the outskirts of Louisville had a quiet mysterious atmosphere. The ebbing light of the sky was lavender with faint particles of dust from the unpaved street in front of the house. Elsie watched the evening star take on its sharp glittering points. From inside the house, she could hear her aunt setting the table. She hit the dishes together, making the glasses ring and the plates give off a hollow sound. Her aunt was getting deaf, and did not hear how much unnecessary noise she made.

Elsie's mother had died nine years before, and the aunt had come in to do her duty by the orphan. She kept Elsie clean, sent her to school but never pretended to be a parent. Also, the deafness gave her association with Elsie a certain formal hauteur. She was respectful, undemanding and lacked motherly affection. The only thing her aunt insisted was that Elsie practice the violin which had once belonged to Elsie's mother. This was an easy duty as Elsie had a mild talent for music, and the accomplishment won her some reputation for charm among boys in the same locale.

Sitting alone, on this particular evening, Elsie thought about everything and nothing. Memories and ideas merged; she enjoyed especially any thoughts of the future, the vague panorama of activities with herself as the center, and as a person of importance. Sitting in a partial dream, with hands clasped and eyes looking past the gate, Elsie was surprised to see a figure approach. In the lavender twilight, it advanced somberly, walking past fence and hedge.

She recognized that the mysterious being was only one of the neighborhood boys, coming to pay a visit.

He stopped in front of Elsie and stood silent, a thin blond fellow who had just obtained his first job in the lumberyard on Standard Avenue, and had just acquired the high airs of unexpectedly dropping in on the homes of possible girls.

"Good evening, Luther," she said. Her voice carried some of the enchantment which had been in her silent dreaming a few minutes before.

"I come to see you, Elsie."

He sat on the lower step, pleased with her manner. It felt like his own romantic mood. The two of them sat in a shell of perfect silence. It was early summer, and in the ditch on Bowling Avenue a cricket chirped rhythmically. Elsie gave a quick sigh and looked up at the evening star again. The star was a spangle she had adopted as her own. She knew it went well in the dark with her long hair and pale dress.

"Here—" Luther was thrusting a box toward her.

It seemed a meaningless gesture. For a brief second she had no idea what it signified. A rather heavily wrapped box—she felt the rough strings against her fingers. Then she realized that the box must contain a present of some sort. Her heart fluttered in an unpremeditated joy.

"Hey, thanks, Luther."

He stood up. The moment was too much. He was just learning how to make it with girls, and became too obviously excited at the thought of real conquest. Rather than look like a fool, he decided to leave.

"Well, I got to be going."

She held the box.

"So soon?"

"Yeah." He placed one foot uncertainly on the gravel walk. "But I'll be coming back. I was thinking of coming back, like if you want."

The last was a tenuous expression of gallantry which seemed to gild both their white disk faces with a strange illumination, bright yet soft. They swayed toward each other.

Luther gulped and said: "G'bye." And staggered away through the gleaming night.

Elsie sat pensively. She began almost at once to open the box. The paper came off quickly, in layers. Underneath was a package smaller than she had expected. But she lifted the lid and a delicious odor was wafted to her. Chocolates! Her inexpressible and secret joy deepened. She put her hand in, among the crisply papered bonbons. The firm round surfaces touched her fingers, while the rich scent of chocolates blossomed on the air like a fresh-cut bouquet.

When she had eaten as much as she wanted, she shut the lid carefully and went inside the house. In her room, she hid the box under the bed. She heard her aunt calling that her father was home and supper was ready. Elsie stood in the dark hall, feeling deliciously fulfilled and secret. She planned that she would save some of the candy for every night, and eat it when nobody else was around. It was not that she had been denied sweets. But Elsie had never been given a whole box of chocolates before, only nickel sacks of grocery peppermints. It was nice to know that a pound box was under her bed.

2

Elsie did not marry Luther as everybody thought she would. He tried hard to get her to. Once or twice he referred to that summer evening when he had brought the candy; romance had been in the air. But Elsie acted as if she had forgotten, and gradually Luther had to give up. At almost the same time, Elsie met another boy named Henry Hubbard. He was dark, with sallow skin and intense coal-black eyes. His body was tall and wiry and he liked to play baseball. His manner was breezy and he had been chewing tobacco for five years. Elsie was sure this was the person she wanted.

Henry was twenty-one, with a steady job at the Jefferson Brewery, and was a hell of a big beer drinker without ever showing a thing. He came to call on Elsie regularly, and seemed to prefer her to other girls around. She was small and demure, with crystal-gray eyes that looked cool and innocent.

Elsie was a sweet little girl, and Henry felt he could just crush her in his big baseball hands.

One evening when they sat on the porch under the honeysuckle, Henry started to kiss her rather intimately. It was a hot evening, nobody else was around, and the two of them had nothing to talk about. Down on the corner of Bowling, the streetlight shone brilliantly; but the porch where the couple sat was shaded by vines.

Henry knew that Elsie was a nice girl. However, she was certainly the softest and most receptive thing he had ever come across. He had been around, and in his time had enjoyed all different types of girls. But Elsie had an unusual childish sweetness that just drew him right to her.

While his thoughts were lazily strumming over these emotions, and he smelled the delicate orange of her perfume mingling with honeysuckle, he suddenly heard her little voice cutting through the warm hazy night, sharp and cool as crystal.

She had mentioned the word *marriage*.

Henry jumped, as if he had been stabbed. He could not believe what he had heard. She said the word again. It struck his brain like a paralysis. The more she said, the less he comprehended. But Elsie did not seem to notice, and talked on reasonably of church weddings, and small houses where young couples might live without great expense. She had an enormous lot of facts at her fingertips, and spoke with an intelligent self-confidence that was almost frightening. Henry listened stupefied. In a situation like this he could not run away, nor could he call for help. He sat, in a cold perspiration of guilt and terror.

It was the sort of thing a man never expected, especially from a little girl like Elsie Linker.

"It's only fair," she said finally, standing up, "to go tell Auntie. And Papa too. Oh—" and her voice did not veer to sounding hypocritical. "Oh, they've been so good to me, Henry!"

In the spattered light from the vine and streetlamp, he saw Elsie's pale dress. She was still the doll creature he had held in his arms. But the new decisive tone of her voice and the strong clasp of her hand gave him the impression that she was two people at once.

"W-well, say, Elsie—"

She clutched his fingers with firm affection.

"Dearest," she said. And regarded him lovingly.

Henry was silenced. He was a man of the world, but had never before encountered the powers of female innocence. With sagging shoulders, his body gone momentarily soft as a puppy dog's, he allowed himself to be led inside the house and back to the kitchen, where Elsie announced to her family the good news.

In the weeks that followed, Elsie alternated between satisfaction at having executed a delicate piece of girlish strategy and a mood of genuine bliss about Henry. She loved him dearly. There was something about him that put her in a fever of passion. The way he walked, agile and cautious, and his independent style. Elsie felt that she had corralled a rare beast into her little domestic den. She would have to be vigilant at keeping him there. But she herself was also a proud unconquerable person. At all church socials and other public affairs now, she played the violin with fresh vigor, her young jaw pressed against the chin-rest, and the curved hand lifting the bow and bringing it down.

3

The marriage took place in early October and the couple moved into a cottage near the brewery where Henry worked. Here they settled down to the day-to-day trials of wedlock. Elsie planned to have a family at once. After a year and a half, with determination, she was able to produce a child. It was a girl, their first and last offspring.

The black light in Henry's eyes became blacker, then showed a small red spark like a cinder that still had fire. He was a reliable husband, but continued to cater to the most famous brew that his company put out, a dark lager beer. Elsie began to suspect that he was mixing rye whisky with this refreshment; but she never felt that she should criticize, and therefore suppressed her fears— learning to take things as they came.

Time passed, the leaves withered and fell under the winter snows, then the trees blossomed again. Henry felt himself withering too, but with no fresh blossoms in his heart. He was working hard, and drinking harder. Since the day of his marriage, somehow, he never felt like playing baseball. All of the adventure had gone out of his life. He knew he was like a million other married men, just barely surviving under the load of responsibilities which sooner or later fell upon everyone.

Just when he thought he could not endure another minute, he was overjoyed to hear that America and Germany were finally to be at war. It was 1917, and this was his chance.

Feeling solemn and patriotic, he quit his job and enlisted at once. There was some trouble about his getting in, being married with a child and all. But as the brewery was not an essential industry, and he was such an eager young man, matters were soon arranged. He came home one afternoon, in uniform, to tell Elsie. Looking rather handsome in khaki, he stood with flushed face and in an excited voice he conveyed the news.

Elsie smelled his breath and realized that her husband was not drunk. If anything, he was marvelously sober, eyes clear and shining.

"Dear little wife," he said. "Write to me."

Her heart broke.

"I will," she promised.

Everyone commented that Elsie had taken the event courageously. Left alone with a dependent and the small sum allotted to soldiers' wives, she managed to get along. Almost immediately, violin pupils appeared. And by October, she had succeeded in renting out part of the cottage, which kept the money coming in.

One cold autumn afternoon, when Henry had been in the army nearly five months, Elsie left her child alone and walked to the drugstore. When she came back, she had a box under her arm which she carried into the living room. Sitting in front of the stove, and forgetting to take off her coat, she opened the box. The sudden appetizing fragrance of chocolates caused her lips to part slightly; she hesitated before biting into the first piece.

Several minutes later, her little daughter toddled into the room. She was three years old, well behaved, and seldom made bids for attention. But entering the room, she smelled the chocolate, and came directly to her mother.

"Mama, gimme?" she said.

Elsie sat in the rocking chair, chewing absorbedly, not seeming to notice.

The child held out her hand.

Elsie looked up. The child gestured with outstretched hand. Elsie paused in her chewing and considered. In a moment, she decided it was better not to try to hide the chocolates.

She swallowed, wiped her mouth and said slowly:

"No, it's not good for you."

The child let her hand fall, and stood expectantly.

4

Henry Hubbard was not killed in the war. Instead, he felt he had become more alive than ever before. At first, he trained out West, and was then sent overseas to France. Henry was in the infantry, but as luck had it he did not see any real action—only the edges of a minor skirmish outside a French town. But there was always the possibility of getting to the *front*. That margin of danger provided him, almost every day of his stay overseas, with a reason for one last fling.

He wrote Elsie with an unerring consistency, two letters a week. And always told what a wonderful thing the army was, "old Uncle Sam is sure good to his boys," and how he was getting a real eyeful of the world. His letters were optimistic and unlabored. He really meant what he said, and never wrote lies to his wife. The only thing he had to leave out was reference to the part of the war that was best of all, and that was the fact that an American soldier was so admired by so many pretty foreign girls. There was not even the necessity of knowing French to get them to step into bed. Easy as pie, just like that.

Every Sunday, Elsie played the violin in church, accompanying the old Methodist hymns with a strident obbligato. People remarked that Mrs. Hubbard was looking well, and had even taken on a little weight. The girlish waist thickened, and her firm chin showed an unforeseen slackness of muscle. It appeared that the addition of heaviness to her already mature manner gave Elsie a maternal look she'd not had before. She began to wear glasses, and the crystal-gray eyes took on an enlarged and fishlike expression. She taught classes in Sunday school, and young girls came to her for advice on domestic problems.

With her own child, she never showed any signs of outrageous possessive affection. At times, she scarcely seemed to notice that the little girl was around. Elsie was, she supposed, very much like her aunt in that respect. She felt it unnecessary to burden a child with too much interest.

"Mama, Mama!" the little girl said, tugging at Elsie's skirt.

When the mother did not answer, the child's voice became shrill.

"*Mama!*"

It was true, she cried too much for a three-year-old, or at other times became stubbornly silent. However, Elsie handled these eccentricities with forbearance.

But occasionally, during those dark cold days of the war, Elsie could not help feeling depressed. Standing by the window and looking out to the snow-crusted street, she found herself saying, "The child needs her father." Then Elsie sighed, as if she had stated the complete key to the puzzle of life.

She awaited Henry's letters with a pathetic eagerness. Before they arrived, she knew what they would say. They came regularly and she answered every one. Whenever she went to post a letter, she got into the habit of stopping at the drugstore and picking up a half-pound box of chocolates. Although this happened on the average of twice a week, Elsie felt that she was not buying too much candy. A person ought to be allowed to splurge on something.

When the Armistice was signed, Henry Hubbard returned home a changed man. Sprawling unconcernedly in the familiar Morris chair, he seemed entirely different. The little girl knelt beside him, playing with one of his loose military leggings. But Elsie sat across the room, with a dignified air, not knowing what to say.

Henry announced that he had important plans. Seeing the world had given him ideas. Not meaning any offense, but Louisville was a kind of hick town. He had seen a lot, big cities and big buildings; and he just figured out that when he got back, he was going to give his family a bigger life. He was now a veteran of the World War and would in time be a full-fledged member of the American Legion. Say what you will, that counted for something.

Elsie noticed that he had a new way of speaking out of the side of his mouth, sending his words off to one corner, although she sat directly across from him. This little oddity of manner excited her strangely. She wanted to do something crazy, throw herself into his arms or burst into tears.

Instead, she sat politely and asked a question.

"So, what are your plans, dear?"

Well, the truth was, a very good pal had offered him a job as a salesman. He would be going from town to town selling high-class goods, meeting high-class people. No more bumming around in a brewery, when you came home from work stinking so that your own wife wouldn't come near you. Henry winked, and gave a loud *ha-ha!* that set the pictures on the walls to swinging.

Elsie's cheeks took color; she looked at the floor. But Henry did not pursue the subject. Instead, he began to tell about what a "good mixer" he was. Being in the army,

he confided, had proved one thing. He was the life of
the party. Give him the right contacts, and the right
experience, and they would be on easy street in no time!

Elsie had never thought of their station in life before.
But now she could see the advantage of rising socially.
They might get a new house, and possibly an automobile.
Involuntarily, the idea of possessions multiplied, a dining
room buffet, a glassed-in sun porch, and a maple bedroom
set. Through Elsie's mind ran little pictures of herself as
the once low-born daughter of a streetcar conductor, now
risen to high honors as the wife of a successful salesman.
Before the conversation had finished, Elsie felt almost
happy.

But after supper, she asked another question.

"When—" she paused, and rubbed her hands together
in the hem of her apron, "when do you think you'll be
starting your new work?"

"Huh?"

"Going out on the road, I mean—?"

"Huh? Well, as soon as I can, I reckon! As soon as
they'll take me, kiddo!" He was smoking a cigar, and
rolled it to one side of his mouth. "Why, what do you
think! I already got my discharge papers. Why listen
here, kiddo," he exclaimed, "I'll be hopping that choo-
choo any day now!"

The next afternoon, Henry went next door to see some
neighbors, to tell them about his war experiences. When
he came home, Elsie was not around. He walked into
the living room.

"Elsie?"

She did not answer.

"Elsie?" he shouted up the stairs.

Finally, he heard her voice, coming from the direction
of the pantry.

He went back and found her standing by the ice chest,
eating something. It was candy, from an open box which
she held in her hand.

She did not speak, but stood munching.

"Well, look what you got." He laughed. "How about
giving the old man some?"

She hesitated. Then held the box toward him.

He selected a piece wrapped in tinfoil, but did not eat it right away.

"Was it," he said, "a birthday?" He glanced at her awkwardly, feeling a little strange to be standing in the cold pantry, taking candy like that.

"No," she answered.

"Huh, you buy it yourself?" He laughed, puzzled. "I never knew you liked candy."

She bent her head in search for a certain favorite kind. She ate it, taffy-nut, with crunching little bites. In the dim pantry light, the expression on her face was rather beautiful. She leaned in profile; an abstracted glance of rare innocence sidled past the flickering edge of her glasses.

Henry stared at her an instant longer.

"Well," he said, "here's sweets to the sweet." He popped the piece of candy into his mouth.

5

True to his word, Henry did well as a salesman. He made contacts and collected orders for a firm called Sheik, Inc., which specialized in men's ties, socks and underwear. He was given the territory in southern Kentucky, and, before five years were out, he had traveled through all the major southern cities.

It was a strenuous time, but he took it in good faith, and sustained a robust cheer that people liked. After eight years of travel and expansion, his once wiry frame was forever hidden under the respectable bulge of good-natured portliness. His sallow face had turned a darkish red, like an overripe apple; his lower lip sagged a little from the way he talked and chewed his cigar.

Henry never overlooked his little daughter, and always brought her gifts from his journeys, small packages of geranium soap from the Pullman lavatories, lumps of sugar from the different hotel restaurants.

On one of his visits home, Henry brought a bottle of cocktail olives. He offered the girl a taste, and simply howled at her expression of fear and nausea.

He patted the child on the shoulder.

"Gotta get used to it, honey," he said, but still grinning in spite of himself.

As a result of her upbringing, the daughter was always obedient and quiet. When she was fourteen, she said she wanted to become a nurse. She was fascinated with gauze bandages and medicine bottles, and always cooking make-believe drugs over the kitchen stove. For a while, Elsie had thought she might interest her daughter in studying the violin. But the girl hated music, and always went away from the house when Elsie practiced scales.

"Well," Elsie thought, "let her go her own way."

And Elsie felt that, considering everything, she was a rather good mother. She was like a *firm foundation*, the one sung about in the Methodist hymn book.

Four years later, when the daughter suddenly announced plans for going to Indianapolis for a job, Elsie did not protest. It seemed the most natural thing in the world to see her only child walk out the front door with a suitcase. It was a hot August afternoon; the girl wore a seersucker suit and a little straw hat, already looking businesslike and competent.

As she turned to wave good-bye, Elsie felt satisfied— and even somewhat relieved.

Elsie had no cause to worry about her daughter these days. She was more disturbed about the problem of her aunt. A while before, Elsie's father had died and left his sister without funds. The aunt was feeble and stone deaf now, wandering around the house where Elsie had grown up like a ghost haunting her own past. She had no friends and never did anything, just puttering about and moaning as some deaf people do.

As Elsie had suspicioned, the old lady began to beg to be allowed to live at Elsie's house. Nothing could have been more upsetting, the thought of the smoothly run household being invaded by the aunt, a person of no use who would come bringing nothing but the certain liabilities of age and sickness.

Elsie now lived in a pretty English-style residence, with shining hardwood floors and built-in kitchen appliances. How could her aunt possibly fit into these surroundings?

She tried to feel that her aunt's unlucky situation was one which the old lady deserved.

"As ye sow, so shall ye reap."

But finally, talking it over with Henry, Elsie could not remember that her aunt had ever done anything bad enough in life to merit living alone and being unwanted. As she thought of this, her throat hardened with an unfamiliar and anguished sense of justice that must be done. When Henry came back at Christmas, she discussed the possibility of giving her aunt the upstairs attic room, and selling the old Linker cottage, which was heavily mortgaged but might bring in a little money at that.

Henry was agreed. He said that her aunt would be company for Elsie, now that her daughter was away.

Elsie looked at him haggardly. His brown tweed sport coat and easy-going male corpulence she loved even more than she had the slim eagerness of his youth. She sometimes found lipstick stains on his handkerchiefs, and guessed that his business pals were not all men. She had gotten used to that. But it hurt Elsie that he could imagine that her aunt, an old woman with an ear trumpet, would be anything like company for her, Elsie Linker Hubbard.

Henry placated, with a smile. He was always in a good humor, seeing his wife, the room, the past, present and future through a genial fog. It was true, he drank all the time these days, and could not stand to be sober. But it was not that he was a real drunkard. It was just that he liked whisky so much, it brought out the best side of himself.

"Well, gotta hurry, kiddo." He looked foggily around for his packed valise. That evening, he had to catch the ten forty-five. There was nothing he liked better than walking into the smoking car—the comfortable leather chairs, and somebody always around with a quart of bourbon to share.

He saw the thick hazy clouds of cigar smoke and the friendly faces of his pals. The smoke would hang motionless in the blurred air, everything always seemed suspended and eternal, himself walking into the car and sitting down in a reclining chair, ready to talk to the boys. Himself talking, or listening to the best good dirty jokes this side of New York—always having a terrific time, no matter where he was.

6

When Elsie's aunt came to live with her, she discovered Elsie's candy-eating habit almost at once. One day, she saw Elsie go into the closet five or six times to get something out of a box on the top shelf. Unlike most old people who live with younger people whom they have raised, she did not feel that her niece was doing a childish thing in sneaking candy from the closet. Instead, she saw a middle-aged woman going calmly, almost stoically to the place where the coats and shoes were kept, opening a box of chocolates and popping several pieces in her mouth at once. The aunt saw Elsie standing there in her flower-print housecoat, quietly eating.

The act seemed so strange and mysterious that the old woman did not even question Elsie about it. She let it remain like all the other unsolved problems and unknown factors of life—which people never understood anyway. Besides, the aunt had more pertinent matters to settle, the task of getting from her niece a hot-water bottle for bedtime, and being sure that Elsie would allow cream in her breakfast tea.

As time went on, she grew more tedious in her demands, always whining and complaining until Elsie was sick of it.

One day, in a fit of annoyance, Elsie exclaimed, "Oh, you damned old nuisance, you!"

"Eh? Eh? What say?" Her aunt held up the ear trumpet, an antiquated black funnel, and put on her most irritating look of incomprehension.

Elsie hated family scenes. She had never allowed her daughter to show her temper. She felt angry and resentful that her aunt had caused her to speak unpleasantly.

That night, Elsie could not sleep. She came downstairs in her bathrobe and walked across the rug, which was alive with moonlight. From the large parlor window the full moon blazed, white and mystical, almost hypnotic.

It was early winter. The furnace had not yet been turned on; the interior of the parlor was like a frozen fairyland, gleaming surfaces of glass and mahogany, the chairs, tables and lamps casting spidery treelike shadows, the moonlight weaving a cold delicacy about the objects of the room.

Elsie moved with softness, and went to the window, where she put the palms of her hands on the cold pane. She did not know why she had gotten out of bed to come downstairs. She only knew that she suddenly felt suffocated with heavy blankets, her thoughts dull and burdensome and the hours of night pressing upon her, each like a separate weight.

In the attic, her deaf aunt was sleeping. The daughter was still in Indianapolis and Henry was completing a sale in Atlanta, Georgia. No one knew that Elsie Hubbard was up in the late night, and alone. She could do whatever she wanted.

She thought she would get some candy from the closet. The saliva gathered exquisitely on her tongue. She did not move. With the instinctive and irrational control that sometimes accompanied her most passionate desires, Elsie curbed the outlandish idea of eating candy at three o'clock in the morning. Putting her cheek against the cold pane, she felt herself swept over by a flood of virtuous emotion, the rare intoxication of having abstained from what she really wanted. The feeling was as clear and radiant as the full moonlight. She stood silently.

And when she went upstairs again, she was tired and had no trouble in falling asleep at once.

7

After the daughter had been away for three years, she wrote Elsie that she was getting married. She said that her mother need not come to the wedding as she understood how busy Elsie was with church activities and taking care of the old aunt. The girl was a practical nurse at Indianapolis, and was marrying the son of one of her patients.

At first, Elsie did not think it queer that her daughter had not claimed her mother's presence at the wedding. But when she told a few of the neighbors, they seemed shocked at the idea. So Elsie wrote the girl immediately that she wanted to attend the ceremony. It seemed only natural, she pointed out.

The letter she got back was a terrible surprise. The girl said she might as well be honest; if Elsie wanted to come to the wedding, she could, but the daughter felt that in the long run it would be a waste of time. Because she had the feeling from Elsie's note that the mother did not care one way or the other. She was not really interested in her son-in-law or in the girl's future happiness.

As Elsie read the letter, she knew that some invisible dike had been opened and the bitter waters of her daughter's rancor were pouring forth. Elsie did not remember exactly what she had said in her own note; it could not have been much. Nevertheless, it had set hidden forces into motion, exposed violent feelings of which she had never thought the girl capable.

The letter said it was the daughter's opinion that Elsie had never given her any real love, respect or assistance. She had been forced to quit her nurse's training course because she had not been offered the money or parental encouragement which was due her. She said that neither Henry nor Elsie had provided her with the warm life she needed. It was not until she got away to Indianapolis that she realized how selfish her parents were, compared with other people.

"When I was a little girl," the daughter wrote, "I used to see you eating candy, but you never let me have any. You ate it all the time and didn't give me anything. That's just an example. You never gave me anything that you wanted. You thought you could get away with it because I was just a kid. But believe me, Mama, I'll never forget. And I'm not forgetting now that you don't care a hoot about my marriage. You just want to look like you're doing right in front of your friends. Well, you can't fool me—"

The letter was cruel, and so vituperative as to be almost unintelligible. Yet there was enough truth in it to keep

Elsie reading anxiously to the end. Stinging tears darted
under her eyelids and the writing danced jaggedly before
her. When she had finished, she sat very still, grinding
questions over and over in her mind, her brain moving
slowly like a millstone, trying to find the little particles of
reason somewhere. She realized that young people are
often prone to hysterics on the eve of marriage.

Getting a grip on herself, Elsie decided that this, indeed, was her daughter's case. She went to the telegraph
office and sent a wire:

Father and I will arrive Thursday for wedding.
Love, Mother

Conveniently, Henry would be home next week and
they could make the Indiana trip together. The idea
pleased her. And by the time she got back to the house,
Elsie felt cheerfully relieved that she had decided to
overlook her daughter's impetuous letter. As she walked
into the parlor, she caught sight of herself in the hall
mirror. Dressed in a cozy brown coat with full-chested fur
lapels, her short tublike figure seemed ample and forgiving.

8

For Elsie, the years had not been the most ideal. Nevertheless, through all the annoyances and disappointments,
she had always maintained a simple domestic equilibrium.
She kept her house in order and reserved an uneffusive
good will for neighbors and friends. Even the death of her
father, which had been the nearest she had come to the
terrible fact of existence, the brutal and extreme penalty
that everyone must pay for the privilege of living—even
that malignant injustice had come as a small shock only.
As if caught in a ripple of electric current, her thoughts
vibrated uneasily, and then subsided. She could always
resume the work of church and household.

However, after the marriage of her daughter, Elsie felt
that time was imposing vast and irrevocable changes. It
was bad enough during those years, having the Depression

and wars all over the world. But worse were the things happening in your own family. No matter what Elsie tried to do, the harsh feelings and natural animosities of her daughter had set in. After the wedding, accusing letters continued to arrive. The charges were disgraceful, references to Henry's character, and Elsie herself always the first target. It seemed fantastic that the girl could feel that way, and for such a long time.

In the sixth year of her marriage, the daughter's husband lost his job. The girl wrote Elsie for money, making her demand so spiteful in tone that the mother wanted to refuse. Nevertheless, a month later Elsie sent a check for forty-five dollars. It was the most she could afford; Henry was not a millionaire. The check was returned without comment, in torn pieces.

After that, the daughter did not write for two years. But then, with the assistance of Christmas cards and birthday remembrances, the correspondence was gradually taken up again. The girl's letters were polite and chilly, the news penned on gray linen stationery, planned and written with a deft disinterest, itemizing facts and leaving out the corrosive elements of feeling. She said that the husband was working in a hardware store, and they were doing fine.

Elsie read the words, but she could not remember what kind of a store it was. The daughter was receding from her, like a figure beyond the horizons she would never reach again.

She felt that she had been moving through veils of time, strange and baffling experiences which did not allow her to see life as the clear and beautiful thing it really was. There was no pleasure in taking care of the whining old aunt, or in suffering ill-treatment from an ungrateful child. Everything seemed without cause, and inevitable.

"But, well," she thought, "that is the way things are."

She was nearing the age of fifty, and in the mellowing sense of her own diminishing strength, she had come to feel that most of wisdom consisted of one motto: *Don't expect too much from anybody*.

Henry's visits were her only comfort. When he came home from a trip now, he usually felt sick and went right to bed. But she was always happy to hear his thunderous snores resounding through the house. Other wives might have been disturbed. But Elsie lay peacefully in her own bed, with the covers up to her chin, listening contentedly to the erratic blubberings of her husband's repose.

The sound came from his room, two doors down. She was lulled, as by the roar of a great waterfall.

9

On a bright September afternoon, Elsie Hubbard sat in her glassed-in sun porch, reading a magazine. Beside her, on a wrought-iron coffee table, was a small dish filled with chocolate-covered cherries. As she read, her eyes wandering to the nice, cheerful illustrations and back down to the entertaining story, her left hand hovered over the table. The plump middle finger and thumb shadowed the candy dish like the stretch of a bird wing.

At that moment, the telephone rang.

Not expecting a call, Elsie did not answer at once. Idly, she turned another page. Then she sighed and got up, waddling into the hall with her slow, languorous gait.

Taking the receiver, she noticed that the maid had not dusted under the dial of the telephone. While Elsie was thinking of this, she heard a man's voice at the other end of the wire. At first she did not understand. But suddenly, the words penetrated like dynamite. She lurched forward and made a howling exclamation.

The person calling was a doctor at a hospital in Nashville, Tennessee. He said that Henry had suffered a stroke, and had lived only an hour afterwards. The word was *dead.*

He said it twice, repeating all the lugubrious information surrounding the shock—the niggling details swam around Elsie's thoughts like sediment in dishwater. She stood dumbly over the telephone, listening; and her desperate feelings strove with the man's voice as with a hostile force.

"Doctor—*who?*"

She spoke in a shrieking annoyed tone. The sunlight froze on the bright wall. She gestured witlessly.

There are times when life shows all its raw possibilities. Familiar elements break up, change color, vanish or explode. Terror, heartbreak and confusion usurp the mind, forcibly seize the place and very spirit of objects which once gave a sense of well-being. So it was at that moment. Elsie shivered. Henry's death was a dream. Everything was unreal, and she felt as if she would never wake up.

The next day when they brought him home, and the daughter arrived, Elsie appeared to take responsibility without trouble. She bustled through the parlor, arranging furniture for the funeral services. At times, she stopped to inquire about the health of sympathetic visitors. She trotted about, carrying candlesticks and flowers, moving with a pronounced heroic vigor.

"For heaven's sakes, Mama!" her daughter exclaimed. "Slow down, why don't you! You act like you're enjoying yourself."

Elsie ceased trotting, and put down a vase.

"I guess it can stay here," she said.

She glanced up, and caught the expression of her daughter's eyes—an unflinching dislike. The girl's face was swollen from crying, and she clutched a handkerchief at her side.

"But I suppose," said the daughter—her tone was hard and conversational—"you're getting pretty used to funerals by now."

Elsie stared, uncomprehending. It was true, this had been a year for funerals. First the old aunt had died, and then several church members. But it occurred to Elsie that her daughter meant something other than that. Elsie's mouth clamped shut. The daughter thought that she did not *care* that Henry, her husband, was dead. The gross accusation cut to the brain. She turned blindly and went toward the stairs.

The numbness had vanished, her body swarmed with pain and fatigue. That her daughter did not understand, and the terrible, useless and unwanted devotion she had always felt toward Henry, put Elsie into a state of panic. It was a loneliness too horrible to be borne, or even to explain. Reaching the top landing, Elsie moved toward her dark bedroom door. She felt the cold knob and pushed. In the black privacy of her room, she burst into a wild soundless weeping. She threw herself on the bed, and rolled back and forth, in a physical agony. Elsie knew that people had to live through such things, but it was terrible all the same.

It was a year later that she wrote her daughter, inviting the girl to come with her husband and two children to live in Louisville. Elsie said they could share the house and pay half the rent. It would be on a purely financial basis, which seemed the most sensible arrangement. There was no hurry. The daughter could look into all the advantages, and possible disadvantages—although of the latter, Elsie could see none.

"You can just suit yourself," Elsie wrote. "You know how easy-going I am about these things. Henry always said that I'm not a Linker for nothing." As she wrote, she smiled briefly at this little fictive boast.

On the next Thursday, Elsie got back a firm and definite refusal. At neither a present nor a future date would the daughter consider such a thing. Her husband's business was established in Indianapolis. They would be crazy to come running down to Kentucky.

"We are doing very well by ourselves, thank you."

Elsie read the letter again. The second time she detected an unapparent, but most serious, omission. No mention had been made that she, Elsie, might be invited to come stay with her own daughter and grandchildren. Not that she would have gone. But it would have been such a friendly thing to ask.

"Nobody wants an old woman," she thought. Then, with a sort of pride: "Even one like me."

But it had not escaped Elsie that, during the past year, certain young people at the church had begun to make unflattering remarks about her violin playing. At first, she felt insulted and argumentative. How much did they know about sacred music! "Brighten the Corner," "Love Lifted Me," "In the Garden," her thoughts skimmed professionally over the tunes. In her time, she must have memorized a thousand. Nevertheless, the young people were against her. She would have to eventually give up her Sunday performances. There was no way to break down the hard wall of youth.

However, she was glad she had her own house, her own front yard and porch. Unlike her aunt, Elsie would never be a burden to anybody. Henry had left enough for her livelihood.

It was early twilight. She looked out of the window to the vast pink-rimmed clouds, with trailing coral fire like the spread of water behind a boat. She moved a little closer. How quiet it was. The day's traffic had ceased, and this was a nice neighborhood after dark. She knew all the houses, the dim roofs and chimneys. Even some of the trees were recognizable, and she remembered which neighbors had planted them. She turned and faced the silent room. She supposed she ought to feel sorry for herself, alone in the house. As usual now, she often thought of Henry. Henry, uncoffined and alive, sprawled in the Morris chair. It was the only memory she could evoke, the consistent reality of her feelings for him. But now *gone*, she thought, accustoming herself to the painful thought.

However, to face the future alone was not a bad thing after all. In fact, she had never faced it otherwise. In certain ways she did not feel any differently from the time when she was a little girl, and had to do things for herself. Some people might have thought she was unhappy. But Elsie knew there was an integral part of herself that had remained aloof from it all.

"Just take things as you find them."

Elsie walked over to the lamp and, snapping it on, experienced a soft pleasure of possessiveness. The full continent of the household came into focus. She crossed the room and opened the closet door. Being short, she had to stand on a footstool to reach the top shelf.

She took down a box of chocolates, half-eaten but still fresh. It was almost time to have supper. But Elsie knew that just one piece before would not hurt.

DREAMY

by Sherry Sonnett

One morning, quite early and without the aid of an alarm clock, I will rise up cleanly from the dreary, dirty sheets of my unmade bed. Slipping my feet into warm soft slippers, drawing a crisp pressed robe around my smooth rounded shoulders, I will enter my orderly kitchen and brew a cup of strong aromatic coffee, which I will sip as I read the morning newspaper, each section and the ads. I will do the crossword puzzle straight through with the exception of two unknown letters. I will dress, washing my face in sparkling water, combing my shiny, lustrous hair, doing each task calmly, quietly, precisely. I will pack a small neat suitcase, mostly sweet-smelling, even folded underwear and safely packaged toilet essentials. Dressed and ready to depart, I will pause before my large, spotless mirror and I will be content with the self-contained image reflected there. Then, silently slipping my key in the lock, I will softly close the door absolutely, and I will take pleasure in this, knowing that such perfect union must be esteemed. I will go to my car, a small blue roadster, and I will place the suitcase securely on the rear seat. I will slip another well-made key into its one perfect opposite, and when the smoothly tuned engine springs into life, I will drive off and disappear forever.

I will drive until nightfall, the only car on miles of unblemished concrete stretching rhythmically through silent green valleys and across rolling molded hills. I will come to a medium-size city, discreet in its boundaries, in a region I have never been in. I will drive through the heart of this city, permanently noting the location of various places of interest, but I will stop a bit removed from the center, somewhere on its perimeter, distanced from the clutter and noise of the heart. I will find and rent at a reasonable sum a furnished room with kitchen in a boardinghouse once grand but now declined genteel. I will sleep that night between clean sheets, although not of the best quality. Long into the night, I shall lie in the darkness on my back. My head will rest comfortably on the supporting pillow beneath it and the covers will be pulled neatly and evenly across my chest, my arms on top of them stationary at my sides. Imprecise sounds will filter through the heavy, old but newly laundered curtains, and I will hear each one separately and trace its source and understand it. I will listen to those sounds and know them.

In the morning, I will dress quickly and go out into the street. Around the corner from my new home, I will find a diner, painted gray, with green plastic on the seats and counter. As I eat bacon and eggs, toast, and coffee, I will search through the job ads listed in the local newspaper. By lunchtime I will be employed as ticket taker at the local movie theater or saleswoman at the five-and-ten. My employer will show me what exactly my job consists of, and at each step I will nod my head and firmly fix it in my brain until I need only do it once or twice for it to be automatic. I will begin that very day and at its end my employer and I will express our mutual satisfaction.

I will stop on my return to my new home at a small neighborhood grocery to purchase the few things I will want—the usual staples, a flavorful tea, imported biscuits, a particularly thin slice of veal. As I enter the boarding house, its proprietor and I will nod to each other, smiling circumspectly, respecting the other's privacy. In my room I will slip off my coat and hang it on a wide wooden hanger made especially for coats such as mine. I will arrange the kitchen in the manner most convenient for me and then I will prepare my dinner. The cooking odors will permeate the room, adding to its warmth.

I will eat this meal on a mahogany table set before the window and, as I slice and swallow precise bite after precise bite, I will view the street below. Two or three old men are quietly talking and enjoying the evening air. Occasionally, they look off down the street at a group of children playing with a ball. By their posture and the movements of their hands as they talk, I can tell they are good men who have lived good lives and I can see that they watch the children with pleasure and not regret. A young man and woman, their arms around each other, come out of a house opposite and amble slowly out of sight, leaving behind the sound of a laugh. A woman appears and calls out to one of the children, a boy of eight, and when he runs to her she offers him a slice of freshly baked chocolate cake.

As I finish my meal and the evening shadows lengthen and seep out into night, I will smoke a cigarette, each inhalation smooth and cool, and I will watch the delicate smoke trail up and out my window, joining the fresh night air which cools my face. I will wash my few dishes, clean the sink, and wipe the counter space. I will neatly fold the dishcloth with which I have dried the dishes and drape it over a rack suitably placed over the sink.

Drawing from my purse a newly purchased book, the characters of which are old familiar friends, I will draw my feet up under me on my easy chair, so comfortable it seems made for the curve of my back and the line of my bottom. For an hour or two, while the night spends itself in comings and goings, I will read this book, turning each page silently and watching it fall flat against its companions. Then I will stretch luxuriously, close the book and place it on a small polished table. I will undress. Again between clean sheets, I will lie on my back in the darkness, although not for so long this night as the last, and I will hear the imprecise sounds and I will understand them.

Each day and each night will be like this. My life will have shape and form. My needs and expectations and desires will coincide perfectly with what my life provides. I will have everything.

I LOVE SOMEONE

by Jean Stafford

My friends have gone now, abandoning me to the particular pallor of summer twilight in the city. How long the daytime loiters, how noisily the children loiter with it! I hear their reedy voices splintering like glass in the streets as they tell their mothers no, they *won't* come in, and call up to the filmed windows of the tenements on the avenue, "Marian!" or "Harold!" dropping, invariably, the final consonant. Abashed by my own indolence, I wish to scold them for theirs, to ask them sharply, as if I were their teacher, "Who on earth is Harol?" I hear their baseballs thudding against the walls of shops, hear their feet adroitly skipping rope, hear them singing songs from *South Pacific*, hear a sudden, solo scream for which there is neither overture nor finale: the moment it is formed, it is finished like a soap bubble. Listening to them half against my will, I think how strong a breed they are, how esoteric a society with their shrouded totems and taboos. What is the meaning of this statement I hear, shouted in singsong suddenly, "My mother is in the bathroom shooting dice"? Or ponder this: a day or so ago, I saw a legend on the sidewalk that haunts me: within a fat, lopsided heart were chalked the words I LOVE SOMEONE. I thought at the time how awful this confession was that concealed the identity both of the lover and of the beloved. In an adult (in myself, say) it would have been a boast or a nervous lie, but in the child who wrote the words, it was no more than an ironic temporizing.

My impatience with the children tonight is not real; I am lorn for other reasons as I sit here in the heat and in the mauve light, facing an empty evening, realizing too late that I should have provided myself with company and something to do. It had been a melancholy day and the events of it have enervated me: I simply sit, I simply stare at a bowl of extraordinary roses. Harriet Perrine and Nancy Lang and Mady Hemingway and I went this afternoon to the funeral of our dear friend, Marigold Trask. Famously beautiful, illustrious for her charm and her stylish wit, inspired with joy, Marigold killed herself with sodium amytal last Thursday night, leaving bereft a husband and two young sons. The five of us had been fast friends since school days, and the death has shocked us badly; in an odd way, it has also humiliated us, and when we lunched today before the service (held in a nonreligious "chapel" fitted out with an electric organ and bogus Queen Anne chairs) we did not speak of Marigold at all but talked as we had talked before, when she was alive and with us. We talked of plays and clothes and we plumbed the depths of the scandals that deluged the world outside our circle. We behaved, even now that it had happened, as if nothing unsightly would ever happen to any of us. But afterward, after we had seen the gray-gloved lackeys close her casket and carry her out to the hearse, we came up here to my apartment and with our drinks we did discuss at length the waste and the folly and the squalor of her suicide. There was a note of exasperation in the tone of all our voices. "If people would only wait!" cried Nancy Lang. "Everything changes in time."

"If it was Morton, she could have divorced him," said Mady. "*We* would have stuck by."

"I don't think it was Morton," said Harriet and we all nodded. Morton was a stick and none of us liked him, but he was not at all the sort of man who would drive a woman to *that*. To lovers, yes, and trips alone, but not to *that*. Then Harriet proposed, "It could have been the Hungarian."

"Oh, but that's been over for months," said Mady. "Besides, *she* chucked *him*." Mady is an orthodox woman. Her mind is as literal as her modern house.

Nancy said, "It must have been something much deeper. If it wasn't, then it was simply beastly of her to do this to the boys."

We talked then of the effects of such catastrophes on children, and though we spoke wholly in banalities (we are

not women with original minds; we "keep up" and that's
the most that can be said of us) and were objective, I
could not help thinking that the others felt it would have
been better if, assuming that one of us had had to take the
overdose of sleeping pills, it had been I. For I have never
married and my death would discommode no one. My
friends would miss me, it is true: to put it bluntly, they
would have no one to coddle and champion in a world unfit
for solitary living. They are devoted to me, I am sure, and
in their way they love me, but they are not *concerned*.
They cannot be, for there is no possible way for them
really to know me now; it would embarrass them, as
married women, to confront the heart of a spinster which
is at once impoverished and prodigal, at once unloving
and lavishly soft. Therefore, out of necessity, they have
invented their own image of me, and I fancy that if I tried
to disabuse them of their notions, they would think I was
hallucinating; in alarm they would get me to a really good
doctor as quickly as possible.

Harriet, who is a tireless and faulty analyst of character, often explains in my presence that I am "one of those
beings whom nothing, but nothing, can bring down to
earth." Does she mean by this that I am involved in nothing? Or does she derive her ethereal vision of me from the
fact that I never appear to change? My moods don't show
and perhaps this gives me a blandness that, for some
reason, she associates with the upper air. I never make
drastic changes in my life; I seldom rearrange my furniture; I have worn the same hairdress for twenty years.
Harriet lives in a state of daily surprise, but surprise only
for things and scenes and people that do not alter in the
least. She begins her day by marveling that her egg is, in
color and constituents, exactly the same as the egg of
yesterday and of the day before and that tomorrow the
same phenomenon will greet her happy, natural eyes.
Whenever she goes into the Frick to look at her favorite
pictures, she stands awed before the El Greco "St. Jerome,"
her hands clasped rapturously, her whole being seeming
to cry out in astonishment, "Why, it's still here!"

But I am grateful that Harriet and Nancy and Mady
have embedded me in a myth. This sedative conviction of

theirs, that ichor runs in my veins and that mine is an operating principle of the most vestal kind, has kept me all these years (I am forty-three) from going into hysteria or morbidity or hypochondria or any other sort of beggary by which even the most circumspect spinster of means is tempted. I have no entourage of coat-carrying young men and drink is not a problem; the causes I take up are time-honored and uncontroversial: I read aloud to crippled children but I do not embroil myself in anything remotely ideological. I know that my friends have persuaded themselves that I once had a love affair that turned out badly—upon this universal hypothesis rests perhaps as much as half the appeal of unmarried women who show no signs of discontent, and there is no tact more beatifying than that which protects a grief that is never discussed. Now and again it amuses me to wonder what their conjectures are. I daresay that when they speculate, they kill off my lover in splendor, in a war, perhaps, or in a tuberculosis sanitarium. I can all but hear them forearming their dinner guests before I arrive: "Jenny Peck has never married, you know. She had one of those really tragic things when she was very young, so totally devastating that she has never said a word about it even to her closest friends."

But the fact is that there has been nothing in my life. I have lived the whole of it in the half-world of brief flirtations (some that have lasted no longer than the time it takes to smoke a cigarette under the marquee of a theater between the acts), of friendships that have perished of the cold or have hung on, desiccated, outliving their meaning and never once realizing the possibility of love. I have dwelt with daydreams that through the years have become less and less high-reaching, so apathetic, indeed, that now I would rather recite the names of the forty-eight states to myself than review one of those skimpy fictions. From childhood I have unfailingly taken all the detours around passion and dedication; or say it this way, I have been a pilgrim without faith, traveling in an anticipation of loss, certain that the grail will have been spirited away by the time I have reached my journey's end. If I did not see in myself this skepticism, this unconditional refusal, this—I admit it—contempt, I would find it degrad-

ing that no one has ever proposed marriage to me. I do
not wish to refuse but I do not know how to accept. In my
ungivingness, I am more dead now, this evening, than
Marigold Trask in her suburban cemetery.

But my reflexes are still lively and my nerves are spry,
and sometimes I can feel the pain through the anesthetic.
Then it is on certain mornings I will not wake, although
my dreams, abstract and horrible, pester me relentlessly
and raucously. The sarcasm of my dreams! All night long
my secret mind derides and crucifies me, "Touché!" All the
same, I do not consciously nurse the wound. Be caught
red-eyed by my friends? It would never do, for their delusion is my occupation: *cogitant, ergo sum.* Unlike Marigold, I will never unsettle these affectionate women, for
whatever would I do without them? I would not know how
to order my existence if they did not drop in on me after
a gallery or a matinee, have me to dine when the extra man
is either "interesting" or "important" (the Egyptologists I
have listened to! The liberals with missions! Shall I forget
until my dying day the herpetologist that Mady once produced who talked to me of cobras throughout the fish?),
have me to come for long weekends in the summer, send
me flowers and presents of perfume in clever bottles, lend
me their husbands for lunch, treat me, in general, like
someone of royal blood suspended in an incurable but
unblemishing disease.

Thus it is I sit and meditate in the ambiguous light
while beyond me and below me the city children vehe-
mently play at stick-ball, postponing their supper hour just
as I postpone mine. I know that I should stir. I must take
the glasses and the ashtrays to the kitchen and rinse them
out because my silent and fastidious maid, who comes to
me by the day, would be alarmed if I departed from my
custom. I must eat what she has prepared for me, I must
read, must bathe, must read again, and finally turn off my
light and commence my nightmares in the heat that lies
like jelly on the city. But thinking of myself, of Marigold
(how secretly she did it!), of the anonymous child who
told the world he loved someone, I am becalmed and
linger exactly where I am, unable to give myself a purpose
for doing anything.

By now my friends are at home in Fairfield County. All three of them are ardent gardeners, and presently they will be minding their tomato vines and weeding between their rows of corn. I imagine their cool, rose-laden drawing rooms where, later, they will join their husbands for cocktails. Is it too late for me to ring up someone and propose dinner and an air-conditioned movie? Much too late. Much too late. Idiotically, I say the phrase aloud, compulsively repeat it several times and try to think how my lips look as I protract the word "much."

Gradually the words lose their meaning and I am speaking gibberish. *Now* what would they think of me, babbling like a cretin? I have just set my tongue against the roof of my mouth to say "late" for the dozenth time when a bumble of voices invades my open windows. The clamor, as of an angry, lowing multitude, is closer than the street sounds and I sit up, startled. Perhaps it is a party in the garden next door; but the voices are harsh and there is no laughter. The sound echoes as if a mass of people were snarling at the bottom of a pit; muted, they are nevertheless loud—and loud, the words are nevertheless indistinguishable. For a minute I remain, true to my character, remote from the tumult; but then, because there is neither pause nor change and because the sound is so close at hand, I grow ever so slightly afraid. Still, I do not move, not even to switch on a light, until suddenly, like the report of a gun, an obscenity explodes in the hot dusk. The voice that projects it is an adolescent boy's and it is high and helpless with outrage. I rise and stand quivering before my chair and then I move across the carpet and open the door to my bedroom.

As I hesitate, I once again take note of the glasses and the ashtrays. And once again, although my heart is pounding rapidly now with a fear that is gathering itself into a shape, I think, quite separately, of Marigold, and I wonder if she knew when it was coming. *It!* Shocked at my circumvention, I revise: when *death* was coming. But does that improve the sentence? *It* means as much to me as *death* does—or, for that matter, *life*. I go further and I say, "I wonder if she finally knew why she wanted nothing else?" For I, you see, dwelling upon the rim of life, see everyone

in the arena as acting blindly. I would know, but did Marigold? Does the bullfighter know, until he is actually in
danger, that the danger itself is his master? Not the glory,
not the ladies' roses, or the pageant, or the accolades, but
the flashing glimpse of the evil and the random and the
unknown? Far from the stage and safe, I, who never act on
impulse, know nearly precisely the outcome of my always
rational behavior. It makes me a woman without hope; but
since there is no hope there is also no despair.

I lean from my bedroom window and discover the source
of the noises in the courtyard of this respectable apartment
house: a huddle of boys stands in the service entry where
the gate has not yet been locked. They are of all sizes and
shapes and colors, and I recognize them at once as a rov-
ing band of youthful hoodlums whose viciousness I have
read about in the tabloids. All their faces wear the same
expression of mingled rage and fascination, and all their
eyes are fixed on something I cannot see. There are twenty-
odd of them and it is from them that comes this steady
snarl. I lean out farther and at my end of the areaway I
see a pair of boys fighting. The fight is far advanced, for
one of them, big and black-haired, has the other down on
the cement. Blood comes from his wide mouth, open in a
gasp, and his hands flutter weakly against his assailant's
shoulders. The engagement is silent. Stunned by its cyni-
cism, I try to pity the loser but I cannot, for his defeat has
made him hideous. Strands of his brown hair lie like
scattered rags on the cement in a parody of a halo.

Now other tenants are aroused and come to their
windows to look in revulsion and indignation. Above me a
man shouts down, "I am going to call the police!" But the
fight continues, silently and maliciously, and the boys in
the gateway ignore my neighbor, who grows very angry
and cries, "Get out of this court! I have a gun here!"

But still they pay no attention. At last the boy on his
back closes his eyes and utters some soft sentence that
is evidently his surrender, for the other, giving him one last
brutish punch in the ribs, gets up, staggering a little. Now
that the excitement is over, the audience instantly quits the
gateway; they vanish swiftly in a body, every man jack of
them, and do not even glance back. But the victor lingers

like an actor on a stage as if he were expecting applause, and seeing that the boys are gone, he looks up at the windows of the apartments. Perhaps he is seeking the man who threatened him with the law; perhaps he wants to challenge *him*. But he finds, instead, myself, and as he looks at me, his feral face breaks into a shameless smile. I suppose he is eighteen or nineteen, but the wickedness in his little black eyes and his scarlet mouth is as old as the hills. He wears a thin mustache, so well groomed and theatrical that it appears to adhere to his lips with gum. He looks at me and then looks down at the other boy, who is just now getting to his feet, and then looks up at me again and shrugs his shoulders. Is he asking me to confirm the justice of his violence? Or the beauty of it? Or the passion?

The blood is driven crudely to my face and I turn from the window. It is my intention at first to lie down on my bed and, if I can, to close my inner eye to what I have just seen. But instead, as will-less as a somnambulist, I go to my door and take the elevator down and let myself out into the street where there is no longer any tumult but, rather, a palpable and sneaky hush. I feel watched and mind-read. With no conscious plan, I walk quickly down the street past the dull buildings with their mongrel doors and their minuscule plots of gritty privet, walking toward the avenue where I reason the boys have gone. A squad car drives slowly by and a bored policeman throws his cigarette stub from the window.

My aim is now articulate. I realize that I want to see the ruffians face to face, both the undefeated and the over-thrown, to see if I can penetrate at last the mysterious energy that animates everyone in the world except myself.

But I do not reach the avenue. Halfway there, I glance down at the sidewalk and I see that swollen heart with its fading proclamation, I LOVE SOMEONE. As easily it could read, beneath a skull and crossbones, I HATE SOMEONE. Now there is no need to investigate further; the answer is here in the obvious, trumpery scrawl, and I go back to my apartment and gather up the glasses and the ashtrays.

My friends and I have managed my life with the best of taste and all that is lacking at this banquet where the appointments are so elegant is something to eat.

SUCCESS IS NOT A DESTINATION BUT THE ROAD TO IT

by Katherine Harding

When I drive anything can happen. Recently I have been daydreaming as I drive: implacable thoughts force their way into my mind. I visualize colliding cars and bodies ripping apart on impact. When I drive on the Sunshine State Parkway I find myself staring at all the snakes, raccoons, and dogs that have been hit, killed, and left on the side of the road.

I first noticed my daydreams seven months ago. I had been with Ian at the O'Brien house, which my office leases and maintains while the O'Briens summer in Europe. Ian had been called in to reengineer the crumbling retaining wall that threatened to let the ocean carry the house out to sea. I had taken Ian there and back to his office-at-home on Worth Avenue, taken him there because Ian didn't drive. A thirty-six-year-old structural engineer familiar with the combustion engine, but an engineer who did not drive. I still can't get over it. "I ride my ten-speed Motobecane very smartly down the Lake Trail," he said to me once. "I'll wager *you* can't ride a *bi*-cycle." That's the way he pronounced it: *bi*-cycle.

At the O'Briens' we examined the buckling and stress in the wall while standing in wet sand that sucked at our feet until we sank to our ankles. The wall was eaten out from below, and waves lapped around the rusted steel beams. The concrete surface had already been eroded up to the high-water mark. "It's not a matter of rebuffing nature's energy; it's a matter of harnessing it and distributing it." Ian told me in his oppressively didactic way. I was bored. "Anderson at your office told me something about you, Jane," Ian went on.

"What's that?"

"That you love cars."

Maybe his bluntness made me uncomfortable, or the detour back to his office, which made me late for the Delray appointment, annoyed me. When I dropped him off I was glad to be alone, even though I liked Ian. In Delray Beach I had an appointment to show New Yorkers the house on Beachway Road. I drove fast, darted in and out of traffic, tailgated relentlessly. The fury I feel behind a car dragging its ass in the left lane! I want to flatten the car, knock it off the road! It was raining in large slanted sheets of water from the east and I could feel, as I whipped around one car, then another, my rear polyglas G6os just beginning to slip out from under me: a tantalizing feeling. I kept everything just barely under control. I cannot say what I did, but there was an edge I could reach out and touch. I would go over that edge or not.

The cars' motion relieves the motion of my thoughts. Some synchronization has finally occurred, some medium has been found for thoughts that otherwise would prey on me.

I always notice cars. The New Yorkers drove a '71 Dodge Dart, black. It was already parked in the carport of the house, as though they were trying to fit two contradictory images together. The Dodge's frame was bent as a result of some collision from the side. Despite the rain, which had drawn lines along the hood, fenders, and through the lettering on the plates, the Dart was still dusty after its trip down from New York. These people didn't care about cars, I thought; if they decided on the house, after a while they'd buy a huge aqua Oldsmobile station wagon—a Ninety-Eight—to match the ocean that can be seen between the split-levels on Sandune Drive. In their new Olds, they'd roll cautiously along South County Road looking at the estates of the rich, and I'd be behind them blaring my horn, trying to get past them, and I'd regret having shown and sold them the house.

I drive a metallic blue Firebird Trans-Am with an SD 455 engine and I am an alert, fast driver. I feel serene behind the wheel of the 455. I like the soothing, guttural rumble of the engine, the encapsulated calm inside. Until recently I hadn't hesitated or concerned myself with avoiding things in the road. I have always followed my father's old advice. Usually I assume cars, people will get out of my way, and I just step on it.

My father put me behind the wheel of his Buck Road-master when I was nine and filmed it. I sat in the driver's seat and peered through the space between the steering wheel with its necker's knob and the rim of the chromium horn. I looked down the country road before me. It went straight to the horizon of pines and palms lining the inland waterway. I wondered if the car would sweep me into that brackish water where you could get ringworm and polio. A story that everyone talked about in those days had run in the Palm Beach *Post*. A man had tried to commit suicide by driving off the Australian Avenue dock. He had failed and explained that he was merely drunk. Later he succeeded.

Before, my father had taught me to drive by sitting me in his lap. Then I became too big and was aware of his thin legs and something else beneath me. Now I was alone behind the wheel. At first he sat next to me, but then he got out, walked down the road fifty yards or so, and pointed his new movie camera at me. He'd bought it since I had seen him last, two months earlier, when he'd left my mother. I didn't ask him where he had been. Anyway, I knew he'd leave again. But he was back, my mother was gone, and now my father and I shared the house, which had been sold. I didn't know where my mother was. My father and I had to be out of the house in two weeks.

"Come on!" my father called. "Drive slowly, and I'll get out of the way as you drive by." I inched the car slowly forward, my right foot tensed over the accelerator: I was afraid by accident my foot would slip and jam the accelerator to the floor. I was concentrating so hard that the periphery of my vision seemed to blacken and encroach on my focus, my father. I began to sweat but I held on to the wheel. As my father moved to the right side of the road, so did the direction of the Buick. Magnetized by him, it followed his lead, and try as I might I could not steer away from him. I slammed on the brakes to avoid running him over, but it seemed the Buick's old drums would never respond.

My father laughed. "Always look at where you want to go, not at what you're trying to avoid."

My mother was afraid of cars and drove as I did when I was nine. In her gray Nash Rambler station wagon she was the terror of the island, and I was scared. Now her driving seems hugely funny and stylish to me, despite what happened to her because of it. It evolved consistently from her preoccupied, myopic, but well-meaning personality. Watching the lamp post so as to avoid it, Mummy steered right for it, slammed on her brakes and slowly maneuvered to the other side of the road and the oncoming cars. It was like all those nightmares where your efforts to save yourself, to run, to scream, lag behind the emotions you're feeling. But Mummy would pretend nothing unusual was happening. She would sing in her shaky contralto "The Surrey with the Fringe on Top" (which reveals how Mummy longed for a past without cars), or "Every Little Breeze Seems to Whisper Louise," which had been played at her lavish wedding: her name was Louise. It makes me laugh. Saturday was the only day she drove to the market because at eleven o'clock she could pretend that it was I who liked to listen to *Let's Pretend*. I can hear the theme music still and feel the sympathetic sway of the Rambler as we worked our way along South County Road to Aiello's Market.

It seems funny to me now. Then I was constantly bracing myself for the impact that was always about to occur. I would stiffen as though slamming on imaginary brakes, thinking childishly that Mummy might notice this and get the hint. I couldn't reason with her, or ask her to let me out. She needed me with her. Maybe the car itself would get the idea, for sometimes I thought it knew what I wanted. Sometimes I thought it had a mind and feelings and could make decisions on its own.

"I disapprove of cars," Ian told me a few weeks after I'd seen him at the O'Briens'. He had called me up expressly to ask for a lift to the old Dodge property in the north end. An architect needed his opinion about an underground tunnel, a passageway for bathers that Mrs. Dodge's architect—probably Mizner—had built. The passageway remained long after the mansion had been demolished, and the architect wanted to know, in planning for the new house, if the tunnel was still sound enough to use. "But I approve," Ian went on pompously, "of well-built tunnels like this one."

"Do you know whose money built this tunnel?"

"Dodge? Oh, motorcars, you mean. It's fantastic how it was built, and the house the architect builds today won't have near the durability of this structure."

"If you disapprove of my car, why do you feel free to exploit it?"

"Actually, I disapprove of your relationship to cars. Can't you see, I'm trying to interject myself—"

"Oh, come on."

"Well, I plan to exploit it some more by having you drive us to some nice restaurant soon. When can we have dinner?"

You know, most men around Palm Beach are rich fags, drunken fags. It's possible to find real men, and in my Firebird I do. Perhaps because Ian didn't drive, I thought at first. Oh well, just another English fag. Ian was a dark, skinny, tall man who seemed fragile and awkward when I first met him. He wasn't bad looking but he also wasn't coordinated enough to shift gears and depress a clutch at the same time. I was uneasy that our relationship had gotten off on the wrong track.

You see, I try to follow my father's advice not to think about avoiding things and just to go, go, but increasingly I get into absentminded thoughts, and my reaction time is slower. Or I just don't see. Once I was turning left into Worth Avenue, delivering some drawings to Ian ("Be a love and fetch the McIntyre drawings from Feruggia, will you?" "Get them yourself. Where's your trusty *bi*-cycle?" "In the shop. Mrs. Goodwillie mistook me and it for the drive-in bank deposit window." "You're kidding!" "No, she was plastered, and nearly plastered me over the stucco of the Palm Beach Bank and Trust." It had made me laugh. "Are you all right?" "I suppose so. She's paying for repairs") and I didn't see, just like Mrs. Goodwillie, the 450 SL coming the other way. It didn't hit me, but only because of the attention of Princess Marina, who was driving. "You fucking nut," she yelled, and gave me the finger.

Occasionally my slow driving thoughts make me think of a man, what we'll do, say, how his gestures and manner will suggest complete intimacy . . . we'll be sitting side by side in a car, speeding calmly through space as though it were the entire course of our life together. We won't need to speak, we'll be perfectly attuned so that each wish will be the other's wish as well. But I become tense thinking about Ian, what we said to one another, what we didn't do. Something gets stuck. I can't follow the sequence of scenes beyond a setting, a certain mood. What will happen next? I do not know, and so I drive fast again. I push everything forward, force these scenes to be played out; I try to make things happen, only they don't.

I pick up men in my Firebird. When races were held at Sebring I met men there. The course was set in the midst of orange groves. I loved the mixed smell of oranges and burning oil, a smell that you drove into like a wall two miles outside of town, long before you heard the fitful roar of engines, long before you saw the Martini/Rossi, the Permalube, the Quaker State signs, long before the track itself.

Now I drive around and meet men in Riviera or in Stuart. There's always the 455, they're always interested in what the Firebird's equipped with. They talk about the reasoning behind the polyglas G6os. I let them drive, we go to dinner, then to a motel. The room sometimes has two beds. I like having two, even single beds. I can fall asleep afterwards in my own space between the sheets; as in my Firebird, it is all my space. I never take a man home.

Ian called me at my office and pried my home phone number out of me by asking if I was frightened of him.

"Of course not," I said.

"I was ringing you to say our dinner reservation's for eight and we can walk over from my flat here. I won't prevail on you to drive. Do you know the restaurant? I forget what it's called, but it's just down the street."

It was uncanny that he had chosen that restaurant. Once, after an argument with my mother, I ran away on my Schwinn to Worth Avenue, where I watched the rich

shoppers hurrying home in their Mercedes and Bentleys.
I would never go home. In front of the restaurant at the
lake end of Worth Avenue was my father's Buick. He was
at the restaurant. I thought, of course, I'd have dinner with
him and we'd go home to his house: I could live with my
father.

Then I saw a man and a lady eating by candlelight in
the outside patio. The lady looked familiar. Her sluggish
voice carried clearly across the lawn. She was talking about
Cuba and began to sing a little song to the man, something
about a "Cuban Moon." I remembered the voice. The lady
was the one who took tickets at the Four Arts at Saturday
afternoon matinees. I'd seen *The Wizard of Oz* and
Cinderella there. I kept telling myself that the man with the
lady was a stranger. He was lifting his glass to her, smiling
and laughing. I told myself I had never seen him before
and I hoped I'd never see him again in my life.

I was cool as ice going home on my bike. I tried out
a few tricks: no hands, no feet. First I was riding Black
Beauty, then a motorcycle; I was tearing through space and
the wind blew into my lungs, making them inflate like a
terrible balloon. They ached and ached. The cops were
after me, but I was too fast for them. I dashed into my
yard, home safe; the cops would never think to look there.

Mummy emerged from the house. "You're damn lucky
I didn't call the cops," she said. How had she known about
the cops? But she always seemed to know what I was thinking. Did she know I had resolved never to be like her? I'd
never get dumped the way she had. Whenever a man wants
to see me again, I stiffen. . . . We'll be in bed smoking
cigarettes, sex is finished, and he'll be telling me something
personal. He'll say then, "What about you?" I'll say, "Oh,
not much, there's nothing much to say." He'll start in again,
his hand moving up my thigh, "What'll we do tomorrow?"
he'll say, making plans, and starting in on sex again, and
this time I'll harden to stone; his kisses and the way he
touches me will do nothing for me, and if we have sex then
I won't come and he'll be surprised, annoyed. "What the
hell is going on?" he'll say. "I was right for you, you liked
me before, what's this cold fish act?" Then he'll relent, remembering the first time round, and he'll say, "When can
I see you?" And I'll say, "You can't see me, not again."

I did see my father after he married Helga Rath. She
was German and her name was pronounced by dropping
the "h" and enunciating a long "a": *Rot*. Over the years
I've enjoyed this mild joke, but now it doesn't seem funny,
it seems only childish. Helga and my father moved to
Naples, Florida, after the wedding. I lived there with them
until after high school. They are still in Naples, but I
don't see them much. When I was eleven his company
was just opening the new branch in Naples, and he and I
made the trip across the state. During the day I visited a
friend, and on Tuesday and Wednesday nights we stayed
in a dingy motel east of town. On the return trip Thursday my father gave me the wheel and we started out fast
on the Tamiami Trail. I knew he drove at 75 mph, and so
would I.

The empty road stretched eastward in a straight line.
Undulating currents of hot moist air rose from the maca-
dam, making water mirages, blurring the edges of the
road. I kept the car—a pea-green Pontiac convertible with
black upholstery, whitewalls, and, inside, the St. Christopher medal that my father had unscrewed from the old
Roadmaster—I kept the car steady. Daddy talked about
his business, but I couldn't concentrate on what he was saying. I murmured "Yeah, really?" to convince him I was
interested, but it was a strain.

Soon my father fell asleep. His head with its hairbrush
bristles fell forward and slightly toward the left, toward me,
and he began to display those neuropathic spasms that
come just before deep sleep. His head would come up in a
jerk, then it would roll downward in an arc to the left,
like the slow, accelerating tumble of a roller-coaster car. I
worried he might hit his head, or fall forward against the
dashboard. Then I thought, What if he put his head on my
shoulder; would it slide down into my lap, just as, when I
was five or six, I feigned sleepiness and laid my head in his
lap? The intimacy of my father's measured breathing, the
trust his sleep implied pleased me, but only momentarily.
I knew it was a misplaced and foolish trust, because I
had begun to see in the narrowing road things that quickly
disappeared when I looked closely at them. Besides, the
Pontiac required increasingly subtle control to keep it on
the road.

The sun had set at our backs. The sky and the Everglades were finished with a pink-gold luster that blurred the distinctions between land and sky, road and swamp, the Pontiac and us inside it. The road seemed to foreshorten and narrow and I imagined it came to a halt just five hundred feet ahead. The road existed for only a few yards before the Pontiac gained on them, ate them up. Sweat was falling into my eyes and I slowed from 80 to 50: my father was sleeping, he'd never know. Then I began to like us there alone in the Pontiac, passing through the Everglades together.

When my father dropped me off, my mother's house was lit up so bright it hurt my eyes to look at it. I was tired, then annoyed to find our neighbor Mrs. Richardson inside. She was standing at Mummy's desk and seemed to be looking for something.

"Where's Mum?"

"Where've *you* been?"

"Naples with my Dad."

"Is he outside? I want to speak with him."

"Mum's Rambler isn't in the drive."

"Did he go home or to the office? I guess not, so late."

"I dunno. Well, he went to Mr. Wickwire's, I guess. How come you want to talk to him?"

"He should come back."

"Can't. Has important news for Mr. Wickwire. Dad was hopping mad how late we were."

"Wickwire. Wickwire . . ." Mrs. Richardson said, thumbing through the phone book. She began to dial.

"What do you wanna talk to Dad for? This is really queer." I knew something was going on. I was used to having my questions go unanswered. I'd been through a divorce, hadn't I? Hadn't I learned to translate what Mummy meant to say from the expressions on her face? I was a pro at that, I read her perfectly, just like she read me, made me nervous. But I couldn't read this Mrs. Richardson.

My father came back and gave me the news that he'd learned from Mr. Wickwire: at two A.M. on Thursday morning my mother had mowed down two old Florida pines, tall, thick-trunked trees that line A1A fifteen miles south, in Manalapan, and she had virtually severed her head on the rebound back through the windshield. She was dead.

I don't like having conventional evenings with men, seeing them regularly. I didn't think Ian was an exception. He was rather handsomely dressed in an expensive beige linen suit and we sat near the bougainvillea in the court-yard. As he talked he kept his bony hands cocked on either side of his plate as though to avoid soiling his fingers. He only occasionally looked directly at me, preferring to address his butter knife. He had been a musical prodigy as a child in England, but owing to a severe illness had given up the piano and the concert stage for MIT and engineer-ing. The northern climate had affected his health adversely and he had had to move south. He loved bridges. He talked at length and boringly about the mathematical structure and symbolism of bridges. I felt vaguely he was trying to say something personal.

"What was the illness?"

"Rheumatic fever. Left my heart rather damaged. But I'm going to hospital." He laughed. "I'm going in for a valve job this winter. Then I'll be right as rain. I imagine you've always lived in Palm Beach and now that I've got your phone number, perhaps we can progress to where you live."

"On Royal Palm Way. I've lived many places. I'm never satisfied and keep moving around. Even when I was a a child we were always selling houses, renting new ones, moving."

"It's become habitual, your moving about. I myself am accustomed to staying put, having been bedridden for so much of my childhood. Have you noticed that difference—how I'm interested in the stability of structures, how to harness entropy and chaos, whereas you're interested in forcing entropy along, interested in movement, speed, change?"

"Not really. I don't want anything to change." But I was thinking that his damaged heart made him kind of a sitting duck. I could see how he might like a friend right now. It could be anyone: he just wanted a lift. "Ian, your bicycle, is it really in the shop?"

"I suppose not."

"Mrs. Goodwillie didn't wreck it, did she? I've never seen you on a bike. Do you have one?"

"A lovely one. But I'm not permitted to ride it until after the winter." His face fell.

"I'll teach you to drive."

"Oh, no. I stay away from cars. I think it's charming for you to love them, very American, like the cowboy loving his horse."

"Ian, how did you manage before I became your chauffeur? You must learn to drive. I'm getting a little put out dragging you from one place to another."

"Actually, I've the idea it's *the* way to see you."

"Is that so important? For your work, isn't being mobile—"

"It's becoming important, yes."

I left him at his apartment later. I became annoyed when he tried to have me stay. I wouldn't. Clumsily he kissed me, and I could feel something dully beating in his lips. It reminded me of some presence I had been marginally aware of before. His clumsiness seemed profound: I couldn't imagine his playing Bach, whom he so adored. When I left him the memory of the pulsing kiss made me tense, so I took off. My mind began to race. It was 12:30 and I headed for Riviera Beach. I met there a guy named Benjy who drove a diTomasso Pantera and who had the Carvel on North Federal Highway. I didn't ask him how he'd financed the Pantera.

I taught Ian to drive in a rented Vega automatic. At the end of the road a yellow scoop was digging trenches for the foundations of a new house. Soon the area would be built up. Ian would be consulting, I'd be renting and selling. The scoop made sporadic grinding noises. We had to shout at one another.

"What if it jolly well goes off on its own? I'm rather frightened."

"You're supposed to be, at first."

"I'm not supposed to become too anxious. Reasons of health."

"Then don't. Do as I tell you." Why couldn't he see how simple it was, how much fun it was? His steering was

absurd. At last I conceived of a plan to teach him not to
oversteer. I straightened the wheel for him and told him:
"Don't steer at all. Just press the accelerator and see where
the car goes." It worked. The car, despite the wheels' needing alignment, rolled almost in a straight line as it was built
to do.

Often after lessons he'd ask me to dinner, would try to
have me stay at his place. I couldn't figure out why I felt so
physically repelled by him at the same time that I smiled
inwardly whenever I saw his skinny figure, his baggy eyes.
We were an absurd pair: me maybe chewing gum very
evenly, coolly driving my Firebird, letting nothing touch
me; he always gesticulating, teaching, explaining. He was
always late for appointments. I never was.

His driving improved gradually over four weeks. We
kept coming back to the road in the south end. The house's
roof was tiled and soon the landscaping would be done: full-
grown coconut palms would be hauled in and replanted,
sea grapes would be lined up in hedges. The workmen all
knew us by sight, and as Ian could now turn, back up, and
parallel park without a hitch, they had stopped laughing.

When Ian could drive without anxiety in traffic, he took
his test, passed it, bought a Volkswagen automatic, and
began to drive himself on his consultations. I didn't see him
much anymore.

The New Yorkers bought the Delray house and I made a
big commission. Soon afterward they bought a huge yellow
Chrysler. I had been wrong about the make and color, but
it was all the same. The O'Briens came back to a new retaining wall that rerouted and dissipated the ocean's erosive
energy. I heard that construction had begun on the Dodge
property. It was December and the winter people were
keeping me busy: I rented eight houses in four days.

Ian called me at home several times. He asked me out
but I avoided him, and anyhow he seemed not to want to
talk. The last time I spoke to him on the phone I asked
pointedly what work he was doing.

"I'm quite back to my old habits. I stay at home rather
much. All that seems to interest me is the piano. I'm
practicing but I'm frightfully rusty. The partitas exhaust
me; I take one at a time. I try to take each thing I do

separately, as though it has no connection with other things. Tomorrow—"

"May be a good policy. One foot in front of the other."

"But still I wonder what's at the end of the road. What tripe! Speaking of 'tripe,' would you come over and fix me supper?"

"I'm meeting the eight o'clock plane from Chicago—clients I must take to The Towers. Anyway, I'm a terrible cook."

"Get Anderson to meet the clients."

"I'd lose the commission."

"Anderson's a decent fellow. You might pick up hamburgers at Hamburger Heaven. *I'd* be in heaven."

"Ian, I can't."

There was a long silence during which I thought, What is this, there's nothing between us. "Very well, I won't beg, but I wonder what you want," Ian said. "Not companionship, not sex, though Anderson said he thought you were promiscuous."

"Jesus, Ian, will you leave me alone!"

He had hung up and it wasn't until the next afternoon that I learned he was in the hospital: his open-heart surgery was scheduled for early the following morning. I called the hospital. A girl with a deep southern accent told me that Mr. Lister could not accept calls. He was resting and undergoing tests in preparation for surgery.

I thought about how there may have been something I'd said that left him vulnerable, precipitated some problem with his heart. . . . What had I done? What could I do? I couldn't think about it, I wouldn't think about it, so, not signing my name to anything, I sent Ian flowers, a basket of oranges, some paperback books. But I knew he'd die under the knife. The lack of coordination in his limbs was a symptom of the malfunction in the exchange between the chambers of his heart. I knew he'd die. I called again later, at six. I was told Mr. Lister was resting comfortably.

Around midnight I drove up to Riviera where I met a young kid named Peter who liked gospel music. Peter felt about gospel music the way I felt about cars; everything else seemed all the same. We went all over Colored Town looking for a group called the Sweetwater Singers and ended up in one sour-smelling bar after another.

Around seven I drove to the Good Samaritan Hospital: the name had always reminded me of the Saint Christopher medals on my father's cars. Ian's surgery had just begun. I sat down in the waiting room on the surgical ward. The room was painted aqua. That color appears all over southern Florida: rooms, cars, the squat cement houses in the developments west of town are all painted aqua. Perhaps without anyone's being aware of it, the ocean once mysteriously rose up in the night beyond the high-water level and engulfed the land, leaving its sick blue mark behind.

Nurses, aides, and doctors in washed-out aqua pajamas sauntered through the room. Their names and strange numbers came over the loudspeaker. "126 on 4 West, 126 on 4 West," came a clipped dry voice suddenly; and soon new aqua figures were running through the room. What did it mean? Was Ian dead already? I imagined his death would come after long, complicated maneuvers in the surgery, not quite yet, not quite so soon. I began to cry.

Later two nurses passed my chair speaking of "that cardiac arrest." I stood up and took hold of one woman's arm. "What cardiac arrest?" I asked. My hand, my whole arm was shaking visibly. I realized I was furious, I wanted to throttle this woman. She looked scared.

"Now, Hon, we can't talk about our patients," the nurse said. She wore a girdle under her uniform and her waist was pinched like putty. Her body might break in half, I thought. I wished it would.

"What about Mr. Lister?" I asked.

"They're still at that valvular repair, if that's what you mean. Are you a relative?" She looked narrowly at me.

"Just a friend."

"Well, don't you worry, now. You'll hear something soon."

I sat down again, listened to more names, numbers, codes, and fell asleep. I dreamed I had died; yet I stood in an empty dirt road at the end of which was Ian's house. He was having a party, and as I watched, limousines filled with laughing people traveled down the road to where he lived. I couldn't go. I was dead. I cried as each car passed and the sound of the engines roared in my ears. Then I head a whirring sound. "Miss? I'm Dr. Angel?" His voice went up at the end questioningly, as though he doubted his own identity. The day had begun with angels: I remembered Peter's cherubic face, gospel music. "Mr. Lister has just come out of surgery. Miss Cross said you were a friend?"

"He's dead, then." I heard "*were* a friend."

"No, everything's fine. The damage made it take longer than we expected, but he's doing very well."

When I drive I feel anything can happen. Sometimes I over-rev it and I wonder, will I blow the engine? Yesterday I drove, tailgating, dodging traffic, slipping slightly on wet pavement, feeling the edge of things but afraid I was late, late. I slammed on the brakes and smelled the slow, sweet burn of rubber, or was it myself I smelled?

Yesterday I drove the Edwardses to some property in Lantana that they think they might buy. They are unsure about the narrow spit of land between the ocean and the inland waterway because of strong and erosive undertows that have carried away five feet of beachfront in the last two years. Ian was there waiting by his Volkswagen when we arrived. He had gained weight and seemed so graceful and confident that I barely recognized him. After business with the Edwardses was finished he politely said, "I believe you sent those nice presents when I was at hospital. Thank you."

"Your surgery was quite successful, then?"

"As you well know. Dr. Angel said you were there the entire time. I must say I was surprised." He paused but I said nothing. "Well," he went on after a bit, "I thought I was a dead man. Now everything's changed, I'm free. I think I shall go north, I've had a super offer in New York. Thank you again for the gifts and thank you for teaching me to drive. I never could have learned otherwise, even now that everything's changed." He walked to his car and I to mine. I had started my engine by the time he opened his door and waved. As I gunned it going past him I thought, I could easily run him over; I could make it look like an accident.

I like to drive on the Sunshine State Parkway. It is only a matter of time. I'll drive for miles at 100 mph, then I'll stop and think. I'll look at myself in my rearview mirror,

I'll look at the person I see. Who is she? I'll pretend I don't know her, I'll try to dredge up thoughts about what this woman is like. I'll try to be a stranger to her: Oh yes, there's an aging, pale, once pretty woman, still futilely trying to make a success of things. But look how she chews her gum in neat circular motions of her jaw. Look at the asymmetry in her body, in her face. She's had it, her life is over.

The Sunshine State Parkway, which often runs in an absolutely straight line north to south, is the crucial road to drive, the easiest road to let the wheel go to see where the car goes. My feelings change between letting go the wheel and moving along slowly, not very fast, having things come to me as they may, or driving fast, hard, running things down: people, animals, woods, tearing things up until I can't anymore.

THE LOVER

by Joy Williams

The girl is twenty-five. It has not been very long since her divorce but she cannot remember the man who used to be her husband. He was probably nice. She will tell the child this, at any rate. Once he lost a fifty-dollar pair of sunglasses while surf-casting off Gay Head and felt badly about it for days. He did like kidneys, that was one thing. He loved kidneys for weekend lunch. She would voyage through the supermarkets, her stomach sweetly sloped, her hair in a twist, searching for fresh kidneys for this young man, her husband. When he kissed her, his kisses, or so she imagined, would have the faint odor of urine. Understandably, she did not want to think about this. It hardly seemed that the same problem would arise again, that is, with another man. Nothing could possibly be gained from such an experience! The child cannot remember him, this man, this daddy, and she cannot remember him. He had been with her when she gave birth to the child. Not beside her, but close by, in the corridor. He had left his work and come to the hospital. As they wheeled her by, he said, "Now you are going to have to learn how to love something, you wicked woman." It is difficult for her to believe he said such a thing.

The girl does not sleep well and recently has acquired the habit of listening all night to the radio. It is a weak, not very good, radio and at night she can only get one station. From midnight until four she listens to "Action Line." People call the station and make comments on the world and their community and they ask questions. Music is played and a brand of beef and beans is advertised. A woman calls and says, "Could you tell me why the filling in

my lemon meringue pie is runny?" These people have
obscene materials in their mailboxes. They want to know
where they can purchase small flags suitable for waving
on Armed Forces Day. There is a man on the air who
answers these questions right away. Another woman calls.
She says, "Can you get us a report on the progress of the
collection of Betty Crocker Coupons for the lung machine?"
The man can and does. He answers the woman's question.
Astonishingly, he complies with her request. The girl thinks
such a talent is bleak and wonderful. She thinks this man
can help her.

The girl wants to be in love. Her face is thin with the
thinness of a failed lover. It is so difficult! Love is concen-
tration, she feels, but she can remember nothing. She tries
to recollect two things a day. In the morning with her coffee, she tries to remember and in the evening, with her
first bourbon and water, she tries to remember as well. She
has been trying to remember the birth of her child now for
several days. Nothing returns to her. Life is so intrusive!
Everyone was talking. There was too much conversation!
The doctor was above her, waiting for the pains. "No, I still
can't play tennis," the doctor said. "I haven't been able to
play for two months. I have spurs on both heels and it's
just about wrecked our marriage. Air-conditioning and concrete floors is what does it. Murder on your feet." A few
minutes later, the nurse had said, "Isn't it wonderful to
work with Teflon? I mean for those arterial repairs? I just
love it." The girl wished that they would stop talking. She
wished that they would turn the radio on instead and be
still. The baby inside her was hard and glossy as an ear
of corn. She wanted to say something witty or charming
so that they would know she was fine and would stop talking. While she was thinking of something perfectly balanced and amusing to say, the baby was born. They
fastened a plastic identification bracelet around her wrist
and the baby's wrist. Three days later, after they had come
home, her husband sawed off the bracelets with a grape-
fruit knife. The girl had wanted to make it an occasion.
She yelled, "I have a lovely pair of tiny silver scissors that
belonged to my grandmother and you have used a grape-

fruit knife!" Her husband was flushed and nervous but he smiled at her as he always did. "You are insecure," she said tearfully. "You are insecure because you had mumps when you were eight." Their divorce was one year and two months away. "It was not mumps," he said carefully. "Once I broke my arm while swimming, is all."

The girl becomes a lover to a man she met at a dinner party. He calls her up the next morning. He drives over to her apartment. He drives a white convertible which is all rusted out along the rocker panels. They do not make convertibles any more, the girl thinks with alarm! He asks her to go sailing. They drop the child off at a nursery school on the way to the pier. The child's peculiar hair is braided and is pinned up under a big hat with mouse ears that she got on a visit to Disneyworld. She is wearing a striped jersey stuffed into striped shorts. She kisses the girl and she kisses the man and goes into the nursery carrying her lunch in a Wonder Bread bag. In the afternoon, when they return, the girl has difficulty recognizing the child. There are so many children, after all, standing in the rooms, all the same size, all small, quizzical creatures, holding pieces of wooden puzzles in their hands.

It is late at night. A cat seems to be murdering a baby bird in a nest somewhere outside the girl's window. The girl is listening to the child sleep. The child lies in her varnished crib, clutching a bear. The bear has no tongue. Where there should be a small piece of red felt there is nothing. Apparently, the child had eaten it by accident. The crib sheet is in a design of tiny yellow circus animals. The girl enjoys looking at her child but cannot stand the sheet. There is so much going on in the crib, so many colors and patterns. It is so busy in there! The girl goes into the kitchen. On the counter, four palmetto bugs are exploring a pan of coffee cake. The girl goes back to her own bedroom and turns on the radio. There is a great deal of static. The Answer Man on "Action Line" sounds very annoyed. An old gentleman is asking something but the transmission is terrible because the old man refuses to turn off his rock tumbler. He is polishing stones in his rock tumbler like all old men do and he refuses to turn it off while speaking.

Finally, the Answer Man hangs up on him. "Good for you," the girl says. The Answer Man clears his throat and says in a singsong way, "The wine of this world has caused only satiety. Our homes suffer from female sadness, embarrassment and confusion. Absence, sterility, mourning, privation and separation abound throughout the land." The girl puts her arms around her knees and begins to rock back and forth on the bed. The child murmurs in sleep. More palmetto bugs skate across the formica and into the cake. The girl can hear them. A woman's voice comes on the radio now. The girl is shocked. It seems to be her mother's voice. The girl leans toward the radio. There is a terrible weight on her chest. She can scarcely breathe. The voice says, "I put a little pan under the air-conditioner outside my window and it catches the condensation from the machine and I use that water to water my ivy. I think anything like that makes one a better person."

The girl has made love to nine men at one time or another. It does not seem like many but at the same time it seems more than necessary. She does not know what to think about them. They were all very nice. She thinks it is wonderful that a woman can make love to a man. When lovemaking, she feels she is behaving reasonably. She is well. The man often shares her bed now. He lies sleeping, on his stomach, his brown arm across her breasts. Sometimes, when the child is restless, the girl brings her into bed with them. The man shifts position, turns flat on his back. The child lies between them. The three lie, silent and rigid, earnestly conscious. On the radio, the Answer Man is conducting a quiz. He says, "The answer is: the time taken for the fall of the dashpot to clear the piston is four seconds, and what is the question? The answer is: when the end of the pin is approximately 5/16" below the face of the block, and what is the question?"

She and the man travel all over the South in his white convertible. The girl brings dolls and sandals and sugar animals back to the child. Sometimes the child travels with them. She sits beside them, pretending to do something gruesome to her eyes. She pretends to dig out her eyes. The

girl ignores this. The child is tanned and sturdy and affectionate although sometimes when she is being kissed, she
goes limp and even cold, as though she has suddenly, foolishly died. In the restaurants they stop at, the child is well-
behaved although she takes only butter and ice water. The
girl and the man order carefully but do not eat much
either. They move the food around on their plates. They
take a bite now and then. In less than a month the man
has spent many hundreds of dollars on food that they do
not eat. "Action Line" says that an adult female consumes
seven hundred pounds of dry food in a single year. The girl
believes this of course but it has nothing to do with her.
Sometimes, she greedily shares a bag of Fig Newtons with
the child but she seldom eats with the man. Her stomach is
hard, flat, empty. She feels hungry always, dangerous to
herself, and in love. They leave large tips on the tables of
restaurants and then they reenter the car. The seats are hot
from the sun. The child sits on the girl's lap while they
travel, while the leather cools. She seems to ask for nothing.
She makes clucking, sympathetic sounds when she sees
animals smashed flat on the side of the road. When the
child is not with them, they travel with the man's friends.

The man has many friends whom he is devoted to. They
are clever and well-off; good-natured, generous people, confident in their prolonged affairs. They have known each
other for years. This is discomforting to the girl, who has
known no one for years. The girl fears that each has loved
the other at one time or another. These relationships are
so complex, the girl cannot understand them! There is such
flux, such constancy among them. They are so intimate
and so calm. She tries to imagine their embraces. She feels
that they differ from her own. One afternoon, just before
dusk, the girl and man drive a short way into the Everglades. It is very dull. There is no scenery, no prospect. It
is not a swamp at all. It is a river, only inches deep! Another couple rides in the back of the car. They have very
dark tans and have pale yellow hair. They look almost like
brother and sister. He is a lawyer and she is a lawyer. They
are drinking gin and tonics, as are the girl and the man.
The girl has not met these people before. The woman leans

over the front seat and drops another ice-cube from the cooler into the girl's drink. She says, "I hear that you have a little daughter." The girl nods. She feels funny, a little frightened. "The child is very *sortable*," the girl's lover says. He is driving the big car very fast and well but there seems to be a knocking in the engine. He wears a long-sleeved shirt buttoned at the wrists. His thick hair needs cutting. The girl loves to look at him. They drive, and on either side of them, across the slim canals or over the damp sawgrass, speed air-boats. The sound of them is deafening. The tourists aboard wear huge ear-muffs. The man turns his head toward her for a moment. "I love you," she says. "Ditto," he says loudly, above the clatter of the air-boats. "Double-ditto." He grins at her and she begins to giggle. Then she sobs. She has not cried for many months. There seems something wrong with the way she is doing it. Everyone is astounded. The man drives a few more miles and then pulls into a gas station. The girl feels desperate about this man. She would do the unspeakable for him, the unforgivable, anything. She is lost but not in him. She wants herself lost and never found, in him. "I'll do anything for you," she cried. "Take an aspirin," he says. "Put your head on my shoulder."

The girl is sleeping alone in her apartment. The man has gone on a business trip. He assures her he will come back. He'll always come back, he says. When the girl is alone she measures her drinks out carefully. Carefully, she drinks 12 ozs. of bourbon in 2½ hours. When she is not with the man, she resumes her habit of listening to the radio. Frequently, she hears only the replies of "Action Line." "Yes," the Answer Man says, "in answer to your question, the difference between rising every morning at 6 or at 8 in the course of 40 years amounts to 29,200 hours or 3 years, 221 days and 16 hours which are equal to 8 hours a day for 10 years. So that rising at 6 will be the equivalent of adding 10 years to your life." The girls feels, by the Answer Man's tone, that he is a little repulsed by this. She washes her whisky glass out in the sink. Balloons are drifting around the kitchen. They float out of the kitchen and drift onto the balcony. They float down the hall and

bump against the closed door of the child's room. Some of
the balloons don't float but slump in the corners of the
kitchen like mounds of jelly. These are filled with water.
The girl buys many balloons and is always blowing them
up for the child. They play a great deal with the balloons,
breaking them over the stove or smashing the water-filled
ones against the walls of the bathroom. The girl turns off
the radio and falls asleep.

The girl touches her lover's face. She runs her fingers
across the bones. "Of course I love you," he says. "I want
us to have a life together." She is so restless. She moves her
hand across his mouth. There is something she doesn't
understand, something she doesn't know how to do. She
makes them a drink. She asks for a piece of gum. He hands
her a small crumpled stick, still in the wrapper. She is sure
that it is not the real thing. The Answer Man has said that
Lewis Carroll once invented a substitute for gum. She fears
that this is that. She doesn't want this! She swallows
it without chewing. "Please," she says. "Please what?" the
man replies, a bit impatiently.

Her former husband calls her up. It is autumn and the
heat is unusually oppressive. He wants to see the child. He
wants to take her away for a week to his lakeside house
in the middle of the state. The girl agrees to this. He arrives
at the apartment and picks up the child and nuzzles her.
He is a little heavier than before. He makes a little more
money. He has a different watch, wallet and key-ring. "What
are you doing these days?" the child's father asks. "I am
in love," she says.

The man does not visit the girl for a week. She doesn't
leave the apartment. She loses four pounds. She and the
child make Jell-O and they eat it for days. The girl remembers that after the baby was born, the only food the
hospital gave her was Jell-O. She thinks of all the water
boiling in hospitals everywhere for new mothers' Jell-O.
The girl sits on the floor and plays endlessly with the child.
The child is bored. She dresses and undresses herself. She
goes through everything in her small bureau drawer and tries

everything on. The girl notices a birthmark on the child's
thigh. It is very small and lovely, in the shape, the girl
thinks, of a wine glass. A doll's wine glass. The girl thinks
about the man constantly but without much exactitude.
She does not even have a photograph of him! She looks
through old magazines. He must resemble someone! Sometimes, late at night, when she thinks he might come to
her, she feels that the Answer Man arrives instead. He is
like a moving light, never still. He has the high temperature
and metabolism of a bird. On "Action Line," someone is
saying, "I live by the airport, and what is this that hits my
house, that showers my roof on takeoff? We can hear it.
What is this, I demand to know! My lawn is healthy, my
television reception is fine but something is going on without my consent and I am not well, my wife's had a stroke
and someone stole my stamp collection and took the
orchids off my trees." The girl sips her bourbon and shakes
her head. The greediness and wickedness of people, she
thinks, their rudeness and lust. "Well," the Answer Man
says, "each piece of earth is bad for something. Something
is going to get on it and the land itself is no longer safe.
It's weakening. If you dig deep enough to dip your seed,
beneath the crust you'll find an emptiness like the sky.
No, nothing's compatible to living in the long run. Next
caller, please." The girl goes to the telephone and dials
hurriedly. It is very late. She whispers, not wanting to
wake the child. There is static and humming. "I can't make
you out," the Answer Man shouts. "Are you a phronemo-
phobiac?" The girl says more firmly, "I want to know my
hour." "Your hour came, dear," he says. "It went when
you were sleeping. It came and saw you dreaming and it
went back to where it was."

The girl's lover comes to the apartment. She throws herself into his arms. He looks wonderful. She would do anything for him! The child grabs the pocket of his jacket and
swings on it with her full weight. "My friend," the child
says to him. "Why yes," the man says with surprise. They
drive the child to the nursery and then go out for a wonderful lunch. The girl begins to cry and spills the roll basket
on the floor. "What is it?" he asks. "What's wrong?" He

wearies of her, really. Her moods and palpitations. The
girl's face is pale. Death is not so far, she thinks. It is easily
arrived at. Love is further than death. She kisses him. She
cannot stop. She clings to him, trying to kiss him. "Be
calm," he says.

The girl no longer sees the man. She doesn't know anything about him. She is a gaunt, passive girl, living alone
with her child. "I love you," she says to the child. "Mommy
loves me," the child murmurs, "and Daddy loves me and
Grandma loves me and Granddaddy loves me and my
friend loves me." The girl corrects her, "Mommy loves
you," she says. The child is growing. In not too long the
child will be grown. When is this happening! She wakes
the child in the middle of the night. She gives her a glass
of juice and together they listen to the radio. A woman
is speaking on the radio. She says, "I hope you will not
think me vulgar." "Not at all," the Answer Man replies.
"He is never at a loss," the girl whispers to the child. The
woman says, "My husband can only become excited if he
feels that some part of his body is missing." "Yes," the
Answer Man says. The girl shakes the sleepy child. "Listen
to this," she says. "I want you to know about these things."
The unknown woman's voice continues, dimly. "A finger
or an eye or a leg. I have to pretend it's not there."

"Yes," the Answer Man says.

SECRETIVE

by Jane Augustine

If I don't tell someone, I'm not sure what will happen. I'll crack perhaps. I'm not sure I can even tell it to you, my secret friend, although you're utterly safe, the receiver of my thought-words. You're comfortable, sympathetic—as if you were somebody's mother (not mine) or a lady psychiatrist, foreign, a little drab, and as if you were sitting across from me at my kitchen table, nodding yes and asking me unformulated questions to which I have exact and full answers, with explanations.

My secret can't even be written in a journal, if I kept a journal. Even my nonsecrets look bad when written out in words. I'd have to write: "I spent all day Saturday downtown looking for the right lining material for my new coat. The lining almost never shows but I was annoyed by the sleazy taffetas and coarse satins and inadequate moires. The inside matters! I kept saying to myself, searching desperately. Almost everything I saw would do, more or less; I could put up with it if I had to, but nothing was exactly right. The lining should pick up one of the colors of the coat's tweed, I decided, but I didn't know which color. It should be a rich fabric but not stiff or heavy. But woven or knit? Or perhaps a contrasting color . . . ?"

You see how my journal would sound—just a list of absurd concerns that burn up my caring. You would probably agree with him that I'm stupid, if you saw my day-to-day life translated into words that way. Now, as you sit absorbing my thoughts, you're sympathetic. You're aware that there's more to me than just that I get involved with trivial matters not worth caring about. My mind latches onto them and labors over them while my secret lies down inside me escaping my attention. I know it's there, but only a little of it makes itself known to me.

If I kept a journal, I'd be tempted to write about him in it. Don't you think people delude themselves when they think that a journal or diary can be kept private? He'd find it and that would set him off again, no matter what I said. He couldn't bear my looking at him and recording him. And if I hinted at the secret, which of course he knows, he'd really blow up. "Who are you writing this to? How can you make up lies like this? You know that I have nothing to do with it—you, *you* bring it on yourself—"

You see why I can't speak out loud, why I have to send thought-words out to you. You understand the way it came about even if I can't explain it properly. You know my secret is a real secret. It really can't be told without showing me up, showing how I bring it on myself, and whatever I do to enrage him—even though I don't know what that is.

He says that I'm weak, and I try to counteract the weakness with misplaced aggressiveness. He says I try to hide my dependency pretending to be independent, learning to sew and getting a job and all that. I don't know about that; it sounds like doubletalk and yet there may be something in it. He's not stupid, he's well educated, a social worker; he's read a lot about what goes on in people's minds.

Writing the secret down in a journal would be bad enough, but worse would be if I ever dropped a hint to any of our friends, as I sometimes wish I could. But there I'd be, talking against my own husband, a complainer, a bitch—I don't want to be like that. It could be just temporary in him too, something that won't last—and then if word of it spread around . . . But it's awkward. Verna came over today, returning the sheath dress pattern, and I showed her how to insert one of those new invisible zippers. You can't see an opening anywhere; all the seams look stitched up—no sign of how to get in or get out.

Of course she looked at me and asked about it. I showed her how the kitchen cupboard door by the stove springs back sharply enough to blacken an eye. That's not so farfetched; after all, he says I do it to myself. Something in me drives him to uncontrollable outbursts. He was never like this before he married me, he says.

So this is what I need you to tell me: what do I do that
I don't see myself doing? It must be huge and obvious and
yet I can't see it. I try thinking back over all the times
it's happened. The last time (before this) was in December; he added up the bills and came into the kitchen yelling
that I'd spent three hundred dollars on the children's
clothing in a year and I had to stop being such a goddam
irresponsible spendthrift. "If you had to work," he yelled,
"you'd understand the value of money—"

Trying to keep him cool, I asked if maybe three hundred dollars wasn't what was spent on all four of us,
which wouldn't be too bad on an income of ten thousand
dollars. That's when it happened. Luckily my face wasn't
involved; I put on a long-sleeved blouse the next day, and
went and got a job typing in an insurance company.

This time—last night—it happened because I hired a
babysitter all day Saturday while I went downtown shopping for the lining material I never did buy. He exploded:
"You hired a goddam babysitter all day for nothing? The
girls are out of school on Saturdays, you ought to be with
them." Then I said—which I guess was a mistake: "You
can think of it this way: I earned the babysitter money."
I was horrified when I looked in the mirror this morning
and remembered that Verna was coming over.

But what's gone wrong? I thought learning to sew was
a good idea, a way to save money and show him I'm not
incompetent. But he says with my Vogue patterns and
highfalutin ideas I spend more on material than I would
on ready-to-wear. How do I know what I would have
spent on ready-to-wear? And he says I just got the job so
I could manipulate him and his money decisions by saying
it's my money. I don't think that's why I got the job, but
I recognize that the mind is full of twistings and turnings,
and mysterious hidden levels. There's more in it than I
can ever know about.

But maybe *you* know more, seeing it from an expert's
point of view. You can tell me about what's going on,
though I understand that I have to be honest with myself
and not block off what's happening even though it frightens
me. I've been reading, and I know that the mind is mostly
unconscious, that we all repress angry and hateful thoughts
and wishes, but at a price. Whenever there's a slip of the

tongue, part of the unconscious is revealed. Whenever there's an accident, there's a reason for it from earliest childhood, a sexual or incestuous reason that's too strong to be concealed and too terrible to be revealed.

So there are no accidents. It wouldn't make any difference if the kitchen-cupboard door *had* sprung back on me. Things like that just don't happen unless something is hidden in the unconscious mind. My abnormality had to earn it. After all he's a respected man, a professional. He works hard on his job and coaches the Little League in the park on Saturdays. When I go to watch a game, the parents tell me how good a coach he is, really driving the kids to win and building their character. But not by getting mad at them, just by keeping everything under control. I'm the only one he blows up at. No one else has ever seen him more than annoyed at a pop fly. I'm the *only* one—

Now you know the depth of my problem. If I told anyone what he's done to me, they wouldn't believe me. They'd whisper behind my back that I must be a real nut to say such things. Or they'd say, so fights happen in the best of families, but it takes two to tango. They'd say I was crazy if they saw me like this in my kitchen talking to yes, myself, in the only way that relieves me, as if I were my own understanding woman, my invented doctor who doesn't charge me twenty-five dollars an hour.

She's almost real, this listener that I imagine. I can almost see her, wavy grayish hair and searching eyes, rather stern. She sympathizes but she isn't going to let me get away with anything. I might be imagining myself too, as a woman who's trying hard to live right and do what her husband wants. But all the time there might be a woman in me to whom those words apply which he uses: manipulative, incompetent, secretive. . . .

Can't you give me some other words for myself? Like "conscientious, thoughtful, a hard tryer . . ." But it takes a friend to speak these compliments; I must only be flattering myself. . . .

Yes, of course I know you must remain impartial; you have to tell me the truth even if it's not on my side. So can't you tell me why I worry about trivial things like zippers and linings? Then I can get over being that way. I'm sure that's one thing he hates me for.

There. Self-scrutiny does help. I've discovered something.

But the next discovery is more frightening. This woman isn't just trivial, she's full of senseless anger. Sometimes it sticks in her throat till she nearly chokes to keep it back. A little thing like his saying, "You didn't sew that button on yet." Only a petty person would flare up over a remark like that. Her feelings aren't right. Really good people have the right kind of feelings deep inside; then the rest takes care of itself.

Oh, she has secrets all right. So now she has to make sure that no one sees more of the inside of her, no more black-and-blue coming to the surface. Then at least they can't say she's crazy, though they'd almost be right; crazy from keeping secrets and holding in. But that's the way it's got to be.

They can just say she wanders around in department stores all the time, with nothing but colors and fabrics running through her head. Sleazy taffeta, slippery nylon, inferior rayon. But the coat must be finished; it has to be properly lined.

And the lining must be a contrast to the outside of the coat, which is a soft blurry pinkish-orange tweed, the color of rubbed flesh, mixed in with knobs of scarlet. It's a fitted pattern. Now the inside will be a bright green, bright as a parrot's wing, an acid green knit of some tough synthetic fiber that will hang nicely but give only when give is needed. It'll do to hold the coat together, and will only show for a moment before it's hidden away, buttoned, on the closet hanger.

WORLD OF HEROES

by Anna Kavan

I try not to look at the stars. I can't bear to see them. They make me remember the time when I used to look at them and think, I'm alive, I'm in love and I'm loved. I only really lived that part of my life. I don't feel alive now. I don't love the stars. They never loved me. I wish they wouldn't remind me of being loved.

I was slow in starting to live at all. It wasn't my fault. If there had ever been any kindness I would not have suffered from a delayed maturity. If so much apprehension had not been instilled into me, I wouldn't have been terrified to leave my solitary unwanted childhood in case something still worse was waiting ahead. However, there was no kindness. The nearest approach to it was being allowed to sit on the back seats of the big cars my mother drove about in with her different admirers. This was in fact no kindness at all. I was taken along to lend an air of respectability. The two in front never looked around or paid the slightest attention to me, and I took no notice of them. I sat for hours and hours and for hundreds of miles inventing endless fantasies at the back of large and expensive cars.

The frightful slowness of a child's time. The interminable years of inferiority and struggling to win a kind word that is never spoken. The torment of self-accusation, thinking one must be to blame. The bitterness of longed-for affection bestowed on indifferent strangers. What future could have been worse? What could have been done to me to make me afraid to grow up out of such a childhood?

Later on, when I saw things more in proportion, I was always afraid of falling back into that ghastly black isolation of an uncomprehending, solitary, oversensitive child, the worst fate I could imagine.

My mother disliked and despised me for being a girl. From her I got the idea that men were a superior breed, the free, the fortunate, the splendid, the strong. My small adolescent adventures and timid experiments with boys who occasionally gave me rides on the backs of their motorbikes confirmed this. All heroes were automatically masculine. Men were kinder than women; they could afford to be. They were also fierce, unpredictable, dangerous animals: One had to be constantly on guard against them.

My feeling for high-powered cars presumably came from my mother too. Periodically, ever since I can remember, the craving has come over me to drive and drive, from one country to another, in a fast car. Hearing people talk about danger and death on the roads seems ludicrous, laughable. To me, a big car is a very safe refuge, and the only means of escape from all the ferocious cruel forces lurking in life and in human beings. Its metal body surrounds me like magic armor, inside which I'm invulnerable. Everybody I meet in the outside world treats me in the same contemptuous, heartless way, discrediting what I do, refusing to admit my existence. Only the man in the car is different. Even the first time I drive with him, I feel that he appreciates, understands me; I know I can make him love me. The car is a small speeding substitute world, just big enough for us both. A sense of intimacy is generated, a bond created between us. At once I start to love him a little. Occasionally it's the car I love first. The car can attract me to the man. When we are driving together, the three of us form one unit. We grow into each other. I forget about loneliness and inferiority, I feel fine.

In the outside world catastrophe always threatens. The news is always bad. Life tears into one like a mad rocket off course. The only hope of escaping is in a racing car.

At last I reached the age of freedom and was considered adult; but still my overprolonged adolescence made me look less than my age. X, a young American with a 2.6 liter Alfa Romeo and lots of money, took me for fifteen or sixteen. When I told him I was twenty-one, he burst out laughing, called me a case of retarded development, seemed to be making fun of me in a cruel way. I was frightened, ran away from him, traveled around with some so-called friends with whom I was hopelessly bored. After knowing X, they seemed insufferably dull, mediocre, conventional. Obsessed by longing for him and his car, I sent a telegram asking him to meet us. As soon as I'd done it, I grew feverish with excitement and dread, finally felt convinced the message would be ignored. How idiotic to invite such a crushing rejection. I should never survive the disappointment and shame.

I was shaking all over when we got to the place. It was evening. I hid in the shadows, kept my eyes down so as not to see him—not to see that he wasn't there. Then he was coming toward us. He shook hands with the others one by one, leaving me to the last. I thought, he wants to humiliate me. He's no more interested in me than he is in them. Utterly miserable, I wanted to rush off and lose myself in the dark. Suddenly he said my name, said he was driving me to another town, said good-bye to the rest so abruptly that they seemed to stand there, suspended, amazed, for the instant before I forgot their existence. He had taken hold of my arm, and was walking me rapidly to his car. He installed me in the huge, docile, captivating machine, and we shot away, the stars spinning loops of white fire all over the sky as we raced along the deserted roads.

That was how it began. I always think gratefully of X, who introduced me to the world of heroes.

The racetrack justifies tendencies and behavior which would be condemned as antisocial in other circumstances. Risks encountered nowhere else but in war are a commonplace of the racing drivers' existence. Knowing they may be killed any day, they live in a wartime atmosphere of recklessness, camaraderie and heightened perception. The contrast of their lighthearted audacity and their somber, sinister, menacing background gave them a personal glamour I found irresistible. They were all attractive to me, heroes, the bravest men in the world. Vaguely, I realized that they were also psychopaths, misfits, who played with death because they'd been unable to come to

terms with life in the world. Their games could only end
badly: Few of them survived more than a few years. They
were finished, anyhow, at thirty-five, when their reactions
began to slow down, disqualifying them for the one thing
they did so outstandingly well. They preferred to die
before this happened.

Whether they lived or died, tragedy was waiting for
them, only just around the corner, and the fact that they
had so little time added to their attraction. It also united
them in a peculiar, almost metaphysical way, as though
something of all of them was in each individual. I thought
of them as a sort of brotherhood, dedicated to their fatal
profession of speed.

They all knew one another, met frequently, often lived
in the same hotels. Their life was strictly nomadic. None
of them had, or wanted to have, a place of his own to
live in, even temporarily, far less a permanent home. The
demands of their work made any kind of settled existence
impossible. Only a few got married, and these marriages
always came unstuck very quickly. The wives were jealous
of the group feeling, they could not stand the strain, the
eternal separation, the homelessness.

I had never had a home, and, like the drivers, never
wanted one. But wherever I stayed with them was my
proper place, and I felt at home there. All my complicated
emotions were shut inside hotel rooms, like boxes inside
larger ones. A door, a window, a looking glass, impersonal
walls. The door and the window opened only on things
that had become unreal, the mirror only revealed myself.
I felt protected, shut away from the world as I was in a
car, safe in my retreat.

Although, after winning a race, they became for a short
time objects of adulation and public acclaim, these men
were not popular; the rest of humanity did not understand
them. Their clannishness, their flippant remarks and casual
manners were considered insulting; their unconventional
conduct judged as immoral. The world seemed not to see
either the careless elegance that appealed to me, or their
strict aristocratic code, based on absolute loyalty to each
other, absolute professional integrity, absolute fearlessness.

I loved them for being somehow above and apart from

the general gregarious mass of mankind, born adventurers, with a breezy disrespect for authority. Perhaps they felt I was another misfit, a rebel too. Or perhaps they were intrigued or amused by the odd combination of my excessively youthful appearance and wholly pessimistic intelligence. At all events, they received me as no other social group could ever have done—conventions, families, finances would have prevented it. Straightaway, they accepted my presence among them as perfectly natural, adopted me as a sort of mascot. They were regarded as wild, irresponsible daredevils; but they were the only people I'd ever trusted. I was sure that, unlike all the others I'd known, they would not let me down.

Their code prohibited jealousy or any bad feeling. Unpleasant emotional situations did not arise. Finding that I was safe among them, I perceived that it was unnecessary to be on my guard any longer. Their attitude was at the same time flattering and matter-of-fact. They were considerate without any elaborate chivalry, which would have embarrassed me, and they displayed a frank, if restrained, physical interest, quite willing, apparently, to love me for as long or short a time as I liked. When my affair with A was finally over, I simply got into B's car, and that was that. It all seemed exceedingly simple and civilized.

The situation was perfect for me. They gave me what I had always wanted but never had: a background, true friends. They were kind in their unsentimental racetrack way, treated me as one of themselves, shared with me their life histories and their cynical jokes, listened to me with attention, but did not press me to talk. I sewed on buttons for them, checked hotel and garage accounts, acted as unskilled mechanic, looked after them if they were injured in crashes or caught influenza.

At last I felt wanted, valued, as I'd longed to be all my life. At last I belonged somewhere, had a place, was some use in the world. For the very first time I understood the meaning of happiness, and it was easy for me to be truly in love with each of them. I could hardly believe I wasn't dreaming. It was incredible; but it was true, it was really happening. I never had time now to think or to get depressed, I was always in a car with one of them. I went on all the long rallies, won Grand Prix races, acted as co-driver or passenger as the occasion required. I loved it all, the speed, the exhaustion, the danger. I loved rushing down icy roads at ninety miles an hour, spinning around three times, and continuing nonstop without even touching the banked-up snow.

This was the one beautiful period of my life, when I drove all over the world, saw all its countries. The affection of these men, who risked their lives so casually, made me feel gay and wonderfully alive, and I adored them for it. By liking me, they had made the impossible happen. I was living a real fairy tale.

This miraculous state of affairs lasted for several years, and might have gone on some time longer. But, beyond my euphoria, beyond the warm lighthearted atmosphere they generated between them, the sinister threat in the background was always waiting. Disaster loomed over them like a circle of icy mountains, implacably drawing nearer: They'd developed a special attitude in self-defense. Because crashes and constant danger made each man die many times, they spoke of death as an ordinary event, for which the carelessness or recklessness of the individual was wholly responsible. Nobody ever said, "Poor old Z's had it," but, "Z asked for it, the crazy bastard, never more than one jump ahead of the mortuary." Their jargon had a brutal sound to outsiders. But, by speaking derisively of the victim, they deprived death of terror, made it seem something he could easily have avoided.

Without conscious reflection, I took it for granted that, when the time came, I would die on the track, like my friends: And this very nearly happened. The car crashed and turned four somersaults before it burst into flames, and the driver and the other passengers were killed instantly. I had the extreme bad luck to be dragged out of the blazing wreckage only three-quarters dead. Apparently my case was a challenge to the doctors of several hospitals, who, for the next two years, worked with obstinate persistence to save my life, while I persistently tried to discard it. I used to look in their cold, clinical eyes with loathing and helpless rage. They got their way in the end, and discharged me. I was pushed out again into the hateful world, alone, hardly able to walk, and disfigured by burns.

The drivers loyally kept in touch, wrote and sent presents to the hospitals, came to see me whenever they could. It was entirely my own fault that, as the months dragged on, the letters became fewer, the visits less and less frequent, until they finally ceased. I didn't want them to be sorry for me or to feel any obligation. I was sure my scarred face must repel them, so I deliberately drove them away.

I couldn't possibly go back to them: I had no heart, no vitality, for the life I'd so much enjoyed. I was no longer the gay, adventurous girl they had liked. All the same, if one of them had really exerted himself to persuade me, I might . . . That nobody made this special effort, or showed a desire for further intimacy, confirmed my conviction that I had become repulsive. Although there was a possible alternative explanation. At the time of the crash, I had been in love with the man who was driving, and hadn't yet reached the stage of singling out his successor. So, as I was the one who always took the initiative, none of them had any cause to feel closer to me than the rest. Perhaps if I had indicated a preference . . . But I was paralyzed by the guilt of my survival, as certain they all resented my being alive as if I'd caused their comrade's death.

What can I do now? What am I to become? How can I live in this world I'm condemned to but can't endure? They couldn't stand it either, so they made a world of their own. Well, they have each other's company, and they are heroes, whereas I'm quite alone, and have none of the qualities essential to heroism—the spirit, the toughness, the dedication. I'm back where I was as a child, solitary, helpless, unwanted, frightened.

It's so lonely, so terribly lonely. I hate being always alone. I so badly need someone to talk to, someone to love. Nobody looks at me now, and I don't want them to; I don't want to be seen. I can't bear to look at myself in the mirror. I keep away from people as much as I can. I know everyone is repelled and embarrassed by all these scars. .

There is no kindness left. The world is a cruel place full of men I shall never know, whose indifference terrifies me. If once in a while I catch someone's eye, his glance is as cold as ice, eyes look past eyes like searchlights crossing, with no more humanity or communication. In freezing despair, I walk down the street, trying to attract to myself a suggestion of warmth by showing in my expression . . . something . . . or something. . . . And everybody walks past me, refusing to see or to lift a finger. No one cares, no one will help me. An abstract impenetrable indifference in a stranger's eye is all I ever see.

The world belongs to heartless people and to machines which can't give. Only the others, the heroes, know how to give. Out of their great generosity they gave me the truth, paid me the compliment of not lying to me. Not one of them ever told me life was worth living. They are the only people I've ever loved. I think only of them, and of how they are lost to me. How never again shall I sit beside someone who loves me while the world races past. Never again cross the tropic of Capricorn, or, under the arctic stars, in the blackness of firs and spruce, see the black glitter of ice in starlight, in the cold snow countries.

The world in which I was really alive consisted of hotel bedrooms and one man in a car. But that world was enormous and splendid, containing cities and continents, forests and seas and mountains, plants and animals, the North Star and the Southern Cross. The heroes who showed me how to live also showed me everything, everywhere in the world.

My present world is reduced to their remembered faces, which have gone forever, which get further and further away. I don't feel alive any more. I see nothing at all of the outside world. There are no more oceans or mountains for me.

I don't look up now. I always try not to look at the stars. I can't bear to see them, because the stars remind me of loving and of being loved.

AND THE SOUL SHALL DANCE

by Wakako Yamauchi

It's all right to talk about it now. Most of the principals
are dead, except, of course, me and my younger brother,
and possibly Kiyoko Oka, who might be near forty-five
now, because, yes, I'm sure of it, she was fourteen then.
I was nine, and my brother about four, so he hardly
counts at all. Kiyoko's mother is dead, my father is dead,
my mother is dead, and her father could not have lasted
all these years with his tremendous appetite for alcohol
and pickled chilies—those little yellow ones, so hot they
could make your mouth hurt; he'd eat them like peanuts
and tears would surge from his bulging thyroid eyes in
great waves and stream down the dark coarse terrain of his
face.

My father farmed then in the desert basin resolutely
named Imperial Valley, in the township called Westmoreland; twenty acres of tomatoes, ten of summer squash, or
vice versa, and the Okas lived maybe a mile, mile and a
half, across an alkaline road, a stretch of greasewood,
tumbleweed and white sand, to the south of us. We didn't
hobnob much with them, because you see, they were a
childless couple and we were a family: father, mother,
daughter, and son, and we went to the Buddhist church on
Sundays where my mother taught Japanese, and the Okas
kept pretty much to themselves. I don't mean they were
unfriendly; Mr. Oka would sometimes walk over (he
rarely drove) on rainy days, all dripping wet, short and
squat under a soggy newspaper, pretending to need a
plow blade or a file, and he would spend the afternoon in
our kitchen drinking sake and eating chilies with my
father. As he got progressively drunker, his large mouth
would draw down and with the stream of tears, he looked
like a kindly weeping bullfrog

Not only were they childless, impractical in an area where large families were looked upon as labor potentials, but there was a certain strangeness about them. I became aware of it the summer our bathhouse burned down, and my father didn't get right down to building another, and a Japanese without a bathhouse . . . well, Mr. Oka offered us the use of his. So every night that summer we drove to the Okas' for our bath, and we came in frequent contact with Mrs. Oka, and this is where I found the strangeness.

Mrs. Oka was small and spare. Her clothes hung on her like loose skin and when she walked, the skirt about her legs gave her a sort of webbed look. She was pretty in spite of the boniness and the dull calico and the barren look; I know now she couldn't have been over thirty. Her eyes were large and a little vacant, although once I saw them fill with tears; the time I insisted we take the old Victrola over and we played our Japanese records for her. Some of the songs were sad, and I imagined the nostalgia she felt, but my mother said the tears were probably from yawning or from the smoke of her cigarettes. I thought my mother resented her for not being more hospitable; indeed, never a cup of tea appeared before us, and between them the conversation of women was totally absent: the rise and fall of gentle voices, the arched eyebrows, the croon of polite surprise. But more than this, Mrs. Oka was *different*.

Obviously she was shy, but some nights she disappeared altogether. She would see us drive into her yard and then lurch from sight. She was gone all evening. Where could she have hidden in that two-roomed house—where in that silent desert? Some nights she would wait out our visit with enormous forbearance, quietly pushing wisps of stray hair behind her ears and waving gnats away from her great moist eyes, and some nights she moved about with nervous agitation, her khaki canvas shoes slapping loudly as she walked. And sometimes there appeared to be welts and bruises on her usually smooth brown face, and she would sit solemnly, hands on lap, eyes large and intent on us. My mother hurried us home then: "Hurry, Masako, no need to wash well; hurry."

You see, being so poky, I was always last to bathe. I

think the Okas bathed after we left because my mother often reminded me to keep the water clean. The routine was to lather outside the tub (there were buckets and pans and a small wooden stool), rinse off the soil and soap, and then soak in the tub of hot hot water and contemplate. Rivulets of perspiration would run down the scalp.

When my mother pushed me like this, I dispensed with ritual, rushed a bar of soap around me and splashed about a pan of water. So hastily toweled, my wet skin trapped the clothes to me, impeding my already clumsy progress. Outside, my mother would be murmuring her many apologies and my father, I knew, would be carrying my brother whose feet were already sandy. We would hurry home.

I thought Mrs. Oka might be insane and I asked my mother about it, but she shook her head and smiled with her mouth drawn down and said that Mrs. Oka loved her sake. This was unusual, yes, but there were other unusual women we knew. Mrs. Nagai was bought by her husband from a geisha house; Mrs. Tani was a militant Christian Scientist; Mrs. Abe, the midwife, was occult. My mother's statement explained much: sometimes Mrs. Oka was drunk and sometimes not. Her taste for liquor and cigarettes was a step in the realm of men; unusual for a Japanese wife, but at that time, in that place, and to me, Mrs. Oka loved her sake in the way my father loved his, in the way of Mr. Oka, the way I loved my candy. That her psychology may have demanded this anesthetic, that she lived with something unendurable, did not occur to me. Nor did I perceive the violence of emotions that the purple welts indicated—or the masochism that permitted her to display these wounds to us.

In spite of her masculine habits, Mrs. Oka was never less than a woman. She was no lady in the area of social amenities; but the feminine in her was innate and never left her. Even in her disgrace, she was a small broken sparrow, slightly floppy, too slowly enunciating her few words, too carefully rolling her Bull Durham, cocking her small head and moistening the ocher tissue. Her aberration was a protest of the life assigned her; it was obstinate, but unobserved, alas, unheeded. "Strange" was the only concession we granted her.

Toward the end of summer, my mother said we couldn't continue bathing at the Okas'; when winter set in we'd all catch our death from the commuting and she'd always felt dreadful about our imposition on Mrs. Oka. So my father took the corrugated tin sheets he'd found on the highway and had been saving for some other use and built up our bathhouse again. Mr. Oka came to help.

While they raised the quivering tin walls, Mr. Oka began to talk. His voice was sharp and clear above the low thunder of the metal sheets.

He told my father he had been married in Japan previously to the present Mrs. Oka's older sister. He had a child by the marriage, Kiyoko, a girl. He had left the two to come to America intending to send for them soon, but shortly after his departure, his wife passed away from an obscure stomach ailment. At the time, the present Mrs. Oka was young and had foolishly become involved with a man of poor reputation. The family was anxious to part the lovers and conveniently arranged a marriage by proxy and sent him his dead wife's sister. Well that was all right, after all, they were kin, and it would be good for the child when she came to join them. But things didn't work out that way; year after year he postponed calling for his daughter, couldn't get the price of fare together, and the wife—ahhh, the wife, Mr. Oka's groan was lost in the rumble of his hammering.

He cleared his throat. The girl was now fourteen, he said, and begged to come to America to be with her own real family. Those relatives had forgotten the favor he'd done in accepting a slightly used bride, and now tormented his daughter for being forsaken. True, he'd not sent much money, but if they knew, if they only knew how it was here.

"Well," he sighed, "who could be blamed? It's only right she be with me anyway."

"That's right," my father said.

"Well, I sold the horse and some other things and managed to buy a third-class ticket on the Taiyo-Maru. Kiyoko will get here the first week of September." Mr. Oka glanced toward my father, but my father was peering into a bag of nails. "I'd be much obliged to you if your wife and little girl," he rolled his eyes toward me, "would take kindly to her. She'll be lonely."

Kiyoko-san came in September. I was surprised to see so very nearly a woman; short, robust, buxom: the female counterpart of her father; thyroid eyes and protruding teeth, straight black hair banded impudently into two bristly shucks, Cuban heels and white socks. Mr. Oka brought her proudly to us.

"Little Masako here," for the first time to my recollection, he touched me; he put his rough fat hand on top of my head, "is very smart in school. She will help you with your school work, Kiyoko," he said.

I had so looked forward to Kiyoko-san's arrival. She would be my soul mate; in my mind I had conjured a girl of my own proportions: thin and tall, but with the refinement and beauty I didn't yet possess that would surely someday come to the fore. My disappointment was keen and apparent. Kiyoko-san stepped forward shyly, then retreated with a short bow and small giggle, her fingers pressed to her mouth.

My mother took her away. They talked for a long time —about Japan, about enrollment in American school, the clothes Kiyoko-san would need, and where to look for the best values. As I watched them, it occurred to me that I had been deceived: this was not a child, this was a woman. The smile pressed behind her fingers, the way of her nod, so brief, like my mother when father scolded her: the face was inscrutable, but something—maybe spirit—shrank visibly, like a piece of silk in water. I was disappointed; Kiyoko-san's soul was barricaded in her unenchanting appearance and the smile she fenced behind her fingers.

She started school from third grade, one below me, and as it turned out, she quickly passed me by. There wasn't much I could help her with except to drill her on pronunciation—the "L" and "R" sounds. Every morning walking to our rural school: land, leg, library, loan, lot; every afternoon returning home: ran, rabbit, rim, rinse, roll. That was the extent of our communication; friendly but uninteresting.

One particularly cold November night—the wind outside was icy; I was sitting on my bed, my brother's and mine,. oiling the cracks in my chapped hands by lamplight—someone rapped urgently at our door. It was Kiyoko-san; she was hysterical, she wore no wrap, her teeth were chattering, and except for the thin straw zori, her feet were bare. My mother led her to the kitchen, started a pot of tea, and gestured to my brother and me to retire. I lay very still but because of my brother's restless tossing and my father's snoring, was unable to hear much. I was aware, though, that drunken and savage brawling had brought Kiyoko-san to us. Presently they came to the bedroom. I feigned sleep. My mother gave Kiyoko-san a gown and pushed me over to make room for her. My mother spoke firmly: "Tomorrow you will return to them; you must not leave them again. They are your people." I could almost feel Kiyoko-san's short nod.

All night long I lay cramped and still, afraid to intrude into her hulking back. Two or three times her icy feet jabbed into mine and quickly retreated. In the morning I found my mother's gown neatly folded on the spare pillow. Kiyoko-san's place in bed was cold.

She never came to weep at our house again but I know she cried: her eyes were often swollen and red. She stopped much of her giggling and routinely pressed her fingers to her mouth. Our daily pronunciation drill petered off from lack of interest. She walked silently with her shoulders hunched, grasping her books with both arms, and when I spoke to her in my halting Japanese, she absently corrected my prepositions.

Spring comes early in the Valley; in February the skies are clear though the air is still cold. By March, winds are vigorous and warm and wild flowers dot the desert floor, cockleburs are green and not yet tenacious, the sand is crusty underfoot, everywhere there is the smell of things growing and the first tomatoes are showing green and bald.

As the weather changed, Kiyoko-san became noticeably more cheerful. Mr. Oka who hated so to drive could often be seen steering his dusty old Ford over the road that passes our house, and Kiyoko-san sitting in front would sometimes wave gaily to us. Mrs. Oka was never with them. I thought of these trips as the westernizing of Kiyoko-san: with a permanent wave, her straight black hair became tangles of tiny frantic curls; between her text-books she carried copies of *Modern Screen* and *Photoplay*, her clothes were gay with print and piping, and she bought a pair of brown suede shoes with alligator trim. I can see her now picking her way gingerly over the deceptive white peaks of alkaline crust.

At first my mother watched their coming and going with vicarious pleasure. "Probably off to a picture show; the stores are all closed at this hour," she might say. Later her eyes would get distant and she would muse, "They've left her home again; Mrs. Oka is alone again, the poor woman."

Now when Kiyoko-san passed by or came in with me on her way home, my mother would ask about Mrs. Oka— how is she, how does she occupy herself these rainy days, or these windy or warm or cool days. Often the answers were polite: "Thank you, we are fine," but sometimes Kiyoko-san's upper lip would pull over her teeth, and her voice would become very soft and she would say, "Drink, always drinking and fighting." At those times my mother would invariably say, "Endure, soon you will be marrying and going away."

Once a young truck driver delivered crates at the Oka farm and he dropped back to our place to tell my father that Mrs. Oka had lurched behind his truck while he was backing up and very nearly let him kill her. Only the daguhter pulling her away saved her, he said. Thoroughly unnerved, he stopped by to rest himself and talk about it. Never, never, he said in wide-eyed wonder, had he seen a drunken Japanese woman. My father nodded gravely, "Yes, it's unusual," he said and drummed his knees with his fingers.

Evenings were longer now, and when my mother's migraines drove me from the house in unbearable self-pity, I would take walks in the desert. One night with the warm wind against me, the dune primrose and yellow poppies closed and fluttering, the greasewood swaying in languid orbit, I lay on the white sand beneath a shrub and tried to disappear.

A voice sweet and clear cut through the half-dark of the evening:

> Red lips press against a glass
> Drink the purple wine
> And the soul shall dance

Mrs. Oka appeared to be gathering flowers. Bending, plucking, standing, searching, she added to a small bouquet she clasped. She held them away: looked at them slyly, lids lowered, demure, then in a sudden and sinuous movement, she broke into a stately dance. She stopped, gathered more flowers, and breathed deeply into them. Tossing her head, she laughed—softly, beautifully, from her dark throat. The picture of her imagined grandeur was lost to me, but the delusion that transformed the bouquet of tattered petals and sandy leaves, and the aloneness of a desert twilight into a fantasy that brought such joy and abandon made me stir with discomfort. The sound broke Mrs. Oka's dance. Her eyes grew large and her neck tense—like a cat on the prowl. She spied me in the bushes. A peculiar chill ran through me. Then abruptly and with childlike delight, she scattered the flowers around her and walked away singing:

> Falling, falling, petals on a wind . . .

That was the last time I saw Mrs. Oka. She died before the spring harvest. It was pneumonia. I didn't attend the funeral, but my mother said it was sad. Mrs. Oka looked peaceful, and the minister expressed the irony of the long separation of Mother and Child and the short-lived reunion; hardly a year together, she said. We went to help Kiyoko-san address and stamp those black-bordered acknowledgments.

When harvest was over, Mr. Oka and Kiyoko-san moved out of the Valley. We never heard from them or saw them again and I suppose in a large city, Mr. Oka found some sort of work, perhaps as a janitor or a dishwasher and Kiyoko-san grew up and found someone to marry.

THE GOOD HUMOR MAN

by Rebecca Morris

All through that hot, slow summer, I lived alone, on ice-cream sandwiches and gin, in a one-room apartment on Carmine Street, waiting while James divorced me. In June he sent a letter saying, "Dear Anne, I have gone West to get the divorce." I was not sure where he meant by "West" and I did not believe he could just do that, without me, until I noticed that he had used the definite article. James was an English instructor at Columbia, and his grammar was always precise. So I knew that he could. The letter arrived two days before graduation. I remember taking it from the mailbox as I left the apartment, stopping just inside the shadow of the doorway to open it. Outside, the sun glanced off Carmine Street and rose in waves of heat, assaulting the unemptied garbage cans by the stoop. For the past week I had been planning to go to graduation. I wanted to see James walk in the academic procession as a member of the faculty, wearing a cap and gown. When the pain struck, I also felt a childish chagrin at having been disappointed.

For the past year, everything had gone badly with us, and James had wanted a separation. He had met someone else. I didn't want him to leave, and for months I alternated between anger and tears. With each new outburst, he became more determined. I never meant to throw his copy of Milton out the window. Finally, just after Christmas, James left, packing his share of our belongings. I didn't know where he had moved to; he wouldn't tell me. I put the rest—one half of everything—in storage and sublet a small walkup in the South Village. I still wanted to see James, though I knew there was someone else, and I began to search for him. He did not want to encounter me; he hated scenes. That winter and spring, I pursued James through the cold, crowded streets of New York like an incompetent sleuth. What I remember of those sad months merges into one speeded-up sequence, as silent and jumpy as an old movie.

It started one January afternoon, chilly and gray. I was wearing a trenchcoat and scarf. Rain blew in on me where I stood, in the doorway of the Chinese laundry on Amsterdam Avenue. My bangs were dripping down onto my dark glasses, so that I could scarcely see who got off the No. 11 bus opposite Columbia. I was coming down with a damn cold. Inside, the Chinaman could be seen talking rapidly to his wife. He pointed repeatedly to me and then to his watch.

In February, I spotted James leaving Butler Library. He glanced nervously over his shoulder. Four girls in scarves and trenchcoats were approaching from various directions of the campus; they were converging on the library. His cheek twitched and he pulled his coat collar high up around his neck.

March, and I sat on a stool looking out the window of the Chock Full O'Nuts at 116th Street and Broadway, watching the subway entrance. The sun burned through the plate glass, and the four cups of coffee I had already drunk were making me so hot that the subway entrance seemed to swim. I ordered an orange drink.

April. James started down the steps of the New York Public Library. Forty-second Street was jammed with marchers. It was a peace demonstration and they were walking—carrying signs, carrying babies—to the U.N. Some were singing. On the other side of Fifth Avenue, a girl in dark glasses and a trenchcoat jumped up and down, apparently waving to him. He ducked his head and slipped in among the New Jersey contingent, whose signs proclaimed that they had walked from New Brunswick. Someone handed him a sign. He held it in front of his face and crossed Fifth Avenue. The girl in dark glasses greeted her friend, a woman in tweeds, and they walked off toward Peck & Peck. I stepped out from behind the south lion and joined the march.

And then May. I was baby-sitting for another faculty

wife, who supplied me with an infant in yellow overalls
and a large aluminum stroller. Under new leaves, cine-
matically green, we traveled slowly back and forth, bumping over the bricks of Campus Walk, courting sunstroke.
It was my most effective disguise. I concentrated my attention on Hamilton Hall, trying to see in the windows. Suddenly there was a rending howl from the stroller. I went
rigid with shock: I had forgotten about the baby. James,
disguised as a Ph.D., left by a side entrance.

June. Once again I was in that doorway on Carmine
Street. I was always standing in that doorway. I was about
to cry, and then I walked down the street unable to stop
crying. I didn't know where I was going.

And so I lived in the one room I had sublet all that
summer. I can still see it. There was a couch, a grand
piano, and a window that looked out onto a tree and the
back of Our Lady of Pompeii School. (The first morning,
I was abruptly awakened by a loudspeaker ordering me to
wear my hat tomorrow to mass. I was confused; I didn't
think I had a hat.) The couch, the piano, and I were the
three largest objects in the apartment, and we felt a kin-
ship. It was very quiet when the school term ended. I slept
on the couch and set my orange-juice glass on the grand
piano. The one or two people whom I knew in New York
seemed to have left for the summer. They were faculty
people anyway—more James's friends than mine. The
part-time job I had in a branch of the Public Library was
over; they had gone on summer hours.

I see it so clearly—the window, the couch, the glass on
the piano. It is as if I am still there and that endless summer is just beginning. I pour a little more gin in my orange
juice. I am drinking orange juice because it has vitamin
C, and I don't like gin straight. Gin is for sleep; it is in-
fallible. I sit on the couch facing the piano and switch the
light off behind me. Through the leaves of the tree I can
see the lighted back windows of Leroy Street. The dark air
coming in my open window is sweet, smelling of night,
garbage, and cats. Sounds hover just outside, hesitating to
cross the sill. I lean to hear them, and sit in the window,
placing my orange juice on the fire escape. Down through
the black iron slats I can dimly make out one . . . two,
three neighborhood cats stalking each other, brushing

through the high weeds, converging toward some lusty surprise. On the top of the piano there is a metronome. I reach over and release its armature. The pendulum swings free—*tock*-over, *tock*-over. I sit looking out across the night. *Tock* in the heavy, slow darkness. *Tock*-over. People framed in the Leroy Street windows are eating at tables, talking soundlessly, passing back and forth. Yellow light filters down in shadows, through the leaves and onto the court, darkly outlining the high wild grass, the rusted cans and gray bottles. I reach over and slide the weight all the way down. The pendulum springs away from my hand, ticking wildly, gathering velocity. Accelerando! In the dark below, the cats dance.

When I awake the next morning, it is already hot and my head hurts. I carefully circle the piano and fill the bathroom basin with cold water. I plunge my face into it, staring down through the cold at the pockmarked porcelain, the gray rubber stopper, until my lungs hurt. After a few minutes, I leave the apartment, bangs dripping, walk through the dark hallway, down a flight of stairs, and out onto the burning pavement of Carmine Street. Pushing against the heat, I cross to the luncheonette on Father Demo Square. This is where I buy my morning ice-cream sandwich. The ice cream is for protein, its cold for my head; the two chocolate-cookie layers merely make it manageable. The sun dries my wet bangs into stiff points over my throbbing forehead. I squint and wish I had my dark glasses. Standing by the corner of Bleecker and Sixth Avenue is a glaring white metal pushcart. A squat man in white pants and rolled shirt sleeves leans a hairy arm on its handle and with the other wipes his brow beneath his white cap. Along the side of the cart, brown letters on a yellow background announce CHOCOLATE MALT GOOD HUMOR. I walk toward the sign, drawn slowly across Bleecker Street. On the sidewalk chairs at Provenzano's Fish Market two old Italians are slipping clams down their throats, sipping juice from the shells. Dead fish, plumped in barrels of ice, eye me, baleful but cool. The air smells of fish and lemon. I confront the Good Humor man and we squint at each other. "Chocolate Malt Good Humor," I say.

The next week, the Good Humor flavor changes. As I

cross Carmine Street, dry-mouthed and stunned in the sunny morning, I read STRAWBERRY SHORTCAKE GOOD HUMOR. The letters, red against pink, vibrate in the glare. Behind the Good Humor cart, Bleecker Street is in motion. Provenzano's has strung black-and-silver eels in the window. The shop awnings are unrolled, and the canopied vegetable carts form an arcade up toward Seventh Avenue. Italian housewives in black are arguing with the vendors, ruffling lettuces, squeezing the hot flesh of tomatoes, fondling gross purple eggplants. Ice melts and runs from the fish barrels. I tear the wrapper of my Good Humor—frozen cake crumbs over strawberry-rippled vanilla ice cream— and, tasting its cold, proceed up this noisy *galleria*. My sandals leak, and I hold my breath passing the clam bar. Loose cabbage leaves scush under my soles, and strawberry sherbet runs down the stick onto my fingers. It is another hot day. At one o'clock, the Department of Parks outdoor swimming pool on the corner of Carmine, where Seventh Avenue becomes Varick Street, is going to open. I have discovered that for thirty-five cents I can stay there until seven in the evening, swimming endless lengths, pastorally shielded from Seventh Avenue by the bathhouse and the two-story Hudson Park branch public library. There my neighbors and I lie and tan on the hot city cement, shivering when the late-afternoon shadow of the building creeps over the pale water and turns it dark green. I stay there late every day, until all warmth is gone and evening falls. I no longer cry. I merely wait.

In the last week of June (Coconut Good Humor—a shaggy all-white confection of shredded coconut frozen on vanilla ice cream), I receive a letter from a Fifth Avenue lawyer telling me that he represents James and that I must consult him in his offices. I find his address formidable. It reminds me that I have not left my safe, low neighborhood for weeks. When I arrive, the lawyer is all smiles and amiability. I sit tensely, feeling strange in white gloves and high heels, while he tells me that James is in Reno, establishing a residence. He asks me if I have a lawyer of my own. I shake my head; I do not want a lawyer. This seems to surprise and annoy him. He shows me a paper that I may sign delegating some Nevada lawyer to represent me. It is only a form, but it is necessary. When it is all over, he says I may have some money, a fair and equable share of our joint assets—if I sign the paper. He offers me a cigarette while I think about it, but I am wearing gloves and I refuse. I do not want to take them off, as if this gesture will somehow make me vulnerable. My gloved hands in my lap look strange, too white below my brown arms. I stare at them and wish I were back on Carmine Street. The lawyer's office is very elegant, with green velvet curtains and an Oriental rug. There is a slim-legged sofa and a low marble-topped coffee table. All of the walls are paneled in dark oak, and there is a fireplace. I wonder who he is trying to kid. The lawyer pretends to reasonableness. I only want to see James. I do not want to sign anything. I shake my head; I will wait. He looks pained. He does not say so, but he manages to indicate that I am being foolish and unreasonable. I nod yes, and sit mute. I want to tell this man that when James comes home I am going to be perfect. I wish someone could tell James now that I have stopped crying. The lawyer sighs and takes out a summons, explaining that he is serving me now, if that is all right with me, because he would only have to send someone to serve me with it later. This is saving us both trouble. I nod and hold my hands in my lap. I wonder what would happen if I suddenly jumped up and hid behind the sofa. He extends the paper over his desk, and I watch it come nearer, until it wavers in front of my chest. I reach out and take it. The summons orders me to answer James's complaint in Nevada within twenty days and give reason why I should not be divorced, or be judged by default. I fold the summons in half and put it in my straw handbag. The lawyer smiles, still talking as he walks me to the elevator and shakes my hand. I am glad I am wearing gloves. He is not my friend.

On the Fourth of July, the Good Humor company exceeds itself and, in a burst of confectionery patriotism, produces Yankee Doodle Dandy Good Humor. I admire it as I turn it around on its stick. Frozen red, white, and blue coconut on a thin coating of white encasing strawberry-striped vanilla ice cream. I salute the Good Humor man as he hands me my change.

I spend most of my time at the pool now. On hot days,

the whole neighborhood lines Seventh Avenue, waiting to get in. We stand outside the brick bathhouse in the sun, smelling chlorine on the city air and eating ice cream to keep cool—children, housewives with babies, retired men, office workers taking their vacations at home. Inside the bathhouse—women's locker room to the left, men's to the right—we hurry into our bathing suits, stuffing our clothes into green metal lockers. The air is steamy from the showers. Children shriek and splash, running through the icy footbath that leads to the pool. Out in the sunlight, we greet the water with shouts, embracing the cold shock, opening our eyes beneath the silent green chill to see distorted legs of swimmers and then breaking the sun-glazed surface again, into the noise and splashing. I wear my old black racing suit from college and slather white cream over my nose. Around the pool edge, four teen-age lifeguards in orange Department of Parks suits rove the cement or take turns sitting astride the high painted iron guard chair. They are neighborhood heroes and accept admiration from small boys with rough graciousness. The pool cop rolls up his blue shirtsleeves and sits with his cap in the doorway of the first-aid room, drinking Coca-Cola. We greet each other and exchange views on the heat. He looks wistfully at the pale aqua water, but he is on duty. I line up behind the crowd at the diving board. I am working on my one-and-a-half this week, pounding the yellow plank, trying to get some spring out of the stiff wood. My form is good, and the board conceals what I lack in daring. Sometimes Ray Palumbo, Paul Anthony, and Rocky (I never did learn his last name), three of the guards, practice with me. We criticize each other and take turns holding a bamboo pole out in front of the board, high above the water, for the others to dive over and try to enter the water neatly. I am teaching Ray's little sister, Ellen, to back-dive, and her shoulders are rosy from forgetting to arch. We all stand around the board, dripping in the sun, and talk about swimming. The boys are shy with me and respectful of my age, but with their friends they are great wits; they patrol the pool, chests out for the benefit of the teen-age girls, swinging their whistles before them like censers.

I have begun to know the other regular swimmers, too. Only the very young and the very old are as free as I am. There is Paul's grandfather, who is retired; he swims a stately breast stroke the length of the pool, smiling, with his white head held high. And Mama Vincenzio, a dignified sixty, who arrives each evening resplendent in a black dressmaker suit three feet wide. She waits her turn with us at the four-foot board, wobbles to its end, and drops off, *ka-plunk*. She does this over and over, never sinking more than a foot or two below the surface before she bobs up again: *pasta*. I am not sure that she can swim, but, on the other hand, she doesn't sink, and she propels herself to the ladder as if she were sweeping floors. We smile shyly at each other for two weeks. When I finally ask her why she comes so late, she tells me she cooks supper for ten people each evening. I also recognize Mr. Provenzano, who closes the store at four-thirty in the summer and comes swimming. I have taught him to scull feet first, and now when I pass his store in the mornings he offers me a peeled shrimp or—I hold my breath and swallow—a raw clam. I sit in the sun, dangling my feet in the water, and think of James. I try imagining him around a roulette wheel or on a dude ranch, but it doesn't work. My idea of Reno is limited. I know he should be studying, and I am sure there can't be a good library there. I wonder what he is doing, but I cannot visualize a thing. When I try, his face begins to look like a photograph I have of him, but I know he never looked like that photograph. This frightens me, so I don't think at all. I swim, and in the evenings I drink.

The thirty-first of July is my birthday. I am twenty-five years old. It is also the day of our trial. I will not know this, however, until the twenty-seventh of August, when the divorce decree arrives in the mail. In the morning's mail I receive a funny card from my mother and one from my aunt. My mother encloses a small check "to buy something you need." I buy a bottle of Gordon's gin. When I announce my birthday to the Good Humor man, he presents me with a Hawaiian Pineapple Good Humor, gratis. It looks like a good day.

My regular friends are already at the pool when I arrive, and we wave to each other. From the two-foot board,

Ellen Palumbo shouts for me to watch. She has lost her
rubber band, and long black hair streams over her
shoulders. Still waving, she turns carefully backward, bal-
ancing on her toes, and then, arching perfectly, as I have
taught her, falls *splat* on her shoulders in the water. I wince
and smile encouragingly as she surfaces. Rocky is in the
water doing laps of flutter kick, holding on to a red
Styrofoam kickboard. I get another board from the first-
aid room and join him. We race through the green water,
maneuvering around small boys playing water tag; our
feet churn spray. Suddenly my shoulder is grabbed and
I am ducked from behind by Rocky's ten-year-old brother,
Tony. My kickboard bobs away, and Rocky and I go
after Tony, who is swimming quickly to the deep end. He
escapes up the ladder and races to the diving board.
Thumbing his nose, he executes a comic dive in jackknife
position, one leg extended, ending in a high, satisfying
splash. It is the signal for follow-the-leader. With shouts,
children arrive from all sides of the pool, throwing themselves off the yellow board in imitation.

On the deck, Paul's grandfather is sunning himself, eyes
closed, smiling upward toward heaven. I pull myself out
of the water and join him. He squints and grins tooth-
lessly, delighted to have someone to talk to. The night
before, he has been to see a free outdoor Shakespeare
performance. A mobile theatre unit is performing in our
neighborhood this week, in Walker Park playground. We
sit together in puddles on the cement, leaning against the
bathhouse wall, and he tells me the story of *King Lear*.
He has been going to the free Shakespeare performances
every summer since they began and has seen each play
two or three times, except for *Richard II*; he saw that one
six times. We watch the boys diving, and he proudly lists
all the plays he has seen. When I admit that I never seen
one of the open-air performances, he says I must. He
thinks for a minute, then shyly offers to escort me. He will
wait in the ticket line at Walker Park this evening and
save me a place. I protest, but he says he has nothing at all
to do in the evening and he probably will go again. I tell
him it is my birthday. He smiles; July is a good month
to be born. See?—he holds up his wrinkled, brown hands

and turns them over in the sun; on the second of July he
was seventy.

When I arrive at the playground that evening, the line
seems endless. It stretches along Hudson Street, and I pass
whole families seated on the cement, eating supper out of
paper bags, reading books, playing cards. Ice-cream vendors wheel carts up and down. I recognize my Good
Humor man, and we wave to each other. He is selling
sherbet sticks to two girls. Frost steams up from the cold
depths when he opens his cart. Mr. Anthony is at the front
of the line; he must have been waiting for hours. He is
wearing a good black wool suit, of an old-fashioned cut.
It is a little too big, as if he has shrunk within it. I suspect
that it is the suit he wears to weddings and funerals, and
I am glad that I have put on my green linen dress, even if
it will go limp in the heat. I have braided my wet hair
and wound it round my head in a damp coronet. I look
like a lady. We smile shyly, proud of our finery.

At eight, the line begins moving into the playground,
where the Parks Department has put up wooden bleachers.
They form a semicircle around the mobile stage; folding
chairs are ranged in rows in front of the bleachers. We
surge through the entrance with the crowd and find seats
quite close to the apron. Behind the gray scaffolding of the
stage I can see the wall of the handball court and the
trees on Leroy Street; to the south, the old Food and
Maritime Trades High School. Trumpets and recorded
Elizabethan music herald our arrival. The crowd fills the
playground, and the sky gradually darkens. Floodlights
dim, and light falls upon the scaffolding. Onstage, Lear
summons his three daughters; the play begins. Mr.
Anthony and I lean forward from our folding chairs,
drawn into the court of Britain. Under the calm, blinking
stars, Lear runs mad, contending with the far-off rumble
of traffic on Hudson Street. High above, an airplane passes.

During intermisson, I tell Mr. Anthony all I can remember about the Elizabethan stage, of the theatre that was a
wooden O. We eat ice cream out of Dixie cups with
miniature wooden paddles, and he compliments me. I
would be a good teacher; in this city they need teachers.
Later, as the final act closes, we sit and weep, on our fold-

ing chairs, for Lear, for Cordelia, for ourselves. "Never, never, never, never, never." Floodlights open over the playground; it is over. We crowd out with a thousand others onto Clarkson Street, past the dark swimming pool that is reflecting the street lights, to Seventh Avenue. On the way home, Mr. Anthony buys me a glass of red wine at Emilio's to celebrate. We walk by the dark steps of Our Lady of Pompeii, and on my doorstep we smile at each other and shake hands.

On August 27, the decree arrives—four pieces of typed paper stapled to heavy blue backing, with two gold seals. It looks like a diploma. I read it in the doorway, then walk back upstairs and drop it inside the lid of the grand piano. It is all over, but just now I am late. I eat my toasted almond Good Humor hurriedly, on my way to the pool. The Parks Department has been giving free swimming lessons to beginners, from ten o'clock to twelve o'clock in the mornings, and I help teach. When I get there, there are at least thirty children waiting for me around the pool edge, kicking their feet in the water.

That summer, Labor Day weekend comes early. Few people in my neighborhood are leaving town, and the pool is crowded; everyone goes swimming. The pool will be closing soon. It is my last swim. Tomorrow I begin at P.S. 84 as a substitute teacher; I want to find out if Mr. Anthony is right. The day is hot, making the water icy by contrast. My bathing suit has bleached to a sooty gray now, and my wet hair drips in a long braid down my back. Children shout and splash, and the tarred seams on the pool bottom leap and break in refracted patterns on the moving water. At the far end, in the playground, old men throw boccie. My dark glasses begin sliding down the white cream on my nose. I push them up and join my friends sunning beyond the diving boards. The Good Humon man has parked his truck in the street, just beyond the wire fence. Children range the fence, handing dimes and nickels through, carefully drawing ice-cream sticks in. Mama Vincenzio has come early today, and she buys this week's special, Seven Layer Cake Super Humor, for her two noisy grandchildren and me. We eat them carefully,

backs to the sun, counting to make sure we get seven different layers of ice cream and alternating chocolate. The children's faces smear with melted chocolate, and ice cream
runs down my arm to the elbow. I toss my stick in the
trash can and dive into the water. The green chill slides
over me, and I move in long strokes toward the bottom,
cool and weightless. Ellen Palumbo passes me and we bubble faces at each other. When my air runs out, I pick up a
stray bobby pin as my civic duty (it would leave a rust
mark on the bottom) and, flexing, push to the surface.
Oooh.

From the guard chair, Ray beckons to me, and I swim
over. For weeks, Rocky and Ray have been working on
flips, somersaulting in tucked position. They have reached
a point where they have perfected a double flip—two of
them, arms linked, somersaulting in unison. All of the
younger boys have been imitating them, working variations
—forward, backward, spinning in twos above the green
water. We have had one broken leg. Now Ray thinks that a
triple flip can be done. No one has tried it yet, but if they
can do a double—why not? It will be dangerous, of course.
If anyone is off, everyone may get hurt. You have to have
reliable buddies. He and Rocky wonder if I will try it with
them. I'm not as daring as their friends, but my form is
better. I won't open at the wrong time. They tell me that I
always keep my head. I swallow, standing there in the sun,
and wonder if they have ever seen me weeping up a fit over
on the Gansevoort Pier, crying into the Hudson as I angrily
skip stones. I nod and promise not to crack us up. I am
apprehensive.

Rocky grins and chases everyone off the board. Children
stand around, dripping puddles, watching us as we carefully pace to the end. The sun burns our shoulders, and the
board wavers and dips as our combined weight passes the
fulcrum. Above, the sky is bright blue. We link upper arms
tightly to make a pivot of our shoulders, and at Rocky's
signal we begin flexing for spring, playing the board.
"Now!" We are lifted and thrown upward, tucking into
the air. The pool turns upside down, sky spins over our
knees, the bathhouse revolves. We turn, holding together
like monkeys, high above the glazed water. I have a snap-

shot Mr. Provenzano took of that historic moment. In it, we hang, crouched against the sky, backsides to heaven; one second later we will cut the water together, perfectly straight, to shouts and cheering. We break apart underwater and surface separately, mouths open, to the applause of our small pupils, who rim the deep end and now flop into the water like seals. On the deck, we congratulate each other, shaking hands. Then Rocky climbs the playground wall and high-dives, just missing the cement, into the deep end. It is the traditional signal to close the pool. He surfaces, puts on his orange Department of Parks poncho, and the guards begin blowing their whistles; everybody out of the pool. Summer is over.

When I leave the bathhouse, the sun is slanting. Walking up Carmine Street, I buy myself a Chocolate Eclair Good Humor as a reward. The long summer is over at last. Summer is over, and I have kept my head.

LUNCH

by Rebecca Rass

The telephone rang. It was for her. Her ex-husband. He'd just heard she had come from abroad. Had five years already passed? They agreed to meet.

On the beach. A small Arab restaurant. The mosques of Jaffa behind. A young, dark-skinned barefoot boy for a waiter. Tahini salad. Strongly scented olive oil. Lots of garlic. Saltwater fish stuffed with fresh spices, grilled on charcoal. He was watching her, his back to the sea.

He had grown fat. A stripe of white hair. The same restless movements. The same deep voice. The same ironic smile. The same inquisitive eyes. The same guy, another edition. The memories, still rippling. Resurrection of long-forgotten images.

First love. The exquisite tension. The trembling heart. The reverberation of the flesh. The wild dark-red tulips on the rocky hills. The wild mushrooms in the musky forest. The poignant odor of sun-soaked soil wet with the first rain. Hand in hand in the shady eucalyptus grove.

The wind playing on the tall trees. The Mediterranean. Yellow sand and naked bodies. Blazing sun burning fiery bodies. Souls on fire.

The wedding—in color prints and on slides. A long white wedding dress. A white lace veil. A white wreath. A golden loop for a ring. A deafening rock band. Glasses clinking: congratulations! A family photo: cheese, everybody. The camera freezes smiles and time. Mazel-tov.

The wedding ceremony under the canopy. The rabbi races through the text. What is it that he says and what is it to do with her? What are they all doing here? Institutionalizing her love? Her intimacy made formal? She can step away and leave it all behind. Too late, she doesn't dare. The price of a coward: love, reduced in scope, made finite and called marriage sealed with a golden ring shamelessly shining on her finger. Why is everybody so happy? She vows never to marry again.

Five years later. Another rabbi rushes through the text. What is it that he says? He unbinds her? What has that to do with her, anyway? Aren't love and separation a personal matter? She vows never to divorce again.

Zealously she keeps her pledges.

At the small restaurant. The roaring Mediterranean sea in the background. They clink glasses, she and her ex-husband. They smile amicably. They examine each other.

You haven't changed, he says. And what about me?

It was not him, yet he kept floating out of layers of past years. Behind him—surging waves and white foam, and five years of her life. Another world. An era from another century. A whole life. Very useful, very necessary, a life workshop. One graduates from school, college, and from marriage.

They smile in embarrassment. In silence. What do you say to a man with whom you lived for five years and haven't seen for another five? Nothing. Nothing to say. Close, familiar, yet strange. So far away, and no bridge in between. They look. They smile. They smile again. They watch. And they wonder. What has the time apart robbed them of, and what has it bestowed on them?

Now she watches him with open eyes, fully aware. Her soul does not surge with love or pain. Memories do not assail her judgment. Only a soft thrill and curiosity; looking back with wonder.

No, he says, he isn't really happy with himself. He looks at her: he misses flying to other spheres, the walks together in the reality of a different world. He misses the dream of first love, the innocence, the naïveté. The eucalyptus grove, the wind in the willows. And what about you, he asks.

Will she tell him, she wonders, that her real life started with the divorce? Just like modern novels, she thinks, and dips the white round Arab bread in the Tahini sauce. 19th century novels ended with marriage, 20th century novels start with a divorce. Her life is divided in two: before and after the divorce. Something like before World War II and after World War II. She was surprised to find out that what the war did to the world, the end of her marriage did to her—it shattered her from top to bottom.

Like the devastated landscape of Europe, her soul was in ruins, wounded and bleeding. With everything inside dead, she groped her way back to life. She had to start the creation of her self all over again, be born in her own image.

Silence. Only the Mediterranean soars and foams. They watch each other motionless. Recollected images rise. Was it as it was? They look back with analytical eyes. They weigh the memories, the plus and the minus, the bliss and the pain. The primal blue water in the background sings of eons, of past civilizations. It sings of eternity. For one short moment they hold hands again, running downhill together; then, embracing in tenderness and facing the sunrise, they promise each other love eternal.

The waiter brings a bottle of white Burgundy. They toast each other, she and her ex-husband. Cheers, skoal! He places a warm, tanned hand—a hand looming from another world—on her own. He presses tightly. A spark lights his eyes. A wild thought: does he want to start it all again from the beginning?

And that is how it started, or rather ended: at midnight he came home, sat in the blue armchair, puffing circles of smoke around her. I fell in love, he said (just like that). I want a divorce. I've already investigated. It can be speedily arranged. In three months— and that was it. A nuclear explosion occurred somewhere in her mind, the earth opened up and she fell into its entrails.

From afar his voice reached her, dividing their property. The double bed for me, the clothes chest for you. The armchair for me, the couch for you. The blue rug for me, the red rug for you, the towels for me, the sheets for you. The wedding presents, the silver cutlery—three spoons for me, three for you. The vortex was raging, spinning around her. She let herself go.

She dips her pita bread in the Tahini salad, and with her fork picks out a slice of tomato soaked with olive oil and marjoram. She slowly sips her white Burgundy.

The whole bottle of wine she had finished all by herself didn't help much. The apartment they were so proud of became a graveyard. The walls closed in on her. Everything around her, once so valued, was reduced in size, in value, in significance, in beauty. Once he had closed the door and left, his steps still echoing down the stairs, everything came awry. The ceiling lowered, the white walls darkened, the furniture crumbled. The mahogany table was only a lifeless pile of planks. The marriage certificate was only a paper bridge between separated hearts.

And this is how it went on: he left and closed the door. He came back and told her he could not live without her, and then left again. He loved her. He loved another. And left again. Alone, she roamed the underworld, visiting the dead. She became a snail. She started to crawl. Crawling, she inched her way through the intricate dark tunnels of the underworld, begging for her lost love, for the scent of eucalyptus at sunset and of daffodils in spring. She begged for the past that had evaporated, for a dream that had crashed, for a yester-world that had blown up.

And when everything around her had tumbled and disintegrated, she still pleaded for time to stand still.

The Mediterranean in the background surges and froths. Arab children play in the sand. The waiter approaches, his arms full: now, says her ex-husband, a surprise. A big tray piled with different kinds of seafood lands in the middle of the table, joined by a chilled bottle of Israeli champagne. You see, he says with a smile, I've not forgotten. Your favorite food. Specially ordered. His eyes sparkle. They clink their glasses. Cheers again. At that moment the sunlight reaches their table. Blinded, she closes her eyes.

With her eyes closed she crawled through the pit of purgatory, at the edge of existence. The debris of the past adhered to her skin. Wherever she crawled, there it was, a cemetery clinging to her back. And again he came and again he left. Each time he closed the door and left, she was seized by an illogical terror that crippled her. Too weak to leave herself, too impotent to lock the door behind him and put an end to the torture, too helpless to make a decision, too crushed to stand, devoid of all will of her own, she snailed on, at the edge of extinction.

With glee they attack the plate of seafood. They pull off the tails and heads of the small red shrimps, peel away the shells and gobble up the soft white meat. Drops of lemon on the oysters and then they suck them in; with a tiny fork they pull the succulent mussels out of their nests. There was a taste of sea in their mouths. He tells her about himself. His life. His work. His loves. And what's happening with you? he asks. They mention common friends.

At that moment in purgatory, it dawned on her that her infernal journey was not singular. Many make it, sooner or later, this journey into purgatory, the underworld of the soul, into the darkest cellars of oneself, an involuntary journey from the conscious into the unconscious, to find meaning in the meaningless, identity in the formless mass.

What are you thinking of? he asks. The sea glitters behind him. Of traveling. Of journeys.

Yes, you've always loved to travel, he says and tells her about his own travels, travels of a successful businessman.

She resumes the travel into herself, struggling in the dark to find the road back to life. It was difficult. No road carved through the devastated landscape of her soul, no paths cut through the charcoal expanses of her mind. Groping her way in the dark, she realized that she was tied by thousands of cords, bound by endless knots that looped along the years from her parents, family, society, school.

Whenever she thought that she'd made her own choice, followed her own path, it was clear to her now that she had simply been led along a well-trodden path cut for her by others.

Then, one day, he came and solemnly declared that everything had come to an end. In a split second, life—detailed, organized and planned for years ahead—dissolved. That moment the process of her liberation began but, reeling in pain, she was too blind to notice. It was so difficult to be free and take full responsibility over one's self, over one's life

She was afraid to be alone, untied, unbound, to be loose. To be free. Blinded, in pain, she snailed on in the desert of her soul, looking for a way out.

Hills of shells piled up between them. One after the other they throw the shells at the sea. Some land on the beach, a few reach the edge of the water. The waiter brings in two Arab coffeepots filled to the brim with aromatic Turkish coffee. He places a small plate of sweet honey cakes on the table. A late-afternoon breeze drives away the heat of the day. She tastes the cakes. Too sweet.

She felt nausea coming up her belly. War waged inside her between what she was and what she wished to be, between the dependent crawling snail looking for a master, and herself as the master of herself. The deep, horrifying sensation of nausea did not leave her. Her inside, soul and flesh, strove to emerge through her mouth.

Then, unexpectedly, the desert winds dropped. Tranquility abided. Sweet exhaustion. Had she reached a land? A country? An independent state? Yes. Her own. But it was a virgin land. She had to build it all from the beginning. To create the borders, to invent a language, compose a constitution all her own, write her own ten commandments, decide on her personal geography.

The restaurant is empty. The waiters stand idle, looking expressionless at the empty street. They are alone, a man and a woman. Apologetically they examine each other. With a sensation of failure. After all, they failed each other, could not keep their promise of love. And when everything collapsed they fled, leaving all questions hanging in air.

A breeze blows up her skirt. His eyes follow the wind and land on her tanned thighs. Blushing, she covers them. He looks straight at her eyes and laughs into them. His eyes slide down her face, down her neck and stop for a moment by the edge of her open-necked dress, hesitating before sliding inside, in between her breasts, saying hello to old friends, weighing the memory against the reality.

Against her will, her breasts stretch themselves under her dress. I wasn't too good at it, was I? he says softly. While married, they never dared to speak about their intimate life. Then, unexpectedly, he starts to talk, quietly, softly, from the depth of his heart, looking far into the sea, never at her. Of his despair he talks, of his pain. Of his failure to keep them both happy and their love intact. Of frustration that increased each day.

The waiter takes away the coffeepots and the glasses. He brings in ice water, but her ex-husband, talking, does not notice. She examines him with new curiosity. For the first time she realizes that he has grown up.

Who is he now, anyway? Her eyes glide over his well-shaven cheeks, down his short beard, roaming freely on his hairy chest, discovering bunches of white hair. She looks for her old self curled against his chest. Her eyes undress him. He looks at her and stretches out his hand. In peace and harmony their hands clasp. Behind them, the waves rise and fall, surges of energy.

She swam alone in that sea, rising and falling with the waves, searching for land. The awareness of her own passivity overwhelmed her. Why had she never challenged their failure? Rising up from the dead, she felt long-subdued energy released inside her.

Sitting in the restaurant, hand in hand, she feels an urge to challenge the past. Their failure. Hers. She feels the urge to bring their failed relations to triumph, the frustration of the past to satisfaction. Can she? Can they?

Without words, they read each other's mind. The sky is blue, the sea is blue and the sun colors a yellow path in between. Slowly they rise and pay the check. They enter the car. It's blue, too. Slowly they drive along the beach. North? he asks. North, she says.

To her surprise, the feeling of aloneness was a source of freedom and strength. It filled her with tremendous joy. She was ready to answer to the world inside her and the world outside her. A vast new land loomed ahead. And it was clear: she had to leave the old world and go.

The car is in perpetual motion. The motion makes their blood run fast. To their left stretches the blue sea. The asphalt road stretches ahead. They sail into a different world, drive in a different dimension outside clocktime. Sea and water move along with them. They hardly talk, a unison of silence. Soon the sun will set. Three tall palm trees appear ahead. They drive off the highway along a dirt road that leads them between high cliffs. They park the car.

On the deck of the sailing ship, against the fiery background of the setting sun, she stood alone, waving good-bye to her parents, her country, her receding past. For the first time in her life she felt no fear, no doubt, no hesitation. A river of fire stretched from the ship's bow to the red ball of the setting sun. It was on this magic path that olden ships sailed to mythical lands in search of the secret of life eternal.

For the millionth time a daughter leaves her father's home in search of the golden fleece.

On the beach, only he and she, and the burning eye of the world to witness. She takes off her clothes and faces him all naked, laughing. He takes off his clothes, faces her with his tanned naked body. A river of fire stretches be-

tween them and the setting sun. Smiling, they let their
eyes travel over each other. Is that the man with whom
she was intimate? He stretches his hand to hold hers. She
slides under his arm and runs to the edge of the water.
Wild rocky beach, primal cliffs rise from the soft waves.
Facing the sea, with her back to her ex-husband, she feels
his eyes fasten on her nakedness, glide along her spine, on
the hills of her buttocks, on the back of her thighs, invading
her secrets. Soft tiny waves lick her feet. Electric waves
shake in her groin. Wave after wave. In a minute she will
be on fire. She plunges into the cool water.

With her heart beating in the rhythm of the waves, on the
deck of the ship, she started to live by the size of her
dreams, and not by the measure of their realization. She
plunged headlong ahead, eager to exercise the life inside
her. With a knapsack and a sleeping bag, she had set her
voyage. Paris. London. Dublin. Oslo. Stockholm. Copen-
hagen. Amsterdam. Berlin. New York. Mexico City. By
bus. By train. By plane. By boat. Distances lost meaning.
The world became a sprawling village. Borders dissolved.
Languages. Cultures. The road circled and circulated, like
the veins in her body, like the blood in her veins. Like the
journey of the sun in the sky. In a world opposite to the
one she was born into, she was a young woman moving
with time. Freed from things, free to go on short notice,
pack her sparse belongings and leave, go with the wind.
Working at odd jobs, she never signed away her freedom,
shunned all contracts. Surprisingly, she found out that life
itself kept her floating. Like water itself, which holds up
the swimmer, and drowns the nonswimmer.

Fast, she swims away from him. He follows, and catches
up with her. She splashes water at his face. He does like-
wise. A moment of joy, of pleasure, of intimacy. The
elements join forces to approximate fulfillment. The setting
sun, the yellow sand, the cool water, the salty air. A man
and a woman laughing in the cradle of the world. Out of
the water she emerges, running along the warm beach. He
follows her, trying to overtake her. When he almost does,
she plunges again into the water, splashing at him. He

escapes. She runs to catch him, and when she almost does, he suddenly turns around. She falls into his embracing arms.

All those years she had refused to be a victim. A victim to despair, to failure, to loneliness, to prowling fear, the common diseases of modern man. She had refused to be a victim to lack of means, to luxury, to pain. To age, to reality, to time. She had refused to serve, but had striven to render the ordinary meaningful, the mundane—the mysterious, the mortal—immortal and to add one single drop of magic to life. Through her dream, she had reached out to the meaning of reality.

For a long time they stand entangled, almost motionless, the water nibbles at their feet. They stream into each other and merge into one flesh. Their bodies forgive past humiliation, overcome once-bitter pain. Then they set out to feast and triumph. The setting sun stretches itself on the water before them, leaving behind a red blazing trail that shines on them as they roll on the sand, in the shallow water.

Alone in the white spaces, a person alone in a living desert, panting desert, a primal beast. A woman—in mellowness, in fulfillment. All she had she would give, all that there was she would receive. And she did.

The past flows into the present, the pain into joy, hate into love, male into female, man into love, love into life.

For one eternal moment she is the goddess of the earth. The goddess of love, sending roots into the soil to fertilize the barren sands. For one eternal moment she is merged with the elements, with the earth and the stones and the sun and the wind. For one eternal moment she is the woman in all women.

The sun has set. Soft gray light embraces the white moon looming in the gray sky. There is peace. There is tenderness. There is mirth. There is soft silence.

It's already dark. The sea soars black and powerful. A soft breeze. Peace and harmony on earth. They dress languidly, and walk to the car. In silence, beyond words. He starts the car and puts on the lights. A stream of white light breaks into the night. They drive in silence, along streets of a different world. The moon rises and hangs up in the air, moving along with them. The motion of the car corresponds to the motion of her blood. The moonlight stretches out to her, moving in the car, a bridge of light.

City lights. City streets. City crowds throng the streets in the warm night. He stops the car on the street corner. It was here that he picked her up a few hours earlier. Their eyes meet for a moment. Their lunch is over. They shake warm hands. See you again. So long. See you again? She gets out and slams the door. The car lingers somewhat before a red light. Green. Here I stand, alone, in the interjunction of city roads, with his blue car speeding out of my life into streets of another world. I turn and head for the sea at the end of the street. I breathe in the salty air. Standing there, leaning on the rusty railing, I feel the constant rhythm of the sea beating in my blood.

REENA

by Paule Marshall

Like most people with unpleasant childhoods, I am on
constant guard against the past—the past being for me the
people and places associated with the years I served out
my girlhood in Brooklyn. The places no longer matter
that much since most of them have vanished. The old
grammar school, for instance, P.S. 35 ("Dirty 5's" we
called it and with justification) has been replaced by a
low, coldly functional arrangement of glass and Perma-
stone which bears its name but has none of the feel of a
school about it. The small, grudgingly lighted stores along
Fulton Street, the soda parlor that was like a church with
its stained-glass panels in the door and marble floor have
given way to those impersonal emporiums, the supermarkets. Our house even, a brownstone relic whose halls
smelled comfortingly of dust and lemon oil, the somnolent
street upon which it stood, the tall, muscular trees which
shaded it were leveled years ago to make way for a city
housing project—a stark, graceless warren for the poor. So
that now whenever I revisit that old section of Brooklyn
and see these new and ugly forms, I feel nothing. I might
as well be in a strange city.

But it is another matter with the people of my past, the
faces that in their darkness were myriad reflections of
mine. Whenever I encounter them at the funeral or wake,
the wedding or christening—those ceremonies by which
the past reaffirms its hold—my guard drops and memories
banished to the rear of the mind rush forward to rout the
present. I almost become the child again—anxious and
angry, disgracefully diffident.

Reena was one of the people from that time, and a main
contributor to my sense of ineffectualness then. She had
not done this deliberately. It was just that whenever she

talked about herself (and this was not as often as most
people) she seemed to be talking about me also. She
ruthlessly analyzed herself, sparing herself nothing. Her
honesty was so absolute it was a kind of cruelty.

She had not changed, I was to discover in meeting her
again after a separation of twenty years. Nor had I really.
For although the years had altered our positions (she was
no longer the lord and I the lackey) and I could even
afford to forgive her now, she still had the ability to dis-
turb me profoundly by dredging to the surface those
aspects of myself that I kept buried. This time, as I listened to her talk over the stretch of one long night, she
made vivid without knowing it what is perhaps the most
critical fact of my existence—that definition of me, of her
and millions like us, formulated by others to serve out
their fantasies, a definition we have to combat at an un-
conscionable cost to the self and even use, at times, in
order to survive; the cause of so much shame and rage as
well as, oddly enough, a source of pride: simply, what it
has meant, what it means, to be a black woman in America.

We met—Reena and myself—at the funeral of her aunt,
who had been my godmother and whom I had also called
aunt, Aunt Vi, and loved, for she and her house had been,
respectively, a source of understanding and a place of
calm for me as a child. Reena entered the church where
the funeral service was being held as though she, not the
minister, were coming to officiate, sat down among the im-
mediate family up front, and turned to inspect those
behind her. I saw her face then.

It was a good copy of the original. The familiar mold
was there, that is, and the configuration of bone beneath
the skin was the same despite the slight fleshiness I had
never seen there before, her features had even retained
their distinctive touches: the positive set to her mouth, the
assertive lift to her nose, the same insistent, unsettling
eyes which when she was angry became as black as her
skin—and this was total, unnerving, and very beautiful.
Yet something had happened to her face. It was different
despite its sameness. Aging even while it remained envia-
bly young. Time had sketched in, very lightly, the evidence of the twenty years.

As soon as the funeral service was over. I left, hurrying

out of the church into the early November night. The
wind, already at its winter strength, brought with it the
smell of dead leaves and the image of Aunt Vi there in
the church, as dead as the leaves—as well as the thought
of Reena, whom I would see later at the wake.

Her real name had been Doreen, a standard for girls
among West Indians (her mother, like my parents, was
from Barbados), but she had changed it to Reena on her
twelfth birthday—"As a present to myself"—and had enforced the change on her family by refusing to answer to
the old name. "Reena. With two e's!" she would say and
imprint those e's on your mind with the indelible black of
her eyes and a thin threatening finger that was like a
quill.

She and I had not been friends through our own
choice. Rather, our mothers, who had known each other
since childhood, had forced the relationship. And from
the beginning, I had been at a disadvantage. For Reena,
as early as the age of twelve, had had a quality that was
unique, superior, and therefore dangerous. She seemed
defined, even then, all of a piece, the raw edges of her adolescence smoothed over; indeed, she seemed to have escaped adolescence altogether and made one dazzling leap
from childhood into the very arena of adult life. At thirteen, for instance, she was reading Zola, Hauptmann,
Steinbeck, while I was still in the thrall of the Little
Minister and Lorna Doone. When I could only barely
conceive of the world beyond Brooklyn, she was talking of
the Civil War in Spain, lynchings in the South, Hitler in
Poland—and talking with the outrage and passion of a rev-
olutionary. I would try, I remember, to console myself
with the thought that she was really an adult masquerad-
ing as a child, which meant that I could not possibly be
her match.

For her part, Reena put up with me and was, by turns,
patronizing and impatient. I merely served as the audience before whom she rehearsed her ideas and the
yardstick by which she measured her worldliness and
knowledge.

"Do you realize that this stupid country supplied Japan
with the scrap iron to make the weapons she's now using
against it?" she had shouted at me once.

I had not known that.

Just as she overwhelmed me, she overwhelmed her family, with the result that despite a half dozen brothers and sisters who consumed quantities of bread and jam whenever they visited us, she behaved like an only child and got away with it. Her father, a gentle man with skin the color of dried tobacco and with the nose Reena had inherited jutting out like a crag from his nondescript face, had come from Georgia and was always making jokes about having married a foreigner—Reena's mother being from the West Indies. When not joking, he seemed slightly bewildered by his large family and so in awe of Reena that he avoided her. Reena's mother, a small, dry, formidably black woman, was less a person to me than the abstract principle of force, power, energy. She was alternately strict and indulgent with Reena and, despite the inconsistency, surprisingly effective.

They lived when I knew them in a cold-water railroad flat above a kosher butcher on Belmont Avenue in Brownsville, some distance from us—and this in itself added to Reena's exotic quality. For it was a place where Sunday became Saturday, with all the stores open and pushcarts piled with vegetables and yard goods lined up along the curb, a crowded place where people hawked and spat freely in the streaming gutters and the men looked as if they had just stepped from the pages of the Old Testament with their profuse beards and long, black, satin coats.

When Reena was fifteen her family moved to Jamaica in Queens and since, in those days, Jamaica was considered too far away for visiting, our families lost contact and I did not see Reena again until we were both in college and then only once and not to speak to. . . .

I had walked some distance and by the time I got to the wake, which was being held at Aunt Vi's house, it was well under way. It was a good wake. Aunt Vi would have been pleased. There was plenty to drink, and more than enough to eat, including some Barbadian favorites: coconut bread, pone made with the cassava root, and the little crisp codfish cakes that are so hot with peppers they bring tears to the eyes as you bite into them.

I had missed the beginning, when everybody had proba-

bly sat around talking about Aunt Vi and recalling the
few events that had distinguished her otherwise undistin-
guished life. (Someone, I'm sure, had told of the time she
had missed the excursion boat to Atlantic City and had
held her own private picnic—complete with pigeon peas
and rice and fricassee chicken—on the pier at 42nd
Street.) By the time I arrived, though, it would have been
indiscreet to mention her name, for by then the wake had
become—and this would also have pleased her—a celebration of life.

I had had two drinks, one right after the other, and was
well into my third when Reena, who must have been upstairs, entered the basement kitchen where I was. She saw
me before I had quite seen her, and with a cry that alerted
the entire room to the presence and charged the air with
her special force, she rushed toward me.

"Hey, I'm the one who was supposed to be the writer,
not you! Do you know, I still can't believe it," she said,
stepping back, her blackness heightened by a white mocking smile. "I read both your books over and over again
and I can't really believe it. My Little Paulie!"

I did not mind. For there was respect and even wonder
behind the patronizing words and in her eyes. The old
imbalance between us had ended and I was suddenly glad
to see her.

I told her so and we both began talking at once, but
Reena's voice overpowered mine, so that all I could do
after a time was listen while she discussed my books, and
dutifully answer her questions about my personal life.

"And what about you?" I said, almost brutally, at the
first chance I got. "What've you been up to all this time?"

She got up abruptly. "Good Lord, in here's noisy as
hell. Come on, let's go upstairs."

We got fresh drinks and went up to Aunt Vi's bedroom,
where in the soft light from the lamps, the huge Victorian
bed and the pink satin bedspread with roses of the same
material strewn over its surface looked as if they had never
been used. And, in a way, this was true. Aunt Vi had seldom slept in her bed or, for that matter, lived in her
house, because in order to pay for it, she had had to work
at a sleeping-in job which gave her only Thursdays and
every other Sunday off.

Reena sat on the bed, crushing the roses, and I sat on one of the numerous trunks which crowded the room. They contained every dress, coat, hat, and shoe that Aunt Vi had worn since coming to the United States. I again asked Reena what she had been doing over the years.

"Do you want a blow-by-blow account?" she said. But despite the flippancy, she was suddenly serious. And when she began it was clear that she had written out the narrative in her mind many times. The words came too easily; the events, the incidents had been ordered in time, and the meaning of her behavior and of the people with whom she had been involved had been painstakingly analyzed. She talked willingly, with desperation almost. And the words by themselves weren't enough. She used her hands to give them form and urgency. I became totally involved with her and all that she said. So much so that as the night wore on I was not certain at times whether it was she or I speaking.

From the time her family moved to Jamaica until she was nineteen or so, Reena's life sounded, from what she told me in the beginning, as ordinary as mine and most of the girls we knew. After high school she had gone on to one of the free city colleges, where she had majored in journalism, worked part time in the school library, and, surprisingly enough, joined a houseplan. (Even I hadn't gone that far.) It was an all-Negro club, since there was a tacit understanding that Negro and white girls did not join each other's houseplans. "Integration, northern style," she said, shrugging.

It seems that Reena had had a purpose and a plan in joining the group. "I thought," she said with a wry smile, "I could get those girls up off their complacent rumps and out doing something about social issues. . . . I couldn't get them to budge. I remember after the war when a Negro ex-soldier had his eyes gouged out by a bus driver down South I tried getting them to demonstrate on campus. I talked until I was hoarse, but to no avail. They were too busy planning the annual autumn frolic."

Her laugh was bitter but forgiving and it ended in a long, reflective silence. After which she said quietly, "It wasn't that they didn't give a damn. It was just, I suppose,

that like most people they didn't want to get involved to
the extent that they might have to stand up and be
counted. If it ever came to that. Then another thing.
They thought they were safe, special. After all, they had
grown up in the North, most of them, and so had escaped
the southern-style prejudice; their parents, like mine, were
struggling to put them through college; they could look
forward to being tidy little schoolteachers, social workers,
and lab technicians. Oh, they were safe!" The sarcasm
scored her voice and then abruptly gave way to pity.
"Poor things, they weren't safe, you see, and would never
be as long as millions like themselves in Harlem, on
Chicago's South Side, down South, all over the place,
were unsafe. I tried to tell them this—and they accused me
of being oversensitive. They tried not to listen. But I
would have held out and, I'm sure, even brought some of
them around eventually if this other business with a silly
boy hadn't happened at the same time. . . ."

Reena told me then about her first, brief, and apparently innocent affair with a boy she had met at one of
the houseplan parties. It had ended, she said, when the
boy's parents had met her. "That was it," she said and the
flat of her hand cut into the air. "He was forbidden to see
me. The reason? He couldn't bring himself to tell me, but
I knew. I was too black.

"Naturally, it wasn't the first time something like that
had happened. In fact, you might say that was the theme
of my childhood. Because I was dark I was always being
plastered with Vaseline so I wouldn't look ashy. Whenever I had my picture taken they would pile a whitish
powder on my face and make the lights so bright I always
came out looking ghostly. My mother stopped speaking to
any number of people because they said I would have
been pretty if I hadn't been so dark. Like nearly every
little black girl, I had my share of dreams of waking up to
find myself with long, blond curls, blue eyes, and skin like
milk. So I should have been prepared. Besides, the boy's
parents were really rejecting themselves in rejecting me.

"Take us"—and her hands, opening in front of my face
as she suddenly leaned forward, seemed to offer me the
whole of black humanity. "We live surrounded by white

images, and white in this world is synonymous with the good, light, beauty, success, so that, despite ourselves sometimes, we run after that whiteness and deny our darkness, which has been made into the symbol of all that is evil and inferior. I wasn't a person to that boy's parents, but a symbol of the darkness they were in flight from, so that just as they—that boy, his parents, those silly girls in the houseplan—were running from me, I started running from them. . . ."

It must have been shortly after this happened when I saw Reena at a debate which was being held at my college. She did not see me, since she was one of the speakers and I was merely part of her audience in the crowded auditorium. The topic had something to do with intellectual freedom in the colleges (McCarthyism was coming into vogue then) and aside from a Jewish boy from City College, Reena was the most effective—sharp, provocative —her position the most radical. The others on the panel seemed intimidated not only by the strength and cogency of her argument but by the sheer impact of her blackness in their white midst.

Her color might have been a weapon she used to dazzle and disarm her opponents. And she had highlighted it with the clothes she was wearing: a white dress patterned with large blocks of primary colors, I remember (it looked Mexican), and a pair of intricately wrought silver earrings —long and with many little parts which clashed like muted cymbals over the microphone each time she moved her head. She wore her hair cropped short like a boy's and it was not straightened like mine and the other Negro girls' in the audience, but left in its coarse natural state: a small forest under which her faced emerged in its intense and startling handsomeness. I remember she left the auditorium in triumph that day, surrounded by a noisy entourage from her college—all of them white.

"We were very serious," she said now, describing the left-wing group she had belonged to then—and there was a defensiveness in her voice which sought to protect them from all censure. "We believed—because we were young, I suppose, and had nothing as yet to risk—that we could do something about the injustices which everyone around us seemed to take for granted. So we picketed and demonstrated and bombarded Washington with our protests, only to have our names added to the Attorney General's list for all our troubles. We were always standing on street corners handing out leaflets or getting people to sign petitions. We always seemed to pick the coldest days to do that." Her smile held long after the words had died.

"I, we all, had such a sense of purpose then," she said softly, and a sadness lay aslant the smile now, darkening it. "We were forever holding meetings, having endless discussions, arguing, shouting, theorizing. And we had fun. Those parties! There was always somebody with a guitar. We were always singing. . . ." Suddenly, she began singing—and her voice was sure, militant, and faintly self-mocking,

> "But the banks are made of marble
> With a guard at every door
> And the vaults are stuffed with silver
> That the workers sweated for. . . ."

When she spoke again the words were a sad coda to the song. "Well, as you probably know, things came to an ugly head with McCarthy reigning in Washington, and I was one of the people temporarily suspended from school."

She broke off and we both waited, the ice in our glasses melted and the drinks gone flat.

"At first, I didn't mind," she said finally. "After all, we were right. The fact that they suspended us proved it. Besides, I was in the middle of an affair, a real one this time, and too busy with that to care about anything else." She paused again, frowning.

"He was white," she said quickly and glanced at me as though to surprise either shock or disapproval in my face. "We were very involved. At one point—I think just after we had been suspended and he started working—we even thought of getting married. Living in New York, moving in the crowd we did, we might have been able to manage it. But I couldn't. There were too many complex things

going on beneath the surface," she said, her voice strained
by the hopelessness she must have felt then, her hands
shaping it in the air between us. "Neither one of us could
really escape what our color had come to mean in this
country. Let me explain. Bob was always, for some odd
reason, talking about how much the Negro suffered, and
although I would agree with him I would also try to get
across that, you know, like all people we also had fun once
in a while, loved our children, liked making love—that we
were human beings, for God's sake. But he only wanted to
hear about the suffering. It was as if this comforted him
and eased his own suffering—and he did suffer because of
any number of things: his own uncertainty, for one, his
difficulties with his family, for another. . . .

"Once, I remember, when his father came into New
York, Bob insisted that I meet him. I don't know why I
agreed to go with him. . . ." She took a deep breath and
raised her head very high. "I'll never forget or forgive the
look on that old man's face when he opened his hotel-
room door and saw me. The horror. I might have been the
personification of every evil in the world. His inability to
believe that it was his son standing there holding my
hand. His shock. I'm sure he never fully recovered. I
know I never did. Nor can I forget Bob's laugh in the elevator afterwards, the way he kept repeating: 'Did you see
his face when he saw you? Did you . . . ?' He had used
me, you see. I had been the means, the instrument of his
revenge.

"And I wasn't any better. I used him. I took every opportunity to treat him shabbily, trying, you see, through
him, to get at that white world which had not only denied
me, but had turned my own against me." Her eyes closed.
"I went numb all over when I understood what we were
doing to, and with, each other. I stayed numb for a long
time."

As Reena described the events which followed—the
break with Bob, her gradual withdrawal from the left-
wing group ("I had had it with them too. I got tired of
being 'their Negro,' their pet. Besides, they were just all
talk, really. All theories and abstractions. I doubt that,
with all their elaborate plans for the Negro and for the

workers of the world, any of them had ever been near a factory or up to Harlem")—as she spoke about her rein-statement in school, her voice suggested the numbness she had felt then. It only stirred into life again when she talked of her graduation.

"You should have seen my parents. It was really their day. My mother was so proud she complained about every-thing: her seat, the heat, the speaker; and my father just sat there long after everybody had left, too awed to move. God, it meant so much to them. It was as if I had made up for the generations his people had picked cotton in Georgia and my mother's family had cut cane in the West Indies. It frightened me."

I asked her after a long wait what she had done after graduating.

"How do you mean, what I did. Looked for a job. Tell me, have you ever looked for work in this man's city?"

"I know," I said, holding up my hand. "Don't tell me."

We both looked at my raised hand which sought to waive the discussion, then at each other, and suddenly we laughed, a laugh so loud and violent with pain and out-rage it brought tears.

"Girl," Reena said, the tears silver against her black-ness. "You could put me blindfolded right now at the Times Building on 42nd Street and I would be able to find my way to every newspaper office in town. But tell me, how come white folks is so *hard*?"

"Just bo'n hard."

We were laughing again and this time I nearly slid off the trunk and Reena fell back among the satin roses.

"I didn't know there were so many ways of saying 'no' without ever once using the word," she said, the laughter lodged in her throat, but her eyes had gone hard. "Some-times I'd find myself in the elevator, on my way out, and smiling all over myself because I thought I had gotten the job, before it would hit me that they had really said no, not yes. Some of those people in personnel had so per-fected their smiles they looked almost genuine. The ones who used to get me, though, were those who tried to make the interview into an intimate chat between friends. They'd put you in a comfortable chair, offer you a ciga-

rette, and order coffee. How I hated that coffee. They
didn't know it—or maybe they did—but it was like offering
me hemlock. . . .

"You think Christ had it tough?" Her laughter rushed
against the air which resisted it. "I was crucified five days
a week and half-day on Saturday. I became almost para-
noid. I began to think there might be something other
than color wrong with me which everybody but me could
see, some rare disease that had turned me into a monster.

"My parents suffered. And that bothered me most,
because I felt I had failed them. My father didn't say anything but I knew because he avoided me more than usual.
He was ashamed, I think, that he hadn't been able, as a
man and as my father, to prevent this. My mother—well,
you know her. In one breath she would try to comfort me
by cursing them: 'But God blind them' "—and Reena's
voice captured her mother's aggressive accent—" 'if you
had come looking for a job mopping down their floors
they would o' hire you, the brutes. But mark my words,
their time goin' come, 'cause God don't love ugly and he
ain't stuck on pretty. . . .' And in the next breath she
would curse me, 'Journalism! Journalism! Whoever heard
of colored people taking up journalism. You must feel
you's white or something so. The people is right to chuck
you out of their office. . . .' Poor thing, to make up for
saying all that she would wash my white gloves every night
and cook cereal for me in the morning as if I were a little
girl again. Once she went out and bought me a suit she
couldn't afford from Lord and Taylor's. I looked like a
Smith girl in blackface in it. . . . So guess where I ended
up?"

"As a social investigator for the Welfare Department.
Where else?"

We were helpless with laughter again.

"You too?"

"No," I said, "I taught, but that was just as bad."

"No," she said, sobering abruptly. "Nothing's as bad as
working for Welfare. Do you know what they really mean
by a social investigator? A spy. Someone whose dirty job it
is to snoop into the corners of the lives of the poor and
make their poverty more vivid by taking from them the

last shred of privacy. 'Mrs. Jones, is that a new dress you're wearing?' 'Mrs. Brown, this kerosene heater is not listed in the household items. Did you get an authorization for it?' 'Mrs. Smith, is that a telephone I hear ringing under the sofa?' I was utterly demoralized within a month.

"And another thing. I thought I knew about poverty. I mean, I remember, as a child, having to eat soup made with those white beans the government used to give out free for days running, sometimes, because there was nothing else. I had lived in Brownsville, among all the poor Jews and Poles and Irish there. But what I saw in Harlem, where I had my case load, was different somehow. Perhaps because it seemed so final. There didn't seem to be any way to escape from those dark hallways and dingy furnished rooms. . . . All that defeat." Closing her eyes, she finished the stale whiskey and soda in her glass.

"I remember a client of mine, a girl my age with three children already and no father for them and living in the expensive squalor of a rooming house. Her bewilderment. Her resignation. Her anger. She could have pulled herself out of the mess she was in? People say that, you know, including some Negroes. But this girl didn't have a chance. She had been trapped from the day she was born in some small town down South.

"She became my reference. From then on and even now, whenever I hear people and groups coming up with all kinds of solutions to the quote Negro problem, I ask one question. What are they really doing for that girl, to save her or to save the children? . . . The answer isn't very encouraging."

It was some time before she continued, and then she told me that after Welfare she had gone to work for a private social-work agency, in their publicity department, and had started on her master's in journalism at Columbia. She also left home around this time.

"I had to. My mother started putting the pressure on me to get married. The hints, the remarks—and you know my mother was never the subtle type—her anxiety, which made me anxious about getting married after a while. Besides, it was time for me to be on my own."

In contrast to the unmistakably radical character of her late adolescence (her membership in the left-wing group, the affair with Bob, her suspension from college), Reena's life of this period sounded ordinary, standard—and she admitted it with a slightly self-deprecating, apologetic smile. It was similar to that of any number of unmarried professional Negro women in New York or Los Angeles or Washington: the job teaching or doing social work which brought in a fairly decent salary, the small apartment with kitchenette which they sometimes shared with a roommate; a car, some of them; membership in various political and social action organizations for the militant few like Reena; the vacations in Mexico, Europe, the West Indies, and now Africa; the occasional date. "The interesting men were invariably married," Reena said and then mentioned having had one affair during that time. She had found out he was married and had thought of her only as the perfect mistress. "The bastard," she said, but her smile forgave him.

"Women alone!" she cried, laughing sadly, and her raised opened arms, the empty glass she held in one hand made eloquent their aloneness. "Alone and lonely, and indulging themselves while they wait. The girls of the houseplan have reached their majority only to find that all those years they spent accumulating their degrees and finding the well-paying jobs in the hope that this would raise their stock have, instead, put them at a disadvantage. For the few eligible men around—those who are their intellectual and professional peers, whom they can respect (and there are very few of them)—don't necessarily marry them, but younger women without the degrees and the fat jobs, who are no threat, or they don't marry at all because they are either queer or mother-ridden. Or they marry white women. Now, intellectually I accept this. In fact, some of my best friends are white women. . . ." And again our laughter—that loud, searing burst which we used to cauterize our hurt mounted into the unaccepting silence of the room. "After all, our goal is a fully integrated society. And perhaps, as some people believe, the only solution to the race problem is miscegenation. Besides, a man should be able to marry whomever he wishes. Emotionally, though, I am less kind and understanding, and I resent like hell the reasons some black men give for rejecting us for them."

"We're too middle-class-oriented," I said. "Conservative."

"Right. Even though, thank God, that doesn't apply to me."

"Too threatening . . . castrating . . ."

"Too independent and impatient with them for not being more ambitious . . . contemptuous . . ."

"Sexually inhibited and unimaginative . . ."

"And the old myth of excessive sexuality of the black woman goes out the window," Reena cried.

"Not supportive, unwilling to submerge our interests for theirs . . ."

"Lacking in the subtle art of getting and keeping a man . . ."

We had recited the accusations in the form and tone of a litany, and in the silence which followed we shared a thin, hopeless smile.

"They condemn us," Reena said softly but with anger, "without taking history into account. We are still, most of us, the black woman who had to be almost frighteningly strong in order for us to survive. For, after all, she was the one whom they left (and I don't hold this against them; I understand) with the children to raise, who had to *make* it somehow or the other. And we are still, so many of us, living that history.

"You would think that they would understand this, but few do. So it's up to us. We have got to understand them and save them for ourselves. How? By being, on one hand, persons in our own right and, on the other, fully the woman and the wife. . . . Christ, listen to who's talking! I had my chance. And I tried. Very hard. But it wasn't enough."

The festive sounds of the wake had died to a sober murmur beyond the bedroom. The crowd had gone, leaving only Reena and myself upstairs and the last of Aunt Vi's closest friends in the basement below. They were drinking coffee. I smelled it, felt its warmth and intimacy in the empty house, heard the distant tapping of the cups against the saucers and voices muted by grief. The wake had come full circle: they were again mourning Aunt Vi.

And Reena might have been mourning with them, sitting there amid the satin roses, framed by the massive headboard. Her hands lay as if they had been broken in her lap. Her eyes were like those of someone blind or dead. I got up to go and get some coffee for her.

"You met my husband," she said quickly, stopping me.

"Have I?" I said, sitting down again.

"Yes, before we were married even. At an autograph party for you. He was free-lancing—he's a photographer—and one of the Negro magazines had sent him to cover the party."

As she went on to describe him I remembered him vaguely, not his face, but his rather large body stretching and bending with a dancer's fluidity and grace as he took the pictures. I had heard him talking to a group of people about some issue on race relations very much in the news then and had been struck by his vehemence. For the moment I had found this almost odd, since he was so fair-skinned he could have passed for white.

They had met, Reena told me now, at a benefit show for a Harlem day nursery given by one of the progressive groups she belonged to, and had married a month afterward. From all that she said they had had a full and exciting life for a long time. Her words were so vivid that I could almost see them: she with her startling blackness and extraordinary force and he with his near-white skin and a militancy which matched hers; both of them moving among the disaffected in New York, their stand on political and social issues equally uncompromising, the line of their allegiance reaching directly to all those trapped in Harlem. And they had lived the meaning of this allegiance, so that even when they could have afforded a life among the black bourgeoisie of St. Albans or Teaneck, they had chosen to live if not in Harlem so close that there was no difference.

"I—we—were so happy I was frightened at times. Not that anything would change between us, but that someone or something in the world outside us would invade our private place and destroy us out of envy. Perhaps this is

what did happen. . . ." She shrugged and even tried to
smile but she could not manage it. "Something slipped in
while we weren't looking and began its deadly work.

"Maybe it started when Dave took a job with a Negro
magazine. I'm not sure. Anyway, in no time, he hated it:
the routine, unimaginative pictures he had to take and the
magazine itself, which dealt only in unrealities: the high-
society world of the black bourgeoisie and the spectacular
strides Negroes were making in all fields—you know the
type. Yet Dave wouldn't leave. It wasn't the money, but a
kind of safety which he had never experienced before
which kept him there. He would talk about free-lancing
again, about storming the gates of the white magazines
downtown, of opening his own studio—but he never acted
on any one of these things. You see, despite his talent—
and he was very talented—he had a diffidence that was
fatal.

"When I understood this I literally forced him to open
the studio—and perhaps I should have been more subtle
and indirect, but that's not my nature. Besides, I was
frightened and desperate to help. Nothing happened for a
time. Dave's work was too experimental to be commercial.
Gradually, though, his photographs started appearing in
the prestige camera magazines and money from various
awards and exhibits and an occasional assignment started
coming in.

"This wasn't enough somehow. Dave also wanted the
big, gaudy commercial success that would dazzle and con-
found that white world downtown and force it to *see* him.
And yet, as I said before, he couldn't bring himself to try
—and this contradiction began to get to him after a while.

"It was then, I think, that I began to fail him. I didn't
know how to help, you see. I had never felt so inadequate
before. And this was very strange and disturbing for someone like me. I was being submerged in his problems—and
I began fighting against this.

"I started working again (I had stopped after the second
baby). And I was lucky because I got back my old job.
And unlucky because Dave saw it as my way of pointing
up his deficiencies. I couldn't convince him otherwise:
that I had to do it for my own sanity. He would accuse me

of wanting to see him fail, of trapping him in all kinds of responsibilities. . . . After a time we both got caught up in this thing, an ugliness came between us, and I began to answer his anger with anger and to trade him insult for insult.

"Things fell apart very quickly after that. I couldn't bear the pain of living with him—the insults, our mutual despair, his mocking, the silence. I couldn't subject the children to it any longer. The divorce didn't take long. And thank God, because of the children, we are pleasant when we have to see each other. He's making out very well, I hear."

She said nothing more, but simply bowed her head as though waiting for me to pass judgment on her. I don't know how long we remained like this, but when Reena finally raised her head, the darkness at the window had vanished and dawn was a still, gray smoke against the pane.

"Do you know," she said, and her eyes were clear and a smile had won out over pain. "I enjoy being alone. I don't tell people this because they'll accuse me of either lying or deluding myself. But I do. Perhaps, as my mother tells me, it's only temporary. I don't think so, though. I feel I don't ever want to be involved again. It's not that I've lost interest in men. I go out occasionally, but it's never anything serious. You see, I have all that I want for now."

Her children first of all, she told me, and from her description they sounded intelligent and capable. She was a friend as well as a mother to them, it seemed. They were planning, the four of them, to spend the summer touring Canada. "I will feel that I have done well by them if I give them, if nothing more, a sense of themselves and their worth and importance as black people. Everything I do with them, for them, is to this end. I don't want them ever to be confused about this. They must have their identifications straight from the beginning. No white dolls for them!"

Then her job. She was working now as a researcher for a small progressive new magazine with the promise that once she completed her master's in journalism (she was working on the thesis now) she might get a chance to do some minor reporting. And like most people, she hoped to write someday. "If I can ever stop talking away my substance," she said, laughing.

And she was still active in any number of social-action groups. In another week or so she would be heading a delegation of mothers down to City Hall "to give the mayor a little hell about conditions in the schools in Harlem." She had started an organization that was carrying on an almost door-to-door campaign in her neighborhood to expose, as she put it, "the blood suckers: all those slumlords and storekeepers with their fixed scales, the finance companies that never tell you the real price of a thing, the petty salesmen that leech off the poor. . . ." In May she was taking her two older girls on a nationwide pilgrimage to Washington to urge for a more rapid implementation of the school-desegregation law.

"It's uncanny," she said, and the laugh which accompanied the words was warm, soft with wonder at herself, girlish even, and the air in the room which had refused her laughter before rushed to absorb this now. "Really uncanny. Here I am, practically middle-aged, with three children to raise by myself and with little or no money to do it, and yet I feel, strangely enough, as though life is just beginning—that it's new and fresh with all kinds of possibilities. Maybe it's because I've been through my purgatory and I can't ever be overwhelmed again. I don't know. Anyway, you should see me on evenings after I put the children to bed. I sit alone in the living room (I've repainted it and changed all the furniture since Dave's gone, so that it would at least look different)—I sit there making plans and all of them seem possible. The most important plan right now is Africa. I've already started saving the fare."

I asked her whether she was planning to live there permanently and she said simply, "I want to live and work there. For how long, for a lifetime, I can't say. All I know is that I have to. For myself and for my children. It is important that they see black people who truly have a place and history of their own and who are building for a new and, hopefully, more sensible world. And I must see it, get

close to it, because I can never lose the sense of being a
displaced person here in America because of my color.
Oh, I know I should remain and fight not only for integration (even though, frankly, I question whether I want to
be integrated into America as it stands now, with its
complacency and materialism, its soullessness) but to help
change the country into something better, sounder—if that
is still possible. But I have to go to Africa. . . .

"Poor Aunt Vi," she said after a long silence and
straightened one of the roses she had crushed. "She never
really got to enjoy her bed of roses what with only Thursdays and every other Sunday off. All that hard work. All
her life . . . Our lives have got to make more sense, if
only for her."

We got up to leave shortly afterward. Reena was staying on to attend the burial, later in the morning, but I was
taking the subway to Manhattan. We parted with the
usual promise to get together and exchanged telephone
numbers. And Reena did phone a week or so later. I don't
remember what we talked about though.

Some months later I invited her to a party I was giving
before leaving the country. But she did not come.

LET THEM CALL IT JAZZ

by Jean Rhys

One bright Sunday morning in July I have trouble with
my Notting Hill landlord because he ask for a month's
rent in advance. He tell me this after I live there since
winter, settling up every week without fail. I have no job
at the time, and if I give the money he want there's not
much left. So I refuse. The man drunk already at that
early hour, and he abuse me—all talk, he can't frighten
me. But his wife is a bad one—now she walk in my
room and say she must have cash. When I tell her no,
she give my suitcase one kick and it burst open. My best
dress fall out, then she laugh and give another kick. She
say month in advance is usual, and if I can't pay find
somewhere else.

Don't talk to me about London. Plenty people there
have heart like stone. Any complaint—the answer is
"prove it." But if nobody see and bear witness for me,
how to prove anything? So I pack up and leave, I think
better not have dealings with that woman. She too cun-
ning, and Satan don't lie worse.

I walk about till a place nearby is open where I can
have coffee and a sandwich. There I start talking to a
man at my table. He talk to me already, I know him,
but I don't know his name. After a while he ask, "What's
the matter? Anything wrong?" and when I tell him my
trouble he say I can use an empty flat he own till I have
time to look around.

This man is not at all like most English people. He see
very quick, and he decide very quick. English people
take long time to decide—you three-quarter dead before
they make up their mind about you. Too besides, he
speak very matter of fact, as if it's nothing. He speak as

if he realize well what it is to live like I do—that's why I
accept and go.

He tell me somebody occupy the flat till last week, so
I find everything all right, and he tell me how to get
there—three quarters of an hour from Victoria Station,
up a steep hill, turn left, and I can't mistake the house.
He give me the keys and an envelope with a telephone
number on the back. Underneath is written "After 6 p.m.
ask for Mr. Sims."

In the train that evening I think myself lucky, for to
walk about London on a Sunday with nowhere to go—
that take the heart out of you.

I find the place and the bedroom of the downstairs flat
is nicely furnished—two looking glass, wardrobe, chest
of drawers, sheets, everything. It smell of jasmine scent,
but it smell strong of damp too.

I open the door opposite and there's a table, a couple
chairs, a gas stove and a cupboard, but this room so big
it look empty. When I pull the blind up I notice the paper
peeling off and mushrooms growing on the walls—you
never see such a thing.

The bathroom the same, all the taps rusty. I leave the
two other rooms and make up the bed. Then I listen,
but I can't hear one sound. Nobody come in, nobody go
out of that house. I lie awake for a long time, then I decide not to stay and in the morning I start to get ready
quickly before I change my mind. I want to wear my
best dress, but it's a funny thing—when I take up that
dress and remember how my landlady kick it I cry. I cry
and I can't stop. When I stop I feel tired to my bones,
tired like old woman. I don't want to move again—I have
to force myself. But in the end I get out in the passage
and there's a postcard for me. "Stay as long as you like.
I'll be seeing you soon—Friday probably. Not to worry."
It isn't signed, but I don't feel so sad and I think, "All
right, I wait here till he come. Perhaps he know of a job
for me."

Nobody else live in the house but a couple on the top
floor—quiet people and they don't trouble me. I have no
word to say against them.

First time I meet the lady she's opening the front door

and she give me a very inquisitive look. But next time she smile a bit and I smile back—once she talk to me. She tell me the house very old, hundred and fifty year old, and she and her husband live there since long time. "Valuable property," she says, "it could have been saved, but nothing done of course." Then she tells me that as to the present owner—if he is the owner—well he have to deal with local authorities and she believe they make difficulties. "These people are determined to pull down all the lovely old houses—it's shameful."

So I agree that many things shameful. But what to do? What to do? I say it have an elegant shape, it make the other houses in the street look cheap trash, and she seem pleased. That's true too. The house sad and out of place, especially at night. But it have style. The second floor shut up, and as for my flat, I go in the two empty rooms once, but never again.

Underneath was the cellar, full of old boards and broken-up furniture—I see a big rat there one day. It was no place to be alone in I tell you, and I get the habit of buying a bottle of wine most evenings, for I don't like whisky and the rum here no good. It don't even *taste* like rum. You wonder what they do to it.

After I drink a glass or two I can sing and when I sing all the misery goes from my heart. Sometimes I make up songs but next morning I forget them, so other times I sing the old ones like "Tantalizin'" or "Don't Trouble Me Now."

I think I go but I don't go. Instead I wait for the evening and the wine and that's all. Everywhere else I live—well, it doesn't matter to me, but this house is different—empty and no noise and full of shadows, so that sometimes you ask yourself what make all those shadows in an empty room.

I eat in the kitchen, then I clean up everything nice and have a bath for coolness. Afterwards I lean my elbows on the windowsill and look at the garden. Red and blue flowers mix up with the weeds and there are five–six apple trees. But the fruit drop and lie in the grass, so sour nobody want it. At the back, near the wall, is a bigger tree—this garden certainly take up a lot of room, perhaps that's why they want to pull the place down.

Not much rain all the summer, but not much sunshine either. More of a glare. The grass get brown and dry, the weeds grow tall, the leaves on the trees hang down. Only the red flowers—the poppies—stand up to that light, everything else look weary.

I don't trouble about money, but what with wine and shillings for the slot-meters, it go quickly; so I don't waste much on food. In the evening I walk outside—not by the apple trees but near the street—it's not so lonely.

There's no wall here and I can see the woman next door looking at me over the hedge. At first I say good evening, but she turn away her head, so afterwards I don't speak. A man is often with her, he wear a straw hat with a black ribbon and goldrim spectacles. His suit hang on him like it's too big. He's the husband it seems and he stare at me worse than his wife—he stare as if I'm wild animal let loose. Once I laugh in his face because why these people have to be like that? I don't bother them. In the end I get that I don't even give them one single glance. I have plenty other things to worry about.

To show you how I felt. I don't remember exactly. But I believe it's the second Saturday after I come that when I'm at the window just before I go for my wine I feel somebody's hand on my shoulder and it's Mr. Sims. He must walk very quiet because I don't know a thing till he touch me.

He says hullo, then he tells me I've got terrible thin, do I ever eat. I say of course I eat but he goes on that it doesn't suit me at all to be so thin and he'll buy some food in the village. (That's the way he talk. There's no village here. You don't get away from London so quick.)

It don't seem to me he look very well himself, but I just say bring a drink instead, as I am not hungry.

He come back with three bottles—vermouth, gin and red wine. Then he ask if the little devil who was here last smash all the glasses and I tell him she smash some, I find the pieces. But not all. "You fight with her, eh?"

He laugh, and he don't answer. He pour out the drinks then he says "Now, you eat up those sandwiches."

Some men when they are there you don't worry so much. These sort of men you do all they tell you blind-fold because they can take the trouble from your heart

and make you think you're safe. It's nothing they say or
do. It's a feeling they can give you. So I don't talk with
him seriously—I don't want to spoil that evening. But I
ask about the house and why it's so empty and he says:

"Has the old trout upstairs been gossiping?"

I tell him, "She suppose they make difficulties for you."

"It was a damn bad buy," he says and talks about selling the lease or something. I don't listen much.

We were standing by the window then and the sun
low. No more glare. He puts his hand over my eyes. "Too
big—much too big for your face," he says and kisses me
like you kiss a baby. When he takes his hand away I see
he's looking out at the garden and he says this—"It gets
you. My God it does."

I know very well it's not me he means, so I ask him,
"Why sell it then? If you like it, keep it."

"Sell what?" he says. "I'm not talking about this damned
house."

I ask what he's talking about. "Money," he says.
"Money. That's what I'm talking about. Ways of making
it."

"I don't think so much of money. It don't like me and
what do I care?" I was joking, but he turns around, his
face quite pale and he tells me I'm a fool. He tells me
I'll get push around all my life and die like a dog, only
worse because they'd finish off a dog, but they'll let me
live till I'm a caricature of myself. That's what he say,
"Caricature of yourself." He say I'll curse the day I was
born and everything and everybody in this bloody world
before I'm done.

I tell him, "No I'll never feel like that," and he smiles,
if you can call it a smile, and says he's glad I'm content
with my lot. "I'm disappointed in you, Selina. I thought
you had more spirit."

"If I contented that's all right," I answer him, "I don't
see very many looking contented over here." We're standing staring at each other when the door bell rings. "That's
a friend of mine," he says. "I'll let him in."

As to the friend, he's all dressed up in stripe pants and
a black jacket and he's carrying a briefcase. Very ordinary looking but with a soft kind of voice.

"Maurice, this is Selina Davis," says Mr. Sims, and Maurice smiles very kind but it don't mean much, then he looks at his watch and says they ought to be getting along.

At the door Mr. Sims tells me he'll see me next week and I answer straight out, "I won't be here next week because I want a job and I won't get one in this place."

"Just what I'm going to talk about. Give it a week longer, Selina."

I say, "Perhaps I stay a few more days. Then I go. Perhaps I go before."

"Oh no you won't go," he says.

They walk to the gates quickly and drive off in a yellow car. Then I feel eyes on me and it's the woman and her husband in the next-door garden watching. The man made some remark and she look at me so hateful, so hating I shut the front door quick.

I don't want more wine. I want to go to bed early because I must think. I must think about money. It's true I don't care for it. Even when somebody steal my savings —this happen soon after I get to the Notting Hill house —I forget it soon. About thirty pounds they steal. I keep it roll up in a pair of stockings, but I go to the drawer one day, and no money. In the end I have to tell the police. They ask me exact sum and I say I don't count it lately, about thirty pounds. "You don't know how much?" they say. "When did you count it last? Do you remember? Was it before you move or after?"

I get confuse, and I keep saying, "I don't remember," though I remember well I see it two days before. They don't believe me and when a policeman come to the house I hear the landlady tell him, "She certainly had no money when she came here. She wasn't able to pay a month's rent in advance for her room though it's a rule in this house." "These people terrible liars," she say and I think "It's you a terrible liar, because when I come you tell me weekly or monthly as you like." It's from that time she don't speak to me and perhaps it's she take it. All I know is I never see one penny of my savings again, all I know is they pretend I never have any, but as it's gone, no use to cry about it. Then my mind goes to my

father, for my father is a white man and I think a lot
about him. If I could see him only once, for I too small
to remember when he was there. My mother is fair-
coloured woman, fairer than I am they say, and she
don't stay long with me either. She have a chance to go
to Venezuela when I three–four year old and she never
come back. She send money instead. It's my grandmother
take care of me. She's quite dark and what we call
"country-cookie" but she's the best I know.

She save up all the money my mother send, she don't
keep one penny for herself—that's how I get to England.
I was a bit late in going to school regular, getting on for
twelve years, but I can sew very beautiful, excellent—so
I think I get a good job—in London perhaps.

However here they tell me all this fine handsewing
take too long. Waste of time—too slow. They want
somebody to work quick and to hell with the small
stitches. Altogether it don't look so good for me, I must
say, and I wish I could see my father. I have his name—
Davis. But my grandmother tell me, "Every word that
come out of that man's mouth a damn lie. He is certainly
first-class liar, though no class otherwise." So perhaps I
have not even his real name.

Last thing I see before I put the light out is the postcard on the dressing table. "Not to worry."

Not to worry! Next day is Sunday, and it's on the
Monday the people next door complain about me to the
police. That evening the woman is by the hedge, and
when I pass her she says in very sweet quiet voice, "*Must
you stay? Can't you go?*" I don't answer. I walk out in the
street to get rid of her. But she run inside her house to
the window, she can still see me. Then I start to sing, so
she can understand I'm not afraid of her. The husband
call out: "If you don't stop that noise I'll send for the
police." I answer them quite short. I say, "You go to hell
and take your wife with you." And I sing louder.

The police come pretty quick—two of them. Maybe
they just around the corner. All I can say about police
and how they behave is I think it all depend who they
dealing with. Of my own free will I don't want to mix
up with police. No.

One man says, you can't cause this disturbance here. But the other asks a lot of questions. What is my name? Am I tenant of a flat in No. 17? How long have I lived there? Last address and so on. I get vexed the way he speak and I tell him, "I come here because somebody steal my savings. Why you don't look for my money instead of bawling at me? I work hard for my money. All-you don't do one single thing to find it."

"What's she talking about?" the first one says, and the other one tells me, "You can't make that noise here. Get along home. You've been drinking."

I see that woman looking at me and smiling, and other people at their windows, and I'm so angry I bawl at them too. I say, "I have absolute and perfect right to be in the street same as anybody else, and I have absolute and perfect right to ask the police why they don't even look for my money when it disappear. It's because a dam' English thief take it you don't look," I say. The end of all this is that I have to go before a magistrate, and he fine me five pounds for drunk and disorderly, and he give me two weeks to pay.

When I get back from the court I walk up and down the kitchen, up and down, waiting for six o'clock because I have no five pounds left, and I don't know what to do. I telephone at six and a woman answers me very short and sharp, then Mr. Sims comes along and he don't sound too pleased either when I tell him what happen. "Oh Lord!" he says, and I say I'm sorry. "Well don't panic," he says. "I'll pay the fine. But look, I don't think . . ." Then he breaks off and talk to some other person in the room. He goes on, "Perhaps better not stay at No. 17. I think I can arrange something else. I'll call for you Wednesday—Saturday latest. Now behave till then." And he hang up before I can answer that I don't want to wait till Wednesday, much less Saturday. I want to get out of that house double quick and with no delay. First I think I ring back, then I think better not as he sounds so vex.

I get ready, but Wednesday he don't come and Saturday he don't come. All the week I stay in the flat. Only once I go out and arrange for bread, milk and eggs to be left at the door, and seems to me I meet up with a lot of policemen. They don't look at me, but they see me all right. I don't want to drink—I'm all the time listening, listening and thinking, how can I leave before I know if my fine is paid—I tell myself the police let me know, that's certain. But I don't trust them. What they care? The answer is Nothing. Nobody care. One afternoon I knock at the old lady's flat upstairs, because I get the idea she give me good advice. I can hear her moving about and talking, but she don't answer and I never try again.

Nearly two weeks pass like that, then I telephone. It's the woman speaking and she say, "Mr. Sims is not in London at present." I ask, "When will he be back—it's urgent," and she hang up. I'm not surprised. Not at all. I knew that would happen. All the same I feel heavy like lead. Near the phone box is a chemist's shop, so I ask him for something to make me sleep, the day is bad enough, but to lie awake all night—Ah no! He gives me a little bottle marked ONE OR TWO TABLETS ONLY and I take three when I go to bed because more and more I think that sleeping is better than no matter what else. However, I lie there, eyes wide open as usual, so I take three more. Next thing I know the room is full of sunlight, so it must be late afternoon, but the lamp is still on. My head turn around and I can't think well at all. At first I ask myself how I got to the place. Then it comes to me, but in pictures—like the landlady kicking my dress, and when I take my ticket at Victoria Station, and Mr. Sims telling me to eat the sandwiches, but I can't remember everything clear, and I feel very giddy and sick. I take in the milk and eggs at the door, go in the kitchen, and try to eat but the food hard to swallow.

It's when I'm putting the things away that I see the bottles—pushed back on the lowest shelf in the cupboard.

There's a lot of drink left, and I'm glad I tell you. Because I can't bear the way I feel. Not any more. I mix a gin and vermouth and I drink it quick, then I mix another and drink it slow by the window. The garden looks different, like I never see it before. I know quite well what I must do, but it's late now—tomorrow. I have one more drink, of wine this time, and then a song come in my head, I sing it and I dance it, and more I sing, more I am sure this is the best tune that has ever come to me in all my life.

The sunset light from the window is gold colour. My shoes sound loud on the boards. So I take them off, my stockings too and go on dancing but the room feel shut in, I can't breathe, and I go outside still singing. Maybe I dance a bit too, I forget all about that woman till I hear her saying, "Henry, look at this." I turn around and I see her at the window. "Oh yes, I wanted to speak with you," I say. "Why bring the police and get me in bad trouble? Tell me that."

"And you tell *me* what you're doing here at all," she says. "This is a respectable neighbourhood."

Then the man come along. "Now young woman, take yourself off. You ought to be ashamed of this behaviour."

"It's disgraceful," he says, talking to his wife, but loud so I can hear, and she speaks loud too—for once. "At least the other tarts that crook installed here were *white* girls," she says.

"You a dam' fouti liar," I say. "Plenty of those girls in your country already. Numberless as the sands on the shore. You don't need me for that."

"You're not a howling success at it certainly." Her voice sweet sugar again. "And you won't be seeing much more of your friend Mr. Sims. He's in trouble too. Try somewhere else. Find somebody else. If you can, of course." When she say that my arm moves of itself. I pick up a stone and bam! through the window. Not the one they are standing at but the next, which is of coloured glass, green and purple and yellow.

I never see a woman look so surprise. Her mouth fall open she so full of surprise. I start to laugh, louder and louder—I laugh like my grandmother, with my hands on my hips and my head back. (When she laugh like that you can hear her to the end of our street.) At last I say, "Well, I'm sorry. An accident. I get it fixed tomorrow early." "That glass is irreplaceable," the man says. "Irreplaceable." "Good thing," I say, "those colours look like they seasick to me. I buy you a better windowglass."

He shake his fist at me. "You won't be let off with a fine this time," he says. Then they draw the curtains. I call out at them. "You run away. Always you run away. Ever since I come here you hunt me down because I don't answer back. It's you shameless." I try to sing "Don't Trouble Me Now."

> "Don't trouble me now
> You without honour.
> Don't walk in my footstep
> You without shame."

But my voice don't sound right, so I get back indoors and drink one more glass of wine—still wanting to laugh, and still thinking of my grandmother for that is one of her songs.

It's about a man whose doudou give him the go-by when she find somebody rich and he sail away to Panama. Plenty people die there of fever when they make that Panama canal so long ago. But he don't die. He come back with dollars and the girl meet him on the jetty, all dressed up and smiling. Then he sing to her, "You without honour, you without shame." It sound good in Martinique patois too: "*Sans honte*."

Afterwards I ask myself, "Why I do that? It's not like me. But if they treat you wrong over and over again the hour strike when you burst out that's what."

Too besides, Mr. Sims can't tell me now I have no spirit. I don't care, I sleep quickly and I'm glad I break the woman's ugly window. But as to my own song it go *right* away and it never come back. A pity.

Next morning the doorbell ringing wake me up. The people upstairs don't come down, and the bell keeps on like fury self. So I go to look, and there is a policeman and a policewoman outside. As soon as I open the door the woman put her foot in it. She wear sandals and thick stockings and I never see a foot so big or so bad. It look like it want to mash up the whole world. Then she come in after the foot, and her face not so pretty either. The policeman tell me my fine is not paid and people make serious complaints about me, so they're taking me back to the magistrate. He show me a paper and I look at it, but I don't read it. The woman push me in the bedroom, and tell me to get dress quickly, but I just stare at her, because I think perhaps I wake up soon. Then I ask her what I must wear. She say she suppose I had some clothes on yesterday. Or not? "What's it matter, wear anything," she says. But I find clean underclothes and stockings and my shoes with high heels and I comb my hair. I start to file my nails, because I think they too long for magistrate's court but she get angry. "Are you coming quietly or aren't you?" she says. So I go with them and we get in a car outside.

I wait for a long time in a room full of policemen. They come in, they go out, they telephone, they talk in low voices. Then it's my turn, and first thing I notice in the court room is a man with frowning black eyebrows. He sit below the magistrate, he dressed in black and he so handsome I can't take my eyes off him. When he see that he frown worse than before.

First comes a policeman to testify I cause disturbance, and then comes the old gentleman from next door. He repeat that bit about nothing but the truth so help me God. Then he says I make dreadful noise at night and use abominable language, and dance in obscene fashion. He says when they try to shut the curtains because his wife so terrify of me, I throw stones and break a valuable stain-glass window. He say his wife get serious injury if she'd been hit, and as it is she in terrible nervous condition and the doctor is with her. I think, "Believe me, if I aim at your wife I hit your wife—that's certain." "There was no provocation," he says. "None at all." Then another lady from across the street says this is true. She heard no provocation whatsoever, and she swear that they shut the curtains but I go on insulting them and using filthy language and she saw all this and heard it.

The magistrate is a little gentleman with a quiet voice, but I'm very suspicious of these quiet voices now. He ask me why I don't pay my fine, and I say because I haven't the money. I get the idea they want to find out all about Mr. Sims—they listen so very attentive. But they'll find out nothing from me. He ask how long I have the flat and

I say I don't remember. I know they want to trip me up like they trip me up about my savings so I won't answer. At last he ask if I have anything to say as I can't be allowed to go on being a nuisance. I think, "I'm nuisance to you because I have no money that's all." I want to speak up and tell him how they steal all my savings, so when my landlord asks for month's rent I haven't got it to give. I want to tell him the woman next door provoke me since long time and call me bad names but she have a soft sugar voice and nobody hear—that's why I broke her window, but I'm ready to buy another after all. I want to say all I do is sing in that old garden, and I want to say this in decent quiet voice. But I hear myself talking loud and I see my hands wave in the air. Too besides it's no use, they won't believe me, so I don't finish. I stop, and I feel the tears on my face. "Prove it." That's all they will say. They whisper, they whisper. They nod, they nod.

Next thing I'm in a car again with a different police-woman, dressed very smart. Not in uniform. I ask her where she's taking me and she says "Holloway" just that "Holloway."

I catch hold of her hand because I'm afraid. But she takes it away. Cold and smooth her hand slide away and her face is china face—smooth like a doll and I think, "This is the last time I ask anything from anybody. So help me God."

The car come up to a black castle and little mean streets are all round it. A lorry was blocking up the castle gates. When it get by we pass through and I am in jail. First I stand in a line with others who are waiting to give up handbags and all belongings to a woman behind bars like in a post office. The girl in front bring out a nice compact, look like gold to me, lipstick to match and a wallet full of notes. The woman keep the money, but she give back the powder and lipstick and she halfsmile. I have two pounds seven shillings and sixpence in pennies. She take my purse, then she throw me my compact (which is cheap), my comb and my handkerchief like everything in my bag is dirty. So I think, "Here too, here too." But I tell myself, "Girl, what you expect, eh? They all like that. All."

Some of what happen afterwards I forget, or perhaps

better not remember. Seems to me they start by trying
to frighten you. But they don't succeed with me for I
don't care for nothing now, it's as if my heart hard like a
rock and I can't feel.

Then I'm standing at the top of a staircase with a lot
of women and girls. As we are going down I notice the
railing very low on one side, very easy to jump, and a
long way below there's the grey stone passage like it's
waiting for you.

As I'm thinking this a uniform woman step up along-
side quick and grab my arm. She say, "Oh no you don't."

I was just noticing the railing very low that's all—but
what's the use of saying so.

Another long line waits for the doctor. It move forward
slowly and my legs terrible tired. The girl in front is very
young and she cry and cry. "I'm scared," she keeps saying. She's lucky in a way—as for me I never will cry
again. It all dry up and hard in me now. That, and a lot
besides. In the end I tell her to stop, because she doing
just what these people want her to do.

She stop crying and start a long story, but while she is
speaking her voice get very far away, and I find I can't
see her face clear at all.

Then I'm in a chair, and one of those uniform women
is pushing my head down between my knees, but let her
push—everything go away from me just the same.

They put me in the hospital because the doctor say I'm
sick. I have cell by myself and it's all right except I don't
sleep. The things they say you mind I don't mind.

When they clang the door on me I think, "You shut
me in, but you shut all those other dam' devils *out*. They
can't reach me now."

At first it bothers me when they keep on looking at me
all through the night. They open a little window in the
doorway to do this. But I get used to it and get used to
the night chemise they give me. It very thick, and to my
mind it not very clean either—but what's that matter to
me? Only the food I can't swallow—especially the porridge. The woman ask me sarcastic, "Hunger striking?"
But afterwards I can leave most of it, and she don't say
nothing.

One day a nice girl comes around with books and she

give me two, but I don't want to read so much. Beside one is about a murder, and the other is about a ghost and I don't think it's at all like those books tell you.

There is nothing I want now. It's no use. If they leave me in peace and quiet that's all I ask. The window is barred but not small, so I can see a little thin tree through the bars, and I like watching it.

After a week they tell me I'm better and I can go out with the others for exercise. We walk round and round one of the yards in that castle—it is fine weather and the sky is a kind of pale blue, but the yard is a terrible sad place. The sunlight fall down and die there. I get tired walking in high heels and I'm glad when that's over.

We can talk, and one day an old woman come up and ask me for dog-ends. I don't understand, and she start muttering at me like she very vexed. Another woman tell me she mean cigarette ends, so I say I don't smoke. But the old woman still look angry, and when we're going in she give me one push and I nearly fall down. I'm glad to get away from these people, and hear the door clang and take my shoes off.

Sometimes I think, "I'm here because I wanted to sing" and I have to laugh. But there's a small looking glass in my cell and I see myself and I'm like somebody else. Like some strange new person. Mr. Sims tell me I too thin, but what he say now to this person in the looking glass? So I don't laugh again.

Usually I don't think at all. Everything and everybody seem small and far away, that is the only trouble.

Twice the doctor come to see me. He don't say much and I don't say anything, because a uniform woman is always there. She look like she thinking. "Now the lies start." So I prefer not to speak. Then I'm sure they can't trip me up. Perhaps I there still, or in a worse place. But one day this happen.

We were walking round and round in the yard and I hear a woman singing—the voice come from high up, from one of the small barred windows. At first I don't believe it. Why should anybody sing here? Nobody want to sing in jail, nobody want to do anything. There's no reason, and you have no hope. I think I must be asleep, dreaming, but I'm awake all right and I see all the others are listening too. A nurse is with us that afternoon, not a policewoman. She stop and look up at the window.

It's a smoky kind of voice, and a bit rough sometimes, as if those old dark walls theyselves are complaining, because they see too much misery—too much. But it don't fall down and die in the courtyard; seems to me it could jump the gates of the jail easy and travel far, and nobody could stop it. I don't hear the words—only the music. She sing one verse and she begin another, then she break off sudden. Everybody starts walking again, and nobody says one word. But as we go in I ask the woman in front who was singing. "That's the Holloway song," she says. "Don't you know it yet? She was singing from the punishment cells, and she tell the girls cheerio and never say die." Then I have to go one way to the hospital block and she goes another so we don't speak again.

When I'm back in my cell I can't just wait for bed. I walk up and down and I think. "One day I hear that song on trumpets and these walls will fall and rest." I want to get out so bad I could hammer on the door, for I know now that anything can happen, and I don't want to stay lock up here and miss it.

Then I'm hungry. I eat everything they bring and in the morning I'm still so hungry I eat the porridge. Next time the doctor come he tells me I seem much better. Then I say a little of what really happen in that house. Not much. Very careful.

He look at me hard and kind of surprised. At the door he shake his finger and says, "Now don't let me see you here again."

That evening the woman tells me I'm going, but she's so upset about it I don't ask questions. Very early, before it's light she bangs the door open and shouts at me to hurry up. As we're going along the passages I see the girl who gave me the books. She's in a row with others doing exercises. Up Down, Up Down, Up. We pass quite close and I notice she's looking very pale and tired. It's crazy, it's all crazy. This up down business and everything else too. When they give me my money I remember I leave my compact in the cell, so I ask if I can go back for it. You should see that policewoman's face as she shoo me on.

There's no car, there's a van and you can't see through the windows. The third time it stop I get out with one other, a young girl, and it's the same magistrate's court as before.

The two of us wait in a small room, nobody else there, and after a while the girl say, "What the hell are they doing? I don't want to spend all day here." She go to the bell and she keep her finger press on it. When I look at her she say, "Well, what are they *for*?" That girl's face is hard like a board—she could change faces with many and you wouldn't know the difference. But she get results certainly. A policeman come in, all smiling, and we go in the court. The same magistrate, the same frowning man sits below, and when I hear my fine is paid I want to ask who paid it, but he yells at me, "Silence."

I think I will never understand the half of what happen, but they tell me I can go, and I understand that. The magistrate ask if I'm leaving the neighbourhood and I say yes, then I'm out in the streets again, and it's the same fine weather, same feeling I'm dreaming.

When I get to the house I see two men talking in the garden. The front door and the door of the flat are both open. I go in, and the bedroom is empty, nothing but the glare streaming inside because they take the Venetian blinds away. As I'm wondering where my suitcase is, and the clothes I leave in the wardrobe, there's a knock and it's the old lady from upstairs carrying my case packed, and my coat is over her arm. She says she sees me come in. "I kept your things for you." I start to thank her but she turn her back and walk away. They like that here, and better not expect too much. Too besides, I bet they tell her I'm terrible person.

I go in the kitchen, but when I see they are cutting down the big tree at the back I don't stay to watch.

At the station I'm waiting for the train and a woman asks if I feel well. "You look so tired," she says. "Have you come a long way?" I want to answer, "I come so far I lose myself on that journey." But I tell her, "Yes, I am quite well. But I can't stand the heat." She says she can't stand it either, and we talk about the weather till the train come in.

I'm not frightened of them anymore—after all what else can they do? I know what to say and everything go like a clock works.

I get a room near Victoria where the landlady accept one pound in advance, and next day I find a job in the kitchen of a private hotel close by. But I don't stay there long. I hear of another job going in a big store—altering ladies' dresses and I get that. I lie and tell them I work in very expensive New York shop. I speak bold and smooth faced, and they never check up on me. I make a friend there—Clarice—very light-coloured, very smart, she have a lot to do with the customers and she laugh at some of them behind their backs. But I say it's not their fault if the dress don't fit. Special dress for one person only—that's very expensive in London. So it's take in, or let out all the time. Clarice have two rooms not far from the store. She furnish them herself gradual and she gives parties sometimes Saturday nights. It's there I start whistling the Holloway song. A man comes up to me and says, "Let's hear that again." So I whistle it again (I never sing now) and he tells me "Not bad." Clarice have an old piano somebody give her to store and he plays the tune, jazzing it up. I say, "No, not like that," but everybody else say the way he do it is first-class. Well I think no more of this till I get a letter from him telling me he has sold the song and as I was quite a help he encloses five pounds with thanks.

I read the letter and I could cry. For after all, that song was all I had. I don't belong nowhere really, and I haven't money to buy my way to belonging. I don't want to either.

But when that girl sing, she sing to me, and she sing for me. I was there because I was *meant* to be there. It was *meant* I should hear it—this I *know*.

Now I've let them play it wrong, and it will go from

me like all the other songs—like everything. Nothing left for me at all.

But then I tell myself all this is foolishness. Even if they played it on trumpets, even if they played it just right, like I wanted—no walls would fall so soon. "So let them call it jazz," I think, and let them play it wrong. That won't make no difference to the song I heard.

I buy myself a dusty pink dress with the money.

DYNASTIC ENCOUNTER

by Marge Piercy

When the knocking came, Maud was taking a sponge bath. Grabbing the sheet from the daybed she stuck her head out. One of the old men from the first floor stood there looking sore. "You got a phone call—why don't you come down when I call? All the way up here on account of you don't listen . . ."

Clutching the sheet she ran for the extension. Hearing Duncan's voice she was sure it was all off. "Duncan, what is it? He can't make it? He won't meet me?"

"Of course, Maud, don't get excited. Didn't I tell you it's all arranged?" His voice playing cool and dependable. "Just a little change of plans. First, we're not meeting at my place."

"Oh." Good-bye to his wife's potato salad, the rye bread and cheeses—port salut, roquefort, camembert. All day she had been figuring the odds on salami, slicing those virgin cheeses. Gorgonzola, gouda, crema danica.

"Bill wants to meet us in town, at the Low Blow. There's a jazz group he wants to hear." The familiarity of the first name hung on the telephone wire as if with clothes pins.

She had an urge to add the last name. The lumpy old man from downstairs had not hung up. He would not know who W. Saltzman was. They hated her in the rooming house, her and the two still sexual men up on three: said they were noisy, said they used the phone too much. Doors opened eyewide behind her in the halls, but when she spoke, the old men answered with suspiciously pursed lips, if at all.

Duncan was warning briskly that she not be late. He would pick her up—he and the wife, chuckle. Damp under the sheet she ran for her room. Duncan was eager to

make her, would like to set up an extracurricular lay on
Fridays after his last class. He taught at the College but
lived in a house adorned with oriental carpets in an older
suburb. With lumbering suaveness he tried to nudge her
guilty for lunches at his expense in an off-campus Italian
restaurant. Often he spoke of his friendship with the poet
W. Saltzman, discovering in her work even more influence than there was, quoting the great man on trivial
occasions. Introducing Saltzman was an attempt to net her
in obligation: rubbing herself dry, she grinned.

Rhoda, his wife, was an excellent cook. Rhoda: chicken
gently sautéed in white-wine sauce, roast sesame lamb,
avocado salad. She would move in if Rhoda would cook
for her. But Duncan was a beefy milk-fed professor; from
dead men's bones he ground plastic bread. He was so sure
she was his proper prey, a rootless, nameless arty girl half
nuts and outside the pale: because it never, never occurred
to him that she might be right.

She put on her good dress—the shade of blue was good,
anyhow. The refrigerator held about a glass of milk and
something in a napkin. She had babysat for a couple
she'd known during her stint teaching at the College.
Besides baby food, she'd turned up maraschino cherries,
cocktail onions and half a box of animal crackers. She
had consumed the cherries and onions and carried off the
box. She poured out a little milk and sat slowly chewing
the crackers, eating each animal paw by paw and the
head last.

She crossed to the john then. The light was on, the
door ajar. The toilet was filled to the brim, splashing over
to puddle the floor. Lazily like a carp in the bowl a long
cigar-brown turd floated. She backed out.

She had as landlady an ex-inmate of Treblinka. She
would go down tomorrow to complain, and Mrs. Goldman would show her her tattoo: Mr. Goldman and the
little Goldmen long since ashes. Mrs. Goldman would
assure her she was lucky to be in the United States and
alive. She would retreat apologizing. Nothing was com-
mensurate, and the plumbing broke down every two weeks.
Mrs. Goldman would hint she was flushing Tampax down
the toilet, and she would deny it. Mrs. Goldman would

bat her large weak eyes in disbelief. She and Mrs. Gold-man would continue the argument as she backed up the staircase. Then Mrs. Goldman would utter a few Yiddish curses for women of loose morals and retire, slamming her door. She would piss in the sink as she did now and go over to the College whenever possible. The College, where she had taught until replaced by a Ph.D., had useful facilities.

She reread the poems she had gone through five times. Saltzman could tell her where to send stuff, give her intro-ductions, even help her find a job, point her out to editors, tell her how to get a book published. He was power. Be-sides it was getting to be winter. Though he was not her only literary pa, surely he would not mind the other influences. He was the local boy and everybody claimed to know him or his ex-girlfriend or his dentist. Imagining this meeting had soothed her to sleep bitter nights. She felt she was moving in darkness about to come round a corner into blinding light and be—not consumed—transfigured. Someday she would make it, why not now? She had to: how else could she survive?

The buzzer rasped. She jumped up. Turned, grabbed the envelope of poems. Clearly saw herself in the bar bearing down on him poems in hand. She took out the bottom three, her cream, shoved them in her purse. Just happened to have on me. Well, shit, he can ask. Shrugging on her mouton coat.

Going slowly down—if she hurried she would fall—she felt the weight of the coat. It had been Sandy's. A year in the state hatch, insulin, electric shock and hydrotherapy had dulled her, but not enough. When Mrs. Gross decided Sandy was getting too wild and must be put away again, Sandy went up on the apartment-house roof and jumped. She saw Sandy's long curious face, her tea-brown hair, her freckled hands with the chewed nails, so vividly she could not take in Duncan. Docilely she followed him to the small Mercedes and got in back.

"What, Rhoda?" She came to. "Oh, Harry the Tailor got robbed. No, they didn't smash the window when they robbed him, it was a man and a woman and they cut him up." She sat with head ducked, assuming Sandy's old position with hands knit, foot tapping shyly. Dead, stone dead. "No, some kids smashed the window, after." Mrs. Gross had acted funny when she gave her the coat. Maud had not wanted it, but she did need a coat. Further, she felt a right to Sandy's things. What she wanted was Sandy's books, but Mrs. Gross brought out the coat. Mrs. Gross kept talking about how much she had paid for it, what good condition it was in, how little Sandy had worn it, till Maud had taken it to please her.

She sat up, her knuckles bumping her teeth. Mrs. Gross had wanted her to pay for the coat. Then she began to laugh, covering her mouth so they would not hear.

Rhoda was sitting turned from Duncan. Her coat had a high fur collar, her reddish hair was done up in smooth whorls, and she radiated a faint smell of hair spray and spicy perfume. Rhoda did not like her because she was young, single and therefore presumably scheming. She and Rhoda were always talking in oblique boring sideways conversations. If they were to talk straight out:

RHODA: See my house! See my pretty things! They cost a lot! See how expensive I am.

MAUD: If you can't get out the door, have you tried the window?

RHODA: See my man. No Trespassing! Keep Off the Grass!

MAUD: It's only lunch I want. I swear it'll never happen while I'm conscious.

Duncan was of middle height but he sat tall: the Man behind the Desk. A sandy thirty-eight, his jaw was square and he thrust it forward like a girl proud of her bosom. "Did you call Julie Norman about the seventeenth? I want her at the party."

"Duncan, I hardly know her," Rhoda whined.

"What do you mean, you don't know her? What do you do at those meetings?"

"You know what I mean." Rhoda's neck arched from the collar: angry goose neck stretching. "She won't remember me."

"Well, make her remember. Doesn't Susan play with her kid?"

"Let's leave Susan out of this."

"Out of what?" Duncan reared back from the wheel. "Can't you make a simple phone call?"

Williams Saltzman (Bill, Duncan had called him: hello, Bill, help!) made and broke reputations. His earlier poems were in the newer college anthologies. He had put out a paperback of younger poets, and why not me, dear God. Would he be queer? He was supposed to have had that affair with a woman anthropologist. Besides, his poems were full of breasts. She reached down the neck of her dress and jerked the bra straps tighter. Made a languorous face of surrender and giggled in disgust.

"There's the Low Blow." She leaned over Rhoda's shoulder to point.

"Yes, love, but do you think I can check the car with the hatgirl?"

Dashboard clock read five to nine. Her stomach dropped.

"There's a lot," Rhoda sang out.

"We're paying through the nose for a sitter. Hold on. Plenty of onstreet parking."

They passed the Low Blow again. If it were like other jazz spots there would be nothing to eat. The rock music she went to hear with her last man never came there. Maybe afterward sandwiches, roast beef or pastrami. The clock hand slipped down from nine.

"Maybe he won't wait, Duncan, if we're late."

"What do you think he'll do, go home? He'll be there."

Around the block again past the Mad Place, past the Squaw Man All Night Hairdressers, past the Low Blow and Orvieto's Pizzeria and Ron's Ale House and around the other corner. She sank back, cradling her cheek in her coat. Open the door and make a break for it. "There's somebody pulling out!" she yelled. He jammed on the brakes and backed jerkily into position, ignoring a Lincoln leaning on its horn.

"See," he said, expansive on the sidewalk with an arm guiding each woman, "why pay a couple of bucks, could be three? A little patience. Keep cool."

She dodged free of Duncan's arm entering and shrank behind him. What was the use, he wouldn't like her stuff. He must have his own protégées.

Duncan got tense, solider. "There he is."

"Where? Which one?" From behind she poked his arm.
"By the bar, talking with that big colored fellow."

Peeking around him, she studied Saltzman. Over what
looked like someone else's army fatigues he wore what
had been a good leather jacket, lined with fleece. He ought
to feel hot in the close room. He was tall with a gaunt face,
a short kinky mustard-yellow beard streaked with gray
and a paunch sloping somewhat over the trousers.

His gaze on them, when finally he ended the conversation and started over, was cold and cat green. She thought
him a fine-looking man, because he was W. Saltzman and
she knew his poems backwards, and because his cheeks
and forehead were textured like weathered bark, and also
because he had a satyr's paunch and must like food. But
his eyes were cold as the sidewalks outside. Shuffling behind came a man his age and seedier, broader built, with a
ruddy face, strong white hair and a knowing grin. Saltzman came at a slow deliberate amble, looked at Duncan's
outstretched hand for a moment, touched it.

Duncan said nervously, "How are you making it?"

W. Saltzman grunted. He said hello to Rhoda, looked
then at Maud, was introduced. "We need a table, Ed,"
he said to the person who asked how many of them there
were.

"Sure, Willy, right up front." They hung back in brief
conversation. The table was tiny and near the stand. Saltzman and his friend, still unintroduced, lolled on one side,
and the three of them huddled on the other. The set was
starting.

"Uh, Bill," Duncan began.

Saltzman looked with his eyelids lowered and then
raised in disbelief. He motioned they should listen. The
first round of drinks was on the house: Saltzman was
known here. The second Duncan bought. The Scotch hurt
her stomach. The tenor sax was a name she had heard,
though she had thought him dead: a contemporary of
Charlie Parker in early bop. She listened conscientiously,
conscientiously not looking at Saltzman. Her hands
sweated cold. Saltzman offered a cigarette. She fumbled.
Politely he lit it. The sound was dull, finally. The music
said little to her, and after a while she was not listening

but daydreaming about her next-to-last man, about getting published and getting laid and getting fed and keeping warm . . . warm with the lax flabby music and the booze, warm . . .

Duncan asked, "What's that smell?"

She felt a stab on her thigh. "Oh, shit." A hot ash had fallen from her cigarette and burnt through the dress. She brushed at it.

"What's wrong?" Saltzman looked halfway interested.

"Nothing, nothing really." Her face heated.

The waitress brought another round, and, after a pause, Duncan again paid. Fixing her eyes on Saltzman's mustard beard she willed him to notice her, to speak. At last when the set finished, he did.

He asked gently, "What do you do with yourself?"

Hadn't Duncan explained? "For a job you mean? I was teaching, and then—"

"Is that how you know each other, from the College?"

They nodded and he leaned back as if his curiosity were satisfied. Quickly she added the important part. "But that's just what I do to support it, you know. I mean, I write poems."

His face shrank. "*Oh.*"

His friend said cheerfully, "Everybody's doing it, doing it, doing it. They think it's poetry, but it's snot."

Her words lay on the table like a fat turd. For a moment she hated him. Did he think he would be the last poet? Duncan, the bastard, had said nothing. Produced her as random female.

Saltzman turned to him. "That workshop, how about it? I expected to hear by now. Is it coming off?"

The friend was staring at Duncan with shrewd assessment. Duncan furrowed his brow. "Arrangements take time. Departments of English move exceedingly slowly and grind exceedingly fine. I'm pushing for it, every chance I get."

"Eh." The friend's mouth sagged. He shrugged his disbelief.

"I have to know soon. Other things depend on it."

pay rent too. Ask the little lady."

"I'm trying to get a decision," Duncan said. "I'm trying to put it through. But you know how encrusted with tradition—"

"Out on the West Coast I had twelve readings in two weeks, including a couple of lectures."

"Kids were standing up outside wanting to hear him," the friend said. "Crowds of college kids."

"By the way, Saturday the seventeenth we're having a sort of pre-holiday thing. Wassail bowl and all, right, Rhoda? Most of the department will be there and the boys from the press, and we'd sure like to see you. And your friend too," he added weakly, but the tone of the invitation was confident.

Saltzman's old tomcat eyes went opaque. Dunc was putting it on the line. Even if Saltzman went, he wouldn't know if Duncan could really get him the workshop or wanted to. Cf. her vague feeling that Duncan could have saved her job. "Sounds fine," said Saltzman. "We'll have to see. I'm spending the holidays in New York, and I don't know when I'm leaving."

The friend did not reply. Rattling the ice in her glass Rhoda came alive to ask, "Don't think I caught your name?"

"Charlie Roach," he said, inclining his head.

"He's one of the West Side Roaches," Saltzman said and caught Maud's gaze as she smiled. She had given up. She pitied him with his grizzled beard and still needing Duncan.

Rhoda was being social. "What do you do?" her voice slurred from the rapid drinking.

Charlie grinned. His teeth were stained and worn down in his ruddy face. "*Any*thing, Ma'am."

"Charlie's a true man of the golden rule, though he likes to operate a little ahead of the beat."

Rhoda was flustered, as designed, but Duncan was enjoying the show. They couldn't shock him if they slit their gullets on his tweeds. Saltzman lolled back, withdrawn. She remembered the poems in her purse and bowed her head, fingering the stiff edges of the cigarette burn.

They were leaving. As they passed the bar people here

and there slapped Saltzman's shoulder. On the sidewalk he halted, turned. For a moment he stared at her and she stared back. His eyes, ice green, were glacial crevasses, his mouth curled in a perhaps amused smile. The eyes said he was bored sick with women wanting to fuck his name, with men wanting to suck his talent: he'd been used and used like an old toothpaste tube, he was well chewed. She looked back posturing, can't you see my ineffable Name, I'm as real as you when you only wanted a young girl to chew on tonight: your mistake, Willy, I'm good and you won't get into my biography for saving me, so there!

Following Duncan and Rhoda to the car she said hopefully, "My, I'm hungry," but nobody answered. In the back seat she huddled into Sandy's coat. The first time she wore it she had found old Kleenexes in the pocket and, unable to have preserved Sandy, preserved them. Then she caught a cold.

Two days ago she had brooded over slitting her wrists: she felt ashamed. There were years, years yet of inventive tortures and deprivations, of hollow victories and bloody defeats. She no longer felt sorry for Saltzman. She would wear the same face. The worst that could happen then might be to meet a kid who had eaten her books and survived.

As for Duncan she could no longer afford his lasagna: she perceived he was her natural predator. The system supported him, and he supported the system. In any attempt to make a deal, he was more powerful than she and he would prevail.

A COLD-WATER FLAT

by Elizabeth Pollet

I am too young; and besides I am a girl. Being young is not a crime, but sometimes I feel as though it were one. For how do I know that what I do is right? The world is so large, and there are many possibilities I have not even heard of. I have decided to keep a secret self—and this is what led me to my definition of consciousness. Consciousness is the adjustment of the unconscious to reality. But all of the unconscious cannot be adjusted to reality and that is why secrets are necessary.

I want you to share my secrets and to sympathize with me. But not too much and only from a distance. I sympathize with other people who suffer and especially children. I cannot see a picture of a Chinese child with its stomach bloated without tears overflowing from my eyes; or the newsreels of Europe's war orphans. Even if the child is lucky and has a relative in America who will substitute for the dead parents, when I see them meeting I cry.

It isn't because people are dead, or because existence is so irrational, that I cry. I realize that my tears are useless, that they will not buy food; and even, that they do not water an emotional seed that will sprout and grow into anything good in me. But even though the constriction of my throat makes me feel at times as if I were strangling, my tears please me.

When I was younger (I have now reached the age of consent) I asked my mother and father, but not together, what made me cry. My mother said that she too was unhappy at my age, that I was now awkward and self-conscious, but that as I got older I would find myself growing more and more attractive to men (for that was what had happened to her). My father said it was natural for young girls to cry, and that some nation, probably the German, had a proverb for it.

I didn't like to say that I was sure they were wrong, that it was neither men nor the Weltanschauung of youth that was bothering me. Now I think that perhaps I cried to gain their attention, and to convince myself that there was some mysterious power in me that set me apart from my brothers and sisters, and my parents too. I opened my mouth to gain attention, just as I have very often since kept it closed for the same purpose.

Nothing they said was any help. I went right on crying. I was baffled: I didn't know what I was like or what the world was like. I felt undefined. My parents had brought me up to be unhappy, having created me, they should know the reason for my existence. But if I asked them, they might get upset. And besides it would be pretentious. I would never climb through the needle's eye that way. And then someone had bound me with a label: She is intellectually overdeveloped but emotionally immature! How did one get out of that?

I decided to run away. This running away was a matter of revenge but I told them ahead of time, and they gave me the money to start out with. At first I went home once a week to see how they were taking it, but gradually the center of my interests shifted. I discovered that there were other people like myself, just as unhappy, and just as proud and resentful. I got involved in Art and Feminism.

But my first problems were a job and an apartment. Instead of a miserable child, I was going to be an independent heroine. My mottoes were *to take life simply* and its corollary *to make the most out of everything*. A job and an apartment would already complicate things: I would have a landlord, an employer, neighbors, and co-employees. The apartment seemed more important to me than the job because it would be more my own. I thought of myself not as innocent but as honest. The great thing to be was *good*. It was how you lived and not what happened to you that mattered.

Perhaps the reader remembers the old tale: The daughter of a family goes to the cellar and sees a rusty sword hanging precariously. She begins to worry about the danger and ends up sitting beneath it sobbing. The other members of the family come down to find out what's wrong. She explains. They all end up sobbing together. Finally the idiot hero, who can't even get into his own trousers but hangs them on a bureau knob and tries to jump into them, appears. He takes down the sword. The family falls on his neck with relief and gratitude. They proclaim his fame. He tells the village that he will imprison the moon for them. He takes them to a pond. But when an eclipse occurs the whole town goes crazy with grief and drowns itself.

The story can be taken in many ways: you can pretend you're the hero, or the idiot. You can be a member of the family. You can be a psychiatrist and take it as a fictional version of the castration complex. You can decide you just like to hear stories. You can worry about the terrible fact: the hero in one instance, through his foolishness and desire to please people, causes the final tragedy.

The novel no doubt ended because of the insupportable attitude of self-irony.

2

Writing is living. Living means talking to people. But I can talk to so many more people if I write.

Getting an apartment was a dramatic event. I was terribly afraid of hurting people's feelings. What if some superintendent wanted me to rent a place that I didn't like! But I was lucky! The first place I saw, I took. I want to tell you about it because the landlord became part of my life, not just accidentally because he was my landlord. One meets so many people like a wall on which the rain falls, never knowing where they came from, or why they're moving, or what they'll do when they reach the ground, or what they would look like if the sun suddenly shone out. That's what upset me about the city at first. My surfaces had not sufficiently hardened. I felt continually bruised. There was so much to take in, and I was able to take in so little.

The landlord's name was Mr. Russala. I can still feel the syllables rolling around on my tongue. He was a shrewd man with gray hair and an aquiline nose. Even in grimy overalls with rough hands and a dirty face, he had force and dignity, the power to be himself.

I was taken to him by his youngest child, a boy with a rosy cherubic face which had not yet hardened into handsomeness. The boy had seen me shuffling my feet on the sidewalk as I looked at the rental sign and thought about how to attract enough attention to get in.

Mr. Russala was painting the floor of a large front room, using two smoking sticks for heat. He went right on painting while I looked around. I did not look too closely for fear of being rude. But I stood in different corners and gazed at the high bleak walls, the empty windows streaked with dirt, the tangle of pipes under the tub and sink, and imagined all the possible transformations these rooms could undergo.

Mr. Russala stood up. "It's a-nice, no?"

I nodded and smiled shyly. The better part of my decision to take it had already been made. But I didn't want to rush into anything. I wanted to hold on to the pleasure of imagining it mine; and also to think of any possible objections.

"It's a-rent at twenty-two." He looked at me sharply. I could tell he thought that was a lot. But I thought it very little. I moved my hand vaguely. "That's all right," I said, "but I have to think it over."

Mr. Russala stood still while I looked around again.

"It's a-nice place for a nice girl."

"It is nice," I agreed. "I want to go out now, but I'll come back this afternoon." I was backing toward the door.

"You come back. If the door is locked, go out back and call me. My name's over the door: Antonio Russala. I won't give it to anyone else until tomorrow. You'll come back?"

"Oh yes!" I sighed in the effort to express my sincerity. "I'm almost sure now. I'll be back at two." I took a last look at my prospective landlord, backed out the door, and rushed clattering down the stairs and out into the fresh air.

That afternoon I was back. I paid my first month's rent and received in return a receipt decorated with an eagle and many fine scrolls and signed by Mr. Russala.

But before I go on with my relationship to the landlord, I must tell you about the rooms. This was my first apartment, my cave, my shell, the extension of my physical habitat. There were three rooms, but since it was already cold and there was no heat, I started out by living in only one. It was meant to be a combination kitchen and bathroom. There was a large tower of a hot water heater, a sink, a tub, and a gas stove. The toilet sat in a water closet with half a window, the other half of which was in the room. The ceiling had a band of ornamented woodwork, and there were huge sliding doors at the end. The room seemed empty, filled with space. Mr. Russala was kind enough to leave a small cast-iron coal stove there for me to use. I moved in with a discarded cot, a straight chair, a desk that had been mine since childhood, and two orange crates. A table, a chair, and a bed. What more does one need? You can eat, work, sit up, or lie down. I spent a day or two cleaning. Hereafter the dirt would be mine.

A place to live! A place to be! To impress the movements of your heart and mind on! The bareness and dilapidation were heartening. The place would grow as I grew. And there were two more rooms for expansion. What patterns of living would animate these objects, what habits of footsteps track these floors? The rooms were empty and full of possibilities.

3

I soon discovered that I had to share possession of the apartment with Mr. Russala. Any change I might make had to square with his feelings as well as mine. He took a fatherly pride in the building: he had invested his savings in it, no doubt during the Depression. It was the only piece of real estate he had, and he couldn't have made much money from it. He was neither practical nor efficient. But he had only one child left, the others were grown and out on their own. And to see Mr. Russala scrubbing the halls and the staircase, shining up the mailboxes, or putting a clean white curtain over the glass of the front door was to know how he felt about this house. His own apartment was not in this building—it was three blocks to the north —but he had kept the backyard for himself, and he had a key to the back door so that when he wanted to he could lock himself out and no one could reach him. He had a den in the cellar. It was several months before I ventured down, though he had invited me before.

It was early one morning and I had gone into the frosty backyard to get a bucket of coal from the coal shed which Mr. Russala had built for me. While I was filling it up, Mr. Russala came out.

"You're up early today?"

"So I am," I said, feeling especially healthy as I watched my breath slide into the air, hover for a moment, and then evaporate.

"Come a-talk a minute. You've never come down," said Mr. Russala.

I started to refuse.

"Come and see. Talk a minute. You're not so busy."

I was very loath, but I agreed. I felt about cellars as an animal might about traps. I set the bucket down and put the shovel away. Mr. Russala went first to turn on the light. What I saw, coming through the door behind him, was a solid mahogany roll-top desk with an upholstered swivel chair in front of it and a wobbly wooden one beside it. The rest of the cellar was a dark pool of broken pipes, rusted plumbing equipment, boards, boxes, rakes, etc. Mr. Russala sat down at his desk, from which all he had in view was a painted calendar leaning against the wall, and me in the wooden chair. He pulled out the bottom drawer of the desk and took out a pint of gin with two shot glasses.

"Not for me," I said plaintively.

"You like it, Bella." He looked knowing.

"I'm sure I won't," I said.

Mr. Russala was not convinced. He felt that I was re-buffing his hospitality. He did not believe my protestations of innocence. Finally I took a timid sip. The expression on my face and the twitch of my throat must have con-

vinced him. He took the glass away from me and swallowed it himself. He was a little shamefaced. Oh the relief
I felt. I had been afraid I would have to swallow it all,
and with the breakfast I had just eaten, I was sure it would
make me sick. Mr. Russala drank three more shots with
exaggerated gestures of pleasure to show me what I was
missing. Then he put the bottle away.

"You're a good girl, Bella," he said.

I smiled. "I have to go now," I said. He got up to show
me out, and bolted the door behind me so that no one
else could come in. It was obvious that he didn't ask for
company; it had been an event to admit me. He admitted
few, and on sufferance as it were. There was no room for
guests. There was only his large desk, his chair, and his
dreams in a dim pool of light against the cellared confusion behind him.

I was moving out in the world. It was true I felt a little
like a kitten who makes a sudden sally into the middle of
the floor and then retreats in haste to a hole in the corner.
But the hole was my own. I was reminded irresistibly of
A. A. Milne:

> I have a house where I go
> Where nobody ever says "No";
> Where no one says anything—so
> There is no one but me*

These lines from *Now We Are Six* always seemed to me
to be very meaningful; a simple statement of the I and
the me, a recognition of the duologue which can take
place in what is nominally a unity. It is no accident that
this was my favorite poem in childhood: it is in a direct
psychic line with my present mode of expression. (Other
children create imaginary playmates or usurp somebody
else's name.) What a difference there is between the child
who announces his presence, "I'm here!" and the child
who waits for the question, "Who's there?" and answers

* From "Solitude" from *Now We Are Six* by A. A. Milne. Copyright, 1927, by E. P. Dutton & Co., Inc., New York.

timidly, "It's me." Me is an object, I a subject. How many adults put their I's together to prove to themselves that their me's are as they would like them to be!

I could be theoretically bold and identify the I as the superego, or in another language, as the soul. But then I am left with the me, which is certainly more than the soul's perceptions of the body, or the ego's recognition of the id.

But I had better scramble back to my hole. Every time I returned to it, it had a different color. Outdoors I felt as I thought other people saw me; indoors I felt as I wanted to be. Even the transitions between my outdoors- and indoors-self varied. I could not move easily from one to the other; an amalgamation of the two was so impossible that the idea of attempting it never occurred to me. It was true: sometimes my feelings turned up in the wrong places. Coming home, I might have to go to sleep before I could wake up into myself; outside, I might suddenly say something that did not belong to my frightened exterior. I did not think of it this way: rather, outdoors, I thought of myself as being extremely polite; and indoors, alive. I preferred indoors, and except that I had to have a job, would have stayed there all the time.

A job! There must be people who can approach their first job with less difficulty than I had. I was overcome with a sense of my own unworthiness; I was ashamed of being unemployed. I was ashamed that up until now life had always been easy for me.

I went first to an agency that I had heard sometimes found interesting jobs for people. A girl I knew had been sent off as an attendant at a sanitarium. I explained that I had had two years' college education, that I had no special talents or training, that I was good at figures. The agent was brusque though the mention of an "interesting job" brought a momentary glance of pity. I nodded at everything she said and soon emerged with two slips of white paper glued to my palms.

I went home first to repolish my shoes, rebrush my coat, rewash my hands, and to hold a cold washrag against my face, which was terribly red, not from rouge which I never wore, but from the anxiety which attacked me like a sandstorm.

The first place I was to go was about a job that had undoubtedly already been filled but the agent had decided to send me there anyway. I was interviewed immediately and the interviewer, a motherly woman, was extremely pleasant. She was sorry the position had already been filled. It was too bad I hadn't come sooner. They didn't have a similar opening. As I was leaving, she said, "I don't suppose you would consider working for a while as a page girl?" I shook my head. If she had said, "I'll give you a job as a page girl," I would have taken it.

Out on the street I opened my mouth wide to let the excitement pour out. I was elated. The wind bit my cheeks. I was now going to the Patriot's Cosmopolitan Bank to apply for a job—as a page girl!

Later, I thought of this incident as an example of neurotic rigidity.

I got the job. I worked in the bank's city collection department. For weeks I was like a mouse in a maze: my feet scurried. Every seventh day I received thirteen dollar bills. It wasn't much. But, standing beside the pneumatic tube, unloading the bundles of mail that pelted down and distributing them according to their texture, size, and color to my superiors at their desks, I felt humble and useful.

Who knows how long I would have stayed if I had not gotten tired? My back ached, my feet shuffled, my hair fell in strings. I could sort the mail in a flash, and the thuds were always waking me out of daydreams.

But the job was not a total loss. To someone who says grandiosely that experience is the aim, nothing can be a total loss. Experience, capitalized or in quotes, banishes discrimination. I might say to myself that possibly with some other job the experience would be more valuable, but how could I be sure? The modern psyche is full of such *a posteriori* tautologies.

My predecessor, I discovered, had run off with a sailor. My cohort—there were two departments in the basement and we shared the same tube station—was engaged to a truck driver. When he was making twenty-five dollars a week they would get married. She was a slight Italian girl with an oval face and a white neck on which there lay a small gold cross. She was a real Madonna, paler and more wasted, her brown eyes more mysteriously sad as the days went by. I always wondered if she married before her spirit slipped away entirely, and if, then, she recaptured the pink cheeks of her first blossom and became the mother, feeding her children and herself with the fruits of this earth. Was she able to forget the murmuring stream of sadness which she had bathed in daily for so many months and which gave her such transparent beauty? The gold cross on her neck could not unlock the mysteries of frustration. If beauty were free, I could have asked her for a miniature.

One day, with a great play of secrecy, one of the elevator men asked me for my name and phone number. I looked at him blankly.

"Union," he hissed, slipping me a folded handbill.

I was very excited, gave him my name and address, and waited impatiently for further contact. Nothing happened, and when I left a few weeks later I had forgotten all about it.

Then one day a strange woman called and began yelling at me over the phone.

"I beg your pardon?" I kept saying.

I couldn't make head or tail of it. The phone was sputtering. She was pregnant; she had a two-year-old son; her family was in debt. I had never heard of the woman before but she had found my name and phone number in an address book in her husband's suit. When she finally mentioned the bank, some of her fury already dissolved by my witless patience, I understood at last. I explained exactly what had happened and told her that I no longer worked there. Then she grew very friendly and, woman to woman, launched into a tirade against the recklessness of men in general, and the dangerous folly of unionization.

After she hung up, I felt that I had participated in a drama that was really life. I had almost been the other woman; I had almost joined a union; I had listened in and heard what poverty and insecurity do to human relationships. Books might be more vivid, but life was more valid.

When I was hired, the literature I was given to read made a great point of the bank's educational program. I decided to take advantage of my opportunities and went up to apply. The director was very pleased that I had come without being pushed and that I had a "native desire for self-improvement." He explained however that the classes were so full I would probably have to wait a year before I could be enrolled.

When I quit, the department head was very friendly. He complimented me on my energy and efficiency and especially on the fact that I had never complained. I was thunderstruck: I thought my whole being had been one living complaint. The department purchased a small cake and everyone had three bites. I acquired a card with twenty-two signatures. I decided that most people were like the three monkeys who say nothing, hear nothing, and see nothing. But this observation, being quite foreign to my nature, while not invalidated, was soon forgotten. . . .

4

I must first announce my dislike of the phrases "cake of custom" and "cultural climate," but having announced it, I must admit that there is such a thing as an atmosphere, a mist of illumination which surrounds us all. Henry Adams speaking of his education makes this impalpable product of circumstances clear. The home from which I had recently escaped had an atmosphere in which, to compare it to the composition of water, the H_2 was a moral perspective and the O whatever dirt had managed to seep in. I carried this atmosphere with me. But gradually new cumuli filled the horizon. The H_2 became whatever was interesting and the O was split between morality and reality. Faced with an extreme—Coca-Cola bottles or perverse exhibitionism—there was a noticeable stiffening and withdrawal. But the line I was trying to draw was no longer between the good and the bad but between the human and the inhuman. The latter is much harder to sight.

In reviewing my actions since the close of the parental era, I was inclined to feel somewhat ashamed. I had really done nothing, but I was no less committed by not making any commitments. I lived in a society that allowed so many possibilities that it was up to me to make my own clear.

I could only answer that in general my life seemed to me interesting, that nothing is simple, and that there are no more majestic roads with *Arcs de triomphe* at the beginning and end. In the modern world all roads do not lead to Rome. There were two fields charged to draw me: one was psychiatry, the other self-expression. I was naturally pulled into the latter. I might say that this allowed more room for eclectic emotions, but psychiatry too could perhaps be characterized as eclectic. It is certainly more than a tool.

When the human fledgling drops out of its nest, but before its routes have been determined by instinct, there is a synaptic and self-conscious interval. But before I discuss the foci of Art and Feminism which my own self-theorizing took, I have another presentation to make. For if my own life did not have to be serious, my adventure began in a period when some persons' did. My mind was razed by the violence of the second world war; cultural monuments seemed to survive only by accident; and life was suddenly too brief to temporize indefinitely with democracy. Another Hundred Years' War on a global scale seemed a likely historical definition for the twentieth century.

I was waked one night by a fumbled but persistent ringing of my bell. My coal stove still glowed, but the room was cold; already the fire banked on the bottom by ashes and on the top by fresh coal had stopped leaping and was slowly smoldering. I looked at my watch: it was one o'clock. The ringing continued while my curiosity grew, and finally I decided to find out who it was. I hurried into the front room and raised the window.

"Who is it?" I called.

A figure backed out of the entrance and into the snowy street.

"Who is it?" I called again. All I could see was an army overcoat and a stiffly visored cap.

"Margaret?"

I recognized my name but that was all.

"It's John Cohen."

"Just a minute," I announced, "and I'll let you in."

I dressed quickly, threw a blanket over the bed, answered the bell, and opened the door.

"How come you're in New York?" I said. "I haven't seen you in years."

He took off his overcoat and shivered.

"Sit here," I said, drawing a round straw chair near the stove. I shook down a few ashes and shoveled them into a pail. I opened the drafts. But I knew it would take at least an hour to warm up the room. In the morning I usually went back to bed for that hour. I lit the hot water heater and turned on the gas.

"I'm afraid it's cold," I said. "I already banked the stove for the night."

"How've you been?" asked John.

"O.K. And you? I see you're a Captain!"

"Major. Army Medical Corps. Can't you tell? Aren't you besieged by officers? A pretty girl like you?"

I was insulted, but his remark was meant to be friendly. He wasn't interested in pursuing his rank. The room was grim. The one lamp, its head turned to the ceiling, barely outlined the shadows.

"I'm sorry if I woke you up," he said. "The train came in at nine. I was sitting in a hotel bar when I thought of you. Why should I spend my last evening in America drinking with a group of men I hardly know and pretending a camaraderie that doesn't exist."

"I'm very glad you came," I said.

He didn't answer. He seemed to have sunk into the straw chair. He was too tired to respond to my politeness.

"God! This place is an awful dump!" he said.

I didn't answer. Such rudeness! I looked at the promontory of bottles in the corner, at the staring black windows, at the newly painted floor which reminded one of an ice rink.

"Would you like to go to a night club?" he asked.

"Sure." But I didn't relish the idea.

"I'm sorry if I woke you up," he said again.

"That's all right," I repeated.

"I'm awfully tired and afraid rather drunk," he said.

"Could I make you some coffee?"

"Don't bother."

"It's no bother." I got up and put some water on to boil. "We'll still have time to go out if you want."

He made an effort to sit up.

"Well, tell me about yourself," he said.

Tell me about yourself. Thus put on the spot, I didn't answer. Though it was true: at a time when I had seen him frequently, I did nothing but talk about myself, a fascinating subject which he put up with to remain in my company.

"Tell me about *yourself!*" I said.

"There's nothing to tell. I was handcuffed, padlocked, and chained from the day I was born."

"Go on!" I said. This was a side of him I had never seen. It was easier to understand my own troubles than his. He had slumped down in his chair again.

"I hear they have a good show at the Jangle," he said.

"I'll have to get dressed up," I said.

"You look well in anything," he said.

I got up to make the coffee. While it was dripping, I shoved at one of the heavy sliding doors and went into the front room to get a small table. A blast of cold air rushed past me. The gas fumes in the kitchen were stifling but it was still cold. I poured him a cup of coffee. It was terribly black.

"I'm afraid I don't have any sugar," I said. He didn't seem to notice. I diluted mine with a lot of milk.

"Do you want to go to a night club?" He couldn't seem to let it alone.

"It would be fun," I said. "But I really don't care. It's up to you."

He thought this over.

"I don't," he said finally.

Later I was glad we hadn't. When I think now of how close we came to going, of how close this conversation came to being as false as all the others, I am horrified. I was perfectly willing to dress up and play at being the soldier's last date before he was loaded into a troopship.

He was almost willing to take me out, to continue his drinking, to make the appropriate politely lewd remarks, to flirt in the face of certain frustration. But not quite. Three years had made us strangers enough to weaken the tonal imperative.

He didn't touch his coffee.

"I'm sorry I don't have anything to drink," I said.

"I was drunk hours ago on the best bonded bourbon," he said. "I still have a bottle in my pocket I think."

"I don't want any," I said.

"I'm keeping you up," he said.

"Don't be silly," I said. "I'm very glad to see you. It's been two years, hasn't it?"

"Three."

"Oh."

"Are you going overseas?" I asked.

"I have to report at ten in the morning." He glanced up at the ghostly face of the alarm clock illuminated by the lamp. An electric marvel.

"I won't keep you up all night," he said. He lifted his coffee cup and grimaced at the taste.

"Are you excited?" I asked.

"What I want to know is why?" he said. "Why? Why?"

"But you don't care," he said. "I'm keeping you up and you're tired and sleepy."

"Go on," I said. "I've talked about myself to you for hours. It's too bad if you can't talk to me for one night."

"You're a nice kid," he said. "Tomorrow I'll sober up. But tonight one little three-letter word is unscrewed. Maybe we should have gone to that night club after all."

"Stop apologizing," I said irritably.

"I feel like a fool," he shouted. "I'm not even drunk any more. I'm just maudlin. What I need is a girl to worry about, and then I'd stop thinking."

"Thinking is more important than anything," I said sententiously, feeling insulted again.

"I'm sorry," he said. "You're being very nice."

I felt like demanding to know what he had come for. You don't go around waking up young ladies at one o'clock in the morning, and then insulting them. I got up

restlessly and stood on one leg in front of the stove, waiting for the coffee to reheat.

"I've always done what I was told," he said quietly.
"And now I'm to risk my life. I feel I should risk it for
something worthwhile. It's not my life that I feel is important. It's life in the face of death. It's not fear; it's the
vacuum that is now to be filled with violence. What for?"

I was uneasy. I felt a tingle up my spine. Here was a
doctor of thirty-five who had worked hard for his education, who had been a success in his profession; who had
always been impatient with introspection, with despair,
with what the intellectuals call the failure of nerve. Was I
to say that he was fighting for democracy, for freedom,
for the end of the gas camps, for the destruction of the
Superior Race, for the freedom of the human race? I felt
as though the flags were flying in a graveyard.

"If I were fighting for the Revolution, or for the Jews,
but I am fighting for a hopeless amalgam of ignorance,
stupidity, and prejudice!"

"But it's what you're fighting against," I said. "You
can't let Hitler win."

"Can't I?" His defiance was wasteful and he knew it.
"Oh, never mind. . . . How've you been?"

"Fine," I said. "I live my life in a permanent state of
excitement."

"You're looking well."

"So are you."

He was still again, a little sullen because of the tide of
words that threatened him. He was not used to banking
and diking ditches for them to run in.

"You wouldn't understand," he said. "You never hated
poverty and ignorance as I did. You never struggled to
get out of it, and having gotten out, felt guilty about those
you left behind. You never struggled for dignity and found
a new kind of farce. You don't know what it means to be
a Jew. . . ."

Here I cut in excitedly. "You have an advantage being a
Jew. You are born facing all the problems of our time:
alienation, internationalism, universality. . . . Why, the
greatest men of the century have been Jews: Marx, Freud,
Proust!" I stopped, breathless.

"Who's been telling you that?" he said.

"What difference does it make? It's true, isn't it?"

"No! And even if it were, what makes you think we face them? America is the great leveler. Being a Jew merely adds a few pounds to the invisible burden of fear we all carry, makes it a little easier for powerful hands to jerk us to attention, adds a few epithets to the destructive range of human nature, a new color to bitterness. My father was a noble man; I am a successful one. My father was a Jew; I am an American. I could not be anything else."

My mouth fell open. I had always had a suspicion that there was a dark place in his head, but except for a slight sense of displacement, a more-than-usual interest and curiosity about other people, it had never shown itself.

"But what am I telling you this for? I'm keeping you up." He made a move as if to rise.

"Don't go," I said. I was excited as if he had suddenly stripped himself naked, uneasy because there was nothing I could answer, a little resentful that he found so many apologies necessary.

"War makes everything so serious," I said.

"If you had seen the boys come back . . . !" he said. "I've been in a central base hospital in the Pacific—very safe for me—and seen them come in. It would be better for most of them if they had been killed outright. It's horrible. I didn't know what horror was before. And I spent a year on accident calls in a big city. Death is nothing to the torture human beings invent. And I patch them up. Many of them would rather go back into battle than face the people at home."

"It must have been awful," I said.

Awful! The meaningless word hung in the air. He slumped again in his chair. The darkness was void.

"This time it's Europe. The boys are making a push. If I'm lucky I'll meet the Russians in Germany.

"Why?" he said again. "What's it all for?"

For Life, Liberty, and the Pursuit of Happiness, I thought. But I couldn't say it.

After he had gone, I rebanked the stove and crawled into bed, although the first streaks of dawn were already slivering the sky. In my sleep I stumbled over rocky wastes and fell into skull-like cavities. I awoke shivering with cold. The stove had gone out and I was already late for work.

John Cohen came back from the war. In a way he had had a good time. He had seen Paris and Rome. He had a choice of several good positions. We never spoke of that night. Our conversation slipped back into its old pattern: we talked about me. And he went off waving a sort of print of my emotional state. A night of darkness is in its own way an inoculation.

Consciousness is often a series of shifting perspectives. Many are permanently lost. Some questions can only be answered by life. But the doctor's life had long been appointed. Success is relative. Few people find it worthwhile going on with their questions when to retain the questions they would have to change their lives. And a question can explode itself and vanish in a puff of smoke. Why is after all only another three-letter word.

5

When I was younger I was inordinately fascinated by the certainties of mathematics. I once tried to write a play in which X, Y, and Z were the constants or main characters, and there were many variables. How I was to translate a series of algebraic equations into human lives was a problem I never solved. At the same period I began to talk to myself; this was an attempt to include the whole world through voices which were all my own. The trouble with this is that there is no satisfaction in having the last word.

While I was becoming a writer I discovered that there were other ways of thinking than that of Descartes, who reduced the truth to a bare bone which he had held in his mouth all along.

As a writer I could consider myself part of an equation which included my relationship to the world. Me plus my experience equaled my art. The equation was wonderful. If I was disgusted with myself, I could think about all the

new things I was experiencing. If I was bored with my
experience, I could read what I had been writing. If I was
afraid that what I wrote was no good, I could think about
how my talents were being improved by exercise. Then
too, the equation gave me a double meaning. Whatever I
was involved in, I was involved in not only actively but
also reflectively.

My days were full of subject matter. My enthusiasm re-
created my world. Ideas could be fused, emotions trans-
fused. I was sometimes afraid that I might explode. But
as I lay looking at the clouds, I felt that gradually the
inchoate sifting of words would purify and perfect itself.

Freud talks about dream states. In such a state the
patient is awake, but his mind operates much as it does
when he is asleep. His mind is like a captain rushing down
the field. His goal is wish fulfillment, a final touchdown.
The umpire is a censor. Repressions block his way. He
tries to confuse the interference.

Dream states work against the reality principle. The
world is never as the imagination would like it to be. Perhaps my life at this time was a special kind of dream in
which I tried to keep the intrusions of reality at a
minimum.

As for feminism, I was a Feminist. At first it was other
people who called me that and I resented it. It was a sort
of catchall to dispose of traits in me that the speakers
didn't like. Then too, no one likes to be generalized: Oh
yes! She is subject to the usual form which the female
neuroses of our day take. But gradually I grew proud of
it. To me, it meant first that I was a female; second, that
I took myself seriously; third, that I had a slow burn
searing my relations with the other sex; and lastly, that I
recognized my co-sufferers in public and looked at them
as if to say: I know, I know. There is more to a girl than
a pretty face and a soft moist body!

Of course there is more to it than that: feminists live in
a continual state of rebellion against real or fancied slights,
and they welcome the friendship of other strugglers and
strivers. To be a feminist does not mean to be aggressive

and rude; to dislike men; to earn your own living. It is a state of being which may or may not concur with or result in the foregoing traits.

I was a feminist. To me, it was almost like saying: I am a human being.

A feminist has expectations, not only for herself but also for her friends, which involve a devaluation of the careers of wife and mother. This tradition goes all the way back to Socrates. Anyone can have a child, but to be brought to bed of a work of art! A friend of mine, nine months swollen and in labor at the hospital, is said to have called through the drugs and pain, "It's such a big world!" Fantastic. But it takes all kinds of people to make a world.

The friends I had were feminists too. We maintained in each other a certain emotional temperature which we very probably could not have managed alone. Friends are like nuclei all swimming in the same liquid. While to us our differences seemed extensive and profound, other people no doubt commented on our sameness. Perhaps fish in a fish bowl feel the same way.

AN OLD WOMAN AND HER CAT

by Doris Lessing

Her name was Hetty, and she was born with the twentieth
century. She was seventy when she died of cold and mal-
nutrition. She had been alone for a long time, since her
husband had died of pneumonia in a bad winter soon
after the Second World War. He had not been more than
middleaged. Her four children were now middleaged, with
grown children. Of these descendants one daughter sent
her Christmas cards, but otherwise she did not exist for
them. For they were all respectable people, with homes
and good jobs and cars. And Hetty was not respectable.
She had always been a bit strange, these people said, when
mentioning her at all.

When Fred Pennefather, her husband, was alive and the
children just growing up, they all lived much too close and
uncomfortable in a Council flat in that part of London
which is like an estuary, with tides of people flooding in
and out: they were not half a mile from the great stations
of Euston, St. Pancras, and King's Cross. The blocks of
flats were pioneers in that area, standing up grim, grey,
hideous, among many acres of little houses and gardens,
all soon to be demolished so that they could be replaced
by more tall grey blocks. The Pennefathers were good
tenants, paying their rent, keeping out of debt; he was a
building worker, "steady," and proud of it. There was
no evidence then of Hetty's future dislocation from the
normal, unless it was that she very often slipped down for
an hour or so to the platforms where the locomotives
drew in and ground out again. She liked the smell of it
all, she said. She liked to see people moving about, "coming and going from all those foreign places." She meant
Scotland, Ireland, the North of England. These visits into
the din, the smoke, the massed swirling people were for
her a drug, like other people's drinking or gambling. Her

husband teased her, calling her a gypsy. She was in fact
part-gypsy, for her mother had been one, but had chosen
to leave her people and marry a man who lived in a
house. Fred Pennefather liked his wife for being different
from the run of the women he knew, and had married her
because of it, but her children were fearful that her gypsy
blood might show itself in worse ways than haunting railway stations. She was a tall woman with a lot of glossy
black hair, a skin that tanned easily, and dark strong eyes.
She wore bright colours, and enjoyed quick tempers and
sudden reconciliations. In her prime she attracted attention, was proud and handsome. All this made it inevitable
that the people in those streets should refer to her as "that
gypsy woman." When she heard them, she shouted back
that she was none the worse for that.

After her husband died and the children married and
left, the Council moved her to a small flat in the same
building. She got a job selling food in a local store, but
found it boring. There seem to be traditional occupations
for middleaged women living alone, the busy and responsible part of their lives being over. Drink. Gambling.
Looking for another husband. A wistful affair or two.
That's about it. Hetty went through a period of, as it were,
testing out all these, like hobbies, but tired of them. While
still earning her small wage as a saleswoman, she began a
trade in buying and selling secondhand clothes. She did
not have a shop of her own, but bought or begged clothes
from householders, and sold these to stalls and the secondhand shops. She adored doing this. It was a passion. She
gave up her respectable job and forgot all about her love
of trains and travellers. Her room was always full of
bright bits of cloth, a dress that had a pattern she fancied
and did not want to sell, strips of beading, old furs, embroidery, lace. There were street traders among the people
in the flats, but there was something in the way Hetty
went about it that lost her friends. Neighbours of twenty
or thirty years' standing said she had gone queer, and
wished to know her no longer. But she did not mind. She
was enjoying herself too much, particularly the moving
about the streets with her old perambulator, in which she
crammed what she was buying or selling. She liked the

gossiping, the bargaining, the wheedling from householders. It was this last which—and she knew this quite
well of course—the neighbours objected to. It was the thin
edge of the wedge. It was begging. Decent people did
not beg. She was no longer decent.

Lonely in her tiny flat, she was there as little as possible,
always preferring the lively streets. But she had after all to
spend some time in her room, and one day she saw a kitten lost and trembling in a dirty corner, and brought it
home to the block of flats. She was on a fifth floor. While
the kitten was growing into a large strong tom, he ranged
about that conglomeration of staircases and lifts and many
dozens of flats, as if the building were a town. Pets were
not actively persecuted by the authorities, only forbidden
and then tolerated. Hetty's life from the coming of the
cat became more sociable, for the beast was always making friends with somebody in the cliff that was the block
of flats across the court, or not coming home for nights at
a time so that she had to go and look for him and knock
on doors and ask, or returning home kicked and limping,
or bleeding after a fight with his kind. She made scenes
with the kickers, or the owners of the enemy cats, exchanged cat lore with cat lovers, was always having to
bandage and nurse her poor Tibby. The cat was soon a
scarred warrior with fleas, a torn ear, and a ragged look
to him. He was a multicoloured cat and his eyes were
small and yellow. He was a long way down the scale from
the delicately coloured, elegantly shaped pedigree cats.
But he was independent, and often caught himself pigeons
when he could no longer stand the tinned cat food, or
the bread and packet gravy Hetty fed him, and he purred
and nestled when she grabbed him to her bosom at those
times she suffered loneliness. This happened less and less.
Once she had realised that her children were hoping that
she would leave them alone because the old rag trader was
an embarrassment to them, she accepted it, and a bitterness that always had wild humour in it only welled up at
times like Christmas. She sang or chanted to the cat: "You
nasty old beast, filthy old cat, nobody wants you, do they
Tibby, no, you're just an alley tom, just an old stealing
cat, hey Tibs, Tibs, Tibs."

The building teemed with cats. There were even a couple of dogs. They all fought up and down the grey cement corridors. There were sometimes dog and cat messes which someone had to clear up, but which might be left for days and weeks as part of neighbourly wars and feuds. There were many complaints. Finally an official came from the Council to say that the ruling about keeping animals was going to be enforced. Hetty, like others, would have to have her cat destroyed. This crisis coincided with a time of bad luck for her. She had had flu; had not been able to earn money, had found it hard to get out for her pension, had run into debt. She owed a lot of back rent, too. A television set she had hired and was not paying for attracted the visits of a television representative. The neighbours were gossiping that Hetty had "gone savage." This was because the cat had brought up the stairs and along the passageways a pigeon he had caught, shedding feathers and blood all the way; a woman coming in to complain found Hetty plucking the pigeon to stew it, as she had done with others, sharing the meal with Tibby.

"You're filthy," she would say to him, setting the stew down to cool in his dish. "Filthy old thing. Eating that dirty old pigeon. What do you think you are, a wild cat? Decent cats don't eat dirty birds. Only those old gypsies eat wild birds."

One night she begged help from a neighbour who had a car, and put into the car herself the television set, the cat, bundles of clothes, and the pram. She was driven across London to a room in a street that was a slum because it was waiting to be done up. The neighbour made a second trip to bring her bed and her mattress, which were tied to the roof of the car, a chest of drawers, an old trunk, saucepans. It was in this way that she left the street in which she had lived for thirty years, nearly half her life.

She set up house again in one room. She was frightened to go near "them" to reestablish pension rights and her identity, because of the arrears of rent she had left behind, and because of the stolen television set. She started trading again, and the little room was soon spread, like her last, with a rainbow of colours and textures and lace and sequins. She cooked on a single gas ring and washed in the sink. There was no hot water unless it was boiled in saucepans. There were several old ladies and a family of five children in the house, which was condemned.

She was in the ground floor back, with a window which opened onto a derelict garden, and her cat was happy in a hunting ground that was a mile around this house where his mistress was so splendidly living. A canal ran close by, and in the dirty city water were islands which a cat could reach by leaping from moored boat to boat. On the islands were rats and birds. There were pavements full of fat London pigeons. The cat was a fine hunter. He soon had his place in the hierarchy of the local cat population and did not have to fight much to keep it. He was a strong male cat, and fathered many litters of kittens.

In that place Hetty and he lived five happy years. She was trading well, for there were rich people close by to shed what the poor needed to buy cheaply. She was not lonely, for she made a quarrelling but satisfying friendship with a woman on the top floor, a widow like herself who did not see her children either. Hetty was sharp with the five children, complaining about their noise and mess, but she slipped them bits of money and sweets after telling their mother that "she was a fool to put herself out for them, because they wouldn't appreciate it." She was living well, even without her pension. She sold the television set and gave herself and her friend upstairs some day trips to the coast, and bought a small radio. She never read books or magazines. The truth was that she could not write or read, or only so badly it was no pleasure to her. Her cat was all reward and no cost, for he fed himself, and continued to bring in pigeons for her to cook and eat, for which in return he claimed milk.

"Greedy Tibby, you greedy *thing*, don't think I don't know, oh yes I do, you'll get sick eating those old pigeons, I do keep telling you that, don't I?"

At last the street was being done up. No longer a uniform, long, disgraceful slum, houses were being bought by the middle-class people. While this meant more good warm clothes for trading—or begging, for she still could not resist the attraction of getting something for nothing by the use of her plaintive inventive tongue, her still flashing handsome eyes—Hetty knew, like her neighbours, that soon this house with its cargo of poor people would be bought for improvement.

In the week Hetty was seventy years old came the notice that was the end of this little community. They had four weeks to find somewhere else to live.

Usually, the shortage of housing being what it is in London—and everywhere else in the world, of course—these people would have had to scatter, fending for themselves. But the fate of this particular street was attracting attention, because a municipal election was pending. Homelessness among the poor was finding a focus in this street, which was a perfect symbol of the whole area, and indeed the whole city, half of it being fine converted tasteful houses, full of people who spent a lot of money, and half being dying houses tenanted by people like Hetty.

As a result of speeches by councillors and churchmen, local authorities found themselves unable to ignore the victims of this redevelopment. The people in the house Hetty was in were visited by a team consisting of an unemployment officer, a social worker, and a rehousing officer. Hetty, a strong gaunt old woman wearing a scarlet wool suit she had found among her castoffs that week, a black knitted tea-cosy on her head, and black buttoned Edwardian boots too big for her, so that she had to shuffle, invited them into her room. But although all were well used to the extremes of poverty, none wished to enter the place, but stood in the doorway and made her this offer: that she should be aided to get her pension—why had she not claimed it long ago? and that she, together with the four other old ladies in the house, should move to a Home run by the Council out in the northern suburbs. All these women were used to, and enjoyed, lively London, and while they had no alternative but to agree, they fell into a saddened and sullen state. Hetty agreed too. The last two winters had set her bones aching badly, and a cough was never far away. And while perhaps she was more of an urban soul even than the others, since she had walked up and down so many streets with her old perambulator loaded with rags and laces, and since she knew so intimately London's texture and taste, she minded least of all the idea of a new home "among green fields." There were, in fact, no fields near the promised Home, but for some reason all the old ladies had chosen to bring out this old song of a phrase, as if it belonged to their situation, that of old women not far off death. "It will be nice to be near green fields again," they said to each other over cups of tea.

The housing officer came to make final arrangements. Hetty Pennefather was to move with the others in two weeks' time. The young man, sitting on the very edge of the only chair in the crammed room, because it was greasy and he suspected it had fleas or worse in it, breathed as lightly as he could because of the appalling stink: there was a lavatory in the house, but it had been out of order for three days, and it was just the other side of a thin wall. The whole house smelled.

The young man, who knew only too well the extent of the misery due to lack of housing, who knew how many old people abandoned by their children did not get the offer to spend their days being looked after by the authorities, could not help feeling that this wreck of a human being could count herself lucky to get a place in this "Home," even if it was—and he knew and deplored the fact—an institution in which the old were treated like naughty and dim-witted children until they had the good fortune to die.

But just as he was telling Hetty that a van would be coming to take her effects and those of the other four old ladies, and that she need not take anything more with her than her clothes "and perhaps a few photographs," he saw what he had thought was a heap of multicoloured rags get up and put its ragged gingery-black paws on the old woman's skirt. Which today was a cretonne curtain covered with pink and red roses that Hetty had pinned around her because she liked the pattern.

"You can't take that cat with you," he said automatically. It was something he had to say often, and knowing what misery the statement caused, he usually softened it down. But he had been taken by surprise.

Tibby now looked like a mass of old wool that has been matting together in dust and rain. One eye was permanently half-closed, because a muscle had been ripped in a fight. One ear was vestigial. And down a flank was a hairless slope with a thick scar on it. A cat-hating man had treated Tibby as he treated all cats, to a pellet from his air-gun. The resulting wound had taken two years to heal. And Tibby smelled.

No worse, however, than his mistress, who sat stiffly still, bright-eyed with suspicion, hostile, watching the well-brushed tidy young man from the Council.

"How old is that beast?"

"Ten years, no, only eight years, he's a young cat about five years old," said Hetty, desperate.

"It looks as if you'd do him a favour to put him out of his misery," said the young man.

When the official left, Hetty had agreed to everything. She was the only one of the old women with a cat. The others had budgerigars or nothing. Budgies were allowed in the Home.

She made her plans, confided in the others, and when the van came for them and their clothes and photographs and budgies, she was not there, and they told lies for her. "Oh, we don't know where she can have gone, dear," the old women repeated again and again to the indifferent van driver. "She was here last night, but she did say something about going to her daughter in Manchester." And off they went to die in the Home.

Hetty knew that when houses have been emptied for redevelopment they may stay empty for months, even years. She intended to go on living in this one until the builders moved in.

It was a warm autumn. For the first time in her life she lived like her gypsy forbears, and did not go to bed in a room in a house like respectable people. She spent several nights, with Tibby, sitting crouched in a doorway of an empty house two doors from her own. She knew exactly when the police would come around, and where to hide herself in the bushes of the overgrown shrubby garden.

As she had expected, nothing happened in the house, and she moved back in. She smashed a back windowpane so

that Tibby could move in and out without her having to
unlock the front door for him, and without leaving a window suspiciously open. She moved to the top back room
and left it every morning early, to spend the day in the
streets with her pram and her rags. At night she kept a
candle glimmering low down on the floor. The lavatory
was still out of order, so she used a pail on the first floor,
instead, and secretly emptied it at night into the canal,
which in the day was full of pleasure boats and people
fishing.

Tibby brought her several pigeons during that time.

"Oh you are a clever puss, Tibby, Tibby! Oh you're
clever, you are. You know how things are, don't you, you
know how to get around and about."

The weather turned very cold; Christmas came and
went. Hetty's cough came back, and she spent most of her
time under piles of blankets and old clothes, dozing. At
night she watched the shadows of the candle flame on
floor and ceiling—the windowframes fitted badly, and
there was a draught. Twice tramps spent the night in the
bottom of the house and she heard them being moved on
by the police. She had to go down to make sure the police
had not blocked up the broken window the cat used, but
they had not. A blackbird had flown in and had battered
itself to death trying to get out. She plucked it, and
roasted it over a fire made with bits of floorboard in a
baking pan: the gas of course had been cut off. She had
never eaten very much, and was not frightened that some
dry bread and a bit of cheese was all that she had eaten during her sojourn under the heap of clothes. She was cold, but
did not think about that much. Outside there was slushy
brown snow everywhere. She went back to her nest thinking that soon the cold spell would be over and she could
get back to her trading. Tibby sometimes got into the
pile with her, and she clutched the warmth of him to her.
"Oh you clever cat, you clever old thing, looking after yourself, aren't you? That's right my ducky, that's right my
lovely."

And then, just as she was moving about again, with
snow gone off the ground for a time but winter only
just begun, in January, she saw a builder's van draw up

outside, a couple of men unloading their gear. They did not come into the house: they were to start work next day. By then Hetty, her cat, her pram piled with clothes and her two blankets were gone. She also took a box of matches, a candle, an old saucepan and a fork and spoon, a tinopener, and a rat trap. She had a horror of rats.

About two miles away, among the homes and gardens of amiable Hampstead, where live so many of the rich, the intelligent and the famous, stood three empty, very large houses. She had seen them on an occasion, a couple of years before, when she had taken a bus. This was a rare thing for her, because of the remarks and curious looks provoked by her mad clothes, and by her being able to appear at the same time such a tough battling old thing and a naughty child. For the older she got, this disreputable tramp, the more there strengthened in her a quality of fierce, demanding childishness. It was all too much of a mixture; she was uncomfortable to have near.

She was afraid that "they" might have rebuilt the houses, but there they still stood, too tumbledown and dangerous to be of much use to tramps, let alone the armies of London's homeless. There was no glass left anywhere. The flooring at ground level was mostly gone, leaving small platforms and juts of planking over basements full of water. The ceilings were crumbling. The roofs were going. The houses were like bombed buildings.

But on the cold dark of a late afternoon she pulled the pram up the broken stairs and moved cautiously around the frail boards of a second-floor room that had a great hole in it right down to the bottom of the house. Looking into it was like looking into a well. She held a candle to examine the state of the walls, here more or less whole, and saw that rain and wind blowing in from the window would leave one corner dry. Here she made her home. A sycamore tree screened the gaping window from the main road twenty yards away. Tibby, who was cramped after making the journey under the clothes piled in the pram, bounded down and out and vanished into neglected undergrowth to catch his supper. He returned fed and pleased, and seemed happy to stay clutched in her hard thin old arms. She had come to watch for his return after hunting trips, because the warm purring bundle of bones and fur did seem to allay, for a while, the permanent ache of cold in her bones.

Next day she sold her Edwardian boots for a few shillings—they were fashionable again—and bought a loaf and some bacon scraps. In a corner of the ruins well away from the one she had made her own, she pulled up some floor boards, built a fire, and toasted bread and the bacon scraps. Tibby had brought in a pigeon, and she roasted that, but not very efficiently. She was afraid of the fire catching and the whole mass going up in flames; she was afraid too of the smoke showing and attracting the police. She had to keep damping down the fire, and so the bird was bloody and unappetising, and in the end Tibby got most of it. She felt confused, and discouraged, but thought it was because of the long stretch of winter still ahead of her before spring could come. In fact, she was ill. She made a couple of attempts to trade and earn money to feed herself before she acknowledged she was ill. She knew she was not yet dangerously ill, for she had been that in her life, and would have been able to recognise the cold listless indifference of a real last-ditch illness. But all her bones ached, and her head ached, and she coughed more than she ever had. Yet she still did not think of herself as suffering particularly from the cold, even in that sleety January weather. She had never, in all her life, lived in a properly heated place, had never known a really warm home, not even when she lived in the Council flats. Those flats had electric fires, and the family had never used them, for the sake of economy, except in very bad spells of cold. They piled clothes onto themselves, or went to bed early. But she did know that to keep herself from dying now she could not treat the cold with her usual indifference. She knew she must eat. In the comparatively dry corner of the windy room, away from the gaping window through which snow and sleet were drifting, she made another nest—her last. She had found a piece of plastic sheeting in the rubble, and she laid that down first, so that the damp would not strike up. Then she spread her two blankets over that. Over them were heaped the mass of old clothes. She wished she had another piece of plastic

to put on top, but she used sheets of newspaper instead.
She heaved herself into the middle of this, with a loaf
of bread near to her hand. She dozed, and waited, and
nibbled bits of bread, and watched the snow drifting softly
in. Tibby sat close to the old blue face that poked out of
the pile and put up a paw to touch it. He miaowed and
was restless, and then went out into the frosty morning
and brought in a pigeon. This the cat put, still struggling
and fluttering a little, close to the old woman. But she was
afraid to get out of the pile in which the heat was being
made and kept with such difficulty. She really could not
climb out long enough to pull up more splinters of plank
from the floors, to make a fire, to pluck the pigeon, to
roast it. She put out a cold hand to stroke the cat.

"Tibby you old thing, you brought it for me then did
you? You did, did you? Come here, come in here. . . ."
But he did not want to get in with her. He miaowed again,
pushed the bird closer to her. It was now limp and dead.

"You have it then. You eat it. I'm not hungry, thank
you Tibby."

But the carcase did not interest him. He had eaten a
pigeon before bringing this one up to Hetty. He fed himself well. In spite of his matted fur, and his scars and his
half-closed yellow eye, he was a strong healthy cat.

At about four the next morning there were steps and
voices downstairs. Hetty shot out of the pile and crouched
behind a fallen heap of plaster and beams, now covered
with snow, at the end of the room near the window. She
could see through the hole in the floorboards down to the
first floor, which had collapsed entirely, and through it to
the ground floor. She saw a man in a thick overcoat and
muffler and leather gloves holding a strong torch to il-
luminate a thin bundle of clothes lying on the floor. She
saw this bundle was a sleeping man or woman. She was
indignant—*her* home was being trespassed upon. And she
was afraid because she had not been aware of this other
tenant of the ruin. Had he, or she, heard her talking to
the cat? And where was the cat? If he wasn't careful he
would be caught, and that would be the end of him. The
man with a torch went off and came back with a second
man. In the thick dark far below Hetty was a small cave

of strong light, which was the torchlight. In this space of light two men bent to lift the bundle, which was the corpse of a man or a woman like Hetty. They carried it out across the danger-traps of fallen and rotting boards that made gangplanks over the water-filled basements. One man was holding the torch in the hand that supported the dead person's feet, and the light jogged and lurched over trees and grasses: the corpse was being taken through the shrubberies to a car.

There are men in London who, between the hours of two and five in the morning, when the real citizens are asleep, who should not be disturbed by such unpleasantness as the corpses of the poor, make the rounds of all the empty, rotting houses they know about, to collect the dead, and to warn the living that they ought not to be there at all, inviting them to one of the official Homes or lodgings for the homeless.

Hetty was too frightened to get back into her warm heap. She sat with the blankets pulled around her and looked through gaps in the fabric of the house, making out shapes and boundaries and holes and puddles and mounds of rubble, as her eyes, like her cat's, became accustomed to the dark.

She heard scuffling sounds and knew they were rats. She had meant to set the trap, but the thought of her friend Tibby, who might catch his paw, had stopped her. She sat up until the morning light came in grey and cold, after nine. Now she did know herself to be very ill and in danger, for she had lost all the warmth she had huddled into her bones under the rags. She shivered violently. She was shaking herself apart with shivering. In between spasms she drooped limp and exhausted. Through the ceiling above her—but it was not a ceiling, only a cobweb of slats and planks—she could see into a dark cave, which had been a garret, and through the roof above that, the grey sky, teeming with incipient rain. The cat came back from where he had been hiding and sat crouched on her knees, keeping her stomach warm, while she thought out her position. These were her last clear thoughts. She told herself that she would not last out until spring unless she allowed "them" to find her, and take her to hospital. After that, she would be taken to a "Home."

But what would happen to Tibby, her poor cat? She rubbed the old beast's scruffy head with the ball of her thumb and muttered: "Tibby, Tibby, they won't get you, no you'll be all right, yes, I'll look after you."

Toward midday, the sun oozed yellow through miles of greasy grey cloud, and she staggered down the rotting stairs to the shops. Even in those London streets, where the extraordinary has become usual, people turned to stare at a tall gaunt woman, with a white face that had flaming red patches on it, and blue compressed lips, and restless black eyes. She wore a tightly buttoned man's overcoat, torn brown woollen mittens, and an old fur hood. She pushed a pram loaded with old dresses and scraps of embroidery and torn jerseys and shoes, all stirred into a tight tangle, and she kept pushing this pram up against people as they stood in queues, or gossiped, or stared into windows, and she muttered: "Give me your old clothes darling, give me your old pretties, give Hetty something, poor Hetty's hungry." A woman gave her a handful of small change, and Hetty bought a roll filled with tomato and lettuce. She did not dare go into a café, for even in her confused state she knew she would offend and would probably be asked to leave. But she begged a cup of tea at a street stall, and when the hot sweet liquid flooded through her she felt she might survive the winter. She bought a carton of milk and pushed the pram back through the slushy snowy street to the ruins.

Tibby was not there. She urinated down through the gap in the boards, muttering "A nuisance, that old tea," and wrapped herself in a blanket and waited for the dark to come.

Tibby came in later. He had blood on his foreleg. She had heard scuffling and she knew that he had fought a rat, or several, and had been bitten. She poured the milk into the tilted saucepan and Tibby drank it all.

She spent the night with the animal held against her chilly bosom. They did not sleep, but dozed off and on. Tibby would normally be hunting, the night was his time, but he had stayed with the old woman now for three nights.

Early next morning they again heard the corpse removers among the rubble on the ground floor, and saw the beams of the torch moving on wet walls and collapsed beams. For a moment the torch light was almost straight on Hetty, but no one came up: who could believe that a person could be desperate enough to climb those dangerous stairs, to trust those crumbling splintery floors, and in the middle of winter?

Hetty had now stopped thinking of herself as ill, of the degrees of her illness, of her danger—of the impossibility of her surviving. She had cancelled out in her mind the presence of winter and its lethal weather, and it was as if spring was nearly here. She knew that if it had been spring when she had had to leave the other house, she and the cat could have lived here for months and months, quite safely and comfortably. Because it seemed to her an impossible and even a silly thing that her life, or rather, her death, could depend on something so arbitrary as builders starting work on a house in January rather than in April, she could not believe it: the fact would not stay in her mind. The day before she had been quite clearheaded. But today her thoughts were cloudy, and she talked and laughed aloud. Once she scrambled up and rummaged in her rags for an old Christmas card she had got four years before from her good daughter.

In a hard harsh angry grumbling voice she said to her four children that she needed a room of her own now that she was getting on. "I've been a good mother to you," she shouted to them before invisible witnesses—former neighbours, welfare workers, a doctor. "I never let you want for anything, never! When you were little you always had the best of everything! You can ask anybody, go on, ask them then!"

She was restless and made such a noise that Tibby left her and bounded onto the pram and crouched watching her. He was limping, and his foreleg was rusty with blood. The rat had bitten deep. When the daylight came, he left Hetty in a kind of a sleep, and went down into the garden where he saw a pigeon feeding on the edge of the pavement. The cat pounced on the bird, dragged it into the bushes, and ate it all, without taking it up to his mistress. After he had finished eating, he stayed hidden, watching the passing people. He stared at them intently with his blazing yellow eye, as if he were thinking, or planning. He did not go into the old ruin and up the crumbling wet stairs until late—it was as if he knew it was not worth going at all.

He found Hetty, apparently asleep, wrapped loosely in a blanket, propped sitting in a corner. Her head had fallen on her chest, and her quantities of white hair had escaped from a scarlet woollen cap, and concealed a face that was flushed a deceptive pink—the flush of coma from cold. She was not yet dead, but she died that night. The rats came up the walls and along the planks and the cat fled down and away from them, limping still, into the bushes.

Hetty was not found for a couple of weeks. The weather changed to warm, and the man whose job it was to look for corpses was led up the dangerous stairs by the smell. There was something left of her, but not much.

As for the cat, he lingered for two or three days in the thick shrubberies, watching the passing people and, beyond them, the thundering traffic of the main road. Once a couple stopped to talk on the pavement, and the cat, seeing two pairs of legs, moved out and rubbed himself against one of the legs. A hand came down and he was stroked and patted for a little. Then the people went away.

The cat saw he would not find another home, and he moved off, nosing and feeling his way from one garden to another, through empty houses, finally into an old churchyard. This graveyard already had a couple of stray cats in it, and he joined them. It was the beginning of a community of stray cats going wild. They killed birds, and the field mice that lived among the grasses, and they drank from puddles. Before winter had ended the cats had had a hard time of it from thirst, during the two long spells when the ground froze and there was snow and no puddles and the birds were hard to catch because the cats were so easy to see against the clean white. But on the whole they managed quite well. One of the cats was female, and soon there was a swarm of wild cats, as wild as if they did not live in the middle of a city surrounded by streets and houses. This was just one of half a dozen communities of wild cats living in that square mile of London.

Then an official came to trap the cats and take them away. Some of them escaped, hiding till it was safe to come back again. But Tibby was caught. He was not only getting old and stiff—he still limped from the rat's bite—but he was friendly, and did not run away from the man, who had only to pick him up in his arms.

"You're an old soldier, aren't you?" said the man. "A real tough one, a real old tramp."

It is possible that the cat even thought that he might be finding another human friend and a home.

But it was not so. The haul of wild cats that week numbered hundreds, and while if Tibby had been younger a home might have been found for him, since he was amiable, and wished to be liked by the human race, he was really too old and smelly and battered. So they gave him an injection and, as we say, "put him to sleep."

TUESDAY NIGHT

by Ann Beattie

HENRY was supposed to bring the child home at six o'clock, but they usually did not arrive until eight or eight-thirty, with Joanna overtired and complaining that she did not want to go to bed the minute she came through the door. Henry had taught her that phrase. "The minute she comes through the door" was something I had said once, and he mocked me with it in defending her. "Let the poor child have a minute before she goes to bed. She *did* just come through the door." The poor child is, of course, crazy about Henry. He allows her to call him that, instead of "Daddy." And now he takes her to dinner at a French restaurant that she adores, which doesn't open until five-thirty. That means that she gets home close to eight. I am a beast if I refuse to let her eat her escargots. And it would be cruel to tell her that her father's support payments fluctuate wildly, while the French dining remains a constant. Forget the money—Henry has been a good father. He visits every Tuesday night, carefully twirls her crayons in the pencil sharpener, and takes her every other weekend. The only bad thing he has done to her—and even Henry agreed about that—was to introduce her to the sleepie he had living with him right after the divorce: an obnoxious woman, who taught Joanna to sing "I'm a Woman." Fortunately, she did not remember many of the words, but I thought I'd lose my mind when she went around the house singing "Doubleyou oh oh em ay en" for two weeks. Sometimes the sleepie tucked a fresh flower in Joanna's hair—like Maria Muldaur, she explained. The child had the good sense to be embarrassed.

The men I know are very friendly with one another. When Henry was at the house last week, he helped Dan, who lives with me, carry a bookcase up the steep, narrow steps to the second floor. Henry and Dan talk about nutrition—Dan's current interest. My brother Bobby, the only person I know who is seriously interested in hallucinogens at the age of twenty-six, gladly makes a fool of himself in front of Henry by bringing out his green yo-yo, which glows by the miracle of two internal batteries. Dan tells Bobby that if he's going to take drugs he should try dosing his body with vitamins before and after. The three of them Christmas-shop for me. Last year they had dinner at an Italian restaurant downtown. I asked Dan what they ordered, and he said, "Oh, we all had manicotti."

I have been subsisting on red zinger tea and watermelon, trying to lose weight. Dan and Henry and Bobby are all thin. Joanna takes after her father in her build. She is long and graceful, with chiselled features that would shame Marisa Berenson. She is ten years old. When I was at the laundry to pick up the clothes yesterday, a woman mistook me, from the back, for her cousin Addie.

In Joanna's class at school they are having a discussion of problems with the environment. She wants to take our big avocado plant in to school. I have tried patiently to explain that the plant does not have anything to do with environmental problems. She says that they are discussing nature, too. "What's the harm?" Dan says. So he goes to work and leaves it to me to fit the towering avocado into the Audi. I also get roped into baking cookies, so Joanna can take them to school and pass them around to celebrate her birthday. She tells me that it is the custom to put the cookies in a box wrapped in birthday paper. We select a paper with yellow bears standing in concentric circles. Dan dumps bran into the chocolate-chip-cookie dough. He forbids me to use a dot of red food coloring in the sugar-cookie hearts.

My best friend, Dianne, comes over in the mornings and turns her nose up at my red zinger. Sometimes she takes a shower here, because she loves our shower head. "How come you're not in there all the time?" she says. My brother is sweet on her. He finds her extremely attractive. He asked me if I had noticed the little droplets of water from the shower on her forehead, just at the hairline. Bobby lends her money, because her husband doesn't give her enough. I know for a fact that Dianne is thinking of having an affair with him.

DAN has to work late at his office on Tuesday nights, and a while ago I decided that I wanted that one night to myself each week—a night without any of them. Dianne said, "I know what you mean," but Bobby took great offense and didn't come to visit that night, or any other night, for two weeks. Joanna was delighted that she could be picked up after school by Dianne, in Dianne's 1966 Mustang convertible, and that the two of them could visit until Henry came by Dianne's to pick her up. Dan, who keeps saying that our relationship is going sour—although it isn't—pursed his lips and nodded when I told him about Tuesday nights, but he said nothing. The first night alone I read a dirty magazine that had been lying around the house for some time. Then I took off all my clothes and looked in the mirror and decided to go on a diet, so I skipped dinner. I made a long-distance call to a friend in California who had just had a baby. We talked about the spidery little veins in her thighs, and I swore to her over and over again that they would go away. Then I took one of each kind of vitamin pill we have in the house.

The next week, I had prepared for my spare time better. I had bought whole-wheat flour and clover honey, and I made four loaves of whole-wheat bread, I made a piecrust, putting dough in the sink and rolling it out there, which made a lot of sense but which I would never let anybody see me doing. Then I read *Vogue*. Later on, I took out the yoga book I had bought that afternoon and put it in my plastic cookbook-holder and put that down on the floor and stared at it as I tried to get into the postures. I overcooked the piecrust and it burned. I got depressed and drank a Drambuie. The week after that, I ventured out. I went to a movie and bought myself a chocolate milkshake afterward. I sat at the drugstore counter and drank it. I was going to get my birth-control-pill prescription refilled while I was there, but I decided that would be depressing.

JOANNA sleeps at her father's apartment now on Tuesday nights. Since he considers her too old to be read a fairy tale before bed, Henry waltzes with her. She wears a long nightgown and a pair of high-heeled shoes that some woman left there. She says that he usually plays "The Blue Danube" but sometimes he kids around and puts on "Idiot Wind" or "Forever Young" and they dip and twirl to it. She has hinted that she would like to take dancing lessons. Last week, she danced through the living room at our house on her pogo stick. Dan had given it to her, saying that now she had a partner, and it would save him money not having to pay for dancing lessons. He told her that if she had any questions she could ask him. He said she could call him "Mr. Daniel." She was disgusted with him. If she were Dan's child, I am sure he would still be reading her fairy tales.

Another Tuesday night, I went out and bought plants. I used my American Express card and got seventy dollars' worth of plants and some plant-hangers. The woman in the store helped me carry the boxes out to the car. I went home and drove nails into the top of the window frames and hung the plants. They did not need to be watered yet, but I held the plastic plant-waterer up to them, to see what it would be like to water them. I squeezed the plastic bottle, and I stared at the curved plastic tube coming out of it. Later, I gave myself a facial with egg whites.

There is a mouse. I first saw it in the kitchen—a small gray mouse, moseying along, taking its time in getting from under the counter to the back of the stove. I had Dan seal off the little mouse hole in the back of the stove. Then I saw the mouse again, under the chest in the living room.

"It's a mouse. It's one little mouse," Dan said. "Let it be."

"Everybody knows that if there's one mouse there are more," I said. "We've got to get rid of them."

Dan, the humanist, was secretly glad the mouse had resurfaced, that he hadn't done any damage in sealing off its home.

"It looked like the same mouse to me," Henry said.

"They all look that way," I said. "That doesn't mean—"

"Poor thing," Dan said.

"Are either of you going to set traps, or do I have to do it?"

"You have to do it," Dan said. "I can't stand it. I don't want to kill a mouse."

"I think there's only one mouse," Henry said.

Glaring at them, I went into the kitchen and took the mousetraps out of their cellophane packages. I stared at them with tears in my eyes. I did not know how to set them. Dan and Henry had made me seem like a cold-blooded killer.

"Maybe it will just leave," Dan said.

"Don't be ridiculous, Dan," I said. "If you aren't going to help, at least don't sit around snickering with Henry."

"We're not snickering," Henry said.

"You two certainly are buddy-buddy."

"What's the matter now? You want us to hate each other?" Henry said.

"I don't know how to set a mousetrap," I said. "I can't do it myself."

"Poor Mommy," Joanna said. She was in the hallway outside the living room, listening. I almost turned on her to tell her not to be sarcastic, when I realized that she was serious. She felt sorry for me. With someone on my side, I felt new courage about going back into the kitchen and tackling the problem of the traps.

Dianne called and said she had asked her husband if he could go out one night a week, so she could go out with friends or stay home by herself. He said no, but agreed to take stained-glass lessons with her.

ONE Tuesday, it rained. I stayed home and daydreamed, and remembered the past. I thought about the boy I dated my last year in high school, who used to take me out to the country on weekends, to where some cousins of his lived. I wondered why he always went there, because we never got near the house. He would drive partway up their long driveway in the woods and then pull off onto a narrow little road that trucks sometimes used when they were logging the property. We parked on the little road and necked. Sometimes the boy would drive slowly along on the country roads looking for rabbits, and whenever he saw one, which was pretty often—sometimes even two or three rabbits at once—he floored it, trying to run the rabbit down. There was no radio in the car. He had a portable radio that got only two stations (soul music and classical) and I held it on my lap. He liked the volume turned up very loud.

JOANNA comes to my bedroom and announces that Uncle Bobby is on the phone.

"I got a dog," he says.

"What kind?"

"Aren't you even surprised?"

"Yes. Where did you get the dog?"

"A guy I knew a little bit in college is going to jail, and he persuaded me to take the dog."

"What is he going to jail for?"

"Burglary."

"Joanna," I say, "don't stand there staring at me when I'm talking on the phone."

"He robbed a house," Bobby says.

"What kind of a dog is it?" I ask.

"Malamute and German shepherd. It's in heat."

"Well," I say, "you always wanted a dog."

"I call you all the time, and you never call me," Bobby says.

"I never have interesting news."

"You could call and tell me what you do on Tuesday nights."

"Nothing very interesting," I say.

"You could go to a bar and have rum drinks and weep," Bobby says. He chuckles.

"Are you stoned?" I ask.

"Sure I am. Been home from work for an hour and a half. Ate a Celeste pizza, had a little smoke."

"Do you really have a dog?" I ask.

"If you were a male dog, you wouldn't have any doubt of it."

"You're always much more clever than I am. It's hard to talk to you on the phone, Bobby."

"It's hard to be me," Bobby says. A silence. "I'm not sure the dog likes me."

"Bring it over. Joanna will love it."

"I'll be around with it Tuesday night," he says.

"Why is it so interesting to you that I have one night a week to myself?"

"Whatever you do," Bobby says, "don't rob a house."

We hang up, and I go tell Joanna the news.

"You yelled at me," she says.

"I did not. I asked you not to stand there staring at me while I was on the phone."

"You raised your voice," she says.

Soon it will be Tuesday night.

JOANNA asks me suspiciously what I do on Tuesday nights.

"What does your father say I do?" I ask.

"He says he doesn't know."

"Does he seem curious?"

"It's hard to tell with him," she says.

Having got my answer, I've forgotten about her question.

"So what things do you do?" she says.

"Sometimes you like to play in your tent," I say defensively. "Well, I like some time to just do what I want to do, too, Joanna."

"That's O.K.," she says. She sounds like an adult placating a child.

I have to face the fact that I don't do much of anything on Tuesdays, and that one night alone each week isn't making me any less edgy or more agreeable to live with. I tell Dan this, as if it's his fault.

"I don't think you ever wanted to divorce Henry," Dan says.

"Oh, Dan, I *did*."

"You two seem to get along fine."

"But we fought. We didn't get along."

He looks at me. "Oh," he says. He is being inordinately nice to me, because of the scene I threw when a mouse got caught in one of the traps. The trap didn't kill it. It just got it by the paw, and Dan had to beat it to death with a screwdriver.

"Maybe you'd rather the two of us did something regularly on Tuesday nights," he says now. "Maybe I could get the night of my meetings changed."

"Thank you," I say. "Maybe I should give it a little longer."

"That's up to you," he says. "There hasn't been enough time to judge by, I guess."

Inordinately kind. Deferential. He has been saying for a long time that our relationship is turning sour, and now it must have turned so sour for him that he doesn't even want to fight. What does he want?

"Maybe you'd like a night—" I begin.

"The hell with that," he says. "If there has to be so much time alone, I can't see the point of living together."

I hate fights. The day after this one, I get weepy and go over to Dianne's. She ends up subtly suggesting that I take stained-glass lessons. We drink some sherry and I drive home. The last thing I want is to run into her husband, who calls me "the squirrel" behind my back. Dianne says that when I call and he answers, he lets her know it's me on the phone by puffing up his cheeks to make himself look like a squirrel.

Tonight, Dan and I each sit on a side of Joanna's tester bed to say good night to her. The canopy above the bed is white nylon, with small, puckered stars. She is ready for sleep. As soon as she goes to sleep, Dan will be ready to talk to me. Dan has clicked off the light next to Joanna's bed. Going out of the bedroom before him, I grope for the hall light. I remember Henry saying to me, as a way of leading up to talking about divorce, that going to work one morning he had driven over a hill and had been astonished when at the top he saw a huge yellow tree, and realized for the first time that it was autumn.

PURE WILL

by Harriet Zinnes

"Birds do not sing in Cages."

—Ezra Pound

She slept on the floor. It wasn't because she liked the coldness under her body or rejected the warmth of his bed. She slept on the floor as an act of pure will. Do this, do that, he always said. And she did this. She did that. Even in bed she did this, she did that. And then he would sleep. He didn't care. It was in November after a snowstorm when, leaving the bed after a long-drawn-out night of lovemaking, at 4 A.M., she went to the window and watched how the flakes fell. They fell effortlessly. No force seemed to direct them in their falling. One by one, sometimes seeming thick as two by two, they fell to the ground; and though as she watched at first there was hardly what could be called even a spread of white, slowly, almost invisibly, the snow covered larger and larger areas, and always each flake could be seen separate, volitionless, falling here there near on top of other flakes to make finally a small mound that turned into a cover of white, through an effortless act of will. That is pure will, she thought, pure will, and I am lacking it.

As she turned away from the window of the bedroom that early morning and looked at her sleeping husband, she yearned to become the snowflake, volitionless, and yet pure will. She would lie on the floor, hug it in her own horizontal position, as if by denying a bed raised on four legs, she would be asserting herself in an act of pure will. She would be in a room with her husband and would sleep on the floor not to deny him but to become WILL.

Mary was up before her husband that November morn-

ing so that it was only that night that he learned of her
new resolution. "Cut the crap," was his response. "Get off
that damn floor." It was then that he began to call her
Mona Lisa because her only response to him was a smile.

She smiled through his curses that night, and since he
was never one to use physical force, she found that her
smile alone allowed her to retain her new bed of freedom,
to achieve that harmony of pure will.

Her son gave her more trouble. Coming into the bed in
the morning little Tom was bewildered to find only his father.
Looking around and seeing his mother almost rigid on the
floor he ran to her frightened that she was ill. She re-
assured him that she was fine, but when he wanted to lie
down beside her she protested. She wanted to be the sole
occupant of her new bed. Tom began to cry but Mary
was adamant. She had gained a new strength. She got up to
make Tom breakfast but he was not even to step on her
spot of floor. "It is mine," she said. "My own."

Mary made Tom his breakfast that morning, and prepared her husband's coffee. When the baby cried, she
went to it. Picking up the infant, kissing it, made her
tremble. For the first time she felt a primeval physical
womanly joy. "Little Annie," she kept repeating. "Little
Annie."

"What about my eggs?" she heard Carl her husband
shout from the kitchen. "I'm coming, Carl," she shouted
back, and when she entered the kitchen, she walked up
to him, kissed him happily on his lips and smiled. He
frowned in response. "What about my eggs?" he said
slowly again. And she thought of the snowflakes and a
line of Pound came into her head: "what whiteness will
you add to this whiteness, what candor?" Mary knew she
would not find candor in Carl, and the whiteness was her
whiteness, her act of pure will. She turned to the pot of
coffee and watched the feather trail of liminous white
steam. She had allowed the coffee to boil.

BIOGRAPHICAL NOTES

MARGARET LAMB

Margaret Lamb has published stories in *Aphra, Mademoiselle, Yale Review,* and other magazines. Her articles on literature and theater have appeared in *The Drama Review, Mosaic,* and *Educational Theater Journal.* She has taught at the City University of New York and Fordham. At present she is working on her second novel.

WILLA CATHER

Willa Cather was born in Virginia in 1873 and educated at the University of Nebraska. Her first novel, *Alexander's Bridge* (1912), is about a man torn between love for his wife and an actress friend. The novels that followed— *O Pioneers!* (1913), *The Song of the Lark* (1915), *My Ántonia* (1918), *One of Ours* (1922)—set the lives of men and women against the new landscape of the Midwest. With *A Lost Lady* (1923), *The Professor's House* (1925), and *My Mortal Enemy* (1926), Cather became more concerned with the destructive pressure of modern life on traditional standards. Other novels by Willa Cather include *Death Comes to the Archbishop* (1927), *Shadows on the Rock* (1931), *Lucy Gayheart* (1935), and *Sapphira and the Slave Girl* (1940). Her short stories and short novels were collected in *The Troll Garden* (1905), *Obscure Destinies* (1932), and *The Old Beauty and Others* (1948). Willa Cather died in 1947.

JOYCE CAROL OATES

Born in 1938, Joyce Carol Oates was graduated from Syracuse University in 1960 and received her Master's Degree in English from the University of Wisconsin. She has won numerous literary awards, among them a Guggenheim Fellowship for 1967–68, the Richard and Hinda Rosenthal Foundation Award of the National Institute of Arts and Letters, the Lotos Club Award of Merit, and the National Book Award in 1970 for her novel *Them* (1969). Her other novels include *With Shuddering Fall* (1964), *Expensive People* (1968), *A Garden of Earthly Delights* (1970), *Wonderland* (1971), *Do with Me What You Will* (1973), and *The Assassins* (1975). Ms. Oates is a professor of English at the University of Windsor, Ontario.

PENELOPE GILLIATT

Penelope Gilliatt is an author whose special talents have won her a popular and well-respected position in each of three separate genres of writing: fiction, screenwriting, and film and drama criticism. Her original script for the John Schlesinger film *Sunday Bloody Sunday* was cited as Best Screenplay of 1971 by the New York Film Critics, and by both the British and American Writers Guilds. It also won an Academy Award nomination. A native of Great Britain, educated in both England and America, Gilliatt now spends half of each year in New York, reviewing films for *The New Yorker*, to which she often contributes short stories as well, and the other half in London, traveling, and writing fiction. Formerly film critic of the *Observer*, she is the author of two novels, *A State of Change* and *One by One*, and two collections of short stories, *Nobody's Business* and *Come Back If It Doesn't Get Better*. She has adapted one of her own stories for a BBC television film.

ELAINE GOTTLIEB

Elaine Gottlieb, a native of New York City, is now teaching creative writing at Indiana University at South Bend.

She has published one novel, and numerous stories of hers have appeared in literary magazines, as well as in *The O. Henry Awards* and Martha Foley's *Best American Short Stories*. She has also published poetry, reviews, and critical essays, and has worked as co-translator on many books and stories by Isaac Bashevis Singer. Her late husband, Cecil Hemley, a poet, fiction writer, and editor, founded Noonday Press where she was the first fiction editor.

APRIL WELLS

April Wells was recently graduated from California State University, Hayward, where she received a B.A. in English, and studied creative writing.

SALLIE BINGHAM

The daughter of a newspaper publisher, Sallie Bingham was born in Louisville, Kentucky, and educated at Radcliffe College. In 1960, she published a novel called *After Such Knowledge*. Since then she has published short stories in *Mademoiselle, Harper's Bazaar*, and *Ms.*, among others. She has a son by her marriage to A. Whitney Ellsworth and lives in Manhattan.

EDNA O'BRIEN

Born in Ireland and educated in a convent, Edna O'Brien lives and writes in London. Her first novels, *The Country Girls* and *The Lonely Girl*, were made into the movie *Girl with the Green Eyes*. *August is a Wicked Month, Casualties of Peace, Girls in Their Married Bliss*, and *Night* are among her later works. Her latest book, *The Love Object*, is a collection of short stories from which the story appearing in this volume was selected. Ms. O'Brien also writes poetry, film scripts, and plays.

SUSAN HILL

Susan Hill is a short story writer, playwright, novelist, and literary critic. She was born in Scarborough, England, in

1942 and educated at King's College, London. Among her novels are *Gentleman and Ladies*, *A Change for the Better*, *The Albatross and Other Stories*, *Strange Meeting*, and *Do Me a Favour*. She received the Somerset Maugham Award in 1971 for *I'm the King of the Castle* and the Whitebread Award in 1972 for *The Bird of the Night*. She is a Fellow of the Royal Society of Literature. Her latest work is *In the Springtime of the Year* (1974).

KATHY ROE

Kathy Roe is a New York-based writer who was brought up near Dover, Delaware, and was educated at the City College of New York. In 1972, she won the coveted De Jur Award for Creative Writing and at present works in the English Department of City College. She has just completed her first novel, *Goodbye, Secret Places*, about a love relationship between two adolescent girls.

JANE MAYHALL

Jane Mayhall was born in 1921 in Louisville, Kentucky. She attended Black Mountain College, the New School, Middlebury College, and Claremont College in California. She has written two novels, *Cousin to Human* and *Ready for the Ha-Ha*, and her stories, poems, and plays have appeared in many periodicals and anthologies. She presently lives in Brooklyn, N.Y.

SHERRY SONNETT

Sherry Sonnett's fiction has appeared in *Redbook*, *Ms.*, and *Glamour*. She also writes screenplays and children's books.

JEAN STAFFORD

Jean Stafford was born in California in 1915. She has studied at the University of Colorado and in Germany. She is best known for her short stories in *Children Are Bored on Sunday* (1953) and *Bad Characters* (1964).

Her novels include *Boston Adventure* (1944), *The Mountain Lion* (1947), and *The Catherine Wheel* (1951). She has written a book on Lee Harvey Oswald's mother, *A Mother in History* (1966).

KATHERINE HARDING

Katherine Harding has published short stories in various reviews and magazines including *The Atlantic Monthly*. She says: "I keep trying to work on a novel, but the problems I write about always seem to be resolved best in the short story form." Harding lives with her husband and their two sons.

JOY WILLIAMS

Joy Williams was born in 1944 in Chelmsford, Massachusetts. She was educated at Marietta College and Iowa State University. Married and divorced, she lives with her daughter in Florida. Her novels are *State of Grace* and *Taking Care*. Her short stories have appeared in *The Paris Review, Esquire, Tri-Quarterly, The Antioch Review,* and *Transatlantic,* and one of them appeared in *Prize Stories 1966: The O. Henry Awards.*

JANE AUGUSTINE

Jane Augustine is a poet and short story writer. Her work has appeared in *Assembling, Greenfield Review, Hanging Loose,* and *Shuttle.*

ANNA KAVAN

Before taking that name by poll-deed, Anna Kavan published several conventional novels as Helen Ferguson in the twenties and thirties. She married twice, had a son, and divorced twice. She lived and traveled widely. In London, she worked as an editor for a literary magazine, and profitably renovated old houses. In 1940, she was admitted to a mental hospital and became a registered drug addict. Her collection of sketches, *Asylum Place,* and a novel called *Ice* were highly acclaimed. The present story comes from *Julia and the Bazooka.* She died in 1968, at the age of sixty-seven, from an overdose of heroin.

WAKAKO YAMAUCHI

The third child of Japanese immigrants, Wakako Yamauchi was born in Westmoreland, California, in 1924. During World War II, her family was shunted off to Poston, Arizona, where she joined the Poston *Chronicle* as a staff artist. Married for 25 years, she lives in Gardena, California, with her husband and daughter.

REBECCA MORRIS

Rebecca Morris was brought up in Ohio and educated at Western Reserve and Columbia universities. Her stories have appeared in *The New Yorker,* and in 1972 "The Good Humor Man" was made into a film called *One Is a Lonely Number.* She presently lives in New York City.

REBECCA RASS

Rebecca Rass attended the University of Tel Aviv, then traveled and taught in Europe, at the Universities of Oslo and Groningen. She has published three books: *From A to Z* (in Hebrew), *From Moscow to Jerusalem,* and *The Fairy of My Mind* (1978). The present story comes from a book in progress called *Carry Me Out.* At present she lives in New York and teaches at the City College of New York, New York University, and Rockland State Community College.

PAULE MARSHALL

The daughter of immigrants from Barbados, Paule Marshall was born in Brooklyn in 1929. After she was graduated Phi Beta Kappa from Brooklyn College, she worked as a journalist for *Our World Magazine* and lectured in black literature at various colleges. She has also spent considerable time living in many of the Caribbean islands. She has published two novels, *Brown Girl, Brown Stones* (1959) and *The Chosen Place, the Timeless People* (1969), and a book of short stories, *Soul Clap Hand and Sing* (1965).

JEAN RHYS

Jean Rhys was born and brought up in Dominica: her father was Welsh and her mother was Creole. She came to England when she was sixteen and began writing in Paris in the 1920's. She wrote four novels before World War II: *Quartet* (1928), *After Leaving Mr Mackenzie* (1931), *Voyage in the Dark* (1934), and *Good Morning, Midnight* (1939). Her collections of short stories include *The Left Bank* (1927), *Tigers Are Better Looking* (1976), and *Sleep It Off, Lady* (1976). She received the W.H. Smith Award for her novel *Wide Sargasso Sea* (1966), the story of the first wife of Mr. Rochester of *Jane Eyre*.

MARGE PIERCY

Marge Piercy was born in Detroit, educated at the University of Michigan and Northwestern University, and at present writes a regular column for *The American Poetry Review*. She has published two volumes of poetry, *Breaking Camp* and *Hard Loving*, and three novels, *Dance the Eagle to Sleep, Small Changes*, and *Going Down Fast*. She lives in New York City.

ELIZABETH POLLET

Born in New York, Elizabeth Pollet has lived in North Carolina (where she studied painting and writing at Black Mountain College), in Ohio, New Jersey, Illinois, and California. After attending the University of Chicago, she worked for the New York City radio station WBAI and wrote a novel called *A Family Romance*. The story included here is the first half of a novella, the second half of which was published in *Botteghe Oscure*. At present she is completing her Ph.D. dissertation at New York University.

DORIS LESSING

Novelist, short story writer, and playwright, Doris Lessing was born in Iran in 1919 and brought up on a Southern Rhodesian farm. After being married twice, she left for England in 1949. Lessing's novels include *The Grass Is Singing* (1950), *Martha Quest* (1952), *Retreat to Innocence* (1953), *A Proper Marriage* (1954), *A Ripple from the Storm* (1958), *The Golden Notebook* (1962), *Landlocked* (1965), *The Four-Gated City* (1969), *Briefing for a Descent into Hell* (1971), and *The Summer Before Dark* (1973). Her short stories are collected in *Five* (1953), *In Pursuit of the English* (1960), *A Man and Two Women* (1963), and *African Stories* (1964).

ANN BEATTIE

Ann Beattie was born in 1948. She is the author of *Chilly Scenes of Winter* (1976), a novel, and *Distortions*, a collection of short stories that mostly appeared first in *The New Yorker*. Her fiction often deals with what has happened to the sixties euphoria for communalism, indiscriminate sex, irreverence for money, and counterculture figures.

HARRIET ZINNES

A professor of English at Queens College, where she teaches a poetry workshop and modern literature, Harriet Zinnes is a widely published poet and literary and art critic. Her work has appeared in numerous publications, such as *Poetry, Chelsea, Confrontation, Choice, Southern Review, The New York Times, The Nation, The New Leader*, and *American Scholar*. She has published three books of poetry: *Waiting and Other Poems* (1964), *An*

Eye for an Eye (1966), and *I Wanted to See Something Flying* (1976). She is working on *Entropisms*, a manuscript of prose poems, and *Ezra Pound and the Visual Arts*, a collection of the art criticism of Pound.